THE LAST DAYS
VOLUME 3

Promised Land

Books by Kenneth Tarr

The Last Days Series
Gathering Storm
Pioneer One
Promised Land

THE LAST DAYS
VOLUME 3

Promised Land

Kenneth R. Tarr

This is a work of fiction, and the views expressed herein are the sole responsibility of the author. Likewise, certain characters, places, and incidents are the product of the author's imagination, and any resemblance to actual persons, living or dead, or actual events or locales, is entirely coincidental.

Promised Land (Last Days Series #3)

Published by Truebekon Books

ISBN: 978-1494396398

Printed in the United States of America
Year of first electronic printing: 2013

To the courageous people who seek and embrace the truth, no matter how painful that truth may be.

Prologue

⚜

The disasters prophesied in scripture began in earnest in the first part of the twenty-first century. Nature was thrown into turmoil and mankind suffered an increase in all kinds of afflictions. There was a rapid disruption of all social, economic, and financial institutions. Because of these tribulations, people of different races, religions, and social ranks rose up in violence against one another in a desperate effort to survive.

The catastrophes occurred mostly in North America but gradually spread around the globe. The American government tried to mitigate the problems and control the lawlessness, but the people had lost respect for government and resisted its efforts to stem the tide.

At the same time, a great secret combination sought to take advantage of the calamities occurring in the United States by acting to overthrow the federal government, and by skillful means it succeeded in doing so. Its goals were to rule the world and destroy the Jewish race.

In spite of all these trials, many decent people displayed unusual courage and kindness.

In the midst of the destruction of American society, the LDS Church summoned a thousand exceptional people to leave Utah in April on a special mission. Their job was to cross the plains in primitive conditions, create the foundations of New Zion in Missouri, and prepare for the saints who would follow. Their name was Pioneer One, and their chosen leader was Steven Christopher.

The modern pioneers endured many hardships during their long journey, but those trials increased their moral fiber and their commitment to God and his purposes. While most faced the tribulations with courage, a few complained incessantly and eventually rebelled, suffering dire consequences as a result.

In spite of all the dangers and obstacles, the pioneers traveled from Provo to Jackson County, Missouri, in ninety-five days. For the most part, they made the thousand-mile trip on what was left of Interstate-80, arriving at Independence in mid-July.

When they entered the land, they felt great disappointment and discouragement, for they beheld nothing but devastation, not the long-awaited Promised Land. But their hope and determination were renewed when their leader had a remarkable vision of a shining city called New Jerusalem. Soon the pioneers moved to a more appealing area near the northern end of Blue Springs Lake, south of Independence, and they quickly began to clear the land, build new homes, and plant late-season crops.

Join the saints now as they struggle to create the greatest and freest nation on earth, their Promised Land, and prepare for the final scenes of the world's history in Old Jerusalem.

PART ONE
The Building of a Nation

Chapter 1

It began to rain around ten in the morning on Tuesday, August 8, and the settlers left the fields and hurried home to their cabins. When Steven and Mary Christopher reached their cabin, they sat on chairs on the small sheltered porch to watch the rain while their three children went inside to play a board game. Half an hour later the rain stopped.

Mary looked at her husband and said, "Look, it stopped raining."

"Yeah, but check out at the clouds to the southwest. A really big storm is heading this way."

"Oh, it's got to be fifty or sixty miles away. We have plenty of time to take a little walk."

"Take a walk! Now?"

"Yes, right now."

"But our feet will get muddy and our clothes wet from the water on the ground and bushes."

"Well, we'll just put on our rubber overshoes and stick to the trail. Listen, dear husband, you're usually so busy solving the problems of our people that we hardly ever spend time alone together. We haven't taken one walk in the three weeks we've been here."

"But you're pregnant. What if you slip and fall?"

"Silly man. I'm not going to slip and fall. Besides, I'm only eight weeks along."

Steven let out a big sigh, knowing she was right. "Okay. Where do you want to go?"

"To my favorite spot north of the camp. It's only about a quarter mile away. There's a small trail most of the way."

After telling the children where they were going, they slipped on rubber overshoes, light jackets, and backpacks and set off on their walk. Unfortunately, by the time they had gone almost a quarter mile in the wilderness, the storm was nearly upon them, much sooner than they had expected. Vast ominous clouds began to streak toward them as if seeking terrified victims. The bolts of lightning that brightened the heavens with growing frequency were followed by distant rumbling, and they felt a light rain touch their faces.

"Now we're in for it," Steven said. Leaning his rifle against a fallen tree, he struggled to pull a raincoat from his backpack.

Mary stared with amusement at his frantic efforts. "Don't be such a baby, Steven. You've told me many times how you never let a little bad weather bother you when you want to do something. I remember with crystal clarity your constant bragging about all the trips you used to take from Provo to Salt Lake in dangerous snowstorms, while everyone else was cowering—as you put it—in their safe, snug homes."

"This wasn't *my* idea."

"What wasn't?"

"To leave our warm cabin and take a merry promenade when we were obviously in danger of being drowned or struck by lightning." Steven looked to the southwest and saw a swirling mass of black clouds. "Look at those clouds! That's a tornado formation. Let's get back to camp."

Mary gazed at him in disbelief and laughed. "A tornado! This is Missouri, not Kansas or Oklahoma."

Steven scowled. "Tornadoes occur frequently in Missouri, and in some of the surrounding states. Let's get going. It doesn't pay to take chances." Ignoring Mary's skeptic look, he drew the raincoat over their heads, took her by the arm, and marched with determination toward the encampment. "When we get back to camp, you can ask Ruther if you don't believe me, and I'm sure—"

He stopped abruptly. In the growing darkness he saw shadowy forms materializing from the bushes fifty yards away. At first he thought they were small trees or clumps of shrubbery, but quickly realized he was wrong when the forms moved toward them with surprising speed. It happened so fast that he was momentarily paralyzed by fear. The apparitions transformed into six men—if that is what they could be called—who grunted and snarled like fiends as they rushed forward, surrounded the young couple, and reached out to take hold of them.

"Lookee here, boys," one of the creatures cackled. "We won't go hungry after all."

From several decent people who had joined their community recently, all of them non- Mormons, Steven had heard frightening stories of widespread cannibalism in Missouri and Kansas. Were these men cannibals? He guessed that the man who had spoken was their leader. The fellow was covered with rags and his depraved countenance betrayed an individual of brutish nature, who indulged in every degenerate vice.

The other animals snorted with glee, and one of them snarled, "Hold it, boss. The little one's a woman. Let's do her first before we dine. It's been so long." The speaker was a hunchback about five feet tall with a huge beak for a nose and eyes that bulged as if they might pop from their sockets.‑

The incredible stench of their filthy bodies assaulted Steven's nostrils. "Stay back, you devils," he yelled as he aimed his rifle at them in the semi-darkness. Unfortunately, he fired too quickly and the bullet went over their heads.

The creatures were too close for him to shoot again. Four of them jumped him while the other two seized Mary. Wrenching the weapon from Steven's grasp and throwing it to the side, the attackers began beating him with fists and clubs. In seconds he was barely conscious and only dimly perceived the dull thuds against his body and head and the strange wetness that spread across his face.

Mary struggled with the men who held her fast, but she couldn't break away. She stared in shock as the other fiends beat Steven. *Oh no! They're killing him! What should I do?* she thought with desperation.

After the thugs had smashed Steven to the ground, the leader threw a short rope to one of them and ordered him to tie their victim's hands and feet. Next he rushed toward Mary, followed by his toadies. The man with the rope dropped next to Steven and began to tie him. Anxious to get his turn with Mary, he did the job in great haste. Then he sprang to his feet, kicked Steven in the ribs, and hurried away to join the fun.

Steven shook his head, trying to clear his mind. He fought to get up but couldn't. Distant shouts and the frantic screams of his wife came to him as if in a dream, and he agonized over his complete helplessness to do anything to help her. Next, he heard hooting and the sounds of struggle. What were those savages doing to Mary? He tried again to rise, but his body refused to respond to his will.

All the brutes had surrounded Mary, grabbing at her clothes in an effort to tear them off. Apparently they had decided to make a game of it, for each man took his turn moving toward her, mocking his victim as he dodged from side to side, and finally reaching out for her. At first Mary was so terrified that she flailed her arms wildly and scratched at each attacker as he drew near, but she forced herself to calm down and to think about the lessons she had learned a year earlier in karate class.

After all, she had earned a brown belt in wado-ryu karate and had also taken a good class in self-defense. At that moment she decided to attack her enemies instead of just trying to ward them off. She realized she had no chance of overcoming the six creatures by herself, but she had heard her husband's rifle shot and knew help would soon arrive from the nearby Mormon camp.

As the next brute moved forward to take his turn, she stepped toward him, swung her right leg upward with bent knee, and snapped her foot forward, striking the man in the belly with the ball of her foot. The man dropped to the ground like a rock, stunned and groaning from pain. The others derided him boisterously for letting a mere woman get the best of him, but soon they returned to their sport.

Another attacker moved in, and this time Mary stood facing him with both fists up in front of her body, with elbows slightly bent. When the man drew close, she stepped forward quickly with her right leg and, at the same instant, pulled her left fist back against her left side as she snapped her right fist forward into the man's chest. This blow, called the *junzuki*, used leverage and opposing body movement to deliver a punishing blow to an opponent. Her enemy toppled over backward, stunned into silence and clutching his chest desperately.

At this shocking sight, the prostrate man's confederates laughed with glee, obviously relishing this unusual contest. Never before had they seen a woman defend herself so effectively and they delighted in the discomfiture of their "rivals." They were full of merriment because they knew that in the end each of them would have his way with her.

Forty feet away, Steven continued to shake his head to clear his mind as he tried to sit up. Soon, in spite of the noise of the approaching storm, he could distinguish some words from the voices shouting nearby. He asked for God's help, praying he'd be in time to save his helpless wife. Frantically he pulled at his bonds and finally felt them begin to loosen.

By this time, Mary's attackers had apparently decided she was no ordinary woman. They rushed her as a group, held her arms, and slugged her until she was unconscious. She slumped to the ground, and they returned to the work of removing her clothes. She was almost naked when she regained consciousness. Suddenly, she felt them stop and move away. But her hope of a reprieve was shattered when she realized they were struggling to remove their own clothing.

Two of the men succeeded in taking off their trousers at the same time and rushed in to throw themselves upon their victim, but they stopped short when they heard a fierce scream from the leader. "Back off! Touch her and you die. First me. After you can do what you want."

He stared at Mary with his eyes full of lust as he finished removing his clothes and began to approach. Mary saw him coming and prepared to use a simple maneuver she had learned for self-protection. In fact, during some special sessions on self-defense, and many times afterwards, she and Andrea Warren had jokingly practiced these moves on each other until they had become automatic, but they had never dreamed they would ever really have to use them.

The terrible thought struck her that these monsters might actually succeed in raping and killing her, but she was determined to give them all the pain she could. The most important thing was to stall them as long as possible, because she believed that Ruther or Steven's brothers or someone else from the settlement would arrive in time.

As the drooling leader dropped to his knees and leaned toward her, Mary punched him with all her might in the Adam's apple using the first two knuckles of her right fist. Bellowing like a bull struck by a sledgehammer in a slaughter house, he rolled over onto the ground, clutching his throat.

While Steven was freeing his hands, he located the loud voices and soon was able to see the enemy. They were almost naked and stood in a semicircle looking down. He searched for Mary and finally caught a glimpse of her lying partly naked on the ground. In a frenzy he groped for his rifle in the gloom. Was it close by or had the men thrown it some distance away?

The brutes roared with laughter when they saw their leader choking and gasping for breath and suddenly falling unconscious. One of his underlings kicked him spitefully in the head. But quickly their attention returned to the prostrate woman. They fought with each other like mad dogs for several minutes until one of them came off victorious, making the others cower by brandishing two long knives.

After making a few final threatening gestures, the victor turned to throw himself on Mary. With surprising calm and determination, Mary met him by slamming the heel of her hand against the bridge of his nose. The man screamed in pain and ran away from the group, his nose broken and bleeding. The other four watched him in surprise for a moment before advancing on Mary as a group, waving knives and clubs and snarling with anger and hate.

At that moment, Steven found his .30-06 a short distance away in the grass. To keep his head clear, he lay close to the ground, supporting the front of his body on his elbows. He trained the weapon on the men threatening his wife. He couldn't tell exactly what they were doing, but he had no intention of waiting to find out. The powerful gun boomed and one of the men, who was about to club Mary, dropped to the ground as if he had been struck with an axe. His confederates froze at once, apparently stunned by the new threat. One of them shouted something, pointed at Steven, and turned to escape. Without hesitating, the others fled after him toward the woods not far away. What a ludicrous sight it was to see three nearly naked men running desperately for their lives!

The leader of the group, after regaining consciousness, struggled to his feet and, still coughing and choking, began to stumble toward the black line of bushes from which the savages had originally emerged. His soul full of fury, Steven aimed carefully and shot the fellow. When the man's back exploded into a bloody mass and he fell headlong into the mud, Steven rejoiced at his success, at the same time feeing ashamed of doing such a violent act. But he told himself it would have been only a matter of time before that evil creature would have raped or killed someone else.

Steven hobbled over to Mary and took her in his arms. "Thank God you're here!" she sobbed, clinging to him.

"Are you all right? What did they do?"

"Beat me and tore off my clothes. The truth is, I think I gave them as much as they gave me."

Mary had not told him what he really wanted to know, and he hesitated over how to ask her. "Did that beast hurt you?"

Mary's face twisted in disgust. "His filthy naked body. Coming toward me . . . No, I stopped him with a punch to the throat. I was so glad when I heard the rifle shots. I knew it was you. How many did you shoot?"

"Two, I believe."

"But I thought those men beat you senseless and tied you up. How did you . . . ?"

Steven could scarcely hear her because of the drenching rain and the deafening roar of the turbulence falling upon them. "I'll explain later," he yelled. "Hurry. We've got to find shelter." As he wrapped his thin jacket around her, he looked at the western sky and was astonished to see a great black funnel spiral down to earth. He guessed it was less than half a mile away. Remembering the gully they had crossed just before seeing the six demons, he grasped Mary's arm and pulled her toward the depression.

When they reached the gully, they descended to its bed and flattened themselves face down against the wet earth. To protect his wife, Steven tried to cover her as much as possible with his own body. The thundering of the tornado was so loud now that they couldn't understand the words they yelled to each other.

The wind whipped around them with terrifying violence, hurling small pieces of rock and wood into their flesh. Steven felt that at any moment both of them would be sucked upward into the black maw of the swirling monster. He flattened himself tightly against the ground and clung to Mary with all his might, praying they would survive the onslaught. It seemed as though it would never end, but then—suddenly—the worst was over.

"Stay down," Steven said. He climbed the embankment and saw the tornado turning abruptly southward and moving away.

"The pioneers are in for it," he said when he returned to Mary.

"You mean—?"

"Yes, it's heading south toward the camp and may hit them face on, unless it turns again."

Mary burst into tears. "The children! Our friends! What can we do?"

Steven realized that his words had expressed more alarm than he had intended. He took Mary into his arms and spoke with as much assurance as he could muster. "Don't worry. I know God is with us. He didn't bring this people clear to Missouri to allow them to be wiped out by a tornado. Just think of all the ways he guided and protected Pioneer One on the trip here."

Mary tried to smile through her tears. "You're right, of course."

"We have to return to camp as fast as possible, but first let's see if we can find some of your clothes."

Since the wind and rain had let up, they returned to the scene of the attack. After searching a few minutes, they found Steven's raincoat and pieces of Mary's clothes. They created a temporary outfit for her from the torn clothes and the raincoat and started off toward the pioneer settlement. Steven guided her carefully over the soaked ground, troubled as to what he might find when they reached their destination. Their progress was particularly difficult, for the muddy earth was strewn with trees, torn earth, and every type of debris. They had plodded along for about ten minutes when they heard a shout from the direction of the camp.

"I think it's Ruther and Paul," Steven said, straining to see the distant figures.

Hurrying even faster, they stumbled and fell in the mud several times as they strove to reach their would-be rescuers. Steven soon recognized the faces of Paul and Ruther and he hoped they could tell him news of the encampment.

Their rescuers finally reached them. "Thank God, you're all right," Paul cried, embracing first Mary, then Steven. "Wow! That was some tornado. Felt like an F4 or F5. Did it come close to you?"

Steven explained how they had found shelter in the gully. "What about you?" Steven asked. "Didn't the tornado head right for you? How did you guys avoid it?"

"We crawled inside a tunnel under a road not far from here. Got knocked around by some pretty bad winds but we escaped the full brunt of the twister." Paul noticed their wounds and the strange way Mary was dressed. "Tell us what happened. How did you get those cuts and bruises? Was it the tornado? And why are you dressed like that, Mary?"

"I'll explain everything later."

"You ornery cuss, Steve," Ruther said with bluster, apparently trying to hide the fact that he'd been worried about them. "I told yuh not ta go traipsin' off like that in this here weather. That's the trouble with this durn world. Nobody never listens to us old folks, even when we is the ones that knows the most."

"But when did you tell me—?" Steven had a terrible headache and was dizzy from the blows he'd received on his shoulders and head. He certainly didn't feel like arguing.

"Don't give me no buts, young feller. I knows it was your wife that drugged yuh away, but a real man knows how ta stand up ta them females."

Steven shrugged. "You're right. I should have been more firm. But the camp. Do you know what happened?"

"You're the prophet of this here company, ain't yuh? How d'yuh 'spect we're supposed ta know? We heard shots and figured we'd better hightail it out your way in case you was in trouble."

Mary gave the old mountain man a big hug. "Thank you so much, Ruther. We love you." Ruther blushed and Paul grinned.

The four of them set out immediately to return to the encampment. As he made his way through the debris, Steven found himself dreading what he might find when they got there.

Chapter 2

As they drew near the camp, they were met by Kent Booth, the colonel in charge of Company One, and several captains.

Kent hurried toward them and spoke first. "We were afraid you got hit by the tornado, but, thank heavens, I see you're both fine."

"What about the people?" Steven said, his voice full of worry.

"The tornado turned east right before it struck the main settlement. Some of the people were injured, but I don't believe we had any casualties. A lot of damage to cabins and fields though."

"Our crops are wiped out," said Frank Hamilton, a young captain. "I was finishing some work on the south edge of the fields when I saw the tornado tear in and devastate the entire area. The worst is, there were at least twenty people still in the fields trying to protect the new crops against the wind by covering them with just about anything they could find . . . " Tears began to flow down his cheeks and he couldn't continue. No one seemed to notice the rain, which was becoming heavier now.

"I understand how you feel," Steven said, "but we need to know. Please go on."

Frank wiped his tears and fought to control himself. "They . . . tried to run . . . but they couldn't get away. The tornado turned so quickly and came so fast. I saw people sucked up like twigs and disappear in the dark churning winds. Nobody on earth could have saved them. I can still hear their screams. I hit the ground and held onto a small tree, but I thought for sure it was going to get me too."

Steven put his hand on Frank's shoulder. "Your wife wasn't out there, was she?"

"No, she's pregnant and I made her stay in camp while I left to help with the plants."

Steven studied the settlement three hundred yards away. He was grateful to see hundreds of people bustling about, cleaning up in spite of the drenching rain. Some of the makeshift buildings were damaged but most remained standing. "Let's get down there, brethren."

The group hurried to check on their families and help in the work of reconstruction. When they reached the town, Steven was stunned to hear the terrible laments of those who could not find their loved ones. He quickly asked for volunteers to scout the region in hopes of finding survivors, and thirty able-bodied men responded. They came back four hours later carrying eight corpses and one woman who was covered with bruises and suffering from a broken leg. The woman was conscious and told the amazing story of being hurled to great heights by the powerful winds of the tornado, and then by some miracle dropping to earth like a leaf carried gently by friendly winds.

Most of those who heard the story believed she had been saved by the hand of an angel, but a few skeptics murmured secretly that the incident, if it happened at all, was fully within the realm of scientific possibility. The families of the victims sadly carried away their dead relatives to prepare them for tomorrow's burial.

Gertrude Jones, one of the practical nurses for Pioneer One, cared for Steven and Mary's wounds and encouraged them to stay in bed as much as possible the rest of the day, especially Steven, who had endured the brunt of the attack.

Mary and Steven obeyed their nurse and spent most of the day in bed trying to recover from the beatings they had received. But around five o'clock they both forced themselves out of bed in order to prepare dinner for the family. The pain of Steven's headache had lessened, but he still felt unstable each time he stood or turned too quickly. In spite of their discomfort, Mary and Steven sent William to their family and friends with a message inviting them to visit after dinnertime. When the guests arrived later, everyone gathered around the fire to discuss the tragic events of the day and what the future had in store for the pioneers. Mary and Steven's children, William, Jennifer, and Andrew, listened to every word the adults said with great interest.

The visitors included John and Tania Christopher, Paul Christopher, Douglas and Elizabeth Cartwright, Ruther Johnston, Andrea Warren, and Jarrad Babcock. After a few moments of subdued discussion on mundane concerns, Mary couldn't help broaching the subject that was heavy on everyone's mind. "Why did these terrible things have to happen? I wish someone would explain it to me. So many people killed! Isn't the Lord supposed to protect his people in the last days?"

Steven understood why Mary was frustrated and upset. He felt the same way. "I don't pretend to have all the answers. I can only say that the scriptures don't promise that the saints will escape the tribulations of the last days. At least not entirely."

Tania Christopher wiped away her tears. "All of us spent weeks in the fields preparing the ground and planting seed. Now it's too late to plant again."

"How will we survive the winter with the meager supply of food we have?" Elizabeth lamented. Elizabeth and Douglas Cartwright and their five children, although not yet Latter-day Saints, had come across the plains to Missouri with Pioneer One.

Andrea Warren's face was dark and her lips tight as she looked around the circle. "I thought the Lord wanted us to prosper so we could build New Zion. Now it seems we'll all be dead before February."

"You may be right," Douglas said. "Today we lost eight people with nine others missing. More likely than not they also died in the tornado."

There was an awkward pause. Finally, Ruther said, "Yuh all know I don't got no say in this group, and I don't have dreams of building no ideal nation like you folks, but I'll give yuh my opinion if yuh want it." Everyone encouraged Ruther to speak his mind. "Well, I'm not sure how ta put this with the proper degree of delicacy. I suppose the best way is ta say it right out clear." He pulled his worn Bible from a pocket inside the long coat he usually wore in the evenings. "This here is the Good Book, and it says the chosen people must suffer trials of fire ta make them strong and pure.

"I know yuh all had some setbacks today, but that's life on this earth. Other groups, some not even chosen, have had it a lot worse than you. And I might add, they done endured it with a heck of a lot more courage than you folks is a showin' today. What did yuh expect? Did yuh think God was goin' ta hand yuh your utopia on a silver platter? Now I ain't got no right ta chastise yuh, but I think yuh ought ta have more faith in God and in your fine leader here. If yuh listen ta him, I reckon you'll be surprised about how wonnerful he'll lead yuh in this present extremity." He inhaled deeply several times, trying to catch his breath, for he had just said more in two minutes than he usually did in a week.

Andrea and Douglas were clearly upset with Ruther's scolding, while others looked sheepish and embarrassed. There was a pause and everyone looked at Steven. Steven swallowed the lump in his throat and said, "Thank you, Ruther. You seem to have more confidence in me than I do in myself. I agree with you that the Lord is giving us trials to make us strong and worthy to build New Zion. Remember that the people who establish the Second Zion must live a heavenly law. They must become righteous enough to receive the direct visit of the Lord Jesus Christ. That doesn't mean they have to be perfect, but they must be worthy enough to endure the presence of Christ. Remember also that our reason for building the holy city is to prepare the world for the Second Coming of the Lord."

Elizabeth looked at him in awe. "Do you mean that Christ will descend personally from heaven to visit the city we're going to build?"

"That's what the scriptures teach," Steven replied. "As soon as we build the city and our new nation and prepare ourselves, he will visit us in the temple and in our homes. Later, many of us will see him again in the great meeting at Adam-ondi-Ahman, which will take place after New Zion is fully established. Or maybe he'll visit us at Adam-ondi-Ahman first."

"Oh, how can I ever be ready to meet him and talk to him?" Mary declared solemnly.

Tania sighed. "I know that when I look into his eyes, I will see his infinite love for *me* as a person, in spite of all my sins and imperfections. I will fly into his arms and kiss his cheek."

Normally Paul would have made some witty remark about his sister-in-law loving another man more than her husband, but her comment impressed him so much that he became uncharacteristically serious. "If I feel then the way I do now, I'll run and hide when I hear he's approaching."

Elizabeth shook her head. "No, Paul. You're a good man and the Lord will be anxious to see you too." Paul was so touched by those words that he couldn't respond. Elizabeth continued, "Can you *imagine* how we'll feel when we learn that in a few minutes he'll come to us and we'll see him in person!"

Even Andrea's eyes were full of tears. "That will be the greatest day in my life."

No one was able to say a word for some time. Steven knew that the Spirit had touched them and changed their doubts into faith and hope, but he noticed a perplexed look on Douglas's face. "What is it, Doug?"

"I'm confused. I thought the scriptures teach that Christ's Second Coming will be a great and dreadful day, that he'll appear to the whole world, and the wicked will be burned. How does his personal visit to us fit in with all that?"

Steven looked at Jarrad. "Would you like to explain it?"

"Well, I understand that Christ will visit us first to accept and dedicate the New Jerusalem and its temple. When he comes to Adam-ondi-Ahman he'll receive reports and keys from Adam, who will have obtained them from all the dispensation heads. Those will be the keys of the Kingdom of God. In other words, that will be the legal creation of the Kingdom of God on the earth, with Christ as King. Most of the people on earth won't know about these two visits to America. Later, he'll come to the world as a whole, and that's when the righteous will be caught up and the wicked burned."

Ruther furrowed his wrinkled brow. "So if and when Jesus comes here to your Zion—speakin' only from your Mormon point of view, naturally— is that what the scriptures are talkin' about when they say Jesus will stand on Mount Zion with his angels and the hundred and forty-four thousand?"

Paul answered before Jarrad could speak. "Yep, that's right, Ruther."

"I don't think so," Jarrad said quickly. "That's when Christ comes to the Mount of Olives in Jerusalem and saves the Jews during the War of Armageddon."

"You're confused, Jarrad," Paul said. "That's *not* what the scriptures say."

"Chapter and verse," Jarrad challenged.

Ruther thumbed through his Bible as if trying to find a scripture, but quickly gave it up. "I cain't find the passage, but I figure Jarrad is right. That's how I remember it."

John couldn't resist joining the discussion. "I'm sorry, Paul, but I have to go along with Jarrad and Ruther. When Christ comes to the Mount of Olives, he stands on Mount Zion with the hundred and forty-four thousand. That coming is what people call the Second Coming of the Lord to the world."

Paul frowned and leaned forward on his chair to emphasize his opinion. "No, no, that's crazy. His coming in glory to the world occurs *after* he descends to the Mount of Olives. It's a separate event."

"There's another possibility," Andrea said. "Maybe Jesus stands on Mount Zion when he comes to the meeting of Adam-ondi-Ahman. That's when he receives the keys of the Kingdom of God. Yes, I'm fairly certain that's right."

"Now I'm completely befuddled and discombobulated," Ruther complained. "How many durn comings are thar supposed ta be?"

Despite his own sadness, Steven preferred to have them bickering a little over the events of the last days than to hear them grieve because of today's disaster. At least it drew their minds away from their pain and fears. He expected to hear Mary jump in with her opinion at any moment, and that thought made him wonder what she believed about the sequence of events of the last days. Never in his life did he expect what came next.

Mary's eyes narrowed as she stared at her husband. "Well, Steven, what's the answer? What's the correct order of events?"

"You're asking me? How should I know?"

"You're the local prophet. Something tells me you know this one."

After hemming and hawing awhile, Steven said, "I don't know for sure. All I can do is give you my opinion."

Andrea smirked. "He knows. He's just trying to be modest."

"I'm not trying to be anything of the sort."

"Please get on with it," Mary said with a scowl. "We're all waiting."

"Okay. I'll try to explain it according to my understanding. Instead of speaking of the Second Coming, we should use the expression Second Comings. The scriptures describe many visits of Christ to earth in the last days. There are at least seven principal ones, maybe more. He visited Joseph Smith in the Sacred Grove. He showed himself to Joseph and Oliver Cowdery in the Kirtland Temple. When the New Jerusalem is built, he will visit its temple and many inhabitants in their homes. At another time he'll appear to a multitude of righteous saints at Adam-ondi-Ahman.

"Later, during the War of Armageddon, he'll descend to the Mount of Olives in Jerusalem and save the surviving Jews. After that he'll appear in the heavens in glory and descend to the entire world with the hosts of the celestial world. That's when the wicked will be burned, and the righteous dead will be resurrected and ascend to meet him, accompanied by the faithful mortal saints who have been transfigured by the Holy Ghost. As part of this visit in glory, or shortly thereafter, he'll again visit the New Jerusalem. This last visit is when he'll stand on Mount Zion with the hundred and forty-four thousand. That's how the scriptures say it will happen, as far as I understand."

With a big smile Andrea clapped her hands several times. "That makes it clear. I think Steve is right."

"I told you he knew," Mary said, grinning with pride.

Steven was a bit surprised and nonplussed at the praise.

Ruther had continued to search for his biblical passage and had finally found it. "I reckon you'll have ta show me where yuh get all that from the scriptures, Steve. But I found one thing in the Bible that seems ta disagree with what yuh folks think about yer New Jerusalem. In Revelation chapter twenty-one it says that the New Jerusalem comes down from God out of heaven. This happens after there is a new heaven and a new earth. So my question is, if it comes down from heaven, how come you folks are tryin' ta build it here on earth. In other words, how can yer Zion be the Mount Zion that Jesus will come to?"

"I'd like to explain our position on that matter," John said quickly, evidently hoping to redeem his earlier confusion. "We believe there are two cities called New Jerusalem. The first is the City of Enoch that was translated and taken to heaven in the days of Enoch. That is called the heavenly city and the one spoken of in Revelation. The second New Jerusalem is the earthly city that the saints will build here in Jackson County. After Christ cleanses the world by fire, the City of Enoch will descend and the earthly city will ascend to meet it. Together they'll descend to earth and rule the world as one Kingdom of God during the Millennium."

Ruther didn't act convinced. "John, why don't you and Steve gather yer scriptures ta prove what yuh say, and we'll discuss these here things another time. I'll have ta warn yuh that I ain't easy ta convince. Try ta see it from my point of view. All my life I've believed that someday I'd leave all the unbelievers behind—and I guess that includes you Mormons—and be lifted up ta join Jesus in the glorious rapture. But now you folks are doin' yer durndest ta throw a monkey wrench inta my plans."

Everyone smiled at Ruther's little joke. Steven grinned too, suspecting Ruther was purposely trying to cheer them up. At any rate, whether he did it on purpose or not, Ruther had succeeded in making everyone feel better because they seemed more willing now to accept the idea that with God's help they could overcome their current dilemma.

However, Steven's friends were not about to let him off the hook easily.

It was Elizabeth who asked him the most crucial questions. "But, Steve, you haven't told us what to do. Should we replant the crops with the seed we have left? Is there time for it to grow? Do we have other sources of food? Are there other measures we should take to insure our survival this winter? Do we need to do more to protect our town from possible enemies?"

Steven's eyes shone with confidence. "The Lord has promised me that if we are diligent, he will give us a good harvest. So far he hasn't revealed to me how this will come about, but I'm sure he will do so at the appropriate time. As for additional food sources, our Cherokee friends will help us hunt wild animals in the surrounding region. The winter will be hard and we'll have trials, but we'll survive them. Concerning defense, I believe our current system of regular day and night patrols is more than adequate."

"That's all we need to know," Douglas declared with surprising faith. "Tomorrow we'll begin to replow and reseed the fields." The others agreed enthusiastically.

"There's somethin' else yuh haven't explained ta us," Ruther said.

"What's that?" Steven was worried that Ruther's concern would lead to another religious discussion.

"Yuh haven't told us why we heard three shots this morning, why you two are covered with cuts and bruises, and why Mary was wearin' torn-up clothes."

Steven looked at Mary and saw panic in her eyes. After thinking a moment, he said, "All I can say is we were attacked and managed to escape without serious harm. The worst of it was, I had to kill two men in order to save our lives."

"Yes, Steven saved our lives," Mary said proudly. "If it hadn't been for him—" She changed the subject abruptly. "That reminds me, Steven. How did you recover so fast from your beating and how did you get free from your bonds?"

"I did a lot of praying and God gave me strength. And, fortunately, our attackers didn't tie me very well. I guess they figured I wouldn't wake up for a long time."

"Yuh sure 'nough live a charmed life, my friend," Ruther declared, gumming a big smile.

"So it seems sometimes, doesn't it?" Steven said. "Now I have a question for you, wifey." The term "wifey" was one of Steven's pet names for Mary. "It took me a long time recovering enough from the beating to be able to help you. How on earth did you manage to hold those savages off for so long?"

Mary's face turned red and she sat there with her mouth ajar, unable to speak at first.

"Yeah, Mary, what happened?" two of the visitors said at once. All the others joined in and encouraged her to speak up and not be embarrassed.

After pausing a few seconds, Mary said, "Well, you see, it's like this." She proceeded to describe her defense moves and delaying tactics in detail. When she had finished, everyone in the room stared at her in amazement.

"That's remarkable," Douglas said.

"It's freakin' unbelievable," Paul chimed in.

"Can women do those things?" John asked.

"That's why I call her Super Mom," Andrew said. William and Jennifer's heads bobbed enthusiastically.

"I need to learn karate," Jarrad added.

"I knew a woman could take on a man if she had some training," Elizabeth said, her eyes narrowed in a sly way.

Steven leaned over and kissed Mary. "That's unbelievable. I'm so proud of you. Now I can give you another pet name: 'Karate Wife One.'"

Everyone chuckled, but Mary said smartly, "Well, that's okay if you mean Karate Wife One and Only." At this correction, everyone burst out laughing.

Steven joined in the mirth, pleased to see them laughing instead of lamenting over their problems.

They continued to discuss the attack and other subjects until around eight o'clock when they grew tired and decided to make it a night. After the visitors left, Steven and his family sat down to make plans for the next day. He was glad he hadn't told his visitors everything. If he had revealed the immense trials and tests that faced them in the future, they wouldn't have left his cabin with such hope and joy.

Later in the evening Steven met with John, Paul, and the four colonels to discuss how the pioneers should proceed in replanting their crops. When his guests departed at ten, Steven checked on his family and saw they were already asleep. As he often did late at night, he sat alone in front of the fireplace, needing time to think in quiet. Not only did he examine the community's immediate problems, but also Zion's long-range challenges.

The greatest challenges concerned the social, economic, and political structures of New Zion. He had discussed these matters many times with the prophet before leaving Utah. President Smith had indicated that he had few answers for him because the Lord had not yet revealed them. However, he had promised Steven that God would show him what to do when the time came. Finally, Josiah had opened the scriptures and other documents and spent an hour reading passages relating to the American Zion.

Now in Missouri, Steven continued that practice, reading the same scriptures over and over. Sometimes Mary came into the room, and when she couldn't get him to go to bed, she read with him and they discussed the meaning of the verses. Steven treasured those prophecies in his heart and prayed frequently that the Lord would give him the direction they so earnestly needed.

Chapter 3

D espite a bad night and the pain of his injuries, Steven arose early the next day. After dressing, he kissed Mary and headed away from camp. He had many things to say to the Lord, but more than anything he desired to find out why God had allowed the tornado to destroy their crops and take so many precious lives. He took his usual route to reach his favorite grove of trees on a rise several hundred yards from the border of the settlement. The storm had passed, but a soft breeze blew a hint of rain against his face, and he was glad he had worn a jacket and boots. Several pioneers waved at him but asked no questions, for they knew he often communed with God in the morning.

He had almost reached his destination when he caught sight of a man emerging from the grove and heading toward him. Steven continued along the same path, keeping his eye on the stranger, intrigued by the man's casual, unconcerned manner. When they were a hundred yards apart, Steven could see the newcomer more clearly, and the man seemed vaguely familiar. He was fairly young and was wearing black dress pants, a white shirt, a silky black tie, and what appeared to be dark cowboy boots. In his left hand he carried a light cane. Steven had the bizarre impression that he was coming across a Mormon missionary on his way to an appointment.

As they drew near each other, the stranger stopped suddenly, smiled pleasantly, and said, "Oh. How nice to see you again. Beautiful morning, isn't it? Fortunately, the storm is over."

All at once Steven recognized him, but there was something different. Now the man seemed older, about thirty-six, had black hair, and was taller. "You!" Steven replied. "What are you doing here? What do you want?"

"You recognize me?"

"Yes. I mean, I think so. You're the man I met in the hills in Wyoming, a few miles west of Rawlins." Once again Steven was amazed at how clean and smart this man appeared.

The handsome stranger raised one foot at a time and tapped the caked mud from his boots with his cane. "I'm delighted you remember. I would have felt bad if you had forgotten."

Steven wanted to ask the question that had been bothering him for some time, and yet he was frightened to do so. "Are you . . . ? My wife believes that you are . . ." He was angry at himself for the fear that prevented him from saying the words.

"Please don't be afraid. Who does Mary believe me to be?" Steven was shocked that the stranger knew his wife's name. "I am sure she has guessed the truth. Women are so intuitive. I call myself Lucas, Lucas Nigel." Steven knew that those names came from Latin, Lucas meaning bringer of light and Nigel meaning dark or black.

The stranger smiled with pleasure when Steven's eyes opened wide and his jaw dropped. "Intriguing, *n'est-ce pas?* I so much prefer those names to the derogatory terms people usually place on me. I have no trouble getting respect where I come from, but it's terribly hard to get even a little respect in this world. The truth is, I am really not a bad person."

"Not a bad person! You must be joking." Steven found it impossible to remove his eyes from those of the stranger. Those dark, penetrating eyes that suggested great knowledge and hidden power. In light of who he claimed to be, it was especially perverse that this personage seemed to pride himself on his careful dress, poised manner, and witty sense of humor.

"Yes, somewhat, but I am serious too. Most of the evils of this world come from the heart of man, not from me. Actually, I am relatively innocent. Just think about it and be honest. You know for a fact that the heart and mind of mortal man—and that includes mortal woman, of course—are a bottomless pit of lust, hate, and greed. As a result, my work is much easier. And the scriptures! They are completely unfair.

"For example, they describe me as the Father of Lies, the Master of Wickedness, a Dark Spirit completely devoid of light, a being who tempts man and oppresses his soul. But all that is just ridiculous propaganda. The truth is, I am quite a pleasant fellow, basically honest and evenhanded, when

you get to know me. I am not an oppressor but a victim. Tell me now. Do
I make you tremble like Moses claimed I made him? Do I bring you to the
point of complete destruction like Joseph Smith said I brought him? Of
course not."

Steven knew he should turn away immediately and leave, but in spite
of himself he was fascinated and wondered if he might learn something
remarkable from this encounter. "I believe you're the last person—if you
are a person—to have the right to speak of innocence, honesty, and truth."

Lucas pointed to two chairs that sat off to the side not far away. "Sit
down and let us discuss it." Steven was astonished because the chairs had
not been there when they had first met. He sat on one of the chairs, and
Lucas took the other. "Why do I not have the right to speak of such
things?"

"Because of who you are. You're the one who rebelled against God and
tempts man to do evil. You only tell the truth when it serves your primary
purpose of leading man into error. You lied to me months ago and you're
lying to me now. Like they say, you're the Father of Lies. You just said that
most evil comes from the heart of man, but I know for a fact that you are
wrong. People make mistakes and they sin, but most are full of goodness
and self-sacrifice."

Lucas smiled and his dark eyes flashed. "My dear friend, you are so
naive. I can see that you are a hard case, and that it will take some serious
work to disillusion you. You are obviously the victim of all that vicious
propaganda against me. Listen, Steven, I would love to discuss religion, life,
and philosophy with you, but I can see it will require more time than I have
available now. I must attend to other business in foreign lands. But before
I go, let me say that I warned you that you would find untold hardship and
destruction as you traveled east into Missouri.

"And now look at what has happened. So many of your people killed
by various types of storms, bands of thugs, and deadly diseases. And now
your crops completely destroyed. You see, I told you the truth back there
in Wyoming, for the most part at least. The fact is, you'll never survive the
winter without the assistance of a person of great knowledge and skill.
Someone who has the power to take care of you."

Steven was aghast. "And who might that be?" He wanted to command
Lucas to depart, but he couldn't end the interview. He was both intrigued
and amazed at the happy, self-confident attitude of this being, especially

in view of his history of grotesque crimes, which spanned thousands of earthly years. Surely this personage must realize that in the end he could not win against the Almighty Father, and that he faced an eternity of unspeakable misery in outer darkness.

"Why me, of course. And then if you insist on building that fabulous utopia of yours, I'll help you do the job. You may have to alter your design a bit, but it will end up being a remarkable nation nevertheless."

"We'll get our help from God and him alone," Steven said, jumping to his feet with impatience.

"Yes, yes, I know what your plan is. He might help you, but you can be sure he will make you suffer, bleed, and die in the process. On the other hand, my assistance will be much more easy and pleasant. You'll accomplish every task in record time and you'll survive to enjoy it."

"My answer is no. We'll never accept your help."

"Never say never. As times goes on, you may have to change your mind."

Finally Steven became angry and shouted, "Leave and don't ever visit me again."

Still smiling pleasantly, Lucas stood. "But why? What harm can it do?"

"Because you're a liar and your goal is always to deceive and destroy!"

"Really! Well, you don't have to become angry and resort to name-calling. I think you're forgetting something. Aren't you the fellow who always says that the Holy Spirit never moves a person to anger and hatred, and that anger is always counterproductive? Personally, I think your attitude is completely illogical and unfair."

The stranger's surprising answer took Steven back. "Unfair?"

"Yes. Quite unfair. Obviously you do not wish to hear the other side of the story. All you know is what those crusty old prophets said about me thousands of years ago in their writings. Their bias is perfectly clear to the honest mind. Have you ever heard my side of the story? How can you ascertain the truth if you don't hear me out? After all, you wouldn't expect a man to approach the Baptists if he desired to discover what Mormons believe." Steven was stunned by the audacity of these arguments. The shocking idea suddenly entered his mind that this devil had obviously overheard their discussions with Ruther Johnston.

"Besides," Lucas continued, "it's traditional for me to make regular visits to mortals, even the opposition—although I don't really see you as an enemy. If you remember correctly, I made visits to Adam and Eve, their sons and daughters, Moses, Job, Jesus Christ, Judas, Joseph Smith, and a host of others."

"Please leave now. I came here to pray to the Lord, not to talk to you."

"As you wish, but I intend to visit you again in the near future." With these words Lucas smiled his maddening smile, waved good-bye, and headed into the wilderness north of the settlement.

Steven watched until the "man" disappeared from view. His mind was in a state of turmoil, and it was very hard for him to believe that he had not been looking at an actual physical body when he was talking to Lucas, because his body looked so real and tangible. But he knew Lucifer had no body and was only a spirit. By the time he reached the grove, he had ceased to tremble.

He knelt and asked God to give him the strength and wisdom to resist the Evil One, and to help the saints prepare for the winter and build Zion according to his wishes. He asked many questions, but finally came to his main reason for coming to the grove. Why had the Lord allowed his people to be punished so severely? After fifteen minutes of fervent prayer, Steven heard a kind, gentle voice whispering to his soul.

The Spirit told Steven that he had sent afflictions to the saints because of their rebellion. Not the rebellion of the majority, but that of a significant minority. The Spirit also said that the pioneers should replant their crops and expect great success, for he would extend the seasons to allow time for their maturity and make their land more fertile than it had ever been. He gave Steven specific directions as to how he should organize the replanting.

The Spirit also promised to protect them from the hardships of the winter and defend them from their enemies. Their main task was to establish the Promised Land of Zion. The Lord also told Steven not to listen to or fear Satan, because the evil one could do him no harm unless Steven gave him permission to do so. Then the Spirit gave further information concerning the Kingdom, but cautioned him to keep those things to himself for the present.

After he had received this message from the Lord, Steven sat against the trunk of a tree and pondered the things he had heard and how to implement them. He chose ten men he felt would be capable of directing the replanting of the crops. An hour later he left the wood with his heart full of joy. He hurried to the settlement, anxious to relate to the people what the Lord had revealed. As soon as he arrived at the camp, he called for a general meeting of all the community to begin at noon. Next he sent word to the ten men he had chosen to supervise the replanting of the damaged fields. All ten came quickly and accepted his call without question. He spent half an hour giving them instructions on how they should organize the work.

Chapter 4

By noon the citizens had arrived, including Steven's family and friends, most of whom were standing in the front. Many in the crowd looked at him anxiously, hoping he would have good news for them. Steven knew that only the people near the front would be able to hear him clearly, but he expected that they would quickly spread the word to those in the back. He wondered if it might have been wiser to discuss the Lord's communication with the pioneer leaders in a private meeting and allow them to spread the word. After stepping onto a bench, he raised his hand to quiet the crowd, and the people responded quickly.

Speaking in a loud, firm voice, Steven said, "Listen, everyone. I will try to speak as loudly as I can so most of you can hear me. This morning I went a short distance into the wilderness to talk with the Lord. I asked him why he had permitted this settlement to be struck with disaster yesterday, and what we should do to recover. The Lord told me that the catastrophe resulted from the selfishness, bickering, and rebellion of some of our people." The expectant crowd suddenly fell quiet. Many lowered their heads.

"The Lord also said that in order for us to escape further chastening, we must work together as one and overcome our selfish desires. If we do not do this, we will be left to ourselves and not be able to complete the great work for which the Lord guided us to this land."

There was a woman with a baby standing directly in front of Steven. With great sadness in her voice, she said, "Why should everyone be punished because some people cause trouble? One of my good neighbors died in that tornado and she was a wonderful person."

Steven looked into her eyes with compassion. "I don't have all the answers for why the Lord does what he does. But I do know that he said those who are most guilty will pay the greatest price." The woman said nothing more, but her face showed she was struggling to understand the answer.

"As for our crops," Steven continued, "the Lord said that we must begin today to repair our fields and replant the crops."

All at once Steven heard people calling and asking questions from farther back in the crowd, wanting to know what he had said, but there was nothing he could do about it. The people who couldn't hear would simply have to get their answers from the others after the meeting.

One of the men in the front—to Steven's left—said in a loud voice, "But we're already well into August. We don't have time to replant the crops. We'll need three to four months of warm, sunny weather with regular rains. It'll be November by that time and too cold for the plants to grow. I don't see how it's possible. We should focus our attention on hunting and trapping to obtain meat."

"It's a test of your faith," Steven declared. "You must trust God and plant the crops. We'll never find enough meat to support this large community, and we'll need the grain and vegetables to maintain our health and to survive. If you repair the fields and replant the crops as soon as possible, the Lord has promised that he will extend the growing season until the plants can be harvested. It will be the same as if we were planting in the spring."

The crowd broke into multiple discussions with their neighbors, whispering and debating the new idea. Most seemed happy and enthusiastic, while others murmured, complained, and scowled. Steven was relieved to see that at least the majority appeared to be pleased with what the Lord had promised them.

After a while the crowd calmed down and gave Steven their attention again. One huge brother, who looked as though he had spent his life in heavy labor on the farm, spoke in a big, imposing voice, "Brother Steve, I'm with you. Some of us have had pretty much the same idea. What I mean is, we sort of figured the Lord was testing us to see if we had any guts. So if you'll direct us concerning what we should do, we'll get to work. I have faith there'll be enough rain and warm weather to produce good crops, just as you said. And if any of these babies here don't believe, let them go hunting or sit on their backsides and spend their time whining about how hard they have it."

"Now that thar's a man after my own heart," Ruther said in a booming voice.

Most in the assembly clapped, showing they agreed with the big farmer and Ruther. Steven debated with himself as to whether or not he should tell them the rest. Finally, he decided to proceed, because the Lord expected him to reveal certain things, and now was as good a time as any. More than anytime in the past year, he wished that the frail but mighty prophet, Josiah Smith, were standing beside him.

"Brothers and sisters, there is more. I have both good news and bad news. First the good news. Most of our loved loves in Utah are safe and free. The Mexican renegade armies have been defeated by a coalition of Mormon and Indian forces. I can't give you assurances about the safety of your own individual families back home, except to say that our people suffered relatively few casualties, considering the size of the invading armies."

This announcement was met with cries of relief and tears of joy. Steven waited five minutes until the jubilation began to subside.

After the crowd quieted down and looked at him again in anticipation, he continued. "I'd like to give you more information on this matter, but I simply don't have any . . . Now for the bad news. Because of the battles in Utah, the Church has not been able to dispatch additional companies of pioneers to Missouri. That means we'll be on our own this year." There were groans from the crowd, and the people at the front looked at one another intently, as if their neighbors could answer their questions. "Nevertheless," Steven added, "the Lord has promised that Pioneer Two will arrive next June."

Seth Crowell stepped forward from the crowd. He was the colonel who had conspired with Dr. Quentin Price and others to mutiny against Steven and his brothers on Nebraska Highway 2. They had convinced two thirds of the pioneers to break away from the other saints and follow a route not authorized by the caravan leaders. While Quentin had perished in the dust storm that struck the rebellious, Seth had lived to fight against the bandit armies at Riss Lake, helping to save the non-Mormon community there.

Steven had decided to postpone relieving Seth of his post as colonel until the saints had set up their semipermanent community near Blue Springs Lake. At that time he chose Michael Stark as the new colonel. Full of jealousy and bitterness, Seth began to spread false rumors against the leaders of the new settlement and continued his secret work of undermining their authority.

"Brother Christopher," Seth called in a loud voice. "Can you tell us if you will continue to lead our community from now until Pioneer Two arrives? And after Pioneer Two comes, will we have a different leadership then? If I understand things correctly, the destiny of this people is to establish the Kingdom of God in this part of the country. I also understand that the kingdom here will have two branches, the ecclesiastical and the political." Steven knew that Seth loved to hear the sound of his own voice, and he wondered how long his discourse would take.

Seth continued, his eyebrows raised and his mouth in a smirk. "Now, we all know—that is, those of us who are Mormons know—that the Church of Jesus Christ is God's ecclesiastical kingdom. And most of us know, or should know, that the Church will be the mother of the political kingdom, which is the great kingdom spoken of by Daniel in the Book of Daniel, chapter two, verses forty-four and forty-five. It's that kingdom that will fill the whole earth and break down all other kingdoms. So I guess my real question is, who will organize and run both branches of the Kingdom of God in Missouri?" Every eye gazed at Steven in expectation.

Steven had asked himself several times in the past few months, and again during the meeting at hand, whether or not the time had come to bring up the thorny question of future leadership. Before Seth's questions, he had decided to postpone revealing more of the Lord's recent revelation, but now the man who had made himself his enemy was forcing his hand. Though he knew Seth and those who sympathized with him would try to use his answers as a way to discredit him in the eyes of the people, he made up his mind to face the problem straight on.

"Seth, I will answer your questions. The Lord told me that we should maintain the same leadership for both church and state until Pioneer Two arrives next summer. At that time the prophet will send two apostles with authority to organize the Church in this land. Meanwhile, the prophet has given me and my brothers the responsibility to guide this people in the establishment of the political kingdom. The two apostles, whoever they may be, will lay their hands on our heads to give us the necessary authority. Of course, the ultimate decision concerning the exact nature of the political system will be up to the people themselves."

"Hah! So you'll still lord it over us," triumphed Seth.

The mouths of many spectators opened wide at Seth's rude remark, and the big farmer slammed his right fist into his left palm. However, a few people glared at Steven and mumbled to their neighbors. Steven noticed that these people were clustered together and seemed to represent a faction.

Without responding to Seth's arrogant comment, Steven said, "Now brothers and sisters, we must get to work. I would like every able-bodied person to go to the fields to help replow the earth and sow our seed once again."

The giant farmer who had supported Steven before called out, "How do you want us to go ahead on this, Brother Steve? What's the plan?"

"Well, Brother Matheson, it's going to take a lot of work and cooperation to replant the two thousand acres that were demolished by the tornado. We'll do it pretty much the way we did it the first time, except we ask every healthy person in Zion's Camp to help. We won't build any more cabins until the replanting is completed. We have nearly twelve hundred people and most of them can do something useful. We'll divide them into ten teams with a hundred and twenty people in each team. I have chosen ten supervisors to lead these teams. Six teams will have the job of replowing the land, and the other four teams will come after them to harrow, plant, and fertilize.

"Our goal is to complete a hundred acres a day, from plowing to planting. If we accomplish that objective, we'll complete the work in the first week of September. The ten supervisors will be my brothers, John and Paul; Kent Booth; Jim Burnham; Jasper Potter; and Michael Stark. Some of you may not know that Michael is our newest colonel. The other four supervisor are José Ramirez, Elmer Gleason, Douglas Cartwright, and Lee Bates."

Steven paused to see their reaction, and was pleased when no one objected because he had chosen two non-Mormons, Cartwright and Bates, as directors. Bates was a former leader of the Riss Community, who had decided to follow the saints to help them build New Zion.

"I have discussed the planting procedures at length with these men, and they know what to do." He started to leave, then stopped, remembering he needed to say one more thing. "I must remind you all that at five this afternoon we'll have a short burial ceremony for those who perished in the storm. If you wish to attend, please meet at the small stand of cottonwood trees just east of the encampment."

He dismissed the meeting, and at once a throng of people rushed forward excitedly and surrounded him. There was a whirlwind of noise, jostling, and confusion. Though he had just mentioned the death and burial of eight people, it was impossible for the crowd to restrain their joy because of the things Steven had revealed. Some of the pioneers, both men and women, embraced him warmly, expressing their happiness that the Lord had given them such a strong, inspired leader, a man who talked with the Lord himself. With tears streaming down their faces, many of them pledged they would help him accomplish everything the Lord desired.

Others who had been farther back in the crowd came up and asked him questions about what he had said, and he was obliged to summarize several times the substance of his message. Nearly all of them joined with the others in rejoicing and giving thanks to God and to their young leader.

Steven was surprised and embarrassed by all the compliments and enthusiasm. Yet, at the same time he was saddened by the conduct of some. He knew they would never be able to create a land of safety and peace unless they loved one another and could work together to reach their great goals. Now he could understand the agony Joseph Smith must have felt when he realized that his people would not be able to build Zion in his day, that is, "redeem Zion," because they were hindered by bickering, selfishness, and lack of unity. Too many of them were unworthy and unwilling to obey the law of consecration. However, Steven had one great consolation. He knew that this time around it would be different.

A short time later, Steven, Mary, and their children went to the fields. Steven was happy to see the people well-organized and working diligently. Nearly the entire population of Zion's Camp, as they now called their settlement, was at work. Steven had never before seen such chatter, laughter, teamwork, and joy. At this rate they would easily finish replanting all the fields according to plan. He and his family wasted no time in joining John's team of workers. However, an hour later Steven and Mary began to suffer because of their injuries. They had to sit or lie down constantly to avoid fainting. Still they did what they could. By the end of the day, the settlers had succeeded in planting a hundred and five acres.

As Steven and his family walked back to the settlement, three sisters, Hannah Baldwin, Rebecca Hale, and Karla Millman, rushed up to him. He recognized Hannah and Rebecca as the two sisters Mary used to take on herb walks on the trail to Missouri to find burdock root and Brigham tea.

"Brother Christopher," Hannah said, "we have an important request.

We want to use an acre or two to plant an herb garden. This community is in desperate need of natural remedies, and the only way we'll get exactly what we want is to grow the plants ourselves."

"What a marvelous idea," Mary exclaimed. "I'd love to help you."

Steven had enjoyed being with his wife all day, but now sensed he'd lose her entirely during daytime to this new project. "Do you have the necessary seeds?"

"Why yes, of course," Rebecca said with a hint of sarcasm. "Well? Do we have your permission?"

Steven knew he had no right to tell them no. And the truth was that since they had no artificial medicines, they were in dire need of remedies for many ailments. "Yes, it *is* a good idea. Let me know if I can help you."

"That was our second request," Hannah said slyly.

"Huh?" Steven grunted.

"We would also like permission to use—to enlist—our husbands," Karla said. "I'm sure you know how hard the work will be. And our guys will be working on something even more important than planting food seeds."

Steven looked at Mary and decided it would be very unwise to refuse. "Certainly, no problem. If your husbands are willing."

Giggling like school girls, the three sisters flew away, no doubt excited to break the *wonderful news* to their husbands. The Christophers followed them at a much slower pace.

"The dears," Mary cried. "They're so happy to be of such great service to the cause of Zion." She said nothing for another twenty paces, then said, "And it's so nice of you to offer to help with the herb garden, Steve."

Steven swallowed hard and smiled. *Women have their ways*, he thought. Yet as he contemplated working on the herb garden with Mary, he decided that's what he preferred to do.

At that moment John came up to them and asked Steven to walk a short distance away with him. He said he wanted to talk to him in private for a minute.

After they had walked fifty feet, John said, "I'm happy you called me to be one of the work supervisors. However, I'd like to spend at least an hour or so every day working on an important personal project." John had accumulated a large supply of electrical components from the modern vehicles some of the pioneers had traveled in and from several auto wrecking yards they had visited in towns on the plains.

"What are you working on?"

"I'd rather not say at this time because it's a difficult project, and I don't know if I can pull it off. I'd rather not look like a fool if it doesn't work. But if it does work, it will really help the community."

"Sounds intriguing. I'll make sure your crew understands why you're not on the job all the time."

"Thanks. Well, I guess I'd better get back to my family."

Steven watched him leave, wondering what marvelous new thing John was inventing.

That night after dinner, the usual family and friends gathered at John's cabin, which was at least twice as large as any other cabin in Zion's Camp. While the children played outside, the adults discussed the events of the day.

"I don't understand why some of those men behave the way they do," Douglas Cartwright said. "They act as though you and your brothers want to be their rulers."

"I'd like to slug that slimy Seth in the snout," Andrea hissed. Everyone looked at her with surprise.

"It's not only Seth Crowell," John said. "I saw groups of men whispering together. It's obvious they were angry about something."

"They appear to be united in secret alliances," Paul added.

"Yes, they do," agreed Steven. "I hope we don't have a repeat of what happened on State Highway 2 in Nebraska."

Tania Christopher frowned and pouted a little. "I thought Zion could only be built by righteous, sanctified people, but in our settlement I see a lot of quarreling, gossip, and downright meanness."

"I've had the same thoughts," Mary said.

"Most of the people are wonderful," Elizabeth said. "It's only a few who are troublemakers." Elizabeth wasn't a member, but she was a better Christian than some of the Mormons.

"Quite a few," Andrea corrected.

"I'm not sure," John said, "that every person has to be righteous for this community to build New Zion. Even in the best of societies there'll always be difficult people. I see them as providing the necessary opposition that sharpens and perfects the decent people. The only people who seriously believe that New Zion must be completely free of sin are a small number of scriptural experts who usually interpret all scriptures literally. Yet no one has ever seen a perfect society in the history of the world. Even in the preexistent celestial world, ruled by the Father, there was a great deal of sin."

"What?" Elizabeth cried. "I thought that was a perfect society."

John shook his head. "No doubt it was perfect in its organization and laws, but still there was sin. Since the law of agency was in power, Lucifer had the right to accept or reject the Father's plan of salvation, present his own plan, exalt his claim for glory, and conspire to seduce others into following him. As a result, he corrupted billions and started the great war in heaven. If warring against God and Christ isn't sin, I don't know what else it could be. As you know, God punished them by casting them out of heaven."

"I think John's right," Paul said. "Now listen, what I'm going to say is just my personal opinion. I don't know if it's doctrine or not. The same situation might exist in the celestial world of the future. People who are assigned to that kingdom will face many challenges and make mistakes. But they will develop gradually until they eventually reach moral perfection. I can't for the life of me imagine spending eternity doing what the Baptists and the fundamentalist Christians think they'll be doing."

"And what's that, pray tell?" Ruther asked, suddenly on the defensive.

"You tell me."

"Tell you what?"

"What you believe all the true believers in Jesus will do throughout eternity."

Steven grinned, amused at how skillfully Paul had turned the subject and lured the old Baptist mountain man into another debate on religion. He knew there was no stopping them now.

Ruther cleared his throat and lifted his hairy chin. "Well, yuh see, young feller, we'll be up thar in heavenly bliss, no doubt lookin' down sadly on you poor Mormons, strugglin' ta build yer paradise. While you folks are a killin' yerselves with all that hard work, we'll be up thar settin' next ta Jesus, praisin' the Lord Almighty, happy as larks, and thankin' Jesus for savin' our souls."

Paul dug in. "What else will you do?"

"What does yuh mean, boy?" Broad grins began to spread across the faces of the others.

"Just what I said. What else will you do when you're not praising Jesus?"

Ruther scratched his head and gazed at the floor for a long moment.

"Oh, I don't rightly know as we'll be doin' much of anything else. The Good Book teaches that the faithful will praise Jesus in heaven forever."

"How long is forever?"

"A real long time, of course," Ruther said scowling, clearly nervous about what trap Paul was leading him into.

Steven didn't interrupt because he understood that Paul and Ruther were very close and often debated religion without a hint of anger. He knew his brother was guiding the old man into a pit from which it would be hard to climb. Next time, perhaps, it would be Paul running for his life.

"A billion years? A trillion millennia?"

Ruther stroked his beard as if in deep thought. Finally, he said, "Well, a heck of a lot longer than that, I'm a guessin'."

Paul shot Ruther an ironical smile. "And all that time—that infinite number of hours—you'll simply be lounging on some silver-lined cloud, strumming your golden harp, and singing the praises of Jesus?"

"Lookee here, boy," Ruther said frowning, "us true believers may be doin' other things, but the Good Book doesn't speculate what exactly."

"You might be building houses, streets, and cities?"

Ruther looked around the room as if searching for help. "Oh, I don't rightly think so. I don't believe there'll be earthly things like that up thar in heaven. We certainly won't be goin' off half-cocked tryin' to be gods and buildin' worlds, like you Mormons plan on doin'."

Everyone in the room laughed because they knew that the LDS doctrine of the quest for godhood was one of the teachings that impressed Ruther the most.

"But with all that strumming and singing you'll be doing—forever and ever—don't you think you might get a little tired of it? Do you think you'll have any time left to talk to angels or friends, visit relatives, explore wildernesses, do some fishing, or go hunting for deer or bear?" Steven realized that Paul knew Ruther adored hunting, fishing, and traipsing through wild country.

"Ah shucks almighty! How does I know? All us Baptists know is what the Good Book says. True believers will be so grateful ta Jesus fer what he done fer us that we'll spend all eternity praisin' his glorious name."

Paul sat back, put his hands behind his head, and continued working on Ruther. "But, brother, don't you think you might get a bit bored doing nothing but praising and singing and praising and singing forever."

"Absolutely not," Ruther declared with powerful conviction and a red face. "You might get bored, but us true believers will never get bored doin' what the scriptures tell us to do."

Seeing that John was almost ready to burst out laughing, Steven decided to jump in and rescue poor Ruther. He felt sorry for the old-timer because he realized that the man was a victim, like so many others, of a religion that placed total faith on the Bible without really understanding its teachings. "Ruther, we're grateful that you're here to give us another perspective on the afterlife. We appreciate you sharing those things with us. But now I'd like to get back to the subject we were discussing a short while ago."

"What subject was that?" Douglas asked. "I've forgotten."

"We were discussing the difficult members of our community. I wanted to say that I agree with John that we may always have some in our midst who are rebellious. But most of our people have come through tests of fire and are worthy, in my opinion, to build New Zion. My conviction is that as the attitude and spirit of the majority gain in strength, most of the rebellious will repent or leave us to join people more like themselves. It's the old principle of like cleaving unto like."

Douglas nodded. "That point John made about there being sin in the preexistence makes me think of something else. The fact that the Father cast the rebellious out of heaven might be a model for us. Someday, as our society becomes larger and more complex, we could handle serious lawbreakers who refuse to repent by simply casting them out of Zion instead of putting them into prisons."

Steven was glad to hear Douglas use the words *our society*. "That's an interesting observation. One I won't forget. By removing such people from the blessings of Zion, we could avoid the huge expense of maintaining jails and a prison system. He stopped a full half minute, finding it hard to speak his mind. "But the thing that touched me most today is the support so many people showed me and the other leaders."

"Personally," said Elizabeth, "I believe the people should be grateful to have you. I've never seen three men who have been kinder and more concerned for their people than you and your brothers."

"Thank you," Steven said with a smile. "I'm sure John and Paul appreciate hearing those words as much as I do." His brothers nodded.

Mary leaned over and hugged Elizabeth. "You and Doug are wonderful friends." Then she turned to Steven. "Okay now, tell us what happened when you went to the grove this morning. I'm dying to know."

Steven related the events in detail. The group listened to every word in awe, asking question after question for twenty minutes. After finishing, he added casually, "Oh, I forgot. Before I reached the grove, I ran into the same stranger that I met in the hills of Wyoming. It wasn't what you'd call a spiritual, uplifting conversation, but it was enlightening and had a certain amount of religious significance."

"You talked with Satan today!" Mary exclaimed.

"Well, he said his name was Lucas Nigel."

They all looked shocked. Mary sat up in her chair, slapping both hands against her knees. "You're kidding. Tell us what he said, and what he did."

After Steven had described his interview with Lucas Nigel, Douglas said, "I'm surprised he would openly make the point that there are two sides to the question of good and evil. It's almost as if he was saying that without evil, good would not exist—"

"And therefore evil serves a useful purpose," Elizabeth added.

"Yep," Ruther said, "that's real interestin'. And I think it's a real hoot to hear that ole devil give hisself a fancy moniker like Lucas Nigel."

"What surprises me," Mary said with a frown, "is his statement that most sin comes from the heart of man, and that he has very little influence in the matter."

"Yeah, that sure shows a lot of gall," Andrea said. "And his appearance. Young, tall, handsome, black hair, better than ordinary clothes, slick and clean, your everyday mortal. Acting as if he were heading for church. Frankly, I don't get it."

Since it was getting late, the visitors started gathering their things and preparing to leave.

"I don't pretend to understand it either, Andrea," Steven said. "But I do know that as long as we don't let him intimidate us and play mind games with us, he can't hurt us or have power over us." Yet even as he said that, he wished that Lucas had not sounded so confident and reasonable.

Chapter 5

~⚜~

G erald Galloway, Supreme Leader of the Universal Government of the Twelve, or UGOT, had arranged for a special conference of his eleven associates on the Inner Council at his mansion in the countryside of Hampshire County, England. This meeting, the eleventh general gathering, was scheduled to begin at five o'clock in the afternoon during the second week of August. Seven of Gerald's associates sat on luxurious armchairs forming a semicircle in his spacious study, waiting for Gerald to arrive and the meeting to begin. At each end of the line of chairs there were two monitors for secure, real-time videoconferencing. The monitors displayed the faces of the four associates who were unable to attend the conference in person. Each of the council members possessed absolute power within the regions of the planet they governed and were subservient only to Gerald himself, whom they revered, feared, and obeyed without question. Gerald's personal secretary had mailed them a list of current council members and their assignments.

Africa North - Francis Bonnard
Africa South - Dominic O'Brien
Australia/Oceania - Coleen Addison (on video)
Eastern Europe - Juliska Ferenci
Eastern Asia (China, Japan, etc.) - Janet Griffin (on video)
Middle East - Randolph Benson
North America - Lucienne Delisle
Russia - Alexi Glinka
South & Central America - Julian Kennedy (on video)

Southeastern Asia - Ernest Hopkins (on video)
Western Europe - Marcus Whitman

The great leader was rather old-fashioned, a hands-on kind of despot. He had contacted each of his council members dozens of times by telephone in the last thirteen months since their tenth general meeting, but he preferred that the members of the Inner Council come to the meetings in person so he could wine and dine them and probe their souls face-to-face. As for Associate Lucienne Delisle, his French mistress, he had spent a great deal of quality time with her at least twice a month since the last big meeting. She was in charge of North America and now was also head of UGOT's Ministry of Religion and Spiritual Welfare.

A few minutes later Galloway entered the study. He went from associate to associate, smiling and extending his hand. As he approached, the associates jumped from their seats, shook his hand, and embraced him warmly. He was pleased at their display of affection, but he wondered how sincere it was. He sat in an armchair facing them and asked each of them what they wanted to drink. As they answered, he spoke into an intercom installed in his armchair, repeating their words to a servant in the wine cellar. Next, he began to ask them, one at a time, questions about their health and the welfare of their families.

Shortly after he had finished his inquiries, four female servants appeared carrying serving trays. Some trays were piled with delicacies, while others bore glasses and bottles of vintage wine. Galloway considered apologizing to the four associates on the video screens for neglecting them, but he noticed that all four of them were being served similar refreshments by their own servants. As they consumed the appetizers and wine, they enjoyed another half hour of pleasant conversation.

When everyone seemed satisfied, Gerald got down to business. "Now that we have enjoyed the pleasantries, I would like to review some of UGOT's main strategies. These strategies will be the means of achieving our two primary goals —to destroy the Jews and to control the destiny of the world. I know that you old-timers know all this, but our two new people, Coleen and Juliska, might need some clarifications regarding their duties."

Recently the Inner Council had voted to replace Ralph Henderson, former associate for Eastern Europe, with Juliska Ferenci; and Brit Young, former associate for Australia and Oceania, with Coleen Addison.

Henderson had been murdered in his bed, and Young had been demoted for incompetence.

The Council had provided their insider manual of five hundred pages to all the associates and their immediate subordinates. There were no more than a hundred people who had a copy of the operation manual, which included their twenty basic strategies and hundreds of detailed procedures for accomplishing those strategies.

Lucienne Delisle, who controlled North America, started the review. "Our first step in overtaking a target nation is too gain control of that country's media."

"And how do we do that, Lucienne?" Gerald asked.

"We send specially trained subversives into the country, sometimes no more than a dozen of them, but at times many more. Those infiltrators speak the native languages. To begin their campaign, the infiltrators locate the key power players and strive to get close to them. Next they use various time-honored methods to do their job. Bribery is usually the best method, but we also use threats and intimidation. Sometimes we simply assassinate uncooperative people and replace them with people we can control. That's about it in a nutshell."

"Excellent," Gerald said. "Without control of the media we can do nothing—except a direct military invasion, which would certainly be wasteful. Okay, what is the next strategy?" Marcus Whitman, who was charged with Western Europe, raised his hand and said, "Well, controlling the media makes the next step much easier. We send additional subversives into the same nation and seize political power in progressive increments. As a part of this effort we also gain control of their courts."

"That's correct," Galloway said. "Marcus, why don't you give us a few details on how we accomplish that takeover?"

"We rely on many of the same techniques used in controlling the media. We infiltrate the nation with dozens of skilled subversives, who also speak the language. We're always recruiting such people. These new operatives gradually work their way into the personal lives of government leaders. Following the tactics of American lobbyists, they wine and dine their victims and offer them fantastic perks. At times it's necessary to entice an official into a compromising situation, which we videotape and pass on to the media for public exposure. Sometimes we browbeat an official into resigning and then replace him with someone more amenable.

"If all that doesn't work, we use bribery, intimidation, and threats of exposure for past misdeeds. Often we secretly plant counterfeit documents into their files and send compliant police to raid their offices. We even threaten them with surreptitious disappearance, incarceration, torture, the elimination of their families, or their own death. When we face the determined resistance of a large number of national leaders, we have even threatened them with an imminent military attack from UGOT's standing army. We assure them that if they force us to invade, we will exterminate them and torture their families. So there you have the basics. In reality, it's a science we have mastered to the utmost. We also have many other cute little tricks to get what we want, many of which we learned from the Nazis."

"I couldn't have summarized it better myself," Gerald said, clearly pleased. "All right, after gaining control of the media, the government, and the courts, what's our next move?" Francis Bonnard, the associate for North Africa raised his hand. "Francis?"

"To disarm the people."

"Exactly. Please be so kind as to explain why."

"If the people have weapons and ammunition, they'll soon take them up and wage guerilla warfare against both us and their corrupt government, whom they see as criminal usurpers. Without disarming the people we have virtually no real chance of controlling a target nation for any length of time. In some nations the people have already been disarmed, as in Japan, China, Singapore, and Luxembourg. For our purposes, those nations are sitting ducks.

"In other nations, like Mexico, Haiti, Guatemala, Brazil, Canada, Australia, England, Germany, and France, guns are permitted but under very strict regulations. Those nations will also be easy to control because gun ownership is fairly low. But in a few nations we will have to work much harder to gain control. For example, Yemen, Switzerland, and the Czech Republic. In the United States the people were originally allowed to own guns under the Second Amendment, but eventually that right was seriously curtailed by multiple nitpicking regulations. Still there were over three hundred fifty million guns of all types in the hands of citizens in that country when it disintegrated. Thanks to the collapse, we don't have to face armed Americans."

"Indeed," Gerald said. "The collapse we helped to orchestrate saved us a lot of trouble and money. That's one of our great success stories."

"Not entirely, Gerald," Lucienne said.

Gerald's face froze. "Explain, please."

"You're forgetting the Mormons. Remember, I told you about them ten months ago when we decided to recruit a Mexican army to attack Utah."

"Yes, of course. I remember." Gerald forced his face to relax. He took pride in always maintaining his composure in front of his subordinates. "Okay, we'll discuss that problem now. Since we've finished reviewing our most important strategies and operations, let's proceed to the second part of this meeting—our recent failures and successes. We need to discuss our Mexican army project, the MOM march in Berne, and the abjuration of Pierre Laborde. Lucienne, fill us in on the result of our attack on Utah."

"Right. Well, as you all know, we used the Mexican cartels to recruit a large army near Mexico City. We gave them promises of vast wealth and the complete possession of the western half of the United States. We also gave them equipment, trucks, tanks, weapons, and supplies. They reached Utah almost a month and a half ago and proceeded to attack on three fronts. The Mexican army numbered about 450,000 soldiers, and the Mormons managed, to our surprise, to raise an even larger army of untrained citizens, armed with nothing but hunting rifles, shotguns, and handguns." Lucienne's lips were tight and her brow covered with sweat.

"Even though the Mexican army was better equipped and had greater firepower, the Mormons were surprisingly well-disciplined and directed by competent leadership. In spite of that, our mercenaries would have defeated them easily if it had not been for an amazing turn of events." Lucienne seemed frustrated and embarrassed and had difficulty continuing.

"What turn of events?" asked Janet Griffin from a video monitor. Janet was the associate for East Asia.

Lucienne clenched her jaw as she struggled for control. "The Indians . . . Thousands of them followed our mercenaries from Morelia, Mexico, all the way into Utah, attacking them in guerilla-style ambushes at night. For the most part using nothing but bows and arrows. By the time the Mexican army met Mormon resistance in Utah, the Indians had been reinforced by other tribes until they numbered about 260,000 braves. Both Mormons and Indians attacked our hired army with such tactical skill and savage determination that they annihilated the three Mexican armies in one week."

The council members looked at one another in shock, without saying a word. Finally, Lucienne said, "I'm sorry, Gerald, I was sure—"

Gerald had already received this report in person from Lucienne, but her rehearsal of it revived his anger and frustration. Yet he quickly regained his usual self-control. "Not to worry. I assure you we'll use other means later to do the job, and nothing will save either the Mormons or the Indians who helped them. Now, the second item—the Mothers Opposing Madness march in Berne." He looked at Marcus Whitman, the associate for Western Europe.

Marcus sat up straight and cleared his throat. His hands tightly clenched the arms of his chair. "Well . . . this should cheer you up. Our MOM march on the House of Parliament was a great success in furthering gun control in Switzerland. It took place about three and a half months ago, at the end of April. As you know, we stacked the deck. We recruited about one hundred and twenty thousand female marchers, who were instructed to weep as they marched and to wave all kinds of heartbreaking signs begging the government to ban guns in Switzerland. We convinced the media that there would be a half million marchers and that's what they reported, much to our delight."

"How many spectators were there?" Lucienne asked.

"I'm not sure exactly. Probably several hundred thousand. We also recruited another thousand people to mix in with the spectators. Their job was to line the march route shouting insults at the demonstrators and waving repulsive placards. The media focused a great deal of attention on the hateful signs and behavior our hired 'pro-gun' people. Almost as much attention as on the weepy, emotional appeals of the anti-gun proponents. I'm not privy to the financing of that project, but I'm sure it cost us a fortune to buy the marchers, the special spectators, and the media."

"Not as much as you might suppose," Gerald said. "Not after I called in a dozen markers owed me by European leaders. But, Marcus, have we gotten any positive results in the Swiss legislature?"

"Absolutely. In the last four months there have been six proposals for legislation to put stricter rules on gun ownership, and they have been met with favor by many legislators and government officials. There certainly won't be a complete ban on guns anytime soon, but definitely an increase in regulation."

"Then it was worth the money and effort. How did Martin Gannt perform?"

"Our Director of Media Relations did an excellent job. I don't think anyone could have done better."

"Good. Martin is dedicated and has done some remarkable things, but that doesn't include his latest effort."

"You mean that fiasco with Pierre Laborde?" Marcus said.

Gerald sniffed and wiped his nose with a handkerchief. "Precisely. Marcus, give us a summary of *that* delightful story, for the benefit of those here who haven't heard the juicy details."

Marcus unclenched his hands and leaned back in his chair with a smile. "I'd be happy to. The whole thing took place in Paris a month and a half ago on prime time television. It seems Martin Gannt decided to use a faithful Mormon named Pierre Laborde, who was incarcerated in a religious concentration camp near Arras, as the star of a special anti-Mormon segment on TV Planète in Paris. This special was to be broadcast to over a half billion viewers. Monsieur Laborde had been given a precise script to read, in which he abjured his Mormon faith and Christianity in general. Of course, if he messed up this renunciation, both he and his wife would be shot.

"Apparently Gannt figured this abjuration would discredit Mormonism and enhance his image in the eyes of UGOT. Unfortunately, however, Gannt arranged the special too rapidly and didn't insist that the segment be taped in advance. So, to the shock and horror of Gannt, the TV producers, and the members of our Inner Council—most of you saw it on TV—Monsieur Laborde bore a fervent testimony of the truthfulness of Mormonism. In short, Laborde sacrificed his life and family for his religion."

With a tight mouth Gerald added, "And immediately afterward he was shot off camera."

"And well he should have been," O'Brien said. "But what I don't understand is why the television control room didn't cut Laborde the instant he went off script."

"Because the technician in charge was drunk as a skunk and couldn't find the right buttons," Gerald replied.

"Another mistake by Gannt for not double-checking," Glinka added.

"Don't worry," Gerald said. "I've had words with Gannt to make sure such mistakes are never repeated."

"You're far too kind, Gerald," Lucienne fawned. "A lot more than I would be."

"Thank you, my dear. Now, on to the next subject. I've heard from various sources that there's another Mormon community being established in the American Midwest. Especially in what used to be Missouri. Do any of you have information on that?"

"Yes," Lucienne said, "it's a small community that left Utah in primitive vehicles to settle in Missouri. I don't know why yet. Some people make the absurd claim that the Mormons hope to establish a worldwide religious civilization, whose capital is in Missouri."

"What a dumb place to choose for a world capital!" Whitman observed. "Out in the boondocks. It's incomprehensible."

"I thought so too," Lucienne said. "But listen to this. I have other reports which assert that thousands of immigrants from all parts of the world, and also many Utah Mormons, are making the nearly impossible journey to join the Missouri settlement."

Again Gerald's face tightened in anger, and he fought to control his temper. "I can see that the Mormons are going to be a much bigger problem than I had imagined. We must take vigorous action and do it quickly. I want all of you to begin recruiting armed forces from various nations under your control to make a little invasion against the Missouri Mormons. Get back to me on your progress within a month. We'll work out the details later. Meanwhile I want each of you individually to give me your input on this problem."

They discussed the new project for an hour and concurred that it would be necessary to organize a large army and transport it, with every modern weapon available, to the eastern coast of the United States. From there, ground troops, supported by tanks and airpower, would travel to Missouri with the goal of ending the Mormon problem once and for all.

Chapter 6

⚜

In the weeks following the great tornado, the pioneers worked together with exceptional diligence and cooperation. Their first goal was to replant the fields, using their last remaining seeds. They were acutely aware of the fact that if these crops didn't grow, many might starve during the coming winter. Fifteen days after the beginning of the reseeding, the first delicate shoots pushed into the bright sunlight, and when the saints beheld that beautiful sight, they danced with joy and gave thanks to their Father in Heaven.

When the replanting was completed, they began once more to build cabins and lodges, finishing about two cabins a day and one lodge a week. The leaders of Zion's Camp regretfully postponed the planned clearing of Independence, the future capital of New Zion, even though it was only a few miles away to the northwest. Since their primary objective was to insure that the people would survive the winter, they focused on the planting and the construction of warm dwellings on the lands they currently occupied.

By the end of August, Steven realized that if they continued as they were, they wouldn't complete the shelters until the end of January. He presented the problem to the leadership of the settlement, and they agreed with him. After discussing the matter for several hours, they decided to suspend the construction of the lodges and focus on family cabins. They had planned on building ten lodges, but would have to be satisfied with five. They could reduce the number of cabins needed by placing the unmarried people in two of the lodges, the females in one and the males in another.

Released from the immediate necessity of spending so much time in the fields and building the huge lodges, the saints should be able to construct at least three or four cabins a day. In this way the leaders hoped to have shelters for every family by the beginning of December so no one would be forced to spend the worst of the winter in a covered wagon. When John Christopher presented the new strategy to the assembled settlers, a few people grumbled and complained that the leaders should have foreseen the problem earlier, but most of the people accepted the plan with good hearts.

On Sunday after church in mid-September, Steven and his family walked slowly back to their cabin. The children were chattering, jumping boulders, and throwing rocks at trees for target practice. But Mary noticed how quiet and pensive her husband was. Finally, about halfway home, she spoke up. "Why so serious? Is there a problem?"

"No, not really. Well, yes, as a matter of fact there is."

"Can I help?"

"Maybe. There's so much going on in the settlement. So many problems and responsibilities. So many decisions to make. I'm constantly approached at our cabin and everywhere else by people needing my help. Frankly, I'm pretty overwhelmed. I can't seem to spend as much time with you and the kids as I want to."

"I know you've been under a lot of stress. Why don't you ask for help?"

"I think we need to do more than just ask for help. I'm wondering if we shouldn't set up a local government to make decisions."

"What a wonderful idea! That way the responsibilities would be spread among a group of people, not just a few. I think you should get started with it today."

"Today?"

"Yes, why not?"

Steven said no more as they covered the hundred yards from the meeting lodge to their cabin. But when they arrived, he said, "You know, you're right." The children disappeared quickly to seek out friends, so the parents entered alone and sat down at the kitchen table.

"Do you think I should ask my brothers and the other community leaders to come here today to discuss forming a local government?"

"Certainly. Let's get moving on it now. Go out and invite them for two o'clock. By that time I can prepare a treat."

Steven kissed her and told her how much he loved her. Then he flew out the door in the direction of John's cabin. He presented the idea to John, and they both set out to invite Paul, Douglas, Ruther, the four colonels, and several others. By two o'clock eleven people were ensconced wherever they could find a place in Steven's cabin, all of them eating apple pie topped with whipped cream. Steven introduced his proposal for creating a community government, and everyone received the idea with enthusiasm.

"It's a great idea," Douglas said. "I've been thinking the same thing for a long time. Why don't we elect a mayor and a city council?"

"Yes, like in Utah towns," Floyd Madsen said. "Then the mayor and the council can select a few administrators to take care of the details. Of course, we should give them some type of recompense. Right now, it might come down to giving them service or maybe special privileges. I don't know."

They decided to post an announcement on the town bulletin board that they would like the citizens to vote for a town mayor and five council members. Nominations for these officers would be accepted until the coming Wednesday at noon and the elections would be held Friday morning.

After they had made these decisions, Ruther frowned a little and said, "Look, since they're goin' ta vote on a government, why don't we have them vote on some city plannin' at the same time. I've seen a few people settin' out stakes and strings for property lines that look like ten acres or more. It's goin' ta be hard ta have a good organized town here, and in Independence too, if everybody claims all different sizes of lots."

"You're right, Ruther," John said, "but the vote on city planning should be conducted by the new city leaders, and then be approved by the voters."

Ruther replied, "Yep, I guess you're right. The new leaders should handle it."

After his guests left at three o'clock, Steven drew up a memo on a large piece of heavy paper. Then he hurried to the town bulletin board and posted his announcement. While he was doing so, several citizens approached, read the memo, and began to ask questions. He answered them as well as he could. Before long, thirty people had assembled and continued to ask more questions. After responding to some of them, he left for his cabin, and the people hurried away to spread the news.

⁂

On Wednesday the citizens nominated five people for mayor: Steven Christopher, Douglas Cartwright, Mary Christopher, John Christopher, and Floyd Madsen. They also nominated eleven other people for city council.

When Steven saw his nomination, he looked at his wife wearily and said, "It looks like I'm still on the hook."

Mary hugged him tenderly. "Well, dear, you can't blame them for wanting the best man.

At least you'll get help."

"But they nominated the best person—you!"

"No, I'm not the best person for the job. It was probably Andrea Warren, my lovely friend, who nominated me. I've no doubt the people will end up choosing you for mayor."

"That's what I'm afraid of." Steven left by two o'clock to post the nominations.

On Friday at three o'clock they officially closed the polls in Lodge Three and began to count the votes. Despite the deadline, a few citizens rushed into the lodge with late votes. The counting of the votes had been turned over to a half dozen sisters, none of whom had been nominated for office, and they couldn't bring themselves to turn away late voters. But by six o'clock they had the results.

It was a landslide in favor of Steven Christopher for mayor. The five council members were Douglas Cartwright, Floyd Madsen, John Christopher, Andrea Warren, and Elizabeth Cartwright. Steven read his name on the bulletin board with sad resignation.

On Saturday morning Steven summoned the city council for a special meeting on city planning at two o'clock. He also asked Tania Christopher to act as recorder. After expressing congratulations on their election and a few other preliminaries, Steven asked the councilors for input on the size of lots and streets for their city.

"Steve," Douglas said, "why don't you choose the sizes? You know more than any of us regarding what the Lord wants in this matter."

Steven paused a moment, wondering how to express his feelings. Then he said, "The Lord hasn't given me instructions on that matter, and I prefer not to decide for others what size their lots should be, or their houses, or their streets. I'm not their master. Therefore, the people should have the freedom to choose for themselves. Frankly, I don't believe the Lord cares a fig about how big our lots are. That said, we do want people within city limits to have lots that are about the same size, or otherwise the organization of the town would be nothing but chaos. But it's up to the citizens to choose how big those lots should be. And when we build other towns, I'll suggest the same thing to the people who live there."

"I agree with Steve," Andrea said. "Why don't we give them several possibilities as to sizes and let them vote on what they prefer."

That idea met with general acceptance. After discussing the matter another hour, they agreed to give the people nine possible lot sizes and several streets widths. Next they decided to write a few general regulations for the settlement. It took another hour to come up with thirty basic rules.

Steven thought the rules were obvious, but while listening to council members suggest and debate them, he was reminded of all the swimming pool rules he used to see when he was a child. Rules forbidding people from running to urinating in the pool. When he read those rules as a child, he concluded that the pool administrators didn't want kids to have any fun. But when he read them as a young adult, he decided the pool bosses were trying hard to avoid lawsuits. He had to admit that people can sometimes act very foolishly and the rules were probably designed to protect them from themselves.

By the end of the following week they had the decisions of the people. The lots would be uniform—a hundred feet across the front and two hundred and seventeen feet in depth. As for the streets, the side streets would be a hundred and twenty feet in width, and the main streets would be a hundred and forty-eight feet wide.

The exceptionally warm, sunny weather, accompanied by regular, gentle rains, continued into December. The crops flourished, including corn, soybeans, wheat, peas, potatoes, carrots, tomatoes, onions, cucumbers, grain sorghum, green grasses for hay, and all kinds of medicinal herbs. The excited saints began to harvest some of the crops in November, working as a united community. After the harvests, the crops were dried, covered with mulch, or put into root cellars, depending on the type of plant.

One day in December a team of thirty men, who had gone on a foraging trip to Kansas City, returned to the settlement with four wagon loads of Mason jars and lids. When the older sisters beheld this treasure, they threw up their hands and squealed with delight. Several demanded to know where the men had found such a marvelous boon. The men explained that they had discovered the jars in an abandoned Kerr manufacturing plant in the city.

A few of the younger women knew what the bottles were because they had been forced to eat food from them in Utah when normal society collapsed, but most of them were not sure why the older sisters were so excited to get tons of empty bottles. But when the uninitiated sisters learned that they could preserve food in the jars for months or even years, they beamed and begged their enlightened sisters to give them lessons immediately.

So the women set up a makeshift outdoors canning factory and got to work. Within five days, fifty-five women, working twelve hours a day—except when they took breaks to nurse babies and discipline children—canned a total of 13,475 jars of vegetables. That meant each female finished an average of 245 jars. They really had fun doing it because as they worked, they laughed, joked, sang happy songs, discussed the foibles of men, and chatted constantly about everything under the sun. Most of all, they knew they were making a real contribution to the survival of the community. When the work was finally done, they lay around the work area, completely exhausted but pleased with themselves. Before they left for home, they vowed to ask the next groups of foragers to bring back even bigger loads of jars.

As the people labored in the fields, they laughed and sang and enjoyed hundreds of conversations. They felt secure because the leaders always posted a few armed sentries around the settlement. The sisters who had planted the giant herb garden had prepared more than forty herbal medicines to administer to the needs of the sick. The Lord had given the people a miracle and they knew it. Even the quarrelsome skeptics helped with the work, shaking their heads in disbelief and grumbling at the "excessive" behavior of the others. They insisted that there must be a natural explanation for the unusual weather and Zion's Camp was simply lucky.

News of the success of Zion's Camp had spread throughout the region, and during December, fifteen good families migrated to the new settlement from the east, seeking food, shelter, and safety. A short time later three more families came from the Riss Community. Steven welcomed all of them and found room for them in the multifamily lodges that were not yet fully occupied.

The families who had immigrated from the east described scenes and conditions of unbelievable horror, most of which they had witnessed themselves. They reported that hundreds of small bands of dangerous vagabonds roamed the country, gratifying their lust for robbery, murder, rape, and destruction. There was disease, famine, and bloodshed everywhere. Neighbors attacked neighbors, and family members assailed one another, even their young, in order to survive. The newcomers declared that they had come to Zion's Camp because they had heard it was the only safe place in the country. Steven interviewed one of these families and was shocked and saddened by their story.

Right after the great Collapse on September 19, Matthew and Linda Newton were boarded up and hunkered down with their family in their home in Boonville, Missouri. They heard frightening sounds in the neighborhood: wailing sirens, horns blaring, people shouting, thunderous pounding, gunshots, and the noise of desperate struggles. Through cracks in the heavy plywood that covered their downstairs windows they could see lights flashing, vehicles racing, and running people. Sometimes there were sights too horrible to mention.

One night the yelling and screaming were almost deafening, directly in front of their home. Matthew was watching through a small hole purposely worked into the plywood.

"What's going on out there?" Linda cried. "Let me see." She approached the front window, but Matthew stopped her.

"No. You don't want to see."

She insisted and took a peek, but quickly pulled her head back, moaning woefully. "Dear God, they're slaughtering people out there."

They decided to wait it out, hoping things would settle down after a while. But it only seemed to get worse. They had stored food—enough for two years—drugs, supplies, and gas for the big generator, and they had put bars on the upstairs windows. They had also stored guns and ammunition, just in case. When the telephone system was still operational, they had tried to call friends who had built a reinforced home in the countryside to protect themselves from marauders, figuring they'd be safer in the wild.

But their friends were wrong, for they were far more vulnerable, out there all alone by themselves. They never did answer the phone.

After a few days they heard the sound of breaking glass, a gunshot, and then terrified screams not far away.

"What's that?" Linda asked.

Matthew ran to the board covering a bedroom side window and looked through a crack. His wife and two of their children followed him and waited anxiously.

"Vandals. They've broken into the Robinson house. Through the windows. A dozen of them inside. I can't see anything else." The loud screams continued, but soon stopped.

"I know Jack Robinson has a pistol," Matthew said, "but it didn't seem to help. Maybe there are too many of them."

Matthew and Linda figured the savage vandals had begun to force their way into the homes of their neighbors, no doubt searching for food and whatever else they wanted.

The Newtons knew it was only a matter of time before it was their turn. So they waited fearfully for the onslaught—eight of them with loaded weapons in their hands watching at strategic spots in the house for attempts at forced entry. Their four children, Brett, Noel, Marcy, and Lucy were teenagers and proficient—all of them—in the use of firearms. Blaine, Matthew's brother, had sought safety for his wife Karen and their small child at their home because Blaine had ignored the growing dangers and had not prepared.

After the utilities went down, Matthew turned on the generator located in a special room attached to the back of the house, and they had light and could cook food on hot plates. Usually, however, he avoided using the generator as much as possible, worried that its noise might alert the wandering marauders. So they usually lighted the house by carrying several oil lamps from room to room.

Then one evening, after a week of anxious watching and waiting, smoke began to swirl into the kitchen while Matthew and Linda were fixing dinner with the help of Karen, Marcy, and Lucy.

"Matt, the smoke, what's causing it?" Linda cried.

"I don't know." He looked around for the source of the smoke as everyone started coughing.

Suddenly it hit him. "The generator," he said. "They've blocked it." He rushed to the back room and switched off the machine. From the outside someone had blocked the exhaust vent located high in a corner of the generator room. Standing on a chair, he removed the vent tube and cleared the blockage. He decided to check the vent every time he used the generator.

At that moment he heard the sound of gunfire and the impact of bullets tearing through the plywood at the front of the house. He ran down the hall toward the living room and nearly collided with Blaine, who was coming to get him.

Weeks ago the two families had agreed upon a plan in case they were attacked from the street by people using guns. The women and children were to lie on the floor as low as possible while the men were to grab their AR-15 rifles and mount the stairs to the front bedroom, from which position they could cover the street.

So when they heard the gunshots that day, everyone went into action, and within two minutes the men were at their posts next to the bedroom windows.

"Do you see what I see?" Matthew asked.

"I think so. Three guys in the street with pistols, taking potshots at our house. They're staggering around like they're drunk."

"See anyone else?"

"Nope," Blaine said. "Do you?" Suddenly he saw two rifle flashes from behind the neighbor's fence directly across the street, and another flash from bushes on the right. "Oops! There are seven or eight of them farther back. My guess is they're using those government-approved bolt-action hunting rifles."

As they readied their "assault rifles," they saw one of the drunks hurl forward violently and slam face down onto the road.

"Geez!" Blaine exclaimed. "Those geniuses shot one of their buddies in the back."

"Let 'em have it," Matthew shouted.

It was growing dark, but their semiautomatics had night vision scopes, and they could see their enemies clearly, even the outline of those sheltered behind the fence. They opened with rapid rounds of fire, targeting each of their enemies carefully, one at a time. Within one minute they had killed seven men, and the few survivors ran for their lives, disappearing into the night.

After that the two families had relative peace for several weeks, and Matthew thought they might survive these perilous times after all. However, during their second month of self-imposed incarceration things suddenly changed.

At about one in the afternoon, everyone was together in the living room, some of them chatting while others were reading books by the light of oil lamps. Their peace was violently interrupted by an axe slamming partway through the plywood covering the big front window. At the same time they heard shouts coming to them from the outside.

"Let us in," a man bellowed. "We're dying out here. We need food and medicine and we're going to get it, even if we have to kill every one of you." The blows continued until the axe went all the way through the plywood.

Linda, Karen and the two teenage girls armed themselves and hurried to their posts farther back in the house. Matthew's two boys, Brett and Noel, grabbed 9mm pistols and took their preassigned positions near the reinforced front door. Someone was hammering on the door with a heavy object but was making little headway. Matthew and Blaine went to the unlocked gun cabinet, seized their rifles, and stationed themselves directly in front of the window. The hole in the plywood was now large enough for Matthew to see the features of the man wielding the axe.

"Is that you, Mr. Campbell?" Matthew called out. James Campbell was his neighbor two houses down. Campbell had often come over to talk to him while he was mowing the lawn or shoveling snow. They considered each other good neighbors if not good friends.

"Yes, it's me, and I know you're hoarding food in there. It's wicked of you not to share with your neighbors. You're going to give me what I want or I'll break in and take everything you have. Then I'll burn your house with you and your family in it."

"Campbell," Matthew yelled, "you'd better leave now while you can."

Suddenly the barrel of a rifle was thrust through the opening and began spitting rounds into the house. The men and boys hit the ground at once and waited for the assailant to run out of bullets. It seemed as though it would never stop, but finally it did, and before his attacker could reload Matthew jumped up, aimed his AR-15 at the hole and blasted away. He enlarged the hole quickly and could see rounds smashing into Campbell and those hovering close by. Soon they were gone, either shot down or scattering for safety.

There was a deathly silence outside, and Matthew decided his enemies had broken off their attack. He walked back into the house and found Karen sitting on the kitchen floor sobbing, her little daughter in her arms covered with blood. One of Campbell's stray bullets had struck her in the head as she got up from the floor for a brief moment. She had died instantly. Everyone did their best to console Karen, but there was really little they could do.

Their life was fairly peaceful and quiet in the following months. Only occasionally did a bullet penetrate the walls of their makeshift fortress, not hitting anyone directly but sometimes causing superficial wounds by forcing slivers of wood and shards of glass into their bodies. When that happened, the occupants rushed to their assigned positions and defended themselves according to Matthew's instructions.

After thirteen months in their prison, Matthew began to get the feeling that things would soon change. He convinced the others to make ready to leave the protection of their home, but he had no definite plan concerning where or when they would go.

One day in mid-November, they heard a knock at their front door. Looking through the door peephole, Matthew saw a pleasant-looking man in his fifties, smiling and waiting patiently.

"Maybe it's a trap," Blaine said. "To get us to open up so they can storm the house."

"I don't think so," Matthew said. He checked the yard through the hole in the plywood and saw several strange vehicles in the street. Each conveyance was attached to horses in traces. "I see families out there. Open the door, Brett." Everyone in the house gathered in the living room to witness this strange new thing.

Brett unlocked the door and pulled it open. What they saw was a man in ragged clothes and wearing a long gray beard. His eyes were bright blue and had laugh lines around them.

"Hello," the man said in a friendly voice. "My name is Howard McDonald. My family has been on the road heading west for three weeks now. Along the way we picked up three other families, good people all of them. Several residents around here told us about you, and we want to invite you to go with us."

"Where are you heading?" Matthew asked.

"To the Mormon Zion in Missouri. It's only a hundred miles to the west and it's the safest place in this part of the country. The people living there are of high caliber and they welcome all those who want to live in peace with their fellow man."

"Can you wait for us a bit?" Matthew said. "We're almost ready to go."

Chapter 7

A t the end of December, Douglas and Elizabeth Cartwright, and three
of their children were baptized members of the Church in Blue
Springs Lake. Steven baptized Douglas, John baptized Elizabeth, and Paul
baptized the children. Mary, who was now over six months pregnant, stood
near the shore, her face bright with happiness to see her good friends make
their commitment.

The weather changed abruptly during the first week in January. A blizzard struck the entire Midwest with a vengeance, as if to make up for the
time that God's hand had held it back. But the leaders of the town were
not worried, for they felt the community was ready. The harvests were in
and the shelters built.

However, news soon reached the settlement that the nearby Riss Community was becoming unsafe because of the growing instability of many of its
inhabitants. Because of this, several good families migrated to New Zion
from Riss, and what they reported was disturbing. Many citizens there were
forming military contingents for the purpose of attacking the saints, their
former friends and allies. These same people did all they could to turn their
fellow citizens against the Mormons. They claimed that the saints were
dangerous neighbors because they selfishly salvaged most of the available
equipment and supplies from devastated cities, prospered by exploiting
their own wives and children, stole other men's wives in order to force them
into polygamy, and indulged in many other unspeakable practices.

But most of all, they accused the Mormons of planning to create a
great religious empire that would destroy all other governments and enslave
every other nation. Two of the leaders of the Riss Community, Austin

Meyer and Lyle Motley, argued against such accusations, contending that the anti-Mormons were nothing but jealous gossipmongers. In spite of this, the enemies of Zion grew in power and influence from day to day.

The winter became so severe in such a short time that the animals began to suffer terribly. Steven condemned himself for not thinking of them earlier. Brother Matheson had warned him, but he had been so intent on protecting the people that he had postponed providing for the livestock. Quickly he organized work teams to build makeshift barns. While the work was in progress, several dozen animals perished from the cold. With happy hearts Steven's enemies took this occasion to accuse him of being a false prophet. If he had really been guided by the Lord, he wouldn't have overlooked such an important matter. Of course, they never tried to explain why they had neglected to suggest it to Steven.

The winter continued long and hard, but few saints complained. At least at first. They understood that the Lord had blessed them and still watched over them. Still, when the bitter winds continued to shriek and the snows buried their cabins even into March, their patience began to falter. It was as if nature was trying to make up for the earlier moratorium. To prevent boredom, laziness, and disorder, the leaders strove to keep the citizens busy. They organized community activities such as snow removal, firewood cutting, hunting expeditions, building projects, and visits to the ruins of Kansas City to salvage tools, supplies, and equipment. They created the first fully organized stake in Missouri, with Steven as stake president, Douglas Cartwright and Byron Mills as counselors, a stake high council, and four small wards. Steven did this at the instructions, and under the authority, of Josiah Smith the prophet, who had prepared him before Pioneer One left Utah.

In spite of the problems, Steven and Mary and their family spent many happy hours in the evening in front of the warm fireplace, studying, talking, playing games, and knitting baby clothes. They had chosen to call the baby Gabrielle if she was a girl, or Daniel if a boy. Some of the parents in the vicinity pooled their expertise to homeschool the children in nearby cabins. Three days a week Steven taught a group of twelve children French and English in their cabin, while Mary gave lessons in science. Other parents offered classes in history, math, music, art, and scripture. News of the success of this homeschool spread throughout the town, and many other parents followed suit.

Steven was proud of his wife and constantly bragged about how healthy and beautiful she looked. Andrea, Mary's best friend, had a different point of view concerning pregnancy and expressed it from time to time with an ironical smile.

One evening during the first week of March, Andrea visited the home-school in order to help Mary give her science lesson. After the classes were done and the children departed, Steven, sitting on a couch in the main room, gazed at his wife and went into another long rehearsal of how lovely she was.

After listening until she could stand it no more, Andrea declared, "Beautiful my eye, Steven. Just look at what you've done to the poor girl. I told her never to marry again, at least to a man who wanted kids, but no, she wouldn't listen. Now look at her. Because of you, she's seriously overweight."

"She's not overweight," Steven objected. "She's pregnant, as you well know."

Andrea glared at him and snapped, "Yeah right. Listen, Mr. Mayor, a pregnant woman weighing a hundred and twenty normally gains about twenty more pounds, not forty. Look at her fat little cheeks."

Mary flashed Steven a smile but didn't bother to refute Andrea.

"But how is that my fault?" Steven said. "I don't force that food down her throat. The fact is, she loves to eat."

"It certainly *is* your fault. Remember back in August, September, and October when she was so ill from morning sickness that the only thing she could do to feel better was stuff herself."

"I see," Steven said. "I'm guilty because I got her pregnant."

Andrea gave a firm nod. "Yep, and not only that. You also dragged her away from civilization and the medicine that could have helped her."

Mary was having difficulty controlling her laughter now.

"But in Utah she couldn't have found—" Steven began.

"And because of the extra weight," Andrea continued without listening, "she'll have such bad stretch marks that I'll have to spend hours of my precious time rubbing her chubby belly with Vitamin E oil and plantain ointment, if we can scrounge those things from somewhere."

Steven threw up his hands in frustration and left the room to tuck the children into bed.

Mary burst out laughing. "Andrea, I promise you that if I want my stretch marks rubbed, I'll asked Steven to do it." Mary felt a special joy at the thought that she would soon experience birth for the first time and give a child to the man she truly loved. In her first marriage she had not borne any children because it was a loveless union and she had learned too late that her husband hated children.

One evening in the third week of March, the Christophers were gathered around the fireplace in Steven and Mary's home. Mary lay on a bed in front of the fireplace and the rest of the family surrounded her. Present also were Andrea Warren and Elizabeth Cartwright, who had come at noon when Mary's labor first started. Gertrude Jones, Mary's midwife, had come several times during the afternoon to check on Mary's condition and then left, saying her patient wasn't dilated enough. She gave Steven instructions as to when things would get serious and he should send for her. He timed her contractions carefully, and when they were forty seconds long and about five minutes apart, he decided it was time. He sent Andrew to alert the midwife and William to inform their friends.

Andrew rushed to the Jones residence, only three hundred yards away. Gertrude arrived within ten minutes and began to prepare Mary for the birth. Soon the other adults rushed into the cabin to greet and encourage Mary. But, after a few minutes, John, Paul, Ruther, Jarrad, Douglas, and Leonard left the room and waited outside the cabin door. Though the weather had grown milder, Steven worried about them getting sick standing in the cold. At midnight he stepped outside and convinced them to go home, explaining that the birth might take all night because this was Mary's first child. They finally agreed to leave when he assured them that everything would be all right.

Between Mary's labor pains Steven rubbed her back and arms, encouraging her in every way he could, in spite of the fact that he was nervous himself. During the contractions Gertrude showed him how to lessen Mary's pain. She told him to push his thumbs into the pressure points on the inside of Mary's upper thighs. Mary claimed that this lowered her pains by at least 50 percent. After four hours of intermittent pushing against the pressure points, he felt as though his thumbs would drop off, but he knew that his little problem was nothing in comparison to what Mary was going through. She moaned during the contractions, but in general was brave and handled the natural birth surprisingly well.

A beautiful baby girl was finally born in a normal birth around three in the morning. She began to breathe immediately without crying. Gertrude suctioned out her nose and mouth quickly and checked her coloring and respiration. Then she placed the baby on her mother's abdomen and covered her loosely with a blanket. Mary gazed at her wonderful new baby, filled with awe and relief that *she* was finally a mother at thirty-two years of age. She stroked Gabrielle's head tenderly and couldn't take her eyes off her. Steven brought the other children into the room to see their new sister and their big eyes revealed their wonderment.

"Okay, Steven," Gertrude said with a sly smile, "are you ready to cut the cord?"

His eyes widened in shock. "What's that? Cut the what?"

"The cord. In a natural birth it's traditional for the father to cut the cord."

"What cord?"

Gertrude touched the umbilical cord. "This is the cord." After ten minutes the cord had become thin and had stopped pulsating.

"But won't that cause them to bleed to death?"

"Of course not, silly man. It won't bleed at all." She handed him a piece of sterilized string.

"I cut it with string?"

"No, Brother Christopher," she said with studied patience. "You tie the string fairly tightly around the cord about an inch from the baby." It was obvious that Gertrude was enjoying teasing him.

He did as directed, trying hard to control his clumsy fingers.

"Very good. You're an expert." She handed him a pair of scissors. "Now you cut the cord here about two inches from the baby."

Steven cut the cord gingerly and was delighted to see that no disaster ensued.

"Excellent. You're all done," the midwife said.

Gertrude wrapped the child more thoroughly and put her at her mother's breast. Gabrielle rooted around, searching for a nipple. Mary had to place it into her mouth, but as soon as the baby got a good hold, she began to suckle contentedly.

Gertrude said, "The suckling will cause Mary's uterus to contract and help her stop bleeding. The contractions will expel the placenta in about half an hour."

An hour later the Christopher family was still staring at the baby, too excited to go to bed. At last Gertrude told them it was important for them to get some sleep and insisted they retire for the night. Then she left with a couple of her assistants, promising to return in the morning to check on mother and baby.

In early spring the pioneers began plowing for the next season's crops. The leaders decided that since the settlement was destined to grow rapidly, especially when more Utah people arrived in the summer, they would expand the number of acres under cultivation to ten thousand. This greatly exceeded their present needs and placed a great burden on the community, but they were determined to help provide for new immigrants.

Steven had wanted to plant twenty thousand acres, but knew it would be far beyond the strength of the pioneers, especially since they also needed to improve their cabins and build new ones for the incoming saints. Mary and Paul chided him on being too conscientious and finally convinced him that the saints from Utah would have plenty of time, if they were able to arrive early enough, to build most of their own cabins and plant late-season crops. Paul had the job of leading a small army of men once a month to Kansas City and the town of Blue Springs to continue foraging for equipment and supplies.

Every week the leaders sent a large party of volunteers to Independence to clear away the rubbish and debris. Paul usually led these groups and had no problem obtaining recruits. Steven hoped to expand their current settlement into Independence the following spring. They always posted sentries day and night to guard Zion's Camp, fearful not only of wandering gangs of outlaws but also of the growing threat from the Riss community.

Chapter 8

Steven heard the boom of a rifle and felt a tremendous force slam into his chest. The pain, weakness, and dizziness were so awful that he thought he was a dead man. He moved a trembling hand to his chest and felt wet gore flowing from a gaping wound. "Why?" he moaned. "Why would my own brethren want to kill me?"

"Steven, Steven! Wake up," Mary screamed in his ear.

Steven shot upright in the bed, his entire body covered in sweat. "What? What's going on?"

"You were having a nightmare. You were yelling and writhing about wildly. What did you dream about?"

Steven struggled to calm himself. "I had a dream that some of the brethren were tracking me through a dark forest and finally trapped me. Then, without a word, one of them shot me point-blank in the chest."

"How awful!"

"Yes, it was." He wiped the sweat from his forehead, feeling better now. "I heard and felt the blast, but it was nothing but a dream. I'm still alive."

Mary shook her head. "But there was a shot. I heard it myself."

"You heard a shot?"

"Yes. I was partly awake and I'm sure I heard a blast from the woods west of the settlement." As she spoke, the sound of gunfire came rolling over the hills and penetrated their room.

"Good grief," Steven exclaimed. "That was real."

The baby began to cry and Mary hurried to the crib and picked her up. Steven rolled from the bed and pulled on his clothes. The three other children burst into the room, their eyes showing a mixture of fear and excitement.

"What was that?" Andrew cried, as he ran to Mary and clung to her.

"Rifle shots, stupid," William said.

Her voice trembling, Jennifer demanded, "Are we being attacked, Dad? I'm—" There were more shots, but then the clamor of people running and shouting outside partially covered the noise of gunfire.

"I don't know." He ran to the bedroom door, and William started to follow. Steven turned and said, "Stay in the cabin—all of you. I'll let you know when I find out."

He grabbed his rifle and a box of cartridges and hurried to the cabin door. As he left the building, several armed men ran by, heading west. He followed them to the edge of the settlement and abruptly caught sight of two men emerging from a nearby stand of trees. He recognized them as Jarrad Babcock and Leonard Reece. They rushed up to him, gasping to catch their breath.

"Looks like we're being attacked by a small army," Jarrad said. The gunfire was steady now.

"How far out?" Steven asked.

Leonard used his sleeve to wipe the sweat from his eyes. "I'd say about four hundred yards due west of town. Ruther was there and told Jarrad and me to take off to let you know."

"Does Ruther have help?"

"Yeah," Jarrad said, still trying to catch his breath. "About twenty of our guys gathered in minutes after they killed our sentries."

"How large is the enemy army?"

"I can only guess," Jarrad replied, "but I'd say about two or three hundred."

Steven felt his chest tighten and his mind reel. "That many?" Suddenly, he decided this was no time to stand there talking. "You two round up as many men as you can. Go from cabin to cabin if you have to." A stream of brethren rushed by, carrying rifles and pistols.

"I don't think we'll have to," Leonard said. "It looks like the men already know what's happening and where to go."

"You're right, of course. Let's go."

They raced toward the battle scene, and a short distance away from the settlement they saw a group of about a hundred brethren gathering around Ruther Johnston, with more coming all the time. As they reached the group, Steven said, "What are we looking at here, Ruther?"

"About three hundred attackers. I checked 'em out with my binoculars and I'd say they're rebels from the Riss Community. But yuh won't believe who I saw with 'em."

"Who?"

"Seth Crowell and several others belonging to Zion's Camp."

"Somehow that doesn't surprise me," Steven replied.

"The lousy traitors," Jarrad said.

"We'll make them pay, all of them," Leonard declared with flashing eyes.

At that point John and Paul joined the defenders.

"How many men would you say we have on the front line?" Steven asked Ruther.

"Oh, I'd estimate we has about a hundred boys out thar in a line several hundred yards long. Our first group formed fast as a cougar can scoot up a tree."

"How did the rebels get so close without alerting our sentries?"

Ruther pulled his beard and scowled. "They snuck up ta them and slit their throats. Seems they hoped to wipe out our settlement in one big sneak attack."

Steven was shocked. "You saw it?"

"Yep, with my very own eyes. Shot one of the assassins from a hundred yards away before the rest turned tail and skedaddled."

"If it hadn't been for Ruther's shot, we wouldn't have had any warning," Jarrad said.

"Well, anyways," Ruther said, "our boys are still holdin' 'em purdy good as yuh can tell by all the gunfire."

By this time over two hundred citizen soldiers had arrived and began to ask for their orders.

Steven was in a quandary as to what to do. More than ever before he realized that being a translator didn't prepare a person for planning military actions. "Any suggestions on how to handle this?"

"Well, I ain't the boss here, but I say we flank 'em right quick before they gits the same idea. Divide these boys inta two troops. Steve, Jarrad, and Leonard can take one troop and head out to the left. John and Paul can take the other half around to the right. Make sure you're past our front line. Then keep on a goin' in a line until you're at their sides. That way we can hit 'em from three positions in a cross fire. Then, as soon as you're in position, let it rip. Make darn sure yuh shoot low and yuh aim carefully ta hit what you're aimin' at. We don't want yuh shootin' our own boys on the other side. I'll go straight ahead with a few of these fellers and join the front line. Those assassins will surely start bitin' their nails and prayin' ta Jesus when this here Sharps starts teachin' 'em the gospel of the Lord."

"Okay," Steven said. "Let's form two detachments now. The leaders need to make sure their men understand Ruther's instructions. When do you want us to begin firing, Ruther?"

"Like I just said, as soon as you git inta position."

As soon as Steven had finished instructing his contingent, he led them toward the left end of their front line. At that point they continued on until they were opposite the enemy, found any kind of protection available, and immediately began firing on the enemy, who was ensconced about a hundred yards away. Many of the attackers, spotting the citizen soldiers on their flank, jumped up and ran to new positions of cover.

After the battle had raged for half an hour, Steven decided to check on a small group of men he had sent to the rear of the rebel troops. He drew back into the woods fifty yards and circled around what he believed to be the enemy position. Fifteen minutes later he concluded he was lost. There was no one in sight and the sound of gunfire seemed more remote now. He worked his way through an extensive thicket, and then began to circumvent a small hill. Suddenly, he heard an unusual sound, and looking up, he saw Seth Crowell twenty feet away, his face transformed by an evil smile.

"Hah! Finally I've got you alone," Seth said, his voice harsh with hatred.

Steven heard running footsteps behind him and turned to see two of Seth's confederates, armed and ready for action. He knew his rifle would be worthless now.

"Alone? But you've brought two of your buddies."

"Oh, I promise you they won't interfere."

"Interfere with what?"

"With the beating I'm going to give you. I plan to beat you to death with these fists." He displayed two big fists for Steven to see, as if the very sight of them should terrify his opponent.

"Why don't you just use the pistol in your holster? A lot easier and quicker if you ask me."

"But a lot less fun than using my hands. I'm going to show you who is the best man."

"You're going to bore me to death with all your talk."

"You don't think I can do it?" Seth growled. He was a little shorter than Steven but outweighed him by thirty pounds. He had huge shoulders and massive arms.

"I think you don't know what you're doing."

"I know perfectly well what I'm doing. I'm going to pay you back for humiliating me and ruining my life."

"You ruined your own life. Besides, it's a lot easier to say you're going to whip a man than actually doing it."

At that Seth roared and charged Steven, swinging both fists in a wild attempt to smash his enemy to the ground. Steven stepped back quickly and blocked four or five blows neatly. Then he stepped forward and jabbed Seth in the stomach with his left, and when Seth dropped his guard to protect his belly, Steven hit him in the jaw with a punishing right. Seth hit the ground like a rock and lay there in the dirt dazed and groaning.

"It's usually better to control your anger when you're in a fight," Steven told Seth. "Ordinarily the belly's the weakest spot." At the same time he thought, *It's also better to avoid taunting your opponent.*

While Seth struggled to get to his feet, the men behind Steven grabbed his arms, making self-defense impossible.

"Just as I expected, Seth. Your promises don't mean much. They never have."

Seth shook his head in an effort to clear his brain. "Well, sometimes you have to do what you have to do."

He stumbled forward and began to slug Steven in the face, chest, and belly. Over and over again until Steven knew he couldn't last much longer. But then Steven decided to fight dirty too, and he kicked Seth between the legs with all his might. Seth screamed and dropped to the ground, grasping his injured parts, groaning in agony. Steven struggled against the grasp of Seth's buddies, but he was too groggy and weak to shake them. After a few minutes of futile tussling and being struck repeatedly in the ribs, he had no more strength to resist.

By this time Seth had partly recovered and, drawing his long hunting knife, he moved in to finish the job. He raised the knife and was about to plunge it into Steven's throat when a huge hand seized his wrist and squeezed so hard that Seth howled like a baby and dropped the knife. Then a giant fist slammed into his jaw and knocked him out cold. It was Neal

Matheson, the gigantic farmer who had always supported and defended the Christopher brothers.

Seth's two confederates released Steven but made a very foolish mistake. They were big and strong and apparently figured they had a good chance against Matheson if they stuck together. So they rushed the big farmer as one, but Matheson seized them by the neck in his big fists, picked them a foot off the ground and slammed their heads together again and again until blood spurted and they fell unconscious.

At that moment twenty armed figures surged onto the scene and surrounded them. Steven's initial panic subsided quickly when he realized they were his brethren. Jarrad also ran up but stopped short when he saw three bodies lying on the ground.

"What happened?" he asked Steven.

"Oh, just a little justice for some traitors." Steven related the story in a few words. "What about the battle? I don't hear firing."

"Ruther's plan worked," Jarrad said. "We wiped out over half their army in about half an hour. The survivors escaped into the countryside when they realized they'd lost. We're still tracking them and hope to catch as many as we can."

"Let them go. I don't want any of you killed or injured, and I'm sure they won't try such a foolish thing again. How many men did we lose?"

"Don't know for sure. Probably fifteen or twenty. We're still counting casualties."

Steven shut his eyes in pain, stunned by that report. After a full minute he looked up and said, "Bring the wounded to the settlement right away. Later in the day we'll transport the dead."

One of the casualties finally brought in was Leonard Reece, who had been shot in the chest and probably died instantly. Steven couldn't bear to look at his body. When Paul and Jarrad saw their friend in the clinic, they stared in disbelief for several minutes, and then had to leave the building. Dozens of wounded, both friends and enemies, received treatment at Mary's tiny hospital, most of them lying on cots outside the clinic. Armed guards kept watch over the rebels to make sure they caused no further trouble. Since the death of Quentin Price during the dust storm in Nebraska, the only medical staff in Zion's Camp was Mary Christopher, who was a registered nurse, and two practical nurses, Gertrude and Karla.

Two days later, on the fifth of April, the settlers held a burial ceremony for their dead, including Leonard Reece, who had been a close friend and companion to Paul and Jarrad all the way across the plains and during the initial establishment of Zion's Camp. Four hundred people attended the ceremony, and there were few among them who could hold back their tears, for all sixteen of these men had given their lives for their families and New Zion.

Seth Crowell and his two friends were found guilty of treason and sentenced to be banished from New Zion permanently. Two other men who had fought against the saints in the battle, and had been brought in wounded, were identified as citizens of the settlement and were also exiled.

Chapter 9

By the middle of April the settlers had finished plowing twelve thousand acres of fertile soil. Immediately they began to plant early-season crops, such as peas, lettuce, and spinach. A few weeks later they added carrots, beets, several kinds of grain, and in May, corn, beans, squash, potatoes, cucumbers, and tomatoes. The Lord blessed the little community by sending warm weather and good rainfall, and the saints were grateful for those gifts. They continued to build cabins for the expected arrival of Pioneer Two from Utah.

Some of the brethren started constructing larger permanent residences. Steven wondered if the settlers should also construct an old-style fort, well stocked with water and supplies. If they did, everyone could run to the fort for protection in case of a full-scale attack. Twice a week crews of nearly a hundred people traveled to Independence to continue the clearing and cleanup. One of their most difficult tasks was to pull out hundreds of charred stumps. The only way they could accomplish this task was to hack through the top layers of roots and then pull out the stumps with chains and teams of oxen.

As Steven witnessed this work, he thought about the great temple and the other buildings of New Jerusalem. Many of them would be built from stone, and he wondered how the saints could ever transport so many massive blocks to the city and erect them into place. He discussed the matter with the other leaders, and they finally decided they would have to use some of the heavy moving and digging equipment that lay quiet and useless at so many Kansas City construction sites.

But in order to use those machines, they would need oil and fuel. They had managed to salvage hundreds of quarts of motor oil, but had found no more than several hundred gallons of gasoline and diesel fuel. That meant they would have to find some way to make their own fuel. After examining the possibilities for several days, they decided to construct a community still and by the end of May began to ferment ethanol. They stored the pure ethyl alcohol in large empty drums that were found everywhere in Blue Springs and Kansas City.

Meanwhile, John Christopher was still working on his special project, which turned out to be a small solar power system. Every time Paul went to Kansas City to recover useful equipment, John gave him a list of solar-related components to bring back.

While a team of workers was clearing a certain spot in Independence the first week of June, they discovered a huge stone lying flat and buried under a pile of debris. After reading the inscription, they realized that the stone marked the site Joseph Smith himself had chosen for the holy temple. With great excitement they sent a couple of boys to inform Steven, who was working on the other side of a nearby hill. Steven came quickly and confirmed the workers' opinion that it was the temple cornerstone. He asked a few of the brethren to help him push the stone upright so it might be visible for future reference.

On Wednesday, June 19, at nine in the morning, a thrill of excitement raced through the community. It was started by a child's word and it galvanized every citizen into feverish action. The small boy had dashed over to Douglas Cartwright, who was working on a new home, and reported that a Cherokee Indian had appeared from the woods on the western edge of the settlement, walked up to him casually and, with a face as unmoving as stone, had told him that a great caravan of covered wagons was moving toward them on the white man's highway.

At first Douglas paid little attention, but realizing finally that the boy was telling him something important, he pumped him for more information. At each question all the child did was shrug and say, "I don't know." Evidently the Cherokee hadn't given the boy more information. Although there was little to go on, Douglas let out a shout of happiness and ran to a group of brethren eating lunch near the cabin they were building. He repeated the boy's words, and the men jumped to their feet and fled in every direction to spread the news.

Though Steven didn't expect the arrival of Pioneer Two until mid-June, the citizens of Zion's Camp were constantly asking him when they would arrive. Because of their fever of anticipation, he had begun sending out parties of scouts, led usually by Ruther, at the beginning of June, to check the highway from Utah. On one occasion the scouts had backtracked on their old route as far as Saint Joseph, Missouri. Steven knew he was putting the scouts at risk, but the men had volunteered for the job and insisted on going.

Unfortunately, they had returned each time with the disappointing report that they had seen no sign of Mormon travelers. After the middle of June had passed, Steven began to fear that Pioneer Two had met with some terrible disaster. Maybe they wouldn't arrive until the end of summer—or maybe not at all. He knew the Lord's promises were usually conditional upon the worthiness of the saints, and perhaps that was the reason for the delay. Mary had teased him many times about being impatient and jumping to conclusions. After all, Pioneer Two was only a little late.

While Steven worked in the fields, it was Paul who rushed up breathlessly and reported the exciting new rumor. Moments later, dozens of people swarmed around him asking for information. Steven had to admit he knew almost nothing. At last, Douglas, who had tracked Steven down, appeared and rehearsed the boy's story. Steven hesitated, unsure as to whether or not the tale was true, but when he looked into the eyes of those around him and saw their joy and anticipation, he couldn't disappoint them. Hoping to form a welcoming party, he asked for volunteers to meet him at the chapel as soon as possible.

Twenty minutes later several hundred people filled the area around the community's only church. There were men, women, and children of all ages, some of them on horseback. The noise was deafening, and the milling people and animals raised so much dust that Steven could hardly breathe or see the faces of those closest to him. He realized he'd made a stupid mistake by asking for volunteers.

At that moment he heard the thunder of hooves on his right and saw Ruther Johnston pound to a stop on his gigantic mule.

Coughing and spitting, Ruther tried to shield his eyes and nose with his dingy red bandana. "This here's a real big problem," Ruther shouted at Steven.

"I know," Steven yelled back.

"Could be dangerous, all these folks chargin' off down the highway, all helter-skelter like."

"I know," Steven repeated.

"Leavin' the settlement unprotected."

"I know."

Steven raised his hand high and called for the crowd to calm down. At first no one paid any attention, but after a minute the throng began to understand what he wanted. Quickly they gained control of themselves and strained to hear what he had to say.

"Brothers and sisters," Steven shouted, "I know you're excited. I am too. We haven't seen anyone from home for over a year. Still, we don't even know Pioneer Two is coming. It's possible the rumor is an evil ruse invented by the same gangs we ran into last year when we came to Missouri. Or maybe by other traitors in our midst. Because of this, we can't just abandon our settlement and charge down the highway in complete disarray. If the rumor came from our enemies, they might be waiting near the highway to ambush us, or they might plan to pillage and burn our settlement as soon as we leave it unprotected. If that happened, our chances for survival in this land might be seriously compromised. For these reasons, I intend to choose a small party of armed men to investigate. I hope you understand and will cooperate. Please arm yourselves and take your assigned defensive positions, as you were instructed in our training exercises."

Steven caught sight of his brothers not far away in the crowd and waved to them. They were on horseback, guiding their mounts through the crowd. When they drew closer, he shouted, "John, Paul, make sure they do what I ask. Ruther and I will check things out on the highway." They nodded, turned their horses, and began shouting instructions to the crowd. Some of the people were visibly upset, but most accepted the directions of their leaders.

Steven chose fifteen men and reminded them of the potential dangers. Ruther cautioned them to be alert for danger and avoid bunching up on the road, but to stay within thirty or forty feet of each other. After these brief instructions, Steven and Ruther led them quickly toward Interstate-470. Because of the excitement that filled his mind and body, Steven had difficulty remaining calm and watching for threats. If Pioneer Two was approaching, led by two apostles, the great burden he had borne so long would be lifted from his shoulders, at least in part.

The group traveled north on Interstate-470 for a mile and a half, and then turned west on Interstate-70. An hour later the highway turned northwest, and still they had seen no sign of either Pioneer Two or ambushers. At noon they were about two miles from the ruins of downtown Kansas City, and Steven's hope began to fade. *It's nothing but a false alarm,* he thought.

As they rode through the center of the ravaged city, Steven had almost decided to turn back, when he heard Ruther shout, "Thar they is!" Steven searched the highway ahead without spotting anything unusual. He scoffed at the idea that an old man like Ruther might be able to see something he couldn't. Apparently, however, the other men hadn't seen any travelers either, for Steven noticed them straining their eyes into the distance without saying a word. "Yep, thar they is, all right," Ruther said again, irritatingly. "About three miles or so down the road."

As Steven continued to stare ahead, he saw a movement that gradually took the form of a covered wagon. "I see them too," he called, spurring his mustang forward.

The others let out a whoop, following him at a gallop. It quickly became a race to see who could get there first. Pierce Hudson, whose horse was known to be the fastest in Zion's Camp, pulled ahead steadily. A few minutes later they drew near the wagon train, and Steven could see a group of men studying them, some using binoculars. By the time his men were several hundred yards from the cavalcade, Steven saw a horde of people rush toward them, laughing happily, gesturing wildly, and shouting words he couldn't hear because of the pounding of the hooves.

When they finally reached the weary travelers, the horsemen reigned to a quick stop. The two groups looked at each other fixedly, all of them suddenly quiet. The swirl of dust from the running horses slowly dissipated. It was as if they were gazing upon lost family members and didn't know what to say. Steven was struck by their appearance. They were gaunt and their clothes were little more than rags, and some had wrapped pieces of cloth around their feet to replace worn-out shoes.

A big man with a flowing white beard eyed Steven and said, "Steven Christopher, I presume." Steven nodded, unable to take his eyes from the man's cadaverous face. The man continued, "Believe me, you people are certainly a sight for sore eyes."

"Welcome to the Promised Land of New Zion," Steven replied. "We were beginning to wonder if you'd ever come."

"We're a week behind schedule. We ran into a lot of problems, but the Lord saw us through every trial."

Then Steven recognized the gaunt man, who was nearing fifty but looked much older after the long journey. "You're Elder Widtsoe, aren't you?" Steven had talked to Jason Widtsoe many times when, as the future leader of Pioneer One, he had traveled to Salt Lake City to receive his instructions from the General Authorities.

"That I am."

The riders descended from their horses and the people of Pioneer Two surrounded them instantly. In spite of their weakened condition, the travelers embraced and kissed Steven and his men, and the two groups asked each other question after question. Twenty minutes later Widtsoe said in a booming voice, "Well, brethren, why don't you show us your marvelous settlement? I hope you have some extra food stored away. And clothes perhaps."

"God blessed us with a bounteous harvest last year," Steven said. "We'll give you everything we can. How many people do you have?"

"Almost fifteen hundred," declared another man as he stepped from the crowd. He was about the same age as Widtsoe, but much shorter. He too wore a long beard, which was a mixture of gray and black.

"Do you recognize this man?" Jason asked with a twinkle in his eyes.

Steven studied the man's face. "No, I'm sorry."

"That's because he was a lot chubbier when you saw him last. He used to have rosy, plump cheeks and a round paunch, sort of like Santa Claus, but this trip has trimmed him down a whole lot. Also, he didn't have that long beard. As you well know, it's mighty hard to shave without regular razor blades." Since Steven said nothing, Jason added, "Why, he's Elder Bartlett."

"Keith Bartlett, of the Quorum of the Twelve?"

"I'm afraid so," Keith said. "After Jason whipped the renegade Mexican army, he forced me to join Pioneer Two. He made the wild claim that he'd never make it without me." Everyone giggled at that, and Steven was surprised to see that these people, who resembled walking skeletons, could still laugh when they were starved half to death.

The riders remounted and began to lead the newcomers to Zion's Camp. Keith Bartlett returned to the rear of the caravan to make sure no one lagged behind, while Jason mounted a horse and rode beside Steven.

"Who's the mountain man?" Jason said, nodding toward Ruther.

"His name is Rutherford Johnston. He came with us across the plains."

"Reminds me of Porter Rockwell."

Steven laughed. "Yes, but our man's much better. Not only is he an expert in wilderness survival and a deadshot with that Sharps, but he's also a philosopher and a Baptist who loves to debate religion with us benighted Mormons. He has saved us from destruction many times."

"I believe it," Jason replied. "The Lord uses all kinds of wonderful people for his purposes."

"From the looks of your people, you don't have much food left, do you?"

Jason gave a weary sigh. "We've been rationing food ever since Cheyenne. For three weeks the people have been living on nothing but water, a half pound of flour per day, and all the bugs they can find. Now we're down to a few barrels of flour."

"You weren't able to shoot wild game?"

"We sent out hunting parties every day. They had some success, but after we portioned out the meat through the caravan, there wasn't much for anyone. I suppose the reason we didn't do better was the scarcity of game and the lack of hunting experience."

Steven wondered about the human savages who had threatened Pioneer One. "Were you attacked?"

"Yes, a dozen times. By small gangs using guerilla tactics. I suppose our numbers intimidated them. That's why the prophet insisted that the caravans be so large. Still, they managed to kill nine saints and wound twenty others."

Steven knew the Lord was using all these terrible trials to perfect his people in the refiner's fire so they might be worthy to redeem Zion, but hearing about the losses made his heart hurt. "It could have been much worse."

Jason looked over at Steven. "I thank God it wasn't. I know your people had a lot of trouble while you were in the Utah mountains. And then we lost contact. Did you have more trouble later?"

Steven spent the next half hour reviewing the struggles Pioneer One had endured coming across the plains.

"Whew! That's quite a story," Jason declared when Steven had finished.

Steven wanted to ask Jason an important question, but was afraid of the answer he would get. Finally he said, "After hunting every day and fighting bandits, you probably don't have much ammunition left, do you?"

"To the contrary. That's one thing we have in abundance. Hundreds of thousands of rounds. Fortunately, most of the saints refused to surrender their guns and ammunition when the federal government declared martial law and forbade the purchase, sale, and possession of all firearms and ammunition. Why? Did you folks run out?"

Steven was so happy that he had difficulty answering. "Not yet but almost." The scavenging crews from Zion's Camp had searched Kansas City and elsewhere for ammunition, but without success. Steven had planned to continue the search at the ruins of individual residences in hopes of getting what they needed.

Jason grinned at Steven's obvious relief. "Well, whatever we have belongs to the whole community."

"I appreciate that," Steven said simply.

"Oh! I can't believe I forgot to tell you one of the most important things. Church leaders planned to have the third wagon train, Pioneer Three, ready to leave Salt Lake City six or seven weeks after our departure."

Steven felt another surge of pleasure. "That's fantastic. How many people?"

"I understand they expected to call and recruit two to three thousand people."

"Unbelievable!" Steven exclaimed. "Now I know why the Lord commanded me to triple the acreage we're cultivating."

"The crops are growing well?"

"Jason—I mean, Elder Widtsoe—you wouldn't believe it. The Lord has made our soil fertile, and our harvests are so abundant that it's everything we can do to store them properly."

Although they were close to total collapse, the weary saints of Pioneer Two somehow found the strength to pick up the pace, inspired by the knowledge that their trail of sorrows and tribulations was nearly finished. It was almost nightfall when Pioneer Two rolled into Zion's Camp, and the welcome they received was indescribable. The joyous settlers invited them into their cabins, fed them, and gave them as many supplies as they could spare.

Despite the fact that the travelers were sick and exhausted, they talked to their hosts late into the night until they could no longer keep their eyes open. The people of Pioneer One especially welcomed the news that the Church had begun to establish permanent towns on the road to New Zion. By the time Pioneer Two passed through, two such communities had already been created in western Wyoming.

Since there were so many newcomers, about a third of them had to spend the night once again in their wagons. Steven noticed that this wagon train, like Pioneer One, had utilized many converted modern vehicles and not just covered wagons.

Steven and Mary cuddled that night and discussed the arrival of Pioneer Two.

"Don't you think things will be a lot easier on you now that the apostles have arrived?" Mary said.

"Probably. They'll take over most of the church leadership matters. Also, we'll have much more talent available to solve community problems."

"Why do you still look so worried then?"

He paused, trying to think of the right words. "Well, the creation of the national government is still my responsibility. If I foul it up, it could seriously compromise the growth of New Zion in America."

"You won't foul it up. You're extremely brilliant. Besides, the Lord is on your side."

"Thank you, dear wife. You're always my best cheering section." Still, he felt an overwhelming dread at the task before him.

Chapter 10

❧

The newly arrived saints did little the next few days, except rest, eat as much as their stomachs could hold, and converse with the citizens of Zion's Camp. They described their trek through the mountains and across the plains—the storms, mud, heat, dust, attacks from bandits, lack of food and clothes, and the endless miles of dreary trudging. Despite the fact that two apostles had led them, they too had met with strife, complaints, stealing, anger, and rebellion.

In turn, the people of Pioneer One related their story, and the new pioneers listened spellbound. When the tales were told, the newcomers admitted that they would never have believed that any other group could have suffered as much as they had.

Fortunately, two doctors and two nurses had accompanied Pioneer Two, and these people worked with the existing medical staff day and night treating sick people in Mary's little clinic.

Within a few days after their arrival, the people of Pioneer Two began helping in the fields and building dwellings of their own. The original settlers had already constructed twenty-five cabins for the new saints, and Steven, Jason, and Keith chose twenty-five of the most destitute families to inhabit them.

Steven was especially grateful when in the following weeks the two apostles reorganized the Church in Zion's Camp, establishing three complete stakes with four wards in each stake. The average membership in each ward was about 225 people. They formed and staffed each ward in the same manner as the Church did in the Rocky Mountains.

The day after the organization of the new stakes and wards began, Elder

Jason Widtsoe approached Steven around noon as he was helping a new family build their home.

"Steven," Jason said, "I'm glad to see you lending a hand this way. Our people need your experience in building log cabins. But I wondered if I could talk to you for a moment."

"Certainly. I could use a break."

They walked to a nearby tree and sat down in the shade.

Widtsoe wiped the perspiration from his forehead and immediately got to the point of his visit. "As you know, when the prophet interviewed you in Salt Lake City, he gave you the responsibility of forming an effective secular government for New Zion." Steven nodded, somewhat embarrassed. "Well, I was wondering if you've decided what kind of government we should have? In other words, I'm asking if you have finished your plans for the political and economic structures of Zion."

"Not yet," Steven said. "I've been giving it a lot of thought but I haven't made up my mind for sure. We've created a small local government but not a government for the future nation of New Zion."

"Have you chosen people to help you?"

"No."

"Then it's imperative that you make up your mind as soon as possible and get the help you need. Someday this land will be covered with millions of people, and they'll need the best government possible and a just tax system."

Feeling a terrible sense of shame and embarrassment, Steven couldn't say a word. He secretly thought there had to be men better qualified than he to take on the enormous responsibility of establishing an ideal government for New Zion.

Widtsoe seemed to read his mind. "You must have confidence in yourself. The prophet chose *you* to be at the head of this work. He knew what he was doing. Nobody can do the job better than you. You already know what to do and how to do it. Just trust in yourself and in God, and don't expect to achieve perfection. In this mortal world there's no such thing as a perfect government or a perfect economic system. You know what to do, so start doing it as soon as possible." Widtsoe put his hand on Steven's shoulder and looked into his eyes with kindness and love. Then he rose and left without another word.

That night Steven felt an overpowering weariness and went to bed early. But in the course of the night he jerked awake and looked around. He found himself standing on his feet and did not see his room but instead a wonderful world of glorious splendor. He couldn't tell whether he was having a dream or seeing a vision. At first the scene was so full of dazzling light that it hurt his eyes. But soon the light softened and turned into a rainbow of soft, beautiful colors. Then he could see objects: buildings, trees, fences, streets of gold, and people gliding smoothly and swiftly over those streets without touching their surface and talking to each other in quiet, gentle tones.

Suddenly he heard a sound and when he turned toward it, he saw a magnificent blue throne, and the Being who sat on that throne was brighter than the noonday sun. Somehow Steven knew he was beholding the Father of an infinite number of children. He wore a gleaming crown and purple sandals and a purple robe that fell almost to his ankles. His beard was short and his dark-brown hair reached halfway to his shoulders. Steven was stunned to see that he appeared to be no more than twenty-five or thirty years old.

On either side of the Father he saw many other thrones, arranged in a semicircle. On the Father's right he saw a beautiful young woman who also wore a shining crown. Without being told, he knew she was the Infinite Mother, the wife of the Father. Next to her on the right, he saw a glorious being who resembled the Father to such a degree that Steven was compelled to look back and forth several times in an effort to distinguish between them. He realized that this personage must be the Firstborn of the Father.

To the right of the Only Begotten, he saw another personage whose beauty and glory were beyond description. He was clean-shaven and had short golden hair that curled around his ears and the upper part of his neck. Steven didn't know who he was, but a small voice spoke to his mind, saying, "*This is Michael the Archangel, whom you know as Adam.*" Still farther on the right he saw several other beings but he couldn't identify them. Next to the Father on his left Steven saw another being who wore a golden crown. The glory of this being rivaled that of the Father and the Son. Yet Steven couldn't identify him, and the secret voice said nothing. Moving to the left he saw other beings he couldn't name either.

Then he turned back toward the people he had first seen on the streets but he saw them no more. Instead, he beheld a multitude of people dressed in robes and tunics, all of them facing toward the semicircle of thrones. The women were bright and beautiful and wore their hair very long. Most of the men had fairly long hair, but some wore it short. Many had beards, some of them short, others long. Steven was especially surprised to see such a great variety in the apparel and appearance of the people. Their number was so great that he could not see the end of them.

As he wondered how many people were in the crowd, he heard the soft voice say, *"Their number is ten million, and there are ten thousand other assemblies of equal size on this globe and its sister globe, all witnessing this same scene by the power of the Father."* Unable to stop himself from making a quick calculation, he came up with the number one hundred billion individuals.

Steven wanted to draw closer so he could see them all better but he was terrified to do so. Then he saw the Father turn and look straight at him, smile in a kindly manner, and beckon him to approach. After he drew nearer, the Father pointed to an empty seat at the end of the semicircle. Steven took the seat and waited expectantly. None of the other beings on thrones seemed to be aware of his presence.

When he had sat down, he heard someone speak. It was God himself. His voice was slow, quiet, and deliberate, but Steven could hear every word distinctly, as if the Father were speaking directly into his ear. He looked at the vast assembly and knew that all of them could hear as clearly as he could.

"My beloved children. The workers have finished their preparations. The home where you will live, in the days assigned to you, is now ready. Soon your first parents will receive tangible bodies and inhabit a paradisiacal world. But they shall be sorely tempted by the Evil One and will choose to partake of the forbidden fruit, and they and the earth shall fall into a mortal state. They will do this so that all of you may enter mortality and thus be enabled to work out your eternal rewards, according to the degree of obedience that you choose to give to my holy word. Yet you cannot work out your salvation alone. None of you have that power. Therefore, to redeem you from the Fall, there must be a Redeemer, and that is why we are assembled here at this time. I must choose a savior in order for you to come back into my presence."

All at once the personage sitting to the left of the Father arose and stood before the assembly. Steven was struck by the beauty and transcendence of his countenance. Raising his arms high, he said with a powerful, grandiose voice, "Here I am, holy and mighty Father, your son from the very beginning. Send me, and I will be your Redeemer. And surely I will do it, for I accomplish all my works, no matter how difficult they may be." Then he turned slowly toward the crowd, his arms still held high. Steven was reminded of an old-time actor performing in a melodrama. As this bright being stood there facing his audience, there arose a roar of applause and cries of approval from a significant portion of the crowd. The noise continued for more than three minutes of earth time, as Steven calculated it.

The Father waited patiently until the crowd quieted down. "Why should I send you, Lucifer? What do you have to offer?"

Lucifer lowered his arms, looked at the Father earnestly, and then turned again to face the audience. "We all know that there are some rulers in this congregation who desire to cheat and deprive this multitude of precious spirits. Deprive them of what? Of protection from sin on a dangerous and uncertain new world. And how do we know that sin will abound on that world? Because where there is agency, there too is sin. In spite of that knowledge, those same rulers insist on having their way, and therefore endanger all these fragile and inexperienced spirits."

Lucifer lifted his arms once more. "All of you know from your life on this celestial globe that most of those poor spirits are not capable of consistently choosing the right. As a result, if we send them to the new world with agency, billions of them will be helpless and fall prey to sin, especially since they will be deprived of the memory of their glorious life here. They will be lost forever to the highest blessings of salvation and never obtain the heritage they so rightly deserve, as sons and daughters of God, to become equal to their eternal parents."

As Lucifer said those last few words, he dropped his arms to his sides, as if overwhelmed by frustration and despair. At this gesture the same segment of the audience as before screamed and shouted their approval, in an outburst that was earsplitting.

Steven knew what the final outcome would be, but he was fascinated and compelled to watch intently as the scene unfolded.

Again the Father waited patiently as the noise gradually diminished. Then he said, "Lucifer, how can we deprive man of his agency? It was decreed by all the Gods throughout eternity that man should have that agency. When the intelligence of sentient beings is organized, agency is an integral component. If man had no agency, he would not be man, but rather more like an animal. I think you are smart enough to know that agency cannot be removed or altered."

"But we can try," Lucifer replied.

"Lucifer, it is impossible to control the mind of one person much less the minds of billions. There is no magical power that you can send across the universe to manipulate the thinking of people on other planets. Not even God can do the impossible."

"But, glorious Father, I can. That is, I can to a degree—at least to the point of greatly minimizing the sin that men can commit."

"How do you intend to accomplish that, my son?"

Steven was fascinated by this incredible dialogue and he knew that the all-knowing Father already understood what Lucifer had in mind. He realized that Christ, Lucifer, and Adam were spirit beings, and the Father and the Mother were resurrected persons who possessed tangible bodies. But he couldn't determine their physical state by simply looking.

"If you give me charge of this new world," Lucifer continued, "I will establish an all-powerful central government, or several of them if necessary, which shall write hundreds, nay, thousands, of detailed laws for men to live by. Those laws will include all your commandments. For each infraction of those laws, men and women will receive an appropriate punishment. If all men know that those punishments are extremely severe, they will avoid breaking them and committing sin. In that way, I will help men and women to become worthy of your love and provide a sure path for them to return into your presence."

Steven thought, *The truth is, all those restrictive, devil-made and man-made laws will make every human being a criminal. Good men will be compelled to break them to maintain their freedom and their beliefs. Evil men will strive to thwart the government and, in order to get what they want, they will lie, steal, betray their neighbors, and engage in all kinds of evil. The result will be chaos.*

The Father smiled at Steven, and then turned again to Lucifer. "But my poor Lucifer, sometimes the worst of sins are done in secret. Your laws and your police would only be able to detect and punish overt physical acts. You would not be able to stop crimes committed in secret or in human hearts."

Lucifer flashed an enormous smile and said, "But there is a way to see secret acts and know the human heart. You, my Father, understand that better than anyone else. You have the power to see into the human heart and to search men's souls. Give me that power, and I will use it for the benefit and blessing of all mankind. With that power my fellow workers and I will detect sin in the mind of man and make the appropriate corrections."

"Yet in order to give you that power I would have to give you all my power," the Father said.

"If that is so, I promise you that I will use it wisely and fairly."

"Is that all you have to say, Lucifer?"

"I repeat what I said before. Send me to be the Redeemer, and I will soothe every pain and meet every challenge which that calling imposes. Also, give me your power, and I will make sure that all men are saved in your glorious kingdom. Of course, for all that work and sacrifice I think I would deserve a certain amount of respect and honor."

Steven glanced at Christ and saw a look of infinite sadness.

The Father also looked at Jesus and said, "What say you, my firstborn son?"

Jesus stood and moved close to Lucifer. He turned to the Father and said, "Beloved Father, Lucifer's plan is one of enormous evil and should be condemned by everyone in this congregation. The agency of man is a sacred gift given to man by God himself and must remain in him. Any effort to curtail that agency in any manner and to any degree must be rejected. By compelling man to do good, Lucifer removes man's worthiness. He removes the tests each man and woman must pass. If a person does no good of his own free will, especially after resisting temptation, he will not learn and grow. He would not be worthy of the rewards Lucifer hopes to give him. Send me, my Father, and I will do your will, and may the power and honor and glory be yours forever."

Christ returned to his throne, and Lucifer to his.

The Father stood and said, "Now I give you my decision. I reject Lucifer's plan and choose my Only Begotten Son to be the Redeemer." He turned toward Lucifer. "Lucifer, it is your pride and blindness that have caused you to offer yourself as the Redeemer of our newest creations and to propose a plan of redemption that has been rejected many times in the past. If you do not speedily repent, you shall be cast out of heaven and sent to the new planet without a body. All those who follow you and rebel against me will receive the same punishment. You will become sons of perdition and forever lose any degree of salvation in the eternities."

Lucifer's face became a horrible mask of anger, hatred, and embarrassment. He sprang from his seat and stormed out of the great council arena. Steven looked at the crowd and saw that they were deathly quiet and paralyzed as if by a stunning blow.

Suddenly the scene changed. Steven found himself in a huge indoor theater, which was brightly lit. He couldn't see the source of the light. To his right there were at least two thousand seats, filled with men and women wearing all kinds of strange, multicolored clothing. Their clothes were loose and revealed portions of their bodies. Most of them had short hair, and only a few of the men wore beards. To his left was a platform upon which a man was speaking. Steven drew closer, trying to see and hear the man better. Soon he noticed that the speaker had very short hair, was clean-shaven, and was wearing some type of blue pants, fastened at the waist by a drawstring. On the upper part of his torso he wore a blue tunic that was open at the front, revealing a bare, hairless chest. Many men in the audience wore similar attire.

Steven was perplexed, wondering where he was, who the speaker was, who the listeners might be, and when this event was taking place. The same secret voice told him what he wanted to know. *"This is Lucifer in the act of rebellion, speaking to his followers. This same speech will be repeated many times and broadcast to tens of thousands of locations. Their apparel and their grooming are symbols of the greatest rebellion in history. It is by these signs and tokens that they identify one another."* Steven examined the speaker more closely because he looked familiar. Then all at once he recognized him—Lucas Nigel. Steven felt incredibly stupid because for some strange reason he hadn't made the connection between Lucifer and that friendly, smiling Lucas Nigel. You can sense something but not really know it. The long hair Lucas had worn at the great council had made the connection more difficult.

Lucifer spoke in a loud, sonorous voice, and his gestures, facial expressions, and grand vocal intonations emphasized his main points and pushed them home. His message was a complex mixture of emotion and cunning arguments. Steven was reminded of the fantastic performance of actor Burt Lancaster in the old Elmer Gantry movie, the story of an alcohol-guzzling evangelical minister who used scripture, fiery rhetoric, vigorous arm and facial gestures, and all his powers of emotional persuasion to separate his gullible listeners from their hard-earned cash. Just like Elmer's audiences, Lucifer's crowd ate it up. They cried, cheered, ranted, jumped up and down in response to their hero's speech, and their faces were contorted by every imaginable emotion. Lucifer, of course, was clearly enjoying himself. All this honor and attention directed at him alone.

The scene changed again. Steven found himself in the cleft of a huge boulder near the top of a high mountain, and before him was a group of men talking animatedly in a clearing ringed by trees. Almost immediately he caught sight of Lucifer, surrounded by forty other spirits. Steven approached them slowly and carefully in order to hear their words better and avoid detection. When he tripped over a rock and fell to the ground, he was sure they would discover him, but they went right on talking as if he weren't there.

Realizing somehow that they were using the Adamic language, Steven was surprised and delighted that he could understand them perfectly well. He silently drew within fifteen feet of them without any means of concealment. Still they seemed unaware of his presence. Steven figured he must be in another plane of existence, but still able to witness their realm. He was there and yet not there. Or maybe it was a vision.

One of the men, standing close to Lucifer, declared, "Master, we are with you to the end. We are ready to visit the council of the Gods and force the Father's hand right to his face." The fact that they were here plotting and willing to challenge God directly impressed Steven a great deal, for it was proof to him that the Father gave his children freedom to act and even to sin on this celestial planet as well as on earth.

Lucifer smiled, and Steven recognized the maddening smirk of Lucas Nigel. "Thank you, Brother Cain, but I have a special mission for you and ten thousand others like you. I now command you not to rebel openly. I want you to hold back and pretend you are obedient to the Father and to the plan of the Only Begotten."

"But why?" said another man. "We're not afraid. We're the greatest and bravest of all the spirits in heaven and we are ready to challenge even the might of the Father. We will sacrifice all to follow you, even if it be to perdition, whatever that is. Let them threaten us with any punishment they desire, for we will continue this path courageously and gain the victory in the end."

"I appreciate your determination, Vladimir, but let me admit something to you. Even though we have forty-four billion dedicated followers, there is a chance—admittedly a small one—that we might lose this conflict in the end. There are two of *them* for every one of us, and in this realm the powers that be have more direct control over us. So we need to have a backup plan in case we cannot convert most or all of heaven to our cause."

"A backup plan?" Vladimir said.

"Yes. If we lose, the Father will exile us to the new earth without giving us tangible bodies. In doing that he intends to punish us and render us relatively powerless. He doesn't seem to realize that as spirits we'll still be able to continue our war against his Master Plan, to deny his Redeemer, and to break his excessive rules. Think of it! Forty-four billion immortal spirits working on the hearts of a vastly smaller population of mortals in each generation. Also, we can be even more effective if we have ten thousand faithful servants who possess mortal bodies and can therefore act more directly upon the everyday lives of mortal men. For that reason, I command you people here and ten thousand others not to rebel openly."

"Not rebel openly?" said a spirit named Adolf.

Lucifer frowned with impatience. "That's right. Keep your rebellion a secret. Keep it quiet. You'll be of more value to me if you pretend you're on their side. That way, you'll be worthy—or at least acceptable—enough to be sent to earth in mortal bodies. The Father has his rules. He can't deprive you of mortal bodies unless your rebellion is open and acted upon. A dozen or so of you will be born in each generation on the new earth, and as mortal beings having physical bodies, you'll be much more useful to me. As I just said, you will be able to influence more effectively the lives of millions of the goody-goodies here who think they're on the side of righteousness.

"When you are born on earth," Lucifer continued, "I'll come to you in secret and show you how to set up powerful governments that can bring about social engineering and force people to follow endless rules, especially my own. You will set up municipalities and powers to promote security and safety for entire nations. All the people will have to do is surrender a little bit of their freedom and independence to acquire all those benefits. Soon they'll realize that our rules are benign and for their own good, whether they understand it or not at first."

"What a brilliant plan!" said in awe a man named Benito. "You are truly a wise leader—wiser than the Father. I think I speak for everyone here, and the ten thousand others you have chosen, when I say that we'll be delighted to perform the marvelous mission you have given us." The other spirits cheered with joy and fell on their master with loving embraces. For Steven it was a terrifying spectacle, and he wanted the terrible scene to end.

Steven received his wish immediately. He looked and saw before him a vast field of fire and a multitude of people standing in the midst. Close to him in the field he saw Lucifer, raising his arms upward toward heaven, his hands clasped together as in prayer, his face a gruesome vision of agony and horror. Then suddenly he was drawn upward in a brief flash of brilliant light and disappeared. Soon multitudes of others began to disappear in the same manner. Not all at once, but a few here and there, and then more and more. Before long the field was empty and turned into a golden plain full of beautiful plants of all kinds.

Not far away sat a small bench, and Steven wondered what the scene meant and why the bench was on the edge of the field. At that moment the still small voice told him what he wanted to know. *"This is the punishment of Lucifer and his children. They are given their reward. By the almighty power of the Father, they are being transported to their new home on the earth, where they will exist as evil spirits, who because of their very nature will tempt and test all mankind. In this way they unwittingly fulfill, by their rebellion, the great plan of God, who uses them to provide an opposition in all things. It is Lucifer's great pride that prevents him from understanding this. Go now and sit on the small bench and ponder the significance of this vision."*

Steven walked over and sat on the bench. As he meditated on the vision, he realized that he had been privileged to witness in detail the plans of the Evil One. Satan would use evil spirits, wicked mortals, and tyrannical governments to continue on earth the War in Heaven. He remembered hearing well-meaning people declare that there was always some good in every human being, no matter how bad they may appear. He believed that was true for the vast majority of the inhabitants of the earth.

Yet now he realized there were many men and women whose souls were completely devoid of any degree of goodness. They may have been good when they were children, but they made many bad choices, one after the other, and gradually they became so addicted to evil that they were beyond repentance, and the chains of sin bound them forever. They had been deceived by Satan and had become themselves the incarnation of evil. He thought of Cain, Judas Iscariot, Stalin, Hitler, Mussolini, Gerald

Galloway, and all the other tyrants whose ambitions and designs had caused the enslavement and slaughter of millions of innocent human beings. As he pondered these things, the vision gradually faded away.

Steven awoke suddenly, his heart racing and his body covered with sweat. He looked around and, in the dimness of the room, saw his precious wife lying next to him. His joy and relief were immeasurable. He lay back down and pondered his dream for a half hour. Soon he understood fully the meaning of his vision and what he had to do here in Zion. Checking his watch, he saw it was already five in the morning and he knew his dream had lasted most of the night. Careful not to disturb Mary, he rolled over and eventually went to sleep.

Chapter 11

❧

The next morning Steven arose at about eight o'clock. The rest of the family was already up and doing their chores. Knowing he had endured a difficult night, Mary let him sleep as long as he needed and saved him some breakfast. As he was eating, he told his family about his dream. They were excited and full of questions, but he asked them to postpone the questions until after dinner. He instructed his three children to find John, Paul, Ruther, Douglas, and Jarrad, and to ask them to visit him as soon as possible.

By ten o'clock the five men were seated with Steven around the kitchen table. Wasting no time, Steven began the meeting.

"I have invited you here for an important reason. Yesterday Elder Widtsoe told me I needed to search Zion's Camp for the wisest people I could find to begin discussions on the establishment of a government for New Zion. I would like you to make inquiries of all the leaders and other people you trust, asking them to provide you with the names of the best people available. I don't want to do this in a general meeting because I don't want a large number of volunteers. It would be especially useful to select people who have had some training in political science or in economics. Also, I want some of those people to be women. Women often think of things that never occur to men."

Ruther scratched his chin and crossed his legs. "If I unnerstand yuh right, yuh don't want a big crowd. About how many names are yuh aimin' fer?"

"Around twenty-five to thirty if possible. Bring them here tonight, and we'll work on the list and narrow it down. Later, when we hear of exceptional people, we'll invite them to join us, especially people from future wagon trains. I hope you'll do this as discreetly as possible because there are people here that I'd rather not have involved in this important task."

"I hear you," Jarrad said. "There are some who might try to throw a lot of crazy ideas into the pot. Do you want only members of the Church?"

"Absolutely not. There are some wonderful nonmembers here who can give us valuable insights. Remember, Zion will be a pluralistic society, at least in the beginning." Steven threw them a subtle grin. "We'll convert the rest of them later." He coughed a little and looked at Ruther. "Especially people like Ruther here. Oh! There's something else. I want all of you on our planning committee and your wives if you have one and she wants to participate." His grin grew wider as he looked at Jarrad, Paul, and then Ruther. "By the way, what do you three have against women?"

Ruther's eyes bulged. "Are yuh crazy, young feller? Don't get me started. Fer some loony reason, them ladies jest don't cotton much fer an old coot like me. Besides, if I got me one of them girlies, I'd have to purdie meself up a mite."

As everybody laughed, Steven turned to Jarrad.

Jarrad blushed and, mimicking Ruther, said, "Why are yuh gawkin' at me, young feller. I'm a doin' my best, but there jest ain't no chicks out thar good enough fer me."

"Okay, okay," Steven said. "I suppose Paul feels the same way." Paul nodded with mock seriousness. "Look, I'll give you boys a few more months, if you need them, but I'll keep checking on you until you get on the ball. By the way, we probably should call our political meetings a second 'constitutional convention' to make people realize how serious this is."

That evening Steven's brothers and friends arrived shortly after dinner. Each of them had a list in hand. Some of the names were repeated on several lists, but the total number was twenty-six. They discussed each of these people and narrowed the names down to fifteen. These fifteen people, plus the six men sitting around the table, brought the total number of committee members to twenty-one.

"Great," Steven said. "Now when and where shall we meet?"

They decided to meet in communal Lodge Two on Tuesdays and Fridays at seven thirty in the evening.

"How do we keep notes on these meetings?" Steven asked. "And how can we make copies of our proposals? In order to get feedback from the community, it's important to distribute copies of the proposals to everyone."

"Yes, of course," Jarrad said. "And later we'll need to make copies of our final decisions. We'll need to post dozens of those copies throughout Zion's Camp at least a week or so before we call for a general vote of acceptance or rejection."

"I think I may have the solution," John said.

"And that is?" Steven asked.

"Brother John Black, the ex-law professor on our list, brought a laptop with him all the way from Utah. He thinks it might still work but he's not sure. He also has a printer, cables, and several reams of paper. All we need is an AC power source to run the computer and the printer."

"Gee! Is that all?" Jarrad piped. "That finishes that. We have no AC power whatsoever. And no DC either."

They all looked at each other as if someone must have the answer. Steven said nothing but stared at John, waiting for him to come up with one of his brilliant solutions.

"Well, that's not quite right," John said, picking his teeth with a toothpick. "It so happens we do have a small source of AC power. After searching every wagon and vehicle in town, with the permission of the owners, of course, and with all the components Paul has brought me from Kansas City, I finally gathered enough parts to make several small solar panels, a charge controller, and a thousand-watt inverter. I have also accumulated some electrical cable, several circuit breakers, and eight deep-cycle batteries to store the power we produce. So I had all I needed to make a small solar system. We can be grateful that so many people decided to convert their trucks and cars for the trip across the plains but were lazy enough—I should say thoughtful enough—to leave most of the electrical parts in the vehicles."

Steven had difficulty concealing his pleasure. "John, you're a genius. How long have you been working on this?"

"I started about a month after we arrived in Missouri. This is the special project I told you about. Paul knew because he found a lot of parts for me in Kansas City."

"He never said a word to me about it," Steven said, gazing at Paul with surprise.

"Yeah, I knew what he was doing," Paul said, "but he asked me to keep it quiet."

"Not to change the subject," Douglas said, "but I have a question."

"Go ahead," Steven replied.

"Why are we concerned about making plans for a large national government when we're only a small town? Aren't we jumping the gun? I can understand planning a county or a state government, but a national one?"

Steven had expected that question. "The General Authorities told me, and Elder Widtsoe reiterated it recently, that we need to structure the national government first because the lower levels of government would model themselves on that, both in form and in principles."

"That makes sense," Douglas said.

"More questions?" Steven asked. No one had any. "Okay, so it's a go for this Friday night. Let's divide up the fifteen names on our final list and contact them tomorrow concerning Friday's meeting. The only problem left is to find a scribe to record the meetings." The second he said "scribe," Paul's hand shot up. "You know how to use a computer, Paul?"

"Well, duh, Steve. I was raised with my nose in a computer, like everyone else *not* of your generation."

Everyone laughed at that, especially since Steven used to earn his living using a computer.

On Friday the new delegates arrived shortly before seven thirty at Lodge Two, where the chairs were arranged in a circle. There was a buzz of excitement as everyone walked around talking to as many people as possible, trying to get their questions answered. At seven thirty Steven raised his voice above the din and asked everyone to take a seat. They did so at once and waited expectantly. Steven looked around the circle and saw many different emotions, including excitement, fear, and nervousness. He noticed with pleasure that two sisters, Fern Mills and Beverly Stark, had joined their husbands in the group. Mary too had decided to come with Steven. After counting the number of people present, Steven began the meeting.

"I would like to begin by welcoming you to this meeting. You are exceptional people and have a special mission to accomplish. Tonight we are blessed to have four sisters with us. You all know them: Sister Mills, Sister Stark, Tania Christopher, and my wife, Mary. We also have two men from Pioneer Two. You may not know them, so I'll ask them to stand when I mention their names. First we have John Black." John stood and waved to the group. "John used to be a law professor at the University of Utah. He is an expert in constitutional law. Next we have James Pratt." James also stood. "James used to be a successful lawyer in Orem." John and James were two of the people on the list Steven had compiled.

"So far, that makes twenty-five of us. My first request is that all of you try hard to be here every Tuesday and Friday evening. If you miss meetings, you won't know what's going on and you'll slow down our progress. Is that understood?" There was nodding throughout the assembly. "Good. Okay, as you know, we're holding these meetings to make some important decisions regarding the future of New Zion. Our church leaders have given me this sacred duty, and I'm enlisting your help. However, tonight's meeting will be shorter than future sessions because I only want to present a general idea of what we need to do.

"Our first responsibility is to establish the political government of Zion. That includes a tax system. Later, this committee, perhaps enlarged by other people, will discuss economic structures, the monetary system, and even energy sources. I know all of you and I believe you're the best people we have to do the work at hand. Some of you have a special knowledge of history and political science."

Byron Mills raised his hand. "Yes, Byron," Steven said.

"I think the problem of political government is easy to solve. We should have a theocracy. After all, we're setting up New Zion, a righteous nation, and it should be religious in nature."

A murmur rose in the assembly as many indicated their agreement.

"But, Byron," Steven replied, "that's what we had at the beginning of our settlement, and I was the head of it."

"Then let's make it that way again," Byron said. "You and your brothers did a great job. You were always fair and made good decisions for our community."

Fern Mills looked shocked. "But I thought that in a theocracy God himself was the supreme ruler."

Steven looked at John Black, the former law professor. "Do you want to clarify that for us, John?"

John Black was a sixty-year-old man of medium height and build. He wore a small moustache and was beginning to bald. His general appearance and bright eyes suggested a serious man of intelligence. "Yes, thank you,

Steven. A theocracy is a government guided directly by a divine being or indirectly by officials who are considered divinely inspired."

Fern blushed a little. "Oh! I didn't know that."

"That's all right," Steven said. "A lot of people get that confused, and I'm glad you asked about it because it's an important point to make right from the start."

"I was already aware of what a theocracy is," Byron Mills replied, "but like I said, let's create a full-blown theocracy. Problem solved."

Steven shook his head. "I'm afraid we can't make the government a theocracy. New Zion will become the home and safe haven, eventually, of millions of good people who flee the violence and evils of a wicked world. They will come to Zion as the only free and safe place on the planet." Steven picked up his scriptures and turned to Section 45 of the Doctrine and Covenants. He began to read:

> *Section 45:68-69*
> *And it shall come to pass among the wicked, that every man that will not take his sword against his neighbor must needs flee unto Zion for safety.*
> *And there shall be gathered unto it out of every nation under heaven; and it shall be the only people that shall not be at war one with another.*

"I assure you that the people who travel to Zion won't come here without their families, and of course we'll welcome them all with open arms. But most important, they will be of all races, nationalities, languages, customs, talents, and beliefs. In other words, Zion will become a great pluralistic society that assures protection and liberty to all people—especially the liberty to enjoy the fruits of their labors and to worship as they see fit. That is how Zion will become the greatest society on earth."

Tania Christopher's mouth fell open in disbelief. "But I thought the people of Zion had to live the law of consecration and the laws of the celestial kingdom. I have even heard some people say we must become translated beings in order to build the New Jerusalem. Also, I thought divine beings, especially the Lord himself, would soon visit us. Won't all the people have to be members of the true Church and live holy lives to be worthy of receiving Jesus? Won't they all have to be translated to bear his presence? And won't Christ himself rule over us and be our King forever?"

Steven smiled at his sister-in-law's list of questions. "Tania, you've asked a lot of good questions. I'll try to answer them one at a time. In the first place, we won't have to be translated to build the New Jerusalem. I know some people have expressed that idea in their writings and speeches, but it's not true. Those who advocate such a doctrine create unrealistic expectations that no one can live up to. It leads to nothing but frustration and disillusionment. Since the time of the Three Nephites around 34–35 AD, no one has been translated, at least that we know of. Those who say we must be translated to do this work depend on statements made in the journals of discourses of various early church leaders in the last dispensation.

"However, those discourses express no more than the wise judgments and opinions of the men who wrote them. Their opinions are not church doctrine. Some of the greatest and most righteous men in history have lived since the Three Nephites. For example, Joseph Smith, David O. McKay, Ezra Taft Benson, Spenser W. Kimball, and many others. Surely those men were good enough to be translated, but none of them were. So don't worry about needing to be translated.

"As for your statement that we must live the laws of the celestial kingdom, and eventually the law of consecration, my answer is that while we have those obligations, there are two basic things we need to consider.

"First, our people are not ready and will need to grow in righteousness. To achieve that, they will have to endure more trials and learning experiences. None of us suddenly became holy just because we entered the boundaries of Jackson County, and in the future we will be joined by hundreds of thousands of additional saints, and they will not marvelously take on holiness just because they come here. There's no such thing as instant righteousness.

"Second, as time goes on, hundreds of thousands of non-Mormons will become citizens of our land. We cannot expect them to become saints—suddenly—the moment they arrive. Of course, we'll preach the gospel to them as best we can, but many of them will not accept it right from the start and maybe not at all. They'll always have their agency, and it will be a gradual process of spiritual development.

"That brings me to your third statement regarding the visitations of divine beings. It's true that someday we'll be visited by ancient resurrected prophets, notably Adam, who is also called Michael the Archangel. Most of our citizens from other nations will be converted when Adam comes to defend us against our enemies. Later, Christ will appear to us in power. Since most of the citizens of Zion will be living at least a terrestrial law when he comes, they won't be consumed by his presence and they won't need to be translated. Still, a few may be transformed by the Holy Spirit, which is a temporary state.

"Even when Christ comes in glory with the hosts of heaven at the end of the world, not everyone will be burned. Only the wicked—those living a telestial law—will be consumed, whereas the celestial and terrestrial people will be protected."

No one said a word as Steven paused to let his ideas sink in. He looked at Tania and realized that she seemed satisfied with his answers.

"So what kind of government will we need, and how long will we need it?" Beverly Stark said.

"That's why we're here," Steven replied. "To decide what kind of government. As for how long we'll need a pluralistic government, I can't answer that one. I suppose as long as it takes. Five years, ten, fifty, or maybe a hundred. " He looked at Jim Pratt, the lawyer. "Jim, you're an expert on the forms of governments. Can you give us a rundown on the various types so we can get a general idea of what the possibilities are?" Steven already knew what kind of government the committee would select but he wanted them to understand the options.

Jim cleared his throat. "Thanks, I'd be happy to. Besides a theocracy, there are three basic kinds of autocratic governments and four types of constitutional governments."

"Please describe those seven forms of government for us," Steven said.

"Well, an autocratic government is an absolute or despotic government. One kind of autocracy is ruled by a dictator who wields absolute power over the people. Next, we have an oligarchy, which is ruled by an elite group who exercise power for their own selfish reasons. Finally, there is the absolute monarchy. This is a government in which the supreme power is in the hands of a monarch or sole ruler. His claim to power is typically hereditary."

With a wide grin Douglas said, "I vote that we reject those three kinds of government without debate. Steven gets a bit autocratic from time to time, but we still love him anyhow." The room filled with laughter, and Steven smiled as Paul gave a thumbs-up.

"I think we all agree that we can eliminate autocratic governments," Steven said.

"Okay," Pratt said with a chuckle. "As for constitutional governments, you have a constitutional monarchy such as that of Great Britain. It includes a king and queen, a prime minister, and a parliament. Then there's the constitutional democracy. This is a system where the sovereign power of the state is vested in the people as a whole, and is exercised directly by them or their elected agents. You'll find this kind of government in France, Canada, and Israel. Well, not Canada after the Collapse of nine nineteen.

"The third type is a republic, as was found in Mexico before the Collapse. Other examples of republics are Brazil, Chili, and Turkey. The fourth type is what we used to have in the States, a constitutional representative federal republic." He looked at Steven. "Do you want me to give a more complete description of each of these political structures?"

"Well, folks," Steven asked, "do we need more information on the four types in order to make our decision?"

Before anyone could answer, Paul quipped, "Jim, can you tell us about some perfect form of government from the past? You know, the governments of those great utopias we've all heard about?"

"I'd like to but I think it would be a waste of time. Many of those so-called utopias were found only in the writings of political scientists and philosophers like Plato." Jim stretched his back and cleared his throat again. "When people tried to set up perfect societies in the real world, they all failed miserably in the end. So there's no such thing as a perfect society, and the word utopia, coined by Sir Thomas More, means 'nowhere' in Greek." As Jim finished, Paul pretended to look terribly disappointed.

"Too bad, Paul," Steven said. "Still you tried. Now, back to my question. Do we need more information or are you ready to decide?"

Floyd Madsen, the former history professor at BYU, said, "Steven, I'm sure you know perfectly well which form of government we'll choose. We're biased and rightly so. The American form of government was inspired by God and is the best we can hope for until we can move into a fully developed theocracy." Everyone in the room clapped at Floyd's statement.

John Christopher had an unhappy look on his face. "I agree that our government was inspired by God in its original form. The Constitution, which was the supreme law of the land, helped to create the greatest and freest nation on earth. The Founding Fathers designed it to respond to the basic, imperfect nature of man, who can be arrogant, greedy, and selfish. In other words, the Constitution was designed to protect us from ourselves. The trouble is, in the century before the Collapse, the Constitution was progressively subverted and undermined until it lost all its authority. Eventually, the only parts that were honored by our leaders were the formalities and procedures. But the heart and soul of the Constitution, which protected the liberty of the people, was gutted by all three branches of the federal government."

Fern Mills's face registered shock. "I thought that when the Constitution was on the verge of falling, the elders of Israel would come forth and save it from destruction."

"A small number of elders tried their best to save the Constitution," John replied, "but the majority of them, as well as the other members of the Church, did very little. They were too busy doing other things."

Steven heard the touch of bitterness in John's voice. "What John says is true, but that's the past. We still have a chance to save the Constitution, and that's exactly what I hope we do right here in New Zion."

"So you knew all along where this was heading, didn't you?" Elizabeth Cartwright said. Steven smiled but said nothing. Elizabeth turned to John. "John, if the Constitution was basically ignored by the time of the Collapse, what kind of government do you think we were living under toward the end?"

"An oligarchy."

"An oligarchy!" exclaimed Jim Burnham, one of the colonels. "You're kidding, aren't you? It was a democracy. Everybody knows that."

John seemed to expect that response. "The Founding Fathers intended our country to be a representative republic. They feared a democratic government as much as they feared an autocratic one. They considered a democracy to be little more than mob rule. What difference does it make if one autocrat tells us how to live or if 51 percent of the people can tell the other 49 percent how to live? In reality, in a pure democracy it's not the people who prevail over the government, but the government that prevails over the people by claiming the blessing of mass opinion.

"Our government and its elite supporters, with great influence and vast sums of money, controlled the media and used it to manipulate and indoctrinate a naive and gullible nation. There is no limit to the size of that kind of government, which uses hundreds of agencies to meddle in every area of people's lives. Those agencies, manned by unelected officials, had the power to make laws, judge laws, and enforce laws, without any real control from congress or the president. In my opinion, that's the very essence of tyranny."

Fern Mills raised her hand and Steven recognized her. "I was wondering why Brother Pratt didn't mention communism and socialism when he reviewed the types of government. Where do they fit in?"

Steven nodded toward Jim and he stood up. "It's not accurate to define communism and socialism as types of government. Actually, they are economic structures, not political systems. This distinction is important but has become confused in the public mind. Usually some type of autocracy is required to create and support communism or socialism."

"Oh," Fern replied, "I didn't know that."

Steven figured it was time to conclude the meeting but he had one thing left to say.

"Brothers and sisters, in later meetings I'll tell you about a tax system I believe is simple and fair, but now I think we should call it a night. For next Tuesday, I ask you to think about how we can reestablish the Constitution as the supreme law of this land, and what changes we might have to make to prevent its future destruction. We'll have it much easier than the Founding Fathers did because those great men did most of the hard work for us." As they left the lodge, John gave each of them a copy of the US Constitution.

Chapter 12

✦

David Omert was studying a new piece of legislation when his friend Chaim Yehoshua burst into his office, which was located in the Israeli Knesset building in Jerusalem.

"Hello, Mr. Prime Minister," Chaim said. "Do you have time for a friend?" Thirteen months ago the unicameral legislative body, the Knesset, had elected David Omert prime minister of Israel, the youngest man elected to that office in Israel's history. Chaim himself was becoming one of the most influential members of Israel's supreme governing body.

"Of course, I always have time for you," David said, putting the bill aside. "What's up?"

"Oh, the same old things, I guess. What are you working on?"

"It's a new bill to be presented soon to the Knesset by one of the legislators."

Chaim took a seat in front of his friend. "Why the frown?"

"The guy who wrote this bill belongs to the liberal bloc. It seems the liberals want us to engage in peace talks with the Palestinians and the Arabs. As a part of these talks, they intend to renew their earlier proposal that we return to the Arabs lands we captured in the last war."

"Peace talks! Return captured lands! They're at it again?"

Twenty-one months ago the Arabs had made a sneak attack against Israel in another attempt to annihilate their traditional enemy, and the Iraqis in their hatred had mistakenly bombed two sacred Islamic sites—the Dome of the Rock and the al-Aqsa Mosque on the Temple Mount in Jerusalem—with Scud missiles. Afterwards the world media had accused Israel of committing that sacrilegious act, and the Arab world went insane,

rioting in the streets, burning Jewish leaders in effigy, and murdering innocent people.

Thanks to the strategies of General Hazony, the Israeli Minister of
Defense, Israel had beaten back Arab forces and had devastated them in a
war that lasted only eight days. At that time the media and the Israeli liberals
had demanded that Israel return captured lands to the Arabs. But Israel had
learned from earlier experiences that the Arabs always used restored lands
as bases for shooting rockets at Israeli communities.

"Yes," David said. "It's the same old story as before. Do you think these
leftist liberals will ever get a clue?" Chaim shook his head several times. "To
promote their causes, the liberals tell us we should 'love our neighbors,' 'seek
peace not war,' and 'forgive their trespasses.' At the same time, the Arabs call
us 'monkeys,' 'devils,' and 'usurpers' who deserve to be wiped from the face
of the earth. The truth is, we need to strengthen our army, not kowtow to
our enemies. Yet we're having trouble keeping our forces up. You probably
aren't aware of it, but we have 50,000 young ultra-orthodox Jews and Arab
citizens who demand exemption from conscription. Fortunately, however,
we'll soon have a law compelling them to do military service."

"What law? I haven't heard anything about such a law."

David took a folder out of his drawer. "This law, the one I'm going to
present at the next session."

Chaim took the folder, put his feet on the edge of David's desk, and
perused the proposal. "Do you think they'll pass this?"

"I think they will, especially if a certain influential legislator gets behind
it."

"You really think the Knesset will listen to me?"

"Yes, you have exceptional powers of persuasion."

Chaim beamed at the compliment. "I remember you telling me last
year that the members of the legislature really did listen to me, and I didn't
believe it . . . But what I really don't get is how the liberals and would-be
exempts expect this nation to survive if we don't have the means to survive.
Why can't the liberals understand that for us a powerful army is a life and
death necessity, and that we always need to be prepared, especially since we
can no longer depend on protection from the United States?"

"Well, frankly, I don't get it. Liberals seem to have very short memories.
The situation is even worse now that UGOT has gained so much power
in Europe."

"What do you mean? I haven't had time to keep track of UGOT with all the new laws being proposed."

"Well, we seem to have far fewer friends in Europe now because of UGOT's influence. But what disturbs me even more is the blasé and worldly attitude that many of our citizens have adopted, even in the face of constant Arab threats and attacks. Don't they realize that if the Arabs defeat us militarily, they'll slaughter every Jew in Israel in a countrywide blood bath?"

"I think they're blinded by the liberal mass media," Chaim said with sadness.

David's face became pale and his lips tight. "Because of the perilous situation Israel is now in, I have been spending many hours praying and doing research. I'm desperately seeking a way to save my beloved country."

"I'm not ashamed to admit that I have said a few prayers myself. But tell me what kind of research you're doing."

"I have been seeking answers in the Bible."

Chaim removed his feet from the desk and sat up straight. "Wow! The Bible. A Jew seeking answers in the Christian Bible?"

"Yes."

"What do you hope to find there?"

"I'm comparing Old Testament prophecies concerning the Messiah with the life of Jesus in the New Testament."

Chaim nearly fell off his chair. "You're comparing—I can't believe it. What do you think you've learned so far?"

"I'm becoming more and more convinced that Jehovah himself is the Messiah, and that the Messiah is none other than Jesus Christ."

"But that would mean our ancestors crucified their own Messiah."

"I know. It explains why God has allowed the Jews to be persecuted for over two thousand years. I have also learned that God is a loving, forgiving father who is ready to pardon us. That's why he has freed us from other nations and brought us here to our land of inheritance. It's all predicted in the Bible. And that's not all. I'm convinced that the Messiah, or Jesus Christ, will descend from heaven in the middle of a great battle and fight for us in person."

"Whew! Does all this mean you're going to become a Christian?"

David smiled at Chaim's worried look. "No, I'm going to remain in the Jewish religion, at least for now. I sincerely believe that as a Jew still adhering to Judaism, I can more effectively teach other Jews about the Messiah and maybe give them hope."

"When do you think the Messiah will come? The Jews have been looking for him for centuries and still there is no sign of him."

"Within the next twenty years."

Chaim looked around David's office and said, "Do you have another copy of the Bible?"

On Tuesday the delegates came to the second meeting with enthusiasm and were well prepared. After a prayer, Steven began immediately.

"Welcome, brothers and sisters. I have thought of a name for this group. I'd like to call it the National Planning Committee. Are there any objections?" No one objected. "Okay, do you all have your copy of the Constitution with you?" A few delegates had forgotten their copies, so John gave them a second one. He also passed around blank paper, but many already had paper or spiral bound notebooks.

"I think we should approach the Constitution in two ways," Steven said. "First, I would like us to read the main articles clause by clause. After each clause, I want to have a discussion of the Original Intent of the Founding Fathers."

Mary Christopher's eyes grew wide with surprise. "You mean we're going to discuss the Original Intent of every clause in the Constitution?"

"No, not the clauses where the meaning is so simple and clear that not even the Supreme Court was able to distort it."

"Whoa, boy," Ruther said, "we'll be takin' a year explainin' all that!" Everyone burst out laughing.

"Well, not quite, Ruther, but almost. No, I'm kidding. It shouldn't take us more than a month or so if we work hard at it. We won't annotate every clause, but only fifteen or twenty crucial ones. What we want to end up with is a copy of the Constitution with a lot of spacing after certain clauses where we'll summarize Original Intent in clear modern English."

"Is all that explaining really necessary?" Tania Christopher said. "In New Zion the people and the leaders won't be unrighteous like many were in Old America. I doubt they'll be promoting evil things like reverse discrimination and abortion."

"You're right. They probably won't. Still, no one is perfect, and there could be misunderstandings, especially in the minds of immigrants from other countries who don't have experience with our political and religious beliefs. So it's important that we explain enough Original Intent to prevent future problems. Also, we might need constitutional laws for a much longer time than any of us expect. In a sense those laws will last forever. It was God himself who inspired the principles of freedom found in the Constitution and I believe he will honor them, even in his eternal kingdom.

"Frankly," Byron Mills said, "I'm excited we're going through Original Intent. I've been studying it for years, and I'd love to clarify a number of things by getting input from others in this room."

"I'm really glad we'll get the benefit of your studies, Byron. In this first approach, we won't alter the original words of the Constitution. All we'll do is write explanations after pertinent clauses. However, those explanations will also have the force of law. In other words, since the Constitution will be the supreme law of the land, the explanations based on Original Intent will also be the supreme law of the land."

"Excuse me for asking a dumb question," Tania said with a frown, "but I don't understand what's so important about Original Intent. Doesn't that just refer to the opinions of men who lived hundreds of years ago? Haven't things changed a lot since then?"

Steven looked at Byron. "Would you like to answer that question?"

"I would. Thank you. The Founding Fathers were some of the wisest men who ever walked the earth. As a group they had an incredible amount of knowledge regarding all the governments of the ages, from the Greeks and Romans down to their own times. They had studied all the great political philosophers, including Plato, Cicero, Polybius, Montesquieu, Locke, and Hobbs, and they were familiar with the teachings of the Bible.

"They used all this knowledge and their own experience concerning the nature of man to form a just system of laws that would provide the highest possible degree of happiness and freedom to the people. The principles they established will always be valid and never die. Original Intent refers to their purposes when they codified those principles into the clauses of the Constitution. Later courts and government leaders betrayed the original intentions and purposes of the framers, and that's why Americans ended up with Big Brother and a grievous loss of freedom and prosperity."

Steven was impressed with that explanation and the others seemed moved also. "Thank you, Byron. All I can add is that the framers were inspired by God in their labors. Okay, do any of you have further questions?"

Jim Burnham, one of the colonels, raised his hand. "You mentioned two ways to approach the Constitution. What's the second way?"

"We'll also make structural changes to the document. In other words, we'll add to the current number of amendments by writing new ones. In that way, certain vital laws will be stated expressly so that no one can ever misunderstand them."

"But what if the Constitution needs to be changed?" Elizabeth Cartwright asked.

"We'll have a special amendment to provide for that. Essentially, it will supersede Article V, which deals with the amendment process. Let me give you some history so you'll understand why we need to alter Article V. Before the Collapse, Congress received hundreds of applications for amendments from state legislatures. Did it act on any of them by calling for a constitutional convention? Absolutely not. They were supposed to but they didn't.

"Instead, Congress simply threw the applications in a waste basket. Ask yourself this important question. Why would Congress want to call for a national convention that might result in curtailing its own power? The Founding Fathers intended that changing the Constitution should be challenging, but not almost impossible as it eventually became. Also, they made the mistake of underestimating the ability of the Supreme Court to go far beyond its constitutional authority."

Elizabeth appeared to be satisfied with Steven's explanation.

Fern Mills squirmed in her seat and waved her raised hand eagerly. Steven nodded to her. "Can you tell us about the new tax plan you mentioned? I'm dying to know what it is."

"All in good time, all in good time. All right! Is everyone ready to start reading and annotating the Constitution?" The members fumbled around opening notebooks, finding pens, and placing a copy of the Constitution on small tables placed in front of them.

He waited until the family left their cabin to work in the fields. Saturday was a full work day so he'd have plenty of time. He slipped into the empty cabin, wrapped the telescope in a sheet and hurried away furtively. But a small boy saw him leave the cabin with the bundle under his arm and hurried to inform the cabin's owner, Daniel Richardson. In a fit of rage, Daniel, who had come to Zion with Pioneer Two, rushed from the field, his family struggling to keep up. Daniel knew right where to go because the boy had identified the thief.

When Daniel reached the cabin of Casey Duff, he burst through the door and immediately caught sight of Casey admiring Daniel's beloved telescope, which had been placed on the kitchen table. Daniel, a large and powerful black man, grabbed Casey by the neck, dragged him outside, threw him on the ground, and began to pummel him with his fists. Several neighbors soon gathered. They tried to stop the violent attack, but to no avail, for Daniel was too strong. Finally, Casey managed to clutch a large stone lying on the ground nearby. He slammed the rock against Daniel's skull and the black man fell back, momentarily stunned.

However, within seconds he recovered. Madder than ever, he pounced on Casey, who was still trying to rise from the ground, seized the rock from his grasp and smashed it against Casey's head until he stopped moving. Seeing his enemy motionless, Daniel stood up, walked a few yards away, and sat on the ground, dazed and uncomprehending. Fortunately, Daniel's family arrived after the attack had ended and didn't witness the killing.

Someone nearby, who had gone to check on Casey, declared in a loud voice, "He's dead. I think he's dead." By that time a crowd had assembled. There were a dozen men, some of them with rifles. Another person examined Casey and confirmed that he was indeed dead. The men surrounded Daniel, and one of them asked him to get up several times. At last Daniel slowly complied, and the men led him away to a temporary jail.

"Quick. Go get the mayor," said one of the women on the scene to her son. "I think he's in his cabin. The boy scooted away on his errand.

A few minutes later Steven appeared and approached the dead man in disbelief. Before he could ask questions, a half dozen people, who had been eye witnesses to the entire episode, explained what had happened. At first Steven had difficulty understanding so many disparate voices, but finally he comprehended the tragedy of the situation. He put both hands against his head and turned slowly in a circle, his face an image of despair and frustration.

Then he said to the crowd, "Will some of you carry this man to my wife's hospital?" Several men picked up Casey and carried him away.

❦

The next day Steven met in Lodge Two with his brothers, six colonels, some of them from Pioneer Two, and the two apostles. In front of them sat Daniel Richardson, tears streaming from his down-turned eyes. His wife, Mariah, was next to him, holding his hand, anxiously trying to console him.

In a gentle voice Steven said, "Daniel, please look at me." Daniel looked up slowly. "Did you strike Casey Duff with a rock?"

"Yes . . . I did," Daniel muttered, "but . . . but I didn't mean to. . . . He stole my telescope. I was mad and wanted it back."

Did you hit him several times?"

"I don't remember . . . Maybe. I don't know. I was so upset. He took my telescope. The one I worked so hard to buy. I used it nearly every night coming across the plains."

Steven looked at the five witnesses sitting not far away. "Did all of you see it with your own eyes? Is that what happened?" The witnesses said "yes" in unison.

Apostle Widtsoe had explained to Steven how much Daniel loved that telescope, his prize possession. He saw Daniel every night with his telescope pointed upward, studying the magnificent constellations. Daniel was an amateur astronomer and was very knowledgeable.

"Do you know Casey Duff is dead?" Steven continued.

"Yes, my wife told me."

"Are you sorry for what you did?"

Daniel hesitated a full minute before answering. "Yes, I'm sorry. Real sorry. I didn't mean to hurt him."

"Do you think you deserve punishment?"

"Yes, of course."

"What kind of punishment?"

"I don't really know, Brother Christopher."

Steven asked two guards standing nearby to take Daniel back to jail, and Mariah followed them. After they left, Steven asked the others, "Well, brethren, what do we do with him?"

One of the colonels suggested that maybe Daniel should be shot in a firing squad, but the others vigorously disagreed. They suggested various jail sentences, varying from a year to ten years.

Finally, Apostle Bartlett said to Steven, "What do you think we should do?"

"Well, elder, I've been thinking about problems like this ever since the prophet called me to this position back in Utah. Before I answer, I'd like this group to tell me what Father in Heaven does to his rebellious children."

He received a number of answers. One brother referred to the Bible and said that sometimes God himself struck down extremely wicked and rebellious children or had others do the job for him. He referred to the Egyptians punished by the collapsing walls of water of the Red Sea in the days of Moses. Another quoted Genesis 9:6, which declares, "Whoso sheddeth man's blood, by man shall his blood be shed." A third man believed that God inspired man in the creation of laws to punish crimes of all degrees.

"Good!" Steven said. "But that's not exactly what I had in mind. For the most part, you're referring to punishments found in the Old Testament. I'm not sure that in New Zion we should create a penal system that executes or imprisons our fellow citizens." Everyone except Elder Widtsoe looked perplexed.

"You wouldn't be thinking about the War in Heaven, would you, Steven?" Elder Widtsoe said.

Steven smiled. "Yes, I am. What did the Father do to Lucifer and one third of the hosts of heaven after they committed the worst crime his children could commit?"

"He cast them out of heaven," Paul said. "Sounds like a Sunday School lesson."

"In a way it is. What will happen to all his children in the hereafter?"

"God will give them their just reward," Paul said. "According to their degree of obedience or disobedience, they'll go to the kingdom they deserve, the celestial, terrestrial, or telestial. Or they'll be cast into perdition." He seemed to have learned those words by rote.

"That's right. So what does God do? He gives his children different rewards and different punishments. But as a part of all this, he separates them physically. He puts significant space between them, as on different planets. He pretty much prevents them from mingling, except with people having a similar degree of holiness." Steven was leading them step-by-step, just as he used to do as a missionary with investigators. "So then, what should we do with people who break our laws?"

Paul smirked a bit and said, "Shoot them skyward onto different planets?" Everyone started to laugh but stifled it quickly, remembering the gravity of the situation. Paul quickly apologized for his levity.

"No, dear brother," Steven said, "but thank you for your input. What's the next best thing to rocketing them to different planets?"

One of the colonels, Kent Booth, brightened suddenly. "Ah! Kicking them out of Zion."

"Exactly. In other words, we can handle minor infractions by making people do service for those they've injured, or do extra work for the community. Perhaps later, we can fine them and make sure the money goes to victims, not to the government. For more serious crimes, we can exile them from Zion for a time, and for crimes like murder and treason we can remove them from the blessings of Zion for many years, perhaps permanently."

"Right!" said Jasper Potter, another colonel. "That way we won't have to establish a prison system in New Zion, and we won't have the gruesome task of executing criminals. All we'll need is some temporary holding cells. Think of the pain and expense the community will avoid."

"That's not all," John said. "Those we exile can take their families with them, if the families are willing to go. Those in the family who might have been victims or fear the offender don't have to join him in exile. That's better than the old penal system where criminals were separated from their wives and children for years."

Steven was pleased with their enthusiasm. "Okay. All of you seem to like the idea of service, fines, or exile. In one of the meetings of the Planning Committee we'll discuss and vote on this matter. If the committee accepts it, we'll add this system to the ballot when we ask the people to vote on the laws of New Zion. Meanwhile, we need to create a universal citizen card in order to identify every legal citizen of Zion. Those who are exiled will lose their identity card until their period of exile has expired. I know the idea of a national identity card might scare some of you, but think of the alternative. Without it, when the population of New Zion grows into the millions, we'll never be able to keep track of our citizens. Consider the identity card to be just another type of temple recommend."

"So what shall we do with Daniel Richardson?" Paul asked.

"We'll have to exile him from Zion," one of the Pioneer Two colonels said.

"But for how long?" Steven asked.

They debated that matter for a half hour. One of the men noted that exile at this time might be nearly the same thing as sending him to his death because it was a dangerous world out there. Another man countered that Daniel could probably find refuge with the Riss Community or some other nearby settlement. There were several mitigating factors: Daniel had acted from momentary rage not from premeditation; he was basically a good man who loved everyone and had contributed to the community; and his victim, Casey Duff, had stolen from others before and tended to be a troublemaker.

Finally, they came to the consensus that they would exile Daniel for a minimum of five years. It was certainly better than imprisoning him. Apostle Keith Bartlett was tasked with the job of informing Daniel and his family. Everyone was sure his family would leave with him, and they decided to give Daniel three weeks to prepare to leave the community. During that time, he would be free to stay in the community and do what he needed to do without hindrance or persecution. After they had made these decisions, the men left the lodge, feeling that their ruling had balanced justice with mercy.

When Apostle Bartlett delivered the sentence to the accused, both Daniel and his family broke out in tears. Somehow, they had expected that Daniel's fate might be much worse, especially since he was African American. Several white families immediately offered to help them in their preparations to depart.

Still sitting in the lodge, Steven asked John and Paul how they could come up with the national citizen card. Paul said that on one of his trips to Kansas City he had searched an abandoned print shop and had come across several laminating machines, both pouch and roll. He had also seen a large quantity of laminating film, heavy card stock, and several good printers. He had not brought them back to the settlement because he didn't realize they would need such equipment. He and John offered to return to the city with wagons and an armed contingent of residents to retrieve the needed equipment.

Three weeks later, at the end of July, Daniel Richardson and his family

were escorted to the western boundary of Zion's Camp, which was the
border the Richardson family had chosen. Three hundred residents
accompanied them to the edge of camp and sadly watched them go, for
the Richardsons were well liked. Many gave them gifts and supplies to
help them survive. Steven made sure Daniel had a weapon and plenty of
ammunition.

Chapter 13

The National Planning Committee spent seven weeks on Tuesday and Friday nights clarifying sections of the US Constitution and writing new amendments. First they annotated dozens of clauses that the Supreme Courts of the former United States had manipulated in order to increase the size and power of the federal government. Those courts had ignored Original Intent and instead had used precedents and activist interpretations of the wording of the Constitution to promote their own social agendas.

In other words, the courts had usurped the authority of Congress by writing new laws. By clarifying all those clauses on the basis of Original Intent and using clear modern English, the committee sought to prevent possible future abuse of governmental powers by arrogant and designing men. They also clarified the meaning of three existing amendments.

After they had finished the work of annotating, the committee took up the job of making structural changes by drafting and approving new amendments.

Before the Collapse of nine nineteen, the Constitution had twenty-seven amendments, so the committee called their first new amendment the Twenty-eighth Amendment, which introduced a new tax system called the Fair Tax. The Sixteenth Amendment, which authorized the income tax, was repealed. The new law provided that government at all levels was to be supported by a single tax—a national retail sales tax. No other taxes or fees of any kind were to be permitted in New Zion.

The retail consumption or sales tax was to be collected by retail merchants and then forwarded to the states. The states would keep 70 percent of the proceeds, which they would use to finance the management of the state, the counties, and the municipalities, and they would send the remaining 30 percent to the central government.

This system was designed to produce multiple benefits. It would prevent the formation of a gigantic federal government. Instead, the central government would be forced to remain small, for it could only receive resources sufficient to deal with national problems and to protect the country from foreign invasion. Thus, the central government would no longer have the means to finance endless foreign wars.

The law would also preclude the development of huge bureaucracies that might meddle in the lives and affairs of the citizens and businesses of New Zion. In other words, it would prevent the formation of gigantic bureaucracies like the IRS and the FDA. As a result, the law would free businesses and citizens from wasting hundreds of millions of dollars and hours keeping records and enduring the onerous task of submitting yearly tax returns, or suffering the humiliation of fines and audits.

No one would pay any tax at all unless they purchased a product or service on the retail market. And the more they purchased, or the more expensive the purchases were, the more taxes they would pay.

In New Zion the tax rate would start at 3 percent, which could be increased incrementally by law to a maximum of 10 percent. Even 10 percent would be far better than the 55 percent Americans paid to government at all levels before the Collapse.

Since it had taken five hours to discuss the tax amendment, and it was getting late, the committee decided to take a vote and adjourn until the following Friday. The vote was unanimous in favor of the Twenty-eighth Amendment. Steven was overjoyed that they had received his proposal with such favor.

Early in July the Christopher brothers and Ruther set out in the morning on horseback for Kansas City, Missouri, with three wagons and twenty armed guards. They saw several bands of vagabonds as they traveled, but the strangers kept their distance when they saw how many armed men there were in the caravan. Traveling as fast as they could on Highway 12, they arrived in the city an hour before noon. Paul led them to the abandoned print shop he had visited before. They found two roll laminators, three pouch laminators, boxes of laminating film, three high-quality printers, stacks of heavy card stock, and several digital cameras. They loaded all of it into the wagons.

Just before they mounted their horses, John said to the others, "Look, guys, while we're in the city, why don't we see if we can find some solar equipment and some other stuff? I could use everything I can get to provide us with more power. Paul, have you ever seen any companies that supply equipment for alternative energy on your other trips to KC?"

Paul looked down and thought a moment. "Um, no, but wait a minute." He hurried back into the shop without saying more. A few minutes later he exited the building with a phone book in hand. "Let's see if we can find a listing." After flipping through the yellow pages rapidly, he stopped abruptly. "Anybody got pen and paper?"

Steven leaned into one of the wagons and grabbed the writing tools from his briefcase.

"Okay, shoot." He wrote as Paul read two addresses.

"I think the first address is only about six or seven blocks from here," Paul said.

They climbed onto their horses and set out immediately, the rest of the caravan following. A half hour later, they found the supply company. The main door was missing, so they walked in and started searching. Soon they found what John wanted, to his great delight. They appropriated four 3,500 watt inverters, several charge controllers, twelve 6-volt deep-cycle batteries, and some miscellaneous wiring and electrical devices.

The prize was a stack of fourteen high-voltage solar panels and several rolls of 10-gauge solar wire. John also found two small wind turbines that he chucked into the same wagon. They took only a small fraction of the equipment available. The stack of panels was very heavy, and it took several strong men to lift them into a wagon. Also, two men had to carry each battery because they weighed 120 pounds each. By the time they were done, they had filled an entire wagon with solar equipment.

They sat on chairs in the company office to rest and eat lunch. As they ate, Steven said offhand, "I sure wish we could find a source of power that would supply all the needs of New Zion for now and forever. A source that wouldn't pollute the environment."

John shrugged. "I'm afraid there's no single magical source of power. Still, we can use several traditional alternative energy sources that will be relatively clean."

Paul stood and stretched his back. "Like what?"

"I'm thinking we can use a combination of solar, wind, and geothermal energy."

Steven stared at his younger brother in disbelief. "Do you really think we can develop all that, John? Do we have, or can we get, the equipment and experts necessary to create those systems?"

"Oh, I think so," John said. "I'm sure I know enough to make a simple one-home system using all three sources of energy. But what we need is larger community systems that supply the needs of hundreds or even thousands of homes. For that we'll need the knowledge and experience of engineers, electricians, geophysicists, geologists, and experts in many other technical fields. We already have some of those people in Zion's Camp right now, and when more people come from other countries and Utah, we'll get all the help we need. We'll also need to scrounge thousands of pieces of equipment, and eventually become capable of producing those things ourselves."

Steven raised his brow. "Are you saying you can build such a system right now for yourself?"

"Of course." John smiled at his brother's disbelief. "Why do you think I wanted to get the solar equipment and the wind turbines?"

At last they started back for Zion's Camp, arriving well before dark. When they appeared on the borders of the town, a troop of wives rushed forward happily and threw their arms around their husbands.

The next morning John and Paul set up the new equipment in Lodge Three. John made sure the computer, printer, and laminator were powered by the electricity from his solar outfit. Afterwards, they designed the new citizen card on paper, using dozens of pages until they got the result they wanted. They made sure they included all the pertinent data and a space for a color photo. After three hours of preparation, they were ready to start making the new citizen cards. They recruited a few children to run through the settlement to invite people to come to Lodge Three to get their new card, and within twenty minutes they had a line of fifteen men, women, and children waiting anxiously.

John had each person fill out an information sheet while Paul took their photos with a digital camera. Next Paul typed the information into the computer and loaded the photos. He used a program called Pictures Plus to design the citizen card, and then printed each card one at a time, after which he laminated them. When the people received their beautiful new cards, they were thrilled and glowed with pride at being legal citizens of New Zion. Only by committing a serious crime would they forfeit the card and their citizenship. Working part time, it took John and Paul four weeks to provide cards for every citizen in the settlement. All were cautioned to protect and guard the cards carefully.

For there shall arise false Christs, and false prophets, and shall shew great signs and wonders; insomuch that, if it were possible, they shall deceive the very elect.
(Matthew 24:24)

On Sunday in mid-August, Colton Aldridge awoke suddenly in his hotel room in Beijing, China. He looked at his illuminated alarm clock. Five thirty in the morning. The room was dark, but he sensed a strange presence there. A minute passed and nothing happened. Yet the feeling that an unknown being was in the room possessed him. Then a tiny light began to appear fifteen feet from the foot of his bed. It grew slowly in intensity until it lighted the entire room. But somehow, by some inexplicable miracle, the light caressed his eyes instead of injuring them. A figure began to materialize in the center of the light, growing more and more distinct until Colton recognized an old friend—his glorious smiling angel.

He had never dared to ask the angel who he was. Was he an angel? The Lord Jesus? God the Father? Today he was determined to find out once and for all. It had to do with his own sense of worth and importance.

He swallowed hard and his heart pounded wildly. "Lord, I'm . . . I'm overjoyed to see you again. What do you require of me, your faithful servant?"

"To bear witness of my glory and power to the people of China."

"Yes, Master. How can I do that?"

"Since this heathen nation does not know me, you must perform a great miracle in this land in my holy name."

"What miracle, Lord?"

"Today the mighty Hairou Reservoir will turn blood red and that crimson poison will kill all life in the reservoir and pollute the waters upon which the city named Beijing depends."

"That's terrible, my Lord, but what would you have me do?"

"Soon you will meet with the leaders of China regarding the role of UGOT in helping China solve its many problems. At this meeting you will use a special tool to encourage China to support UGOT's future objectives."

"What kind of tool will I use?"

"You will tell those leaders you have the power to heal the waters of their reservoir."

"Lord, will you give me that power?"

"No, my son, you already have it."

"But I'm not sure—"

"Promise them that you will heal the reservoir before their very eyes."

"Still, how can I—"

"Do as I say, and at the moment you need further knowledge, I will whisper into your mind."

"Yes, Master, I'll do as you say. May I ask you a question?"

"Ask as you desire."

"Who are you? Are you the Lord Jesus Christ? Or are you the Father? Or are you a—"

"No, I am not the Only Begotten. You are he."

"Me! That's not possible. I'm just a pro—"

"You are the very reincarnation of the crucified Lord." The bright personage began to disappear. "You have the power within you to perform the miracle . . . And I am your Father."

The last few words were spoken in a diminishing voice as the image gradually vanished.

Colton was dressed and ready by eight o'clock. He hurried to the adjoining room and knocked on the door. Janet Griffin opened almost immediately because she was expecting to accompany him to the meeting at ten with the Chinese leaders. Since she was UGOT's associate for East Asia, China was one of her areas of responsibility. Colton entered quickly and asked her to sit down to hear his story. With utmost solemnity he related his vision to her in as much detail as possible.

Janet was primarily a cynic and normally would have ridiculed him for such a ludicrous rehearsal. But Lucienne Delisle had told her many shocking things regarding Colton's miraculous powers. Besides, Gerald Galloway held Colton's ability to convince in high regard. She also knew UGOT had other miracle-producing prophets working hard in many parts of the world to promote its designs. She decided to go along with Colton and wait to see for herself.

As they headed down the street to hail a taxi, they heard people talking—most in Chinese but a few in English—about the great disaster that had occurred at Hairou Reservoir early that morning. When Janet heard those reports, she gazed at Colton, her face aghast. He shot her a sly smile and said, "Just what I told you, and you pretended to believe."

They caught a taxi and told the driver, who spoke some broken English, that they wanted to go to the Great Hall of the People. They arrived on time, and after passing two guards, found the office of Xi Jinping, the seventy-year-old General Secretary of the Communist Party, who met them in the hall and bowed to show his respect. They also bowed in response. After they introduced themselves, Jinping ushered them into his office and, using impeccable English, asked them to take a seat on chairs near his massive desk. Colton felt intimidated because he knew this was the head man among the seven members of the ruling Politburo.

It was obvious, however, that the General Secretary considered himself a very important person and really too busy to talk to UGOT's underlings. So he got right to the point. "How can I help the honored representatives of the great association of UGOT? We have already acquiesced to several of Gerald Galloway's *suggestions*. We have allowed him to create special offices in this very building so his people might act as *consultants* for some of our policies and to serve as a basis for his China operations. We have also accepted, with our utmost gratitude, his billions in loans to help stabilize our economy, which has been in a temporary state of crisis for the last few years." Both Janet and Colton squirmed a bit in their chairs.

The Chinese economy had boomed immensely for two decades after the year 2000, but then had taken a nosedive, due to many unwise Politburo decisions. The leaders had allowed the deficit to skyrocket and had approved many unsecured loans to foreign nations unable to repay those loans later. The problems of pollution, the supply of clean water, and a vastly expanding population, seemed unsolvable.

Xi Jinping smiled at their discomfiture. "We even supplied him with ten thousand troops to encourage the Mongolians to behave, for they were causing him so many problems."

Neither Colton nor Janet said anything for a minute, waiting to make sure the great prince had finished his recital. Finally, Colton said, "But now, Mr. Secretary, you have a new problem."

Jinping stared at him through unblinking eyes. "A new problem?" Colton suspected the prince was wondering what he knew.

"The Hairou Reservoir, filled with poisonous pollution." The Hairou Reservoir was a crucial source of water and environmental replenishment for the entire Beijing region.

"How do you know about that? It only happened a few hours ago."

"I have my sources," Colton said in a cryptic voice.

"Oh, you mean your Christian God told you." Jinping hesitated, then added, "I've heard your God gives you special powers. Powers to perform miracles."

"Yes, and I'm ready to perform one for you."

"For me? What possibly can you do for me?"

"Purify your polluted reservoir."

"That's impossible. We have thirty scientists working on the problem. So far, they have no idea as to the causes or the solutions."

"I can do it if you will permit me."

Jinping stood suddenly. "I have a meeting to attend, Mr. Aldridge. Thank you for your time." Colton knew it was only a matter of seconds before he and Janet were escorted from the building by security, so he decided on a desperate measure. "Gerald Galloway has promised to provide you with another loan of three billion pounds, or thirty billion yuan, interest free if I cannot heal the waters of your reservoir."

"Galloway knows about the reservoir already?"

"He knows, of course," Colton lied.

Galloway's incredible offer got Jinping's attention. "One moment, please. I am phoning a friend to ask him to accompany us to the reservoir." After talking on the phone for a minute, he made a second call. Completing his call, he said, "Mr. Aldridge, I'll be happy to take you up on that offer of three billion from your employer. Can you put it in writing?" He handed

Colton pen and paper, and Colton wrote the offer down, signed it, and gave it to Janet to sign. Janet did so with a shaky hand.

Before long, another Politburo member entered the room. It was Zang Gaoli, the Executive Vice Premier in charge of economic affairs. The Chinese leaders consulted in Chinese for a few minutes and then led their guests out to Tiananmen Square. Ten minutes later a helicopter appeared. The four of them hopped in, with several security guards, and the helicopter took off. By automobile the Hairou Reservoir was about an hour and a half away, but they covered the distance in twenty minutes in the copter, landing on a small plateau near the reservoir. The lake before them was blood red and was a shocking sight to behold. By that time, fifty scientists and water specialists had gathered at the shore of the lake. There was equipment strewn everywhere, and the experts were taking and analyzing water samples. Xi Jinping walked over to a group of them and had a quick consultation. He looked grim when he returned to his party.

"Unfortunately, they have not yet been able to discover the source of the pollution." He grabbed the elbow of Zang Gaoli, and they walked twenty paces away. Colton knew he was filling Zang in on the details of their intentions. A few minutes later, they returned, and Jinping said, "Okay, Mr. Aldridge, let's see your miracle. Do you wish me to tell my people to distance themselves from the edge of the lake?"

Colton shook his head and turned toward the lake. In his mind he said, *"Dear God, please help me. Now is the time for your instructions, as you promised in my hotel room."* He began to panic when he heard nothing at first, realizing what a disaster it would be if God did not tell him what to do.

Finally, a voice spoke to him. *"My son, raise your hands high toward heaven and in a loud voice command fire to descend onto the lake. Remember, you are the Only Begotten Son of God."*

Following his master's instructions, he raised his arms and shouted, "In the name of my Father, I, the Lord Jesus Christ, command thee, oh heavenly fire, to descend and cleanse these adulterated waters."

Since nothing happened immediately, the spectators began to look at one another with skepticism. But soon a huge flaming ball began to form slowly in the sky. It appeared to be several thousand feet up and as large as a small cloud. Then suddenly a jet of fire burst from the blazing cloud, curved gradually downward, and fell onto the lake with a violent snapping sound, like a great bolt of lightning. Immediately the waters around the area struck by the jet began to turn greenish blue, the normal color of the lake. The color change progressed with surprising rapidity and spread throughout the vast reservoir.

The crowd cheered as they beheld the miraculous change. When the lake seemed back to normal, the two Chinese leaders approached Colton and shook his hand in gratitude. Janet Griffin stood off to the side, staring at the water, her mouth half open.

"I promised you a miracle, and now you have it," Colton said to Jinping. "This miracle was performed for your benefit, but I want you to know I can perform even greater miracles that might *not* be for your benefit."

The two Chinese leaders left their guests in order to examine the lake water up close. Seeing they were alone, Janet said to Colton, "Did Gerald really give you permission to offer them that loan?"

"Of course not. I made it up."

In subsequent meetings the National Planning Committee approved eleven additional amendments to the Constitution. These laws were designed to correct many of the problems that had undermined the freedom of the people in Old America.

The designers reinstated the provision that senators should be elected by state legislatures, and not by the vote of the people, thus reinforcing the principle of the separation of powers between the states and the federal government. They also required a balanced budget and provided that any federal statute might be repealed by the vote of the legislatures of two-thirds of the states.

In another amendment they prohibited the federal government from promoting public works and institutions such as libraries, theaters, and schools. Since the federal government would have no power over education, it would not be able to introduce a program like Common Core, which in Old America worked to brainwash and indoctrinate children, teaching them *what* to think, not *how* to think.

The modern framers also prohibited the central government from financing or regulating doctors, hospitals, pharmacies, and healthcare in general. Such actions could only be taken by the states.

They wrote an amendment authorizing the president to have the power to hire and fire bureaucratic chiefs working under him, thereby preventing the rise of petty czars who could not be fired and were not responsible to the people. However, the same amendment prohibited the president from engaging in military actions abroad, since only Congress had the power to declare war. It also prohibited him from issuing executive orders other than those dealing directly with his enumerated powers.

Another amendment set term limits so that congresspeople could not make lifetime careers out of government service. Other amendments forbade abortion in New Zion except under specific conditions, rejected conscription as involuntary servitude, and took the amendment process out of the hands of Congress and made it the responsibility of state legislatures. The final amendment authorized the new penal code, which provided for the loss of citizenship and residence in Zion for serious crimes instead of resorting to imprisonment or capital punishment.

Therefore, the Planning Committee wrote twelve new amendments, making a total of thirty-nine amendments to the Constitution. After they had completed their difficult task, the members disbanded, and the final approval of their work was left up to the people. They were grateful for their experiences on the committee and left with a new appreciation for the majesty of the US Constitution.

PART TWO
The Triumph of New Zion

Chapter 14

❦

And Zion grew and prospered. Within the next fifteen years, a million and a half immigrants flooded into the land. About half of these people were from Utah, arriving in one wagon train after another every three months in good weather. Each caravan brought more than a thousand new pioneers, and in time the travelers began to arrive in powered vehicles. The other half came from all the other nations on earth. The foreign immigrants were the best people those countries had to offer. They rejoiced as they traveled to the land of freedom and goodness, desperately trying to escape the hatred, violence, and sin found in their native lands. Most of all, they hated the tyranny and evil of UGOT.

The citizens of New Zion welcomed all the newcomers with joy and tears. As the people poured into Zion, the atmosphere was unbelievable. Laughter, exuberance, excitement, bustle, dancing, happy songs, kind deeds, hard work, and the sharing of burdens filled the new nation. Their greatest problem was adjusting to the burgeoning population. Everywhere one looked, in every valley and hill, in every community, there was construction. And no one had to do his work alone, but had many helpers until the job was completed.

Every new person, including the young, was given a precious citizenship card, after they had built their homes and had been in New Zion three months. They considered the card to be a symbol of freedom and hope. Mormon and non-Mormon alike showed the same kind of love and service, and there was almost no animosity or dissension.

So God blessed them and made their land fruitful. Fields that had yielded little fruit before became rich and produced magnificent harvests. Forests grew where none had grown before, providing the inhabitants with all kinds of wood for building their homes and adding to the building materials they already had. Cities and towns sprang up everywhere in Missouri, and then spread to Arkansas, Tennessee, Kentucky, Indiana, Illinois, Iowa, Nebraska, Kansas, and Oklahoma. Communities became counties, and counties became states.

The people living within old state boundaries voted to keep the cherished state names of the past. And why not? In the early days, America with its component states had become the greatest and freest nation in the history of mankind, and the citizens for the most part had loved their states as much as their nation. This dual love continued almost without interruption until the terrible Civil War, which turned America upside down. But that dual love was restored again in Old America after a few difficult decades. It continued for many years until eventually most of the people, especially the leaders, gradually turned away from goodness and freedom and instead chose riches, influence, security, slavery, and sin.

In New Zion the citizens of every town and city elected their own type of government, which usually consisted of a mayor and a council. They also planned the basic organization of their own communities. Usually they followed the plans established by the leaders of Zion's Camp and approved by the voters of that community. But some communities chose other government forms and planning structures, unhampered by controlling national laws.

The citizens of the states chose governors, lieutenant governors, bicameral legislatures, and court systems. And finally, near the end of the first eleven years, delegates from the ten new states gathered at Independence, Missouri to create a federal government similar to that created by the original Founding Fathers. It was not hard to do because they had excellent models. Their first action was to approve the revised US Constitution as the supreme law of the land. The annotations and the twelve new amendments that Steven Christopher and his National Planning Committee had written were also accepted as the supreme law of the land.

The work of the state delegates was then approved by all ten state legislatures. Because of the new laws and the unique tax system—the Fair Tax—small government at all levels was assured. Since the people had to pay no more than one simple tax at a small rate, they had plenty of money left over to help the sick and the poor, which the Church and the communities encouraged as much as possible. Since the government didn't steal people's money and property by taxing them to death, they felt more compassionate toward the unfortunate and more inclined to assist them. The tax agency of the federal government consisted of one small office employing less than a hundred people, and state tax agencies were even smaller.

All commerce and trade was based on the free enterprise capitalist system. Shortly after its foundation, the federal government began to print currency. However, constitutional law required that the currency could not be fiat money, or currency created by government and not backed by silver or gold. Fiat money was outlawed as being a plague to society and a grave danger to freedom. The leaders of New Zion passed statutes rejecting any kind of government manipulation of the money supply, and thus forbade the creation of a Federal Reserve, which would only serve to profit the rich and impoverish the poor. Only privately owned banks were permitted.

Zion warmed and powered its homes and businesses by renewable energy. Each district created its own power installations. They built geothermal plants, huge arrays of solar panels, or great wind farms, often combining more than one of those energy sources. In the countryside, individuals—usually farmers—provided their own small power plants, choosing from a half dozen different power producers.

Towns and states were aggressive in rebuilding the infrastructure. Long-distance power lines were a necessity, but they were always buried underground in well-marked trenches. Many types of factories and industries arose and provided the people with most of the old machines and technologies, and many new ones also. Where possible, old-style machines were converted to run on natural energy sources. Many factories produced battery-run or solar-run automobiles, and it was a joy for the citizens to see these vehicles zip from place to place on shiny new streets. From time to time, they saw small airplanes fly overhead, powered by the sun. There were a few small factories extracting oil from the ground, but that oil was used only to lubricate moving metal parts.

As a result of the consistent use of alternative energy sources, the air, water, and soil of New Zion became increasingly pure and clean.

The growth of industry and small business benefited enormously from the freedom the people enjoyed from government taxes, regulations, and unending interference.

In New Zion there was room for many types of occupations: farmers, builders, masons, teachers, scientists, researchers, chemists, government officials, engineers, soldiers, and many others. But there were very few lawyers, doctors, nurses, pharmacists, policemen, and judges. Every citizen from age sixteen to eighty was trained in the use of firearms and was expected—not required—to own at least one weapon. It was by these citizen soldiers that New Zion would be defended from the dangers of foreign invasion.

In contrast to Old America, the people of Zion, in general, sought kindness, righteousness, and service rather than money and position. Self-worth was determined by how good you were and how much you served others, not by how wealthy you were or how large your home was. The people of Zion had a great mission to prepare the world for the Second Coming and in general they pursued that mission with all their hearts.

To prepare for the coming of the Lord, the church members built a great new temple at Independence, Missouri, using consecrated funds. A short time later, Christ appeared privately to his apostles and others in the temple and gave them instructions. The people also constructed four smaller temples in other regions. Many non-Mormons helped them by supplying both funds and labor. After working on the temples with their hands and tools, many of those good people joined the Church. They too developed a yearning for truth, peace, righteousness, and justice.

Indeed, New Zion was well on its way to becoming the greatest nation and society that ever existed on the planet. And in this free land the Church blossomed and prospered as never before. Two years after Steven Christopher's Nation Planning Committee had created the new version of the US Constitution, plans for societal organization, and new energy sources, all their hard work was taken back to the Rocky Mountains, and within sixteen months Old Zion embraced most of those advances. The people of the western branch of the Church were especially delighted with the Fair Tax system.

While the two branches of Zion communicated mostly by radio, they began to repair I-80 and string telephone lines along its course. Both nations were harassed by constant attacks from bands of renegades, seeking greedily to benefit from the labors of the diligent. Thus they were forced to maintain strong citizen armies. They didn't realize that this preparation would soon lead the two Zions to join more effectively in a common cause. Since the Prophet Josiah Smith had died eleven years earlier, the Church had ordained senior apostle Wilford Benson as the new prophet, with Bennion Hicks as first counselor and Samuel Law as second counselor. The Church had sent a total of six apostles to New Zion to govern the Church in that region. The senior apostle was Jason Widtsoe, who lived at Independence and was now seventy years old.

A few years after the establishment of the Republic of Zion, the Church began the construction of a natural open-air amphitheater at the future site of the great council of Adam-ondi-Ahman. In the center of this great amphitheater there was a small level square occupied by a few altars and a large table made of rock. In a circle around that square the ground rose steadily to an elevation of two hundred feet and extended outward for a quarter of a mile.

The construction crews worked on the site for nearly a year. They removed all the trees that might obstruct one's view from the top of the circular hill to the square and they planted the entire arena with a hardy green grass. After you walked over the top of the hill heading away from the square, the grass continued for another four hundred yards.

To house the people who would be invited to the council, the Church constructed nine five-story hotels about a hundred yards beyond the planted grass. In that area also, the Church installed forty pairs of temporary outhouses for the convenience of visitors who would have no access to the restrooms in the hotels. All this work was done according to the original instructions of the Prophet Josiah Smith.

Yet the primary question on the minds of the people who knew about the preparations being made in Daviess County, Missouri, was when the meeting at Adam-ondi-Ahman would actually take place.

Chapter 15

At the beginning of August the army came from the east and rolled relentlessly westward, winding slowly across the broken terrain like some great metallic serpent. At what used to be Indianapolis it hesitated as if trying to decide whether to take the northern path or the southern. Finally, it made its choice, divided into two branches, and then advanced once more, hungrily, toward its prey.

Nearly six thousand vehicles, including light tanks, trucks, APCs, tankers, and jeeps, carried the great invasion army of 300,000 troops from eastern United States to the west. From time to time, segments of the army stopped, and patrols dressed in ugly green uniforms vomited from its innards to rape and pillage the countryside. The thousands of ragged, starving creatures who inhabited the land were no match for the highly trained invaders, who carried sophisticated weapons and delighted in blasting their helpless victims from great distances. Their lust for supplies and human blood was insatiable. Their destination was New Zion.

Gerald Galloway met with his eleven associates in Le Bristol Hotel, located at 112 rue du Faubourg Saint Honoré in Paris. It was their annual meeting and they had a great deal to discuss. At age sixty-seven Gerald was still alert and active. His eyes displayed a strange glow and excitement, for he was only a few years away from his goal of destroying the State of Israel. His mistress, Lucienne Delisle, was still svelte and striking at age forty-five. She too sensed that soon their great mission would be accomplished. Gerald had extended a special invitation to Colton Aldridge, the prophet, who was not a member of the Twelve but had used his miraculous powers to enlist the cooperation of numerous governments. Gerald would use the armies of those nations against the despised Jews.

After spending a few days enjoying the food and many amenities of the spectacular hotel, including the remarkable swimming pool, the leaders of UGOT gathered at eight in the evening to get some work done.

As usual, Gerald began the discussion. "Have you all got to know Colton better since we've been here? You knew him before from his reputation only, but now you've had a chance to get to know him personally. He is my favorite prophet because he has found many new allies for us." They all raised glasses of wine and gestured toward Colton to show their approval. Colton smiled in return but secretly thought these people to be worldly hypocrites and great sinners. He knew God would punish them too someday. Perhaps even by his hand.

After they had discussed Colton's operations for some time, Gerald said, "Now we'll give Lucienne, our associate for North America, the floor. Give us your report, Lucienne."

"Well, right now it's all about the Mormons. They are the only people in the old United States to have an organized society. Actually, two societies, one in the Mountain West and the other in the center of the country. Both these groups are rebuilding the infrastructure of their regions and are becoming more and more powerful. They also have made it a point to organize extensive citizen armies. But to cut to the chase, you're all aware of my plans to send an army, or several armies, into the country to wipe out the Mormons."

Francis Bonnard, the associate for North Africa, said, "You know, I still don't understand why we concern ourselves with the Mormons. How much trouble can such a small religious community give us, after all? Can't we just annihilate them anytime it's convenient? Why several armies?"

Lucienne scowled and glared at Francis. It wasn't the first time she had explained her plans to the other associates and to Francis in particular. "Because the Mormons aren't a small religious community. They have millions of members worldwide. And in the States their numbers are growing exponentially. It seems that all they do is reproduce like rabbits. Worst of all, the Mormons support Israel. If we don't deal with them now, we'll have to face their armed militias in Israel when we move against the Jews. Besides, it's useless for me to try to convince you now."

Juliska Ferenci, the associate for Eastern Europe, said, "Why is that, Lucienne?"

"Because, with Gerald's permission, I've already dispatched an army of over 300,000 troops to the States. It's the most modern and best-equipped army in recent history. They landed on the east coast in mid-July and are heading toward Mormon lands in the Midwest as we speak. I expect them to attack within three weeks."

❦

John Christopher opened the door to the governor's office at Independence and entered without waiting for an invitation. After all, the governor of Missouri was his older brother, Steven Christopher, who was serving his second term in that office. Steven was now fifty-three years old, and John was forty-nine, and both brothers had streaks of gray in their hair. Today John had a grim look on his face.

Instead of jumping up and hugging his brother, Steven remained in his chair, sensing immediately the gravity of this unannounced visit. "What's up, John? Why so serious?"

"I just got a radio message from Paul." Although there was landline telephone service within the boundaries of Zion, there was still very little such service just outside those limits.

"Oh? How's he doing?"

Paul, who was now forty, and Jarrad Babcock had led a troop of two hundred militiamen on horseback to Columbus, Ohio, on Highway 70 to reconnoiter the area. Many of the incoming groups of immigrants from Europe had been viciously attacked by bands of outlaws in that vicinity, and Paul was charged with eliminating that constant threat.

"He's fine, but the report he's giving me is very disturbing."

"What's he saying?"

"He rescued a group of immigrants from outlaws. They were headed for Zion, and if he and his boys hadn't arrived when they did, the travelers would have been slaughtered. Anyway, to make a long story short, one of the men he rescued, an elderly man from Holland, told him that when his caravan turned south to move onto Highway 70, they saw a great column of soldiers moving west. This was back near Washington, Pennsylvania, about a hundred and fifty miles east of Columbus."

Though Steven had known that someday New Zion would be attacked by a large, powerful army, he hadn't realized it would come so soon. "Did the old man say how many troops there were?"

"He didn't know for sure, but he said his people hid themselves quickly and watched the column continue westward for at least half a day. Yet that's only part of the story. He described an army that seemed equipped to wage World War III. They had massive battle tanks, armed vehicles of all kinds, and even air support."

"Air support?"

"Yes, the old man saw squadrons of modern warplanes roar in and then out suddenly. He couldn't figure out where they came from or where they went, except that sometimes they flew off to the north."

"Probably flying up and down the column to provide reconnaissance and support. The fact some of them flew north suggests they were also communicating with another army to the north. Well, we need to inform the president immediately." The president resided in Independence and was usually in his office in the capitol building at this time. Steven picked up the handset and dialed the number. He waited with furrowed brow and tight lips as the line rang a half dozen times.

Then he heard the familiar voice. "Douglas, this is Steve." The president was none other than his old friend Douglas Cartwright, who had recently been elected president of the Republic of Zion. "How are you? . . . And the family? . . . That's great! Listen, I need to get right to the point." He reviewed Paul's message and said, "What do you want to do?" He listened carefully to the answer, which took five minutes. "Okay, I understand. I'll get right on it." He replaced the handset.

"What did he say? What does he want to do?" John asked, his face lined with worry.

"He believes the army in question was raised by UGOT and is coming here to destroy our nation. I'm sure he's right. He said he's going to declare martial law and he wants all the governors to mobilize their state forces as quickly as possible."

John smiled with pleasure. "I always knew Douglas was a man of action, and I agree with him completely. But how do we mobilize our forces?"

"We'll simply inform the military leaders we have in place and instruct them to prepare for war."

"Do we stay at our posts here in Missouri or what?"

"The president wants to move most of our troops to the eastern boundaries of Zion, in hope of intercepting the invaders. He said he'd give us more details shortly."

As John got up to leave, he said, "Steven, is this the end of New Zion?"

"Don't be silly. No army can destroy Zion."

John paused for a moment and then said, "Yes, you're right, of course. What do you want me to do?"

"Well, since you're a member of the legislature, you can seek out your colleagues and warn them. I'll start making calls to government officials and to the military."

John turned to leave but Steven stopped him. "Wait. I want to give you the rest of Douglas's message."

"Yes."

"He wants Paul and Jarrad to disregard their original orders. Because of the new threat, he wants them to lead their troop east following I-70 to reconnoiter the approaching army. They are to stay off the freeway and travel instead on the terrain adjacent to the road. They must stay far enough away to avoid being spotted, but close enough for their scouts to keep track of the advance units of the enemy. Their job is to follow the army, give us regular updates on their movements, and continue this tactic until instructed otherwise.

"Douglas also wants Paul to detach a platoon with instructions to ride north to I-80 to see if there's a second army on that highway. He should dispatch the platoon immediately before he leads the main body east. Above all, they are not to engage the enemy in any way. Douglas is also calling an emergency meeting of governors and other leaders in Independence at ten in the morning. His secretary is making the phone calls as we speak."

"Is there anything else?"

"Only something personal. When you talked to Paul, did he happen to mention how the boys were doing?" Steven's two sons, William and Andrew, and John's three sons, Patrick, Raymond, and Cory, had gone with Paul on the patrol to the eastern boundaries of Zion. All of them were in their twenties.

"Oh, yes. I was so traumatized by the threat that I forgot to tell you. The boys are fine and very proud to be doing their part to protect the immigrants."

"Are they giving Paul any trouble? I know Andrew can be a handful at times."

"No, according to Paul, he's been as good as gold. Paul made William and Patrick patrol leaders and he says they're showing real promise."

Steven smiled with relief. "That's good news. Okay, we need to get things moving."

John left and Steven picked up the phone handset and began to call.

⚬

Within one day the people of New Zion learned of the great threat to their nation. They quickly began to put into practice the procedures for self-defense that their leaders had been teaching them for the last fifteen years. Most families had already obeyed the leaders and stored sufficient food, clothes, and essential supplies to last them a year. Nearly a fifth of the citizens had built reinforced underground bunkers permanently stocked with supplies for a month. They loaded weapons and barricaded windows and reinforced doors. When that work was done, thousands of crews set out for strategic locations in each community to dig trenches and erect barricades.

While they waited for reports on enemy movements, they expanded national defensive efforts. On the eastern borders of their land, they began to block the main arteries with thousands of large blocks of cement, which fit together neatly to form massive barricades. They had been pouring those blocks for over ten years on the counsel of Steven, John, and Douglas. They also started the work of positioning hundreds of high-caliber artillery guns, which they had collected from abandoned army and National Guard posts. From storage they removed over four thousand machine guns, Gatling guns, howitzers, and grenade launchers and positioned them strategically around the entire periphery of the nation, especially the eastern front.

⚬

About thirty miles east of Cambridge, Ohio, Captain Paul Christopher's advance scouts spotted UGOT's army moving slowly westward. Paul posted his main contingent in a hidden valley five miles south of I-70 and approached the freeway with three of his best scouts. A mile from the freeway, they tied their horses and climbed a small rise. Near the top they began to crawl on their bellies until they reached a good position. Paul removed his binoculars from his pack and studied the enemy for fifteen minutes. The scouts were also using their binoculars. The green line of the enemy appeared like a blight against the magnificent landscape.

"Well, men, what do you think?" Paul said.

The scout on his right was looking up the enemy line as it moved from the east. With the binoculars he could see almost twenty miles. "I can still see them until they disappear on the horizon. I'd say we're dealing with a lot more than 100,000 troops."

"I guess there's no way of accurately assessing the total force," Paul returned. He addressed the scout on his left, who had the radio equipment. "Matt, get on the horn and see if you can raise Lieutenant Babcock." Several days earlier, Second Lieutenant Jarrad Babcock had left the main troop with forty cavalrymen. His assignment was to check I-80 to the north for enemy troop movements.

After cranking his radio, the radioman said, "Little Miss Muffet, come in, please. This is Mother Goose." He repeated this several times until the radio finally crackled and a voice said, "Yes, Mother Goose, this is Little Miss Muffet. Lay your egg, please. Over." The radiomen had made up the nursery rhyme code ahead of time, thinking it might confuse the enemy, which they knew came from foreign lands.

"Have you sat on your tuffet yet? Over."

"Yes, Mother Goose, I have and I'm eating my curds and whey. Over."

"Did the black spider sit down beside you? Over."

"Yes, Mother Goose the spider did exactly that. Over."

"Did the spider frighten you away? Over."

"Yes, Mother Goose, the spider worked his magic. Over."

"Okay, Miss Muffet. Get yourself a stick and smash the spider fast. Over."

"Will do, Mother Goose. Over and out."

The radioman turned to Paul and said, "They say they've reached I-80 without problems and have spotted the enemy moving west on the freeway. They believe the enemy army to be over 100,000 troops. Lieutenant Babcock's platoon still has enough supplies to reconnoiter for at least two weeks." Paul smiled at the youthful exuberance of his radiomen.

"Okay," Paul said, "now get me headquarters so I can transmit Lieutenant Babcock's information and what we've seen ourselves." After watching the enemy forces another half hour, Paul was shocked to see huge fuel tankers that rolled by every half mile or so.

⚙≈⊚

In Independence, President Cartwright met with key leaders at ten o'clock on August 11 in a conference room down the hall from his office. He had invited all ten governors, the vice president, the minister of defense, four generals, the secretary of state, and the president's chief of staff. The latter two were women. He had also invited a young major named Chad Nelson. They sat around a big rectangular table with a pot of red roses in the center. The room was sparse and utilitarian, decorated only with filmy blue curtains and a few paintings of early American leaders on the walls.

After asking Governor Christopher to give a prayer, the president said, "Thank you, Steve. Okay, people, I've called this emergency meeting to deal with a grave threat to our nation. As you all know, we've received confirmed reports that two great armies are bearing down on us from the east. From the uniforms and equipment our scouts have seen, it seems that UGOT has sent these armies against us. We believe UGOT is the great secret combination described in the Book of Mormon, and since it has gained so much power and influence in the last thirty years, today it no longer needs to remain secret."

"What numbers are we looking at, Mr. President?" General Michael Jamison asked. Jamison had been chosen as the Commander in Chief of all Zion's forces.

"Captain Paul Christopher encountered the enemy just east of Cambridge and has been following them since. After observing them for days, Christopher and Babcock estimate that the combined armies total more than 300,000 troops." With wide eyes they all looked at one another in consternation.

"Whew!" another general said. "More than 300,000. What type of military equipment do they have?"

Cartwright looked down at his written list. "Very modern and extremely varied. The troops are carrying improved M16 assault rifles, Beretta M9 pistols, sniper rifles, shotguns, machine guns, and grenade launchers. As for bigger stuff, they have rockets, missile launchers, and mortars. Their vehicles include troop trucks, armored fighting vehicles with machine guns, motorcycles, flat beds carrying artillery guns, the Humvee and M1 Abrams main battle tank, and fuel tankers. Worst of all, they have air support, including attack helicopters and F-15E Strike Eagle warplanes. Also, Captain Christopher thought he saw several air-to-surface missiles under the wings of the F-15Es."

"We're in deep trouble," said the minister of defense.

Cartwright struggled to smile as he said, "It's not all bad. I have good news also. As soon as we had confirmed that UGOT's army was headed this way, we contacted Salt Lake City and apprised them of the situation. President Benson assured me that the Lord would come and fight our battles, as long as we did our best to defend ourselves. He has informed government authorities, and they promise to send us reinforcements as soon as feasible."

"How many troops can they spare?" the secretary of state asked.

"A substantial number. President Benson has asked all bishops and stake presidents to recruit volunteers. A quick assessment suggests they might raise between 150,000 to 200,000 soldiers."

"But they're so far away," a third general said. "It'll take them at least two months to recruit and transport those forces. By that time, we'll be history."

"Not at all. I asked President Benson when was the earliest we might expect help, and he said they could start arriving in less than two weeks. Most of the armed volunteers are already in place because of their ongoing need for defense. They now have hundreds of cars, trucks, and buses powered by high-tech batteries and solar energy. Interstate 80 has mostly been repaired and is ready for use. Don't worry. They'll get here in time to help us, especially if we can find ways to delay the enemy advance. They also plan to bring a lot of heavy firepower."

The chief of staff frowned and shook her head. "But the enemy can easily make I-80 unserviceable by using airpower to blast it to pieces with rockets and guided missiles."

Steven Christopher chuckled and said, "I don't think UGOT has any idea that reinforcements are on the way. Of course, it's wise to consider every contingency, but we should also remember that God didn't redeem New Zion so UGOT could destroy it."

Douglas's face showed he agreed. "We also have a number of tricks we can use against them. I don't think we should sit back and wait for the enemy to reach us. We need to take the fight to them. I have already ordered Major Chad Nelson here to form a battalion and plan preemptive strikes. It's part of our delaying tactics. He already began assembling the men he needs early this morning."

Chapter 16

President Cartwright had handpicked Major Chad Nelson, an experienced warrior, to conduct the difficult operation. He was tall, slender, golden-haired, aggressive, intelligent, sure of himself, and in his mid-forties. He wore a blond goatee and a long mustache. When history buffs first caught sight of him, they thought of General Custer of the early American Indian wars. After accepting his assignment, Major Nelson chose a select group of men he trusted implicitly. There were three hundred and forty of them. Twenty-four of these men were expert marksmen, the best Zion had to offer. They carried sniper rifles, scrounged from gun shops and abandoned army posts.

Nelson also selected subordinate officers to lead the troops. His friend, Major James Ellwood, was his first choice. Major Nelson summoned all the men to assemble at the restored National Guard armory in Springfield, Illinois, early on the morning of Saturday, August 14. When the men first arrived, they were so excited that they filled the huge auditorium with bustle and noise. But the major demanded silence and got it quickly. Immediately he began to explain their mission.

They were to depart that same day, and their job was to meet up with Captain Paul Christopher's troop of two hundred men near Columbus and delay the enemy advance by executing preemptive strikes. When as he had explained in detail what he and his lieutenants planned to do, the major ordered the men to collect their weapons and gear and load them quickly into waiting trucks, for there was not a minute to lose. They also loaded bombs, mines, and Thompson submachine guns. By nine o'clock the trucks and the soldiers on horseback moved onto I-70 and headed east as fast as the terrain permitted, with three hundred and eighty-three miles ahead of them. They didn't know how fast UGOT's armies were moving, but reports had indicated that most of their infantry was on foot.

❦

General Liu Dejiang, Commander in Chief of the great offensive against the religious fanatics called Mormons, rode in his personal staff vehicle a quarter mile back from the front on I-70. With him were two orderlies and a machine gunner. His friend and second in command was General Zhang Qishan, who controlled the northern army heading west on I-80. They consulted with each other regularly by radio. The northern army was proceeding about fifty miles behind the southern army.

Lieutenant General Li Gaoli, Dejiang's subordinate, hopped into the staff car, noting that Dejiang was very upset. Speaking in Chinese, Dejiang said to Gaoli, "This snail's pace is driving me crazy. If only they had listened to me, we would have totally annihilated the enemy by now." Being Chinese, he was normally stolid, calm, unreadable. Never before had he told Gaoli how he felt, but this was just too much.

"I don't understand, sir. Please be so kind as to explain."

"That arrogant War Office in Paris. They listened to that crazy woman and insulted my honor. After all, I'm the leader of this expedition and I should make the crucial decisions."

"What crazy woman, honorable leader?"

"Lucienne Delisle! They listened to her and she knows nothing about war or battle strategies. She's just one of Galloway's lackeys. Nothing but a paper pusher."

"Please explain further, sir. I am sure you are right to object to their treatment of you."

Dejiang decided to favor his subordinate by explaining himself. "I wanted to insert these troops and materiel into attack positions using transport aircraft like the Airbus A400M Atlas, not walk halfway around the world."

Gaoli's face became pale as he stared hard at his leader. Dejiang had never gotten out of his vehicle once except to eat, sleep, and relieve himself. "But won't the airbus carry only about a hundred and twenty troops? To transport 300,000 men would take—"

Irritated at being contradicted, Dejiang snarled, "We don't need 300,000 troops to eradicate a few backward peasants who have no modern weapons. We could do it with a few thousand men and some warplanes and tanks."

"But, honorable general, the War Office said the provincials will have at least 150,000 troops."

"I don't believe it. I have done my research and found that Mormons are basically pacifists and will probably fall down at our feet and ask for mercy."

"But, my honorable leader, they say—"

"And they are wrong! At the very least the War Office should have given us more transport trucks. Half my men are on their feet. By the time we get to Mississippi or wherever the Mormons are, the Mormons will have time to escape to the great desert to the west."

"Noble general, don't you mean Missouri, not Mississippi? And isn't the land west of them the Great Plains, not a desert?"

"Yes, of course, that's what I meant. My main point is, this operation is taking too long."

"But, sir, I'm sure we will get there in time to punish the peasants for what they have put us through."

"I assure you, Gaoli, we will punish them. Still, I wish my entire army was Chinese. The Chinese are so obedient and respectful. Trying to control all these Japanese, Koreans, Frenchmen, Englishmen, and Germans is nearly impossible."

SATURDAY, AUGUST 14–SUNDAY, AUGUST 29

Major Chad Nelson led his cavalry eastward at a slow trot. They stopped frequently to water, feed, and rest the horses. He limited the distance covered to no more than forty miles a day. To lose horses from injury or exhaustion would be a disaster and result in the loss of human life, and even compromise their mission. The trucks rolled along behind the cavalry at about eight miles per hour. At six in the afternoon of the tenth day, they spotted Captain Paul Christopher's troop in a camp south of the freeway.

According to Paul, the enemy was still a hundred miles away. After joining Paul's camp, Major Nelson gave precise instructions to the twenty-four snipers. He also organized ten demolition teams of five soldiers each and gave them their orders. Later that night, Major Nelson, Major

James Ellwood, Captain Christopher, and the other officers discussed their strategies around a campfire until late in the evening.

Early Tuesday morning the battalion of 550 men split into two contingents of cavalry. Nelson sent one detachment north to meet up with Lieutenant Babcock on reconnaissance near I-80. They were led by Major James Ellwood, and half of the trucks followed them. After dispatching advance scouts to determine the location of the enemy, Nelson led the second detachment east on I-70.

At noon the following day the scouts came charging up to the main group and reported to Nelson that the enemy front guard was less than twenty miles away. Nelson ordered his twelve marksmen to proceed east until they spotted hostiles. They already knew what to do. Then Major Nelson ordered the first demolition team of five soldiers to dig a hole in the middle of the freeway, install a mine, and cover it with enough debris to prevent the enemy from discovering it. The first team would remain there to ignite the powerful explosive at the appropriate time with a remote control from five hundred yards away. When Nelson had finished his instructions, the troop rode westward to deposit the second mine twenty miles down the highway. In this same manner, they would try to plant fifteen mines.

By eleven o'clock in the evening the snipers of Squad One were in position seven hundred yards south of the UGOT camp. They lay on their stomachs on a low hill, watching the movements of the enemy. Some of the greencoats were rolled up in sleeping bags, but many were sitting around campfires or strolling through camp. The snipers carried powerful, long-range rifles with telescopic sights equipped with night vision, which were steadied at the front by bipods.

Their goal was to spread terror, demoralize the enemy, and hinder their progress. It was a gruesome assignment for these innocent young men, but they stayed strong by reminding themselves that the monsters before them planned to murder their families, burn their homes, and destroy everything they held dear. There was no stopping now. There were three other squads somewhere nearby in the darkness, ready to do the same work. Each squad was composed of three men. Squad Two was a hundred yards to their right on the same side of the freeway, and the other two groups were positioned north of the highway.

At precisely ten minutes after eleven the twelve snipers opened fire, almost in unison. Their rifles spat flame and bullets in the blackness, and there was instant pandemonium in the enemy camp. The snipers were searching for officers and they seldom missed what they targeted. Bullets slammed into the enemy from both sides of the freeway, and the helpless greencoats ran to and fro screaming and seeking shelter. Many hid behind tanks and other armored vehicles, but the fire came from both sides of the road so they found little protection.

A few minutes after the attack had started, fifty greencoats lay on the ground, either dead or wounded. Finally, however, their officers began to control the situation. They quickly sent dozens of soldiers into the night to track their attackers. Searchlights mounted on vehicles shot beams of light back and forth along both sides of the road, hunting for the enemy and lighting the path of the first responders. Some of the responders carried flashlights, making them easier targets. Squads One and Two dispatched another ten greencoats as they approached. By the time the searchers reached the top of the hill, the snipers had already disappeared like ghosts. They would wait patiently until later in the night to perform the same work on a different section of the enemy line. The same operation was executed simultaneously by the snipers on the north side of the freeway.

❧

The next day General Liu Dejiang was furious beyond words. Angry at his troops, his officers, and the cowardly assassins who had attacked his army under the cover of night. Most of all, his honor had been compromised. He screamed at everyone, especially Li Gaoli, who cowered in the back of the staff vehicle next to the machine gunner. After radioing General Zhang Qishan on I-80 at seven in the morning, he had learned that Zhang's troops had also been attacked by snipers the previous night at the same time, with a loss of fifty-six men. Now Dejiang was dying to get revenge and planned to do so that very night.

To ensure his own safety, he positioned his vehicle farther back on the line, about a half mile from the front. It was safer, but there was a drawback. One of the huge tankers carrying fuel for the motorized vehicles rolled along a hundred and fifty yards ahead. All of the army's forty tankers leaked somewhat, exuding fumes for some distance behind them. Dejiang cursed UGOT and Lucienne Delisle for not providing better equipment, and he tried to console himself by reasoning that the tankers would smell less bad as the volume of fuel diminished.

The five militiamen who had buried the land mine around noon the preceding day were hiding in a thicket five hundred yards from the freeway. One of them, a young man named Anderson, held a radio control device. They waited patiently as the enemy army rumbled by, like a herd of cattle to the slaughter.

Another militiaman, a young man nicknamed "Donald Trump," shouted to the others, a little too loud for comfort. "Look! A tanker."

The others shushed him angrily. They couldn't take chances. Maybe the army had special listening devices that could detect sounds miles away. All of them wanted the operation to be a success, for their own benefit and that of their families. They waited for what seemed an eternity.

"That has to be the slowest damn—darn—army in the world," Anderson growled.

"For Pete's sake," one of his buddies said, "Chill out. Look, why don't you give me the remote. I'm better at this."

"No. I've got it. Back off."

"It's coming. It's coming," Donald Trump said, again too loudly. "Not yet. Not yet."

"Shut up, Trump," Anderson snarled. "You're driving me crazy." He waited another thirty seconds and pressed the button on the remote.

Dejiang was busy planning what he would do to capture the snipers. Or better, to exterminate them like Japanese beetles. After a while he stood up in his vehicle, looking for the front of the line. It was such a beautiful, sunny day that his confidence had begun to return. Especially since a cross breeze was blowing the tanker fumes away. He raised his nose into the air, proud of how clever his ideas were.

At that very instant there was a deafening roar and a blinding flash of light. An immense wall of pressure slammed Dejiang backward violently, right onto the lap of Gaoli. A mushroom of flames rose hundreds of feet into the air. Somehow the tanker ahead and its thousands of gallons of fuel had exploded.

The explosion had destroyed the tanker and fifteen nearby vehicles, and had damaged another twenty vehicles. It killed nearly a hundred men as it blew a hole in the freeway ten feet deep and thirty feet wide. Dejiang and the other occupants of his staff car had been knocked unconscious and suffered burns. It took the general five minutes before he came to. Dazed, he looked around trying to comprehend what had happened.

Moments later a dozen people arrived to help, taking him and the others out of the car and laying them on the side of the road. Within minutes a medical vehicle arrived and the trained personnel began to give treatment. Officers sent jeeps and infantry everywhere to pursue an invisible enemy.

The bomb crew, stunned by the magnitude of the explosion they had unleashed, watched in awe as vehicles and men flew forty feet into the air. It was impossible for them to turn their eyes away from the devastation. But when they saw jeeps and infantry leaving the enemy column and heading their way, Anderson commanded them to run for their horses. They raced as fast as they could to their mounts posted over a rise two hundred yards away, and as they leaped upon the horses, they caught sight of the first jeeps bouncing toward them. The occupants were shaking fists and weapons at them.

The troopers reined their steeds southward and galloped away, hearing high-powered rifle blasts and seeing dirt kicked up all around them. Soon they saw the jeeps losing ground behind them, for the terrain was far too rough for wheeled vehicles to keep up with fast horses. They galloped for some time until, seeing no sight of the pursuers, they slowed to a walk. Then they turned west in hopes of rejoining the main battalion as soon as possible.

The enemy recovered quickly. They salvaged everything they could and used giant bulldozers to shove damaged vehicles out of the way, and with a backhoe they dug a trench at the side of the freeway and threw the dead into it. At the same time they put the wounded into medical vehicles and treated their injuries. Afterwards, the column rolled off the side of the freeway to circumvent the huge hole in the road.

General Liu Dejiang had almost completely recovered from his trauma and injuries, but his face and hands were plastered with Bacitracin. As usual, he was violently angry, particularly since the patrols they had sent out to capture the Mormon terrorists had returned empty handed.

He summoned Li Gaoli and several other important officers to join him in his staff car as they rolled westward. They positioned themselves near the front of the column and at least a mile from the nearest tanker. Their goal was to make plans for countermeasures. Although it was somewhat hard for Dejiang and Gaoli, the officers spoke to one another in English, the world's universal language.

Dejiang began the analysis. "Okay, gentlemen, let's talk about the snipers and then the bomb squads. How can we catch or thwart them before they do further damage? The snipers first."

"They attacked us late in the evening when it was completely dark," Gaoli said, "but before most of our troops had retired for the night. Obviously, they chose nighttime because the dark makes it harder for us to detect them. They must have night vision capabilities on their weapons, so the dark doesn't prevent them from being extremely deadly. Chances are they will follow the same pattern for future attacks."

Dejiang was surprised and pleased. "Thank you, General Gaoli. Good analysis. But now do any of you have suggestions for countermeasures?"

Before Gaoli could continue, an officer named Chen said, "I believe that when we stop for the night, we should send out small patrols on both sides of the freeway. They could be assigned to walk up and down within a certain perimeter, perhaps six or seven hundred yards from the main army. They should be armed with sniper rifles with night vision and also night vision binoculars. In that way, they would be close enough to locate the enemy by flashes from rifle fire."

"Excellent, Chen," Dejiang said. "That's a good possibility. Other suggestions?"

A German officer nicknamed "Bird Dog" said, "The problem is, the patrols might be too late to reach the snipers before the damage is done. Besides, it would take thousands of troops to patrol two sides of the freeway for thirty miles, and we don't have thousands of rifles equipped with night vision telescopic sights."

Dejiang smiled, impressed. "Good objections, Bird Dog. What's your alternative?"

"I say we hunker down before it gets dark. Hide behind boulders, dig one-man holes, get as many people as possible into armored vehicles."

"Yes, I like that," said an Iranian officer named Abdullah. "I remember that in some of the big wars of the past, every soldier had to dig in to protect himself from enemy fire."

"The problem with that is I don't want to spend the whole night hiding behind rocks or in a filthy hole while terrorists take potshots at me." This was from a Russian officer named Nicolai.

Bird Dog offered a solution for that. "The snipers wouldn't dare attack for more than a few minutes. That's why they broke off after only about five minutes, which was all the time they needed to intimidate and terrorize our troops. If they did continue their attack, we could get them quickly with a tank or two."

"With a tank or two?" Nicolai asked.

"Yes. As soon as their attack begins, we could have a few lightweight tanks poised to take off after them, using their built-in searchlights, machine guns, and cannons. As you know, we have such tanks every fifteenth vehicle or so. We could transmit that plan today to every tank in the army in a matter of minutes."

"I like everything you've said, Bird Dog," Dejiang said. "Okay, are there any further suggestions or comments?"

After discussing the proposals already given and several others for some time, they decided to go with Bird Dog's plan. Next they turned to the bombing of the tankers.

"That's an easier problem to solve," Gaoli said. "We could simply have a line of minesweepers precede the main column on foot, using our dual-sensor mine sweepers." These sweepers combined ground-penetrating radar and metal detectors. "That way we could clear the highway and fifty yards or so on each side of it."

Nicolai grinned and said, "Absolutely! All we'd need is forty mine-sweepers and forty devices. That's completely doable. We probably wouldn't even need that many since the saboteurs must make a direct hit—or a near hit—in order to explode the tankers."

Bird Dog scowled, apparently having a better plan. "Why don't we just send a rapid-moving detachment up the freeway until we catch the mine-burying team in the act. Then we blast them to kingdom come."

"The problem I see with that is we don't know how many of them are out there," Dejiang said with a touch of smugness. "There might be hundreds with lots of firepower, just waiting to ambush a small detachment."

They spent another forty minutes debating the various options and at last decided to go with the minesweeping plan. After the officers returned to their own vehicles, General Dejiang radioed General Zhang Qishan on I-80 to inform him of their new strategies.

Dejiang's countermeasures worked, at least for the most part. The next attack by the four squads of snipers took place the following night and was largely ineffective because the enemy soldiers were safely dug in. Only one greencoat was killed as his curiosity got the best of him and he raised his head above the level of his hole. Several lightweight tanks chased the snipers and wiped out one team before they could reach their horses. The same thing occurred on I-80, except that two complete sniper teams were blasted by the tanks tracking them.

But on Saturday the fifteen remaining snipers changed their tactics on both freeways. They attacked at two in the afternoon as the enemy soldiers strolled along the road, confident they were safe. The snipers shot sixty greencoats in ten minutes. The pursuing tanks had more trouble spotting them in their hiding places because the rifle flashes were less visible in the bright sunlight. However, when they did locate the snipers, they could see them clearly as they galloped away on their horses. The tanks laid down withering gunfire and quickly killed six riflemen and their horses. Three more were wounded and lay on the ground helpless, groaning in pain. An enemy officer walked over casually and executed them one at a time with his pistol.

After reaching safety, the six remaining snipers radioed each other and decided they would attack again that same night. They grieved for their fallen buddies but were proud of the fact that they were accomplishing their mission of slowing the enemy's advance. Most wanted justice, but two desired revenge, so they changed tactics again. This time they would wait until midnight, approach the enemy camp stealthily, tie their horses, and then walk boldly into the UGOT camp. Once there, they would shoot as many of the prone figures as they could, and when the enemy began to rally, they would flee to their horses and try to escape.

Surprisingly, that turned out to be an effective tactic, especially since the enemy had hunkered down again, still fearing a nighttime attack from a distance. The snipers killed twenty greencoats in just a few minutes, and the enemy was so stunned and confused that all the assailants escaped without harm. Later, at two in the morning they talked and decided to change their attack methods regularly until they were recalled or killed. Shortly after four in the morning Major Nelson contacted them and ordered them to return to the battalion. Their mission was over.

The mine countermeasures were more successful. The Mormon battalion succeeded in detonating only two additional tankers, but they too had accomplished their mission, for they had struck terror into the hearts of the enemy and had forced them to slow their progress. As a result, the reinforcements from Utah arrived in plenty of time to help in the war effort, and with them came the prophet himself, President Wilford Benson, despite the fact that he was now seventy-six years old.

Chapter 17

In the early afternoon on Monday, the reinforcements from Utah began to pour into New Zion. By midnight almost 200,000 citizen soldiers, half the total military forces of the Mountain West, had arrived and found lodging with the residents or used the shelters they had possessed on the trip across the plains. They had organized their forces and arrived in record time because it was only twenty-six days since President Cartwright had asked for help. It was especially fortunate they had been able to make the journey in powered vehicles. The citizens of the Republic of Zion welcomed them and began to feel a surge of hope. The next day the government started sending the new troops to the eastern front to join New Zion's forces already stationed there.

General Michael Jamison was Commander in Chief of all Zion's forces and was headquartered at Marshall, Illinois, near I-70. He had already sent a dozen scouts to watch the region around Indianapolis, Indiana, at the junction of I-69 and I-70, where he and his staff expected the two UGOT armies to join forces. In a few days he would add the new Utah forces to his two-hundred-mile defense line, which stretched roughly along the eastern border of Illinois. Already the citizens of Indiana had abandoned their homes in fear because they had lived on the eastern borders of New Zion where there was little protection and they had decided to move to a safer location west of the defensive line.

Three weeks later several scouts returned to Marshall to report to General Jamison, and he received their report in his private bunker. They informed him that the two UGOT armies had joined forces, traveled about forty miles west in a twenty-mile front, and then gradually expanded their front into a giant pincer movement, which was almost three hundred miles long. It seemed as though the enemy desired to swallow Zion whole like a hungry lion devours a piece of meat.

"What about the hundreds of concrete blocks we put on the freeways and on dozens of access roads?" Jamison asked.

"Basically, they shoved them out of the way with bulldozers," replied a scout named Rickles. "They sure had a heck of a time doing it, and dozens of blocks fell on greencoats, crushing them like the bugs they are. Still, their leaders didn't seem to care and pushed the bulldozer work ahead without even stopping. I'd say the blocks cost them several days' time."

"Well then, they served their purpose."

As they were talking three warplanes flew in from the east. When they reached the defensive line, they shot several missiles and strafed the defenders with .50 caliber cannons. Then they continued west at five hundred miles an hour in search of other targets. At least sixty men died instantly.

Jamison struggled to get out from under a collapsed bunker wall and looked around, seeing a scout and two officers doing the same. They staggered toward him in an effort to help, blood and debris covering their heads and clothing.

"Well, gentlemen, I guess it's started," Jamison said, shaking his head and blinking his eyes. "I hope they don't have many of those cursed jets. Are you boys okay?" His men told him they would survive, and they all slumped against fallen blocks of concrete, stunned and silent for some time, still dazed from the onslaught.

Jamison shook the dust from his hair and checked his painful left arm. "How far away would you boys say their front is?"

"I'd guess they're no more than twenty miles from our line," said a scout named Priest.

"Okay. Thanks, men. Now let's find a medic and get our wounds taken care of."

Steven Christopher was the governor of Missouri, but in spite of Mary's pleadings, he had traveled to the front with the new warriors from Utah. Because of Steven's military experience, General Jamison had made him a colonel in the citizen militia. He was in charge of a 4,000-man brigade near Elbridge, Illinois, about two miles west of the state line and ten miles north of central command. Standing beside two lieutenants and a sergeant, he looked over a barrier at the enormous army approaching six miles to the east. He was shocked as he studied them through his binoculars because of their numbers and weaponry. At the same time, he held a radio in his hand, waiting for the signal from General Jamison to commence firing.

When the enemy was four miles away, the signal came, and Steven shot a pistol round into the air, which was the signal for his men to open fire with howitzers and field guns. The noise was deafening as nearby batteries fired shells into the enemy. Steven watched the result and saw many direct hits, but then the enemy opened fire with all their big guns. Steven and his aides hit the ground as explosions and fire erupted everywhere around them. Huge chunks of flying earth and debris covered them, and an airborne truck barely missed their bunker. After ten minutes the firing ceased, but the enemy advanced still, relentlessly.

Steven got to his feet and looked around, seeing nothing but devastation: dead bodies, wounded soldiers moaning pitifully, destroyed vehicles, broken barriers, and mangled weaponry. Basically, the enemy had devastated his entire emplacement. Yet soon he saw medics and others rise from the rubble and begin to search, looking for the wounded. He was grateful many of his men had survived but he knew the worst was soon to come. He hunkered down with his lieutenants and waited, pondering what to do. A few minutes later, his radio crackled, and he put the handset against his ear.

"Colonel Christopher, what's your status? Over," General Jamison asked.

"Sir, my brigade has been hit hard. I'd say about 30 to 40 percent casualties. What shall we do? Over."

"The same has happened all along the defense line. They just have too much firepower. Withdraw to Position B posthaste. Over and out." Position B was a predetermined front in eastern Missouri just west of the Mississippi River. The central command at Position B was near St. Louis.

Steven hurried up and down the line, ordering his men to withdraw immediately. As they rushed from the battlefield, Steven wondered how Zion could ever survive these onslaughts to fulfill its ultimate destiny.

Two hundred thousand survivors struggled forlornly to cross the state of Illinois, heading west to their new point of rendezvous. Continuous squadrons of enemy warplanes attacked them, destroying men, equipment, and countryside, but after several days they finally reached Position B and dug in, waiting for instructions. Steven, John, and Paul Christopher were among the survivors and eventually found one another. Their reunion was full of tears—tears of joy and of grief. They rejoiced to see their brothers had made it, but wept bitterly over the loss of their sons.

The body of Andrew, Steven's youngest son, who was only twenty-five years old, had been found and brought to his father. John had suffered the loss of Patrick, who was twenty-seven, and Raymond, who was twenty-four. Fortunately, Paul's three sons, Matthew, Mark, and Luke had been too young to fight in the war, although Matthew, who was twelve, had begged his parents incessantly to permit him to go to the front, claiming he could shoot better than 90 percent of the militiamen.

General Dejiang laughed with glee. He had finally taught those cretinous infidels a lesson. How dare they think they could stand against him with their puny weapons? However, he was angry that the cowards had retreated after only half an hour of fighting because they should have stood their ground and fought like men. He estimated that enemy casualties were about 150,000, while he had lost only ten thousand and no more than fifty armored vehicles. Now he would pursue them deeper into their den and utterly destroy their holy kingdom. He gave the signal to proceed into Illinois. His order was passed along the entire UGOT front, and the great army moved in to finish their work.

A week later, near the end of September, the armies of Zion formed a new front on the eastern borders of Missouri. The central command was at St. Louis, and the defensive line extended north and south a hundred miles. Now even women joined their ranks, especially unmarried women without children. The first thing General Jamison did was to order every bridge spanning the Mississippi River destroyed, for a hundred miles upstream and another hundred downstream. The Mississippi was a natural barrier that protected them because UGOT's army would find it extremely difficult to cross over without bridges.

General Jamison and his staff had also decided to place all their heavy artillery on flatbeds pulled by trucks. They would concentrate them along a thirty-mile line near St. Louis and be ready to move the fifty flatbeds at a moment's notice. They knew that in their first battle they had made the mistake of not firing on the enemy when they were much farther away. Yet in spite of the positive attitude of the generals, the citizen soldiers and the people looked at the future with fear and foreboding. The consensus was that they had no chance whatsoever in defeating such a formidable enemy, and there was much weeping and complaining in New Zion. Many lost faith and decided the end was near.

The generals received all kinds of suggestions from citizens concerning how to escape or defeat the enemy. Some proposed they flee to the plains or even to Utah. Some said they should form bands of snipers and attack the enemy like guerillas. Others declared they ought to send troops to the far north and south to go around the enemy and attack them from the rear. The generals laughed at those proposals as being founded on nothing but fear and desperation.

On the first day of October, Steven, John, and Paul Christopher were stationed together a few miles north of St. Louis, Missouri, on a point of land jutting into the Mississippi River, and their brigade was stretched several miles along the western shore. The brothers stood in a pleasant park looking directly east toward the small town of Hartford, Illinois, across the great river. The brothers were accompanied by several militiamen on a day that was bright and sunny without a hint of air pollution, and they were straining to see as far as possible in hopes of detecting signs of the mighty army bearing down on them. They saw no army but they felt its evil presence and knew it was less than twenty miles away. Since September 23, the day they learned of the death of their sons, Andrew, Patrick, and Raymond, the three brothers had consoled one another often with tears in their eyes. The death of loved ones was a bitter pill to swallow.

"Well, guys, I guess this is it," Paul said with resignation. Both John and Paul had also served in the defense line in eastern Illinois when the UGOT army had attacked, and they knew what they were in for. "Do you think New Zion will survive this day?"

"Don't worry, Paul. We'll survive," Steven said.

"I'm sure you're right," John said, "but so many have died already. They estimate that over 100,000 of our guys died in Illinois. We may survive as you say, but at what cost?" Steven knew Paul felt the same way but his youngest brother said nothing, which was unusual for him.

Steven heard a swishing sound nearby and, turning to look, he saw a man walking slowly through the grass toward them from the south. Steven was amazed at the sight of the man. He was about six feet one, the same height as Steven, and he had golden blond hair that reached halfway to his shoulders, was parted in the middle, and curled around his face like a protective shield. He wore no beard or mustache and was extremely well-built, giving the impression of immense physical strength.

The strange idea popped into Steven's mind that he was looking at a blond superman. The man's stride was powerful and effortless, and he seemed to glide over the lawn. As he drew nearer, Steven saw piercing blue eyes full of intelligence, and his handsome face was transformed by a kind, pleasant smile. He was surrounded by unusual brightness, and instinctively Steven knew that the glow came from the man himself.

The stranger's clothes were glistening white as though lit by an internal source of power. His top was a light-weight, long-sleeved tunic, of a kind Steven had never seen before. It was tucked into a trouser that was held in place by a golden belt. On his feet he wore gold-colored sandals tied with laces of the same color.

As the stranger reached them, he held out his right hand to Steven. "Beautiful day, isn't it, gentlemen? It's very sad that a day like this has to bring such a terrible reckoning."

Steven shook his hand, not fully understanding what the man meant. "Yes, it's a beautiful day. Who—"

"Michael. In your language my name is Michael."

"Nice to meet you, Michael." As Michael shook hands with the others, Steven asked himself why the young man was there, especially without weapons or military gear. For some reason, he felt like a child in this man's presence and he was reluctant even to question him.

"Thank you, Steven. Don't be afraid. I'm here to help you."

Steven wondered how the man knew his name and why he was so sure of himself. "You want to help? Shall I get you a rifle?"

"Oh no. I have other means at my disposal."

Steven was more perplexed than ever, but he decided the man would probably be no help in the coming struggle. "Maybe you should leave this area, sir. It's going to get violent and ugly."

Michael dropped his smile. "And well it should, considering what they have done to my people. I'm here to end this and to exact justice."

Steven thought, *His people. Exact justice. What does he mean?*

"They *are* my people, Steven. Don't you recognize me? We did many great things together in the previous life, such as create the earth, organize planets, and exile Satan and his followers. You and others had the power to do all that. Of course, I was your boss, second in command, and you had to follow my instructions. Still, you've forgotten all that. The veil of forgetfulness. Maybe it would have helped if I had descended from heaven in blazing white robes and a flowing white beard.

"But really now, you don't think all of us have to sport beards and wear all that uncomfortable clothing, do you? The truth is, the Father lets us wear pretty much what we want, as long as it's decent, and there's no rule about beards. Think of the angel Moroni, who was clean-shaven, short-haired, and wore nothing but a loose robe, not even sandals. He died an old man but appeared to Joseph as a young man in his prime . . . Steven, my name is *Michael!*"

Suddenly Steven understood. He was talking to one of the greatest of God's sons, Michael the Archangel, who had cast Lucifer from heaven and had become Adam, the father of the human race. He was the being second in rank only to Christ himself, and now he stood before him, a great and powerful resurrected being.

"Yes, now I know who you are."

"Who is he, Steve?" Paul asked, his face blank.

Steven handed his rifle to one of the militiamen. "Michael the Archangel."

Paul's mouth dropped open. "The Archangel. But that's—"

"How can we bear his presence?" John interrupted. "He's a celestial being."

"Not to worry," Michael said. "Sometimes we have to tone down the glory stuff a little so we can talk to mortals. When Moroni appeared to Joseph, he was a resurrected man, but young Joseph endured his presence just fine."

Steven was delighted to see that Father Adam had a sense of humor. "You have a good sense of humor, Michael." He was also impressed by Michael's total self-confidence, a confidence without pride.

"Well, Steve, a sense of humor is very important. Can you imagine what it would be like to live forever with a bunch of sourpusses? Nothing could be worse than spending eternity with millions of celestial beings who couldn't take a joke and have a little fun. The real celestial kingdom isn't like that. It's a place of joy, laughter, and excitement, not one of excessive solemnity, worry, and endless toil."

"Why are you here, Michael?" Steven said.

"I already told you. To end this charade. But also to prepare for Adam-ondi-Ahman and the visit of the Holy One."

At that moment Steven realized that the Father had sent Adam himself to redeem New Zion, and he was going to do it with power. What could be more logical? Adam or Michael was the warrior God in the preexistence. He was the being who would save them in this extremity. He was the personage who would come to Adam-ondi-Ahman to receive all the keys from the ancient prophets, those who would soon come in person. He was the one who would transfer those keys to Christ and ordain him the great King of the eternal kingdom.

Steven stared at Michael with anticipation. "How are you going to end this charade?"

"You'll soon see. In a minute we'll be visited by three of those flying contraptions. What do you call them?"

"Warplanes!" one of the young militiamen said, a little too loud.

"Yes, warplanes. Thank you, my son."

It seemed incongruous to Steven that a man who looked twenty-five years old would call another man of the same age "son." But such is the eternal world where looks don't mean very much.

"What are you going to do, Ada— Michael?" Paul asked.

"You'll see. Just a bit more patience."

They waited about a minute, and the mortals gazed into the heavens, mimicking Michael. At last they heard a faint roar coming from the east, and three spots appeared in the sky, growing larger and larger, and finally turning into death-dealing hornets. As they flew past at supersonic speed, Michael quickly waved his hand at them, as if signaling the pilots. After glowing a few seconds, they suddenly disappeared, with no explosions at all.

"Don't worry, boys," Michael said. "They didn't suffer. All they felt was quick heat and then poof. It was a lot easier for them than what they have dealt to others. In handing out justice, we try hard to be kinder than Satan's minions."

"Why didn't they fire their missiles as they approached?" John asked.

Michael shot him a sly look. "Well, for some strange reason, their missile-releasing mechanisms refused to work."

Everyone laughed, except one eighteen-year-old militiaman who interpreted Michael's words literally.

"Now we have to handle that overgrown army coming this way," Michael said.

Steven felt frustrated. "But we have to wait, don't we? I can't even see them yet through my binoculars."

Michael smiled, his eyes glowing with irony. "You need to realize, Steve, that my eyes are a lot better than yours, even when you're using that vision-enhancing gadget. You'll understand better someday when you get your own resurrected body. We'll let them draw closer, say, about ten miles away."

Steven knew that when the enemy reached the ten-mile line, just beyond Hartford, the Mormon army would open fire with their long-range artillery, and the enemy would also start firing. While they were waiting, Steven wanted to ask a question, but he figured it would be stupid to do so. Even if he did ask and Michael answered, he doubted he'd understand the answer.

Michael looked over at him and said, "You want to know how I relocated those pilots and their planes."

Steven's jaw dropped with surprise. This celestial man could read his mind. "Well, uh, yes. I'd like to know."

"You'll remember when you pass over. You used to do it yourself quite often, in your spirit body, but for a different purpose, of course. Basically, it's a matter of using the power of thought to control matter. I could explain further, but it would take hours for you to understand, and simply understanding is not the same thing as actually doing it. It's not at all like the magicians' miracles in your science fiction films."

"Okay, thanks. You've answered my question."

With a hint of annoyance in his voice, John said, "What I'd like to know is why you didn't come to help us sooner."

Michael gave John a kind, understanding smile. "You're a brave man, John. All of you were wondering the same thing, but were afraid to ask. The answer is, the Father told me when to come. The reasons he does what he does are extremely complex, but you know the answer already, all of you. You learned it in Sunday School class when you were twelve years old. But wait . . . The enemy is upon us."

"I don't see a thing," Paul said. "Where are they?"

"Keep looking and you will see."

Like the other men, Steven stared intently at the land east of the Mississippi, straining to catch sight of UGOT's army. Then the angle of his line of sight gradually changed and he could see farther and farther away. At last he saw the enemy. "There they are—about fifteen miles away."

"Right," Michael said. "A little elevation helps."

"Elevation!" exclaimed several of the men. Steven looked down and saw they were forty or fifty feet from the ground.

"Don't worry. I've got you," Michael said. "You're not going to fall. We can go down now."

They watched the ground as they descended slowly and alighted gently to the earth.

"Whew! That was great," Paul said.

Michael grinned but quickly grew serious. "Okay, the enemy is now preparing to fire upon our people, and your general is also about to give his signal. I must act speedily." He raised his hand toward the north and moved it slowly in a half circle to the south. As he proceeded, a bright glow bubbled forth and progressed around the semicircle, changing colors from yellow to orange to red. The entire gesture took less than one minute, and the glow remained after he let his hand drop. "There. It's done. Your foes and their weaponry have been changed and relocated."

They stood there a long time in shock, all of them except Michael, gazing eastward at the remarkable miracle they had seen with their own eyes. For Steven it was incredible to think that such a formidable enemy could be dispatched in only a few seconds, and he marveled at the infinite power of God and those like him.

Steven squinted as he looked north, then south. "I can see the bright fire ahead of us, but how do you know the entire army has been relocated? It stretches for hundreds of miles."

"Like I told you before, my eyes are much better than yours. Also, I can assure you that only our adversaries have been relocated, not the innocent, because the fire, as you call it, is very selective. And remember, they suffered very little pain."

Steven believed every word Michael said. "We're so grateful to you. You have saved us, our families, and our nation."

"Give thanks to the Father only. I am just his servant. Your people have suffered much and have felt the refiner's fire. All these things will prepare them for even greater trials in a land far away . . . Now, I must go for a short season. Soon we will meet in the land of Adam-ondi-Ahman in the great council of God's people. Prepare for that."

"Do you want us to organize and prepare the council?" Steven asked.

"No. I will send an angel to visit those who have the keys in order to instruct them concerning what they must do."

Steven knew that Michael was referring to President Benson and the six apostles. Michael embraced each of them tenderly, called them his beloved sons, and then turned and walked slowly away to the south. As he proceeded, he gradually disappeared.

General Jamison was waiting for the call from his scouts that would tell him the enemy was in optimum firing range. If it was a go, he'd communicate the fire order to all his artillery units on a special frequency. Finally the call came, and he grabbed the horn. "Jamison here. Report."

The scout's voice was shrill with excitement. "General! They're gone!"

"Gone? What do you mean, gone?" The scout was breathless and unable to respond immediately. "Speak up, corporal."

"They're just not there, sir. None of them. No greencoats, no guns, no tanks, nothin'."

"How can that be? Explain yourself."

"Sir, I was watchin' real good. Using my binoculars and waitin' till they got to the line. I was hid real good, about a mile away, not far from the river. Then there was this bright light that hit them quick and wrapped around them. It spread my way and covered me too. I was right in the middle of it, but it just gave me a pleasant charge. It changed colors again and again, and I couldn't see nothin' of the enemy. Nothin' at all. But I kept on watchin' real good. After about five minutes or so, things started clearin', and—guess what?—they weren't there anymore. Completely disappeared. Can you explain it to me, sir? Do we have some kind of new secret weapon?"

Jamison was stunned. "No. I can't explain it. Keep watching and report back if anything changes."

Within the next ten minutes Jamison received three calls from other scouts, reporting the same phenomenon.

Zion's military leaders launched boats and crossed the Mississippi. They reconnoitered the area east of the river, sending patrols forty miles into Illinois. To the amazement of all, there was no sign whatsoever of the great army that had threatened them—no bodies, guns, tanks, weapons, or trucks.

It took only a few hours for this wonderful news to spread throughout the entire nation of New Zion, and the people praised God, danced, sang, and embraced family and friends in happiness.

Most had no idea how the miracle was accomplished, but they gave the Lord all the credit. The president radioed church leaders in Utah to tell them that their supposedly invincible enemy had been destroyed, and the western saints celebrated just as if they themselves had been freed from the forces of Satan.

Steven spent a long time on the radio with Mary that night, describing in detail what had happened. She asked many questions, most of which he couldn't answer, but when he could answer, her responses varied from amazement and shock to excitement and happiness. She was especially surprised at his description of Adam and the apparently simple means by which he had brought about the destruction of UGOT's army.

Chapter 18

⏤❦⏤

The great land of Shee Lo was in turmoil because of wickedness and war. Although the ancient scriptures had prophesied that the appointed day would come for the people to leave the land in the fullness of times, most were not ready for it. The prophets had told the people to prepare themselves spiritually and materially, but many were seduced by lives of comfort, safety, and the vain attractions of the world.

So when the prophets finally received God's command for the people to depart, there were objections, disagreements, and bickering. The disobedient ridiculed the old prophecies and those who were foolish enough to believe them. Some formed bands of marauders, who made secret oaths to commit murder for profit and gain. They sought to destroy the prophets and the leaders who trusted in God and wanted to migrate to Zion. Gathering their rebel forces into one great army, they attacked Shomron, the capital of Shee Lo.

However, the faithful banded together, and putting their lives in the hands of God, they fought valiantly and overcame the rebels. The brave defenders drove the surviving renegades, about two thousand in number, away from Shomron and scattered them into the wilderness. After peace and order were reestablished in the land, the obedient sent missionaries throughout Shee Lo in order to convince the inhabitants that they should obey the new command of God. Yet, in spite of the efforts of the righteous, the most part of the people still refused to make the journey.

The land of Shee Lo was vast. To the north, snow-covered mountains, hundreds of miles long, raised their forbidding peaks. Beyond those mountains, there was a no-man's-land of gigantic glaciers, isolated peaks, and great fields of snow and ice. No one could survive there very long. Many expeditions of brave men and women had gone to explore that wilderness, but few had returned. The people who did return told stories of traveling for weeks, only to find the land becoming colder and more barren the farther they went. At first they saw bears, strange birds, and sea animals in rare open waters, but later, no life at all.

The prophets knew the Lord didn't want them to journey beyond the snow-clad mountains. In past ages, it had been traditional for their people to travel northward in an effort to escape their enemies and find freedom, but now they were commanded to go south. So they spent months making preparations. The first group chosen to leave, ten thousand of them, waited for winter to release its grip on the land. Then, at the first signs of approaching spring, they began their great journey.

In the lead wagon Chava threw her black braids behind her shoulders and turned to her husband, Mosheh. "I'm so cold. You told me the weather would get warmer as we went south, but it's getting colder. It looks like a blizzard ahead, and I can't see anything but white."

"I'm sorry. I can't explain it. I'm going to stop the caravan."

They had been traveling for two weeks. At first the weather had been excellent and the caravan had made good time without unusual hardships, but at the end of the second week the weather had turned bitterly cold, and flakes of snow had begun to blow in their faces.

Mosheh was the tribal leader in command of the caravan. He was thirty years old, six feet six inches tall, and weighed about two hundred and thirty pounds. His wife was tall and beautiful and wore a multicolored robe, with her long black hair in braids wrapped with pieces of red cloth.

Mosheh reined to a stop the two great shaggy horses. As he climbed down from his wagon, five bronzed warriors hurried up to him.

"Looks like a big one headed this way," one of the warriors said, pulling up the collar of his heavy fur coat.

"Yes," Mosheh replied. "Pass the word along that we're going to stop here and hunker down. Tell everyone to pitch tents and build fires."

The men ran to their steeds tied to the back of their wagons not far away. They trotted down the caravan, which was over two miles long, to pass the word. The blizzard hit them with a vengeance an hour later, but by that time most of the pilgrims had succeeded in erecting tents and making fires. Even though they tried to protect the fires from the wind by building rock and wood barriers, it wasn't enough, and soon every fire was extinguished. The only thing the pilgrims could do was climb into their tents and roll themselves up in blankets and warm furs. They cooked no meals, but nibbled on scraps of prepared food from their storage containers.

Two days later the storm was over, and they scrambled out of their shelters and gazed with disbelief at the stark whiteness surrounding them everywhere. It was still very cold, but the wind had died and the sky was blue and clear. Their livestock was spread out over the land near the wagons, scraping the frozen ground in search of patches of brown forage. Fortunately, their shaggy coats had protected them from the cold. Mosheh commanded his people to load up and make ready to depart.

In the late afternoon of that day Chava said to her husband, "Look up ahead. I see areas of earth now on the snow-covered terrain."

Mosheh grinned at her. "You're right. Look off to the left. There's a small huddle of trees. I think we'll see nicer country soon."

The cavalcade continued to travel over cold hard ground for another two days, and the stretches of snow became less frequent. They often saw stands of trees where they could get firewood for their nightly campfires.

On the third day after the storm, they saw before them at midday what looked like a mountain of ice. It was a huge glacier with sheer walls rising three hundred feet into the sky, and it extended to the east and west as far as the eye could see. Mosheh ordered the caravan to stop, and he and Chava clambered down from their wagon and cautiously approached the frozen barrier. Within minutes they were joined by a crowd of babbling people.

"How are we going to cross this wall?" Chava said, her lips tight. "It's immense and seems impassable to me."

Mosheh hushed the people near them. He reached out, pushed his hand tentatively against the hard ice, craned his neck upward to look at the top of the wall, and finally looked at Chava.

"I don't know, but we'll find a way."

"How? When?"

"Again, I don't know. We'll pitch our tents in this area and stay here until we figure it out. Maybe our prophets will know the answer."

After the pilgrims had made camp, their leaders and prophets gathered to discuss the problem. The three prophets said they hadn't envisioned such a dilemma and didn't know what to do. The leaders debated for some time and decided to send out two parties, one to the east and the other to the west, with the task of discovering a passage through or around the glacier. The searchers were instructed to travel no longer than three days before they returned to the encampment.

A week later, the eastern party came back, saying they had found no passage through. Later the same day, the second group returned with the same disappointing news.

The next day, one of the leaders had a suggestion. "Let us gather great quantities of wood from the nearby groves and pile them up against the foot of the glacier and set the mound on fire. This ice wall might be no more than twenty or thirty feet thick, and maybe our fire will burn a path through it."

"All right," Mosheh said. "Your idea is worth trying. I can't think of a better way, at least not now. Are there any objections?"

Since no one objected, Mosheh gave the order, and hundreds of people began to gather wood. Two hours later, they had built a huge mound of wood that extended upward fifty feet. They set fire to it and moved away to a safe distance. It quickly became a blazing inferno, heating the atmosphere for over a hundred feet around, and it took the fire an hour to reduce the wood to ashes. At that point, dozens of warriors started raking away the ashes and smoldering embers with improvised tools. The leaders assessed the results as the work was being done.

"The fire did nothing but put a little dent in it," said Karmiel with a scowl. He was one of the prophets traveling with the caravan.

"You're right," Liron said. "The hole looks to be about seventy feet high and thirty feet deep, but the wall is still there. It may be miles thick." Liron was Karmiel's friend and the second most prominent prophet of the nation.

"I guess we acted out of desperation, not knowing what else to do," Mosheh said, frowning in frustration.

"Maybe it did more than just make a dent," said another chief. "Let's find out." Without waiting for permission from Mosheh, he ordered the warriors around him to attack the wall with instruments and weapons. The men rushed forward and began to chop wildly at the ice with swords, spears, and farm tools.

"Get out of there, you fools!" Mosheh shouted with anger.

However, the men were making so much noise they couldn't hear him. As they continued their work, the ceiling of the hole suddenly caved in and tons of ice buried the foolhardy warriors, who screamed as the ice crushed them. Their countrymen rushed forward to help at the risk of their own lives, for the overhanging ledge of ice, one hundred and fifty feet above them, still posed a deadly threat. After working for some time, they managed to free several victims, but only one was still alive. His broken body was bruised and bleeding.

Seeing this disaster and the impassable barrier still, the people raised their voices high, lamenting and complaining, asking why God had sent them this terrible tribulation.

Karmiel, Liron, and Amon, the third prophet, did their best to console them.

"Be of good cheer, my compatriots," Karmiel declared in a loud voice. "We, your prophets, will inquire of the Lord, and he shall guide us past this great barrier." Karmiel secretly thought that was what they should have done in the first place.

He talked to the distressed people for a long time and finally consoled them, for they returned to their families and shelters with renewed hope.

That same night the prophets walked away from camp and knelt in the snow. They prayed fervently to God, and soon he answered them. He told them they had not been able to defeat the ice barrier because they had depended too much on their own strength, and he commanded them to have faith and use the power God had already given them to clear the way.

The next morning, the prophets instructed the people to arise and prepare to continue their way southward. They looked at the holy men in disbelief. Some laughed and ridiculed them, and a few called them false prophets. Yet they followed the prophets' instructions. As soon as the people had readied themselves for the trail, they stood some distance away looking at the barrier with apprehension, wondering how the miracle would happen. Liron and Karmiel went to opposite sides of the gaping hole, carrying ordinary sticks they had found in the snow.

In a loud voice Karmiel declared, "In the name of the Lord I command this ice to melt." He touched the ice with his stick and Liron did the same on the other side.

Then they stepped back fifty feet and watched. In less than a minute the people felt violent shaking and heard loud rumblings as if from a mighty earthquake. All of a sudden a deep crevasse opened before them and raced along the front edge of the glacier. Everyone quickly moved even farther back. Then the ice in front of them began to melt, and the water flowed in great streams into the crevasse. It was as if a gigantic red-hot rod had been plunged into the glacier from the heavens above, but the glacier as a whole didn't melt, but only a corridor directly in front of them.

They waited about an hour as the ice melted away and the corridor extended deeper and deeper into the glacier. Before long, they couldn't see the end of it.

As they waited, the voice of the Lord came to Karmiel, saying, *"Be not afraid, my son. Lead your people into the passageway, and I will protect them as they go."* Karmiel knew Liron had heard the same message, so he gave the signal and both prophets entered boldly into the corridor. The people hesitated, but finally a few ventured forth, and then more and more. The wall rose high above them on each side, and it was a terrifying sight to behold. Hundreds of feet up Karmiel could barely see a tiny slit in the ice at the top and the sky above that.

As Karmiel walked deeper into the glacier, a small girl rushed over to him and clung to his leg. With tears and desperation in her eyes, she cried, "This looks like the jaws of a great beast waiting hungrily to chew us up."

"No, my child. This is the work of the Lord, and he has promised to protect us." He picked her up and set her on a passing wagon.

As they trudged forward, streams of water rushed past their feet, flowing in the direction from which they had come. But the water was not freezing cold as Karmiel had expected, but rather was lukewarm. To him that was another confirmation of God's protection, because had the water been extremely cold, their feet and legs would have frozen and they would never have been able to make the passage.

They continued along in the ice corridor for about a mile, and when they finally exited the glacier, they saw before them rolling hills and valleys full of grass as high as their waists. Karmiel was astounded at the sudden transformation. It was still very cold, but he could see several streams flowing down the center of the valleys in narrow gullies, and clumps of trees here and there. He didn't recognize the kind of trees they were.

The path was much easier now as they wended their way south. They forded several shallow streams and had little difficulty doing so. Just before sunset, they pitched their tents in a wide glen protected by a line of ridges, and their camp spread out for over two miles to the east and west. Before eating their evening meal, the entire encampment gave thanks to God in a prayer led by one of the tribal leaders.

Two days after the victory over UGOT's army, the Mormon prophet was alone in his office in Independence, Missouri. After the recent trials and tribulations, he was exhausted, for the recent trip from Utah to New Zion had been hard on him. When he had worked three hours, he put his head on his desk and quickly dozed off. At seventy-six years old he found it increasing hard to do the same work he had done in earlier years, and these catnaps really helped. But after no more than fifteen minutes, he was awakened by a bright light beginning to form in his office. He looked up and saw a man standing ten feet in front of him and a foot or two in the air.

The dazzling light was brightest around the man himself and lessened in brightness as it shone farther away from his glorious body. His hair and short beard were light brown, but seemed snow white because of the light they emitted. He wore no hat or sandals, but only a loose white robe, girdled by a golden belt. He gave the impression of being about twenty-five or thirty years old. The prophet realized quickly that this man was a resurrected angel sent to him from God. He was amazed that the exquisite brightness didn't hurt his aging eyes, but rather seemed to caress them.

"Wilford Benson?" said the angel.

"Yes, Lord." Wilford was pleased to hear the angel call him by name.

"The Father has sent me to give you a message."

"I am here and ready to obey."

"You are commanded to prepare for the great council in the land called Adam-ondi-Ahman, in Daviess County, Missouri. The place was called Spring Hill, then Cravensville, now Spring Hill again."

"Yes. We have built many lodgings in that vicinity. When will the council take place?"

"It shall begin in twenty-two days. The council will span the time of six days, from Monday, October 25 through Saturday, October 30."

"And who shall participate in that council?"

"You will summon the First Presidency of my Church, the apostles, stake presidents, bishops, and branch presidents, and others as you see fit. The leaders just mentioned will represent the entire Church, and indeed, all the peoples and nations of the earth. It shall be the greatest and most important church meeting since the beginning of this planet. However, you may permit others to attend as is proper and necessary, following your own discretion."

The angel proceeded to give the prophet many details, especially concerning the import of the council and what events would take place. But he didn't specify on which days they would occur. He also indicated that many heavenly beings would attend the conference, some in resurrected form, others as spirit beings. After finishing his message, the angel ascended in a channel of light, leaving the prophet's office as it was before he appeared.

The prophet remained in his chair, rehearsing the angel's message and writing notes. He made a quick calculation and estimated that the number who might attend the council would be about fifteen thousand men, if all those called were able to attend. He left his office and summoned his secretary, who sat at her desk at the end of a short hall. She hurried toward him.

Seeing the unusual look on the prophet's face, she said, "Yes, President Benson. What do you need?"

"I want you to summon as many of the apostles as you can locate for a special meeting in our conference room at three o'clock this afternoon. How many of them are in the city?"

"Two are in the building now. Elder Widtsoe and Elder Bartlett. I believe two others are at home in Independence. The rest are visiting LDS communities in Kansas."

"Contact the four who are close by as soon as possible. What about my counselors?"

"President Hicks is also in the building, but President Law is on assignment in southern Missouri."

"Okay, be sure to invite President Hicks to our meeting."

"Yes, President."

"Good. Thank you. I would also like you to telephone as many bishops and stake presidents as you can in the vicinity before the meeting. Do you have some help?"

"I can recruit three or four other sisters to help with the telephoning."

"All right. Please give me a report on your efforts by two o'clock if possible."

⚜

By three in the afternoon, twenty-nine leaders were assembled in the prophet's conference room. One of them was Steven Christopher, who was not only the governor of Missouri but also the bishop of a local ward. Also, the president of the Republic of Zion, Douglas Cartwright, was present. He too was a local bishop.

After one of the bishops had offered an opening prayer, the prophet turned toward Douglas and Steven and said, "We want to recognize President Cartwright and Governor Christopher. We're honored by your presence." Both men nodded in appreciation. Next he recognized President Hicks and Elders Widtsoe and Bartlett.

The prophet continued by telling the group about the visitation of the angel and the content of his message. When he had finished, ten hands shot into the air. Raising his hand high, he asked them to hold their questions for a few moments. He instructed them to help spread the word concerning the future council meeting at Adam-ondi-Ahman to all the bishops and stake presidents of the Church, cautioning them to make sure the meeting was not announced to church members at large. He didn't want hundreds of thousands of people swarming to the tiny county of Daviess, possibly compromising the solemnity of the occasion.

"Okay," he said. "I'm ready for your questions."

"When will the council start, President, and how long will it last?" Elder Widtsoe asked.

The prophet sneezed several times and put a tissue to his nose. "Darn hay fever. Hits me in all seasons. Gets worse as I get older. Well, where were we? Oh, yes. As I just mentioned, the angel told me it will begin on the morning of October 25 and end on Saturday, October 30. In other words, the council will last six days." Those who had not written that information down before did so now.

"Can you tell us what the agenda will be?" Apostle Bartlett asked.

"Frankly, I'm not sure. Others will decide that when the time comes."

Steven raised a hand and said, "President, can you tell us who will decide the agenda?"

"I'm not sure of that either, but I believe it will be Father Adam or even the Lord."

Everyone was stunned. They had read the prophecies on the legendary council of Adam-ondi-Ahman, but still they were astounded to think that soon they would see Father Adam and the Lord himself. It was hard for them to accept the fact that they would be participants in such a wondrous event.

"I understand that Adam and the Lord are divine resurrected beings," Douglas said. "So will I—we—see them face to face?"

The prophet gave him an understanding smile. "Of course. All of you will see them and other resurrected beings, including Abraham, Moses, Isaiah, and many others. And that's not all. You'll also see holy men in spirit bodies." A buzz filled the room as the leaders turned to their neighbors and expressed many different emotions.

The prophet raised his hand to quiet them. "Brethren, are there any other questions?"

A bishop raised his hand anxiously, looking worried. "President, how can we weak, sinful men endure the presence of celestial beings without being consumed? Don't we have to be translated or transformed in some way?" He was feeling guilty because he had been having a lot of arguments with his wife the last few weeks, and his worry concerning the UGOT threat had caused him to gain thirty pounds from pigging out on junk food.

The prophet chuckled. "No, I think you're all good enough to survive. Anyhow, it seems that celestial beings can withhold a portion of their physical splendor when they want to. Remember that after his resurrection, Jesus appeared to eleven of his apostles and other men in a room in Jerusalem, and none of them were consumed. Some say that's because he had not yet ascended to his Father and received his full endowment of glory, and that may be true. But don't forget that in the nineteenth century he and the Father both appeared to Joseph Smith, and Joseph was not consumed. So, I think you should stop worrying about it."

He held up a pile of papers. "I have here a three-page handout, which includes two pages of instructions and a page listing the supplies and clothing people should take with them to Daviess County. My secretaries and I worked on this material for hours today. Please make copies and distribute them to as many bishops and stake presidents as you can reach."

Later that afternoon, Steven parked his solar car in the driveway next to his house on the outskirts of Independence. He sat in the car for a while, wondering how Mary was. Both of them had experienced bouts of depression since September 23, the day they learned that their son, Andrew, and John and Tania's sons, Patrick and Raymond, had been killed in the UGOT offensive in eastern Illinois. He finally slid out of the car and headed up the walkway.

Mary was waiting just inside the front door, with a few questions for him. "Sweetheart, what happened? What did the prophet say? Why did he call a special meeting? Who was at the meeting? Why don't you answer me? Is there going to be another invasion? Are you going to command another brigade? Why don't you say something? Did the prophet call you to a special church job?" Her voice became more strident. "Steven, you need to tell me these things. After all, I'm your wife." At last she paused because she was out of breath.

Steven pulled her down next to him on the couch. Drawing her head toward him, he kissed her full on the mouth, not letting her speak despite the fact she was trying hard to do so.

She slipped her mouth sideways away from his, and muttered, "Wh— Why—Don't . . . you—Answer m—"

"I can't answer you when you ask me fifty fast frivolous questions in a row."

She put on an angry expression. "Very funny, Lord Governor Christopher. My questions are never fast or frivolous. I only asked you one or two simple little questions, in an extremely patience manner, and you didn't even have the decency to answer one of them."

"Can I do so now?" He kissed her hand as he asked that question.

"Please do."

At that instant he remembered he couldn't tell her about the special priesthood meeting at Adam-ondi-Ahman. He hesitated, thinking fast. After coughing several times, sneezing once, and mumbling a little, he finally came up with an answer. "Oh, um, well, it's nothing important. In a few weeks the prophet wants me to take a little jaunt with several of the brethren."

"Where are you going?"

Oh, oh. More questions, Steven thought. *I won't lie to her, but I've got to be careful.*

"Well, uh, I think we're going to Daviess County, about seventy miles north of here."

"Aah hah! That far. Who's going with you?"

"Doug Cartwright, Elder Widtsoe, President Hicks, and a few others. Not all in the same car, of course."

Mary looked pleased and suspicious at the same time. "Oh, how nice. Soo, why are you going to Daviess County? That's kind of out there in the sticks."

"Oh, it's just a little priesthood meeting. Men only, obviously."

"I see. Seventy miles for a little priesthood meeting in the boonies with some general authorities and the president of the republic. Sounds a bit fishy to me."

"Fishy! What's fishy about it? Priesthood meetings are serious business."

"Steven, you wouldn't be going to that place where the Church built all those hotels and that open-air amphitheater, would you?"

"Uh . . . no. I mean, yes. Well . . . maybe."

"But those facilities are supposed to handle over twenty thousand people. Are you sure it's just a teeny-weeny little ole priesthood meeting?" As she said this, she chucked him under the chin endearingly with her index finger.

"Oh, my heavens! We won't have anywhere near twenty thousand brethren there. Not by a long shot."

"How many exactly?"

"Mary, you're asking me questions I can't answer. I'm not the prophet."

"Okay then. Here's a question you should be able to handle. How long are you going to be gone?"

"Oh, I'd say around, um, probably, uh, let's see, maybe about five or six days."

"Five or six days! Listen here, my tricky husband. Don't tell me that's a little ole regular priesthood meeting." All at once she noticed he was holding some papers in his hand, and when she tried to see what they were, he slid them behind his back. "What do you have there? Why are you hiding that?"

"Hey, don't get excited. It's nothing you'd be interested in. Just some papers the prophet gave us."

"You can't fool me. I know what this is all about."

"You do? Come on. What are you thinking?"

"You're going to the council meeting at Adam-ondi-Ahman. The one that was prophesied centuries ago in the scriptures. The greatest meeting to date in the history of the earth. And you're going without me!"

"But, Mary, it's for men only. It's a priesthood meeting."

"Look, big boy. Can you give me a ballpark figure as to how many priesthood holders will attend the meeting?"

"Oh, I'd say about fifteen thousand, maybe more. That's what the prophet told us."

"That doesn't surprise me. That's about what I'd already figured. Tell me now. Are all those men married?"

"Most of them, I'm sure. After all, they're bishops, stake presidents, and general authorities."

"Okay. Now give me a straight answer to another question, my sneaky, duplicitous husband."

Steven was really starting to sweat and his mouth was tight. "All right. Shoot."

"When these fifteen thousand married men leave home for a week to attend a small, insignificant priesthood meeting, what do you suppose their wives are going to think?"

"I have no idea. What man can ever understand what women think?"

"Don't give me clichés. They'll think exactly what I think."

"Which is?"

"I just told you, Steven. They'll know their husbands are sneaking off by themselves to Adam-ondi-Ahman to see Jesus, Adam, and other divine beings. They'll pump their husbands just like I'm pumping you. And don't you think every one of those fifteen thousand wives will be ticked off and think she's been slighted?"

"Yeah, I suppose that's a possibility. Still, it's a priesthood meeting for men. That's the established order of things."

"Established—smablished. There's no sacred rule that women can't attend a priesthood meeting when there's a good reason for them to be there. And I can assure you of one thing."

He tried to hug her, but she pulled back. "What's that, dear?"

"You'll have at least ten thousand women go to that insignificant priesthood meeting too. Probably a lot more. And thousands of children also.

I guarantee you one thing: there won't be one square inch of space in those hotels and that natural amphitheater that isn't jam-packed."

Steven became serious and decided he needed to come clean. "Mary, the prophet didn't want this meeting to be announced to the Church at large. He was concerned it would produce immense crowds of people, and that those crowds would overrun the area and destroy the sacredness and solemnity of the occasion."

Mary matched his serious demeanor. "Yes, I'm sure he had the best of intentions, but it's impossible for the Church as a whole not to know what's happening. It's too big for that. And remember that when Christ had multitudes, including women and children, surrounding him in Palestine, he often paid special attention to the little children. I'm sure he'll do the same at Adam-ondi-Ahman. Obviously, he doesn't believe that the presence of women and children are a detriment to sacredness."

"You may be right . . . Yes, I'm sure you're right."

Chapter 19

꧁꧂

The morning after the pilgrims from Shee Lo passed beyond the wall of ice, their sentries caught sight of an army coming toward them from the direction of the glacier. Two of the sentries rode quickly back to camp to report the bad news to their tribal leader, Mosheh.

"How large is the army?" Mosheh asked.

"I'd say about two thousand warriors," the first sentry said.

"How far away are they?"

"About fifteen miles distant," said the second sentry.

Mosheh paused, thinking hard. "Okay," he said at last, "take five other men with you and return to keep an eye on the strangers. We need to know who they are, if possible, and what their intentions are. Send riders to me regularly with any new information you get."

When the riders galloped away, Mosheh alerted his people, warning them to prepare for battle.

In the early afternoon, several lookouts returned and reported that they recognized the army as the two thousand warriors who had rebelled against their nation in Shee Lo. These men, their sworn enemies, seemed to be pursuing them, probably hoping for revenge. However, they had temporarily suspended their chase and were now camped some ten miles away. At once Mosheh summoned the other leaders for a meeting so they could decide what to do. Several chiefs wondered how their enemies knew they had left Shee Lo, traveled south for many weeks, and passed through the great ice barrier.

One of Mosheh's closest friends, a chief named Yaakov, said, "They knew that many of our citizens had decided to obey the prophets and planned to set out for Zion in the near future. Therefore, some of them might have secretly returned to Shee Lo after we departed to find out who had left the country, and how many. No doubt they hid their identity." Yaakov and Mosheh had fought many campaigns together and trusted each other's judgment.

"I agree with Yaakov," said another chief. "They dared not attack us in Shomron because of the size of our combined armies. Yet when they heard that we, a fairly small group, had left the capital, they knew we were much more vulnerable. So they followed us, waiting for their chance."

Since Mosheh and Yaakov had fought the same rebels in many battles, they knew much about their battle tactics and their fundamental nature. Mosheh told the other chiefs that he believed the rebels posed a great threat to their company, for they were young men and experienced in war. Also, they had only to watch after themselves—which is exactly what they would do—because no children or women accompanied them, except for the type of women who often followed troops on the trail. The chiefs agreed that the enemy must have passed through the glacial corridor in the darkness of night.

"Brethren," Mosheh said at last, "while waiting for news from our sentinels, I thought much about the danger, and after a while a plan of action came to me." Mosheh secretly hoped his inspiration had been genuine. "Since these renegades are evil men and basically cowards, they will seek every opportunity to destroy us without danger to themselves. They seldom show bravery unless they possess overwhelming odds against their enemies."

Another chief named Akiba frowned and said, "But now the renegades have that superiority. I do not understand why they have not commenced their attack."

"It has to do with their character," Yaakov said laughing. "They broke off their advance because they are afraid, and they are waiting until nightfall to attack us in our sleep so they can kill all of us with little or no loss to themselves." Mosheh felt as though Yaakov had been reading his mind.

"Mosheh," Akiba said, "we await your wise orders."

Mosheh searched the circle of leaders, pausing briefly at each man to look into his eyes. At last he said, "We will leave three hundred warriors behind to guard our people here. The rest of us will advance to meet the enemy, but we will do so in a special way. After riding within four or five miles of the enemy camp, making sure we avoid detection, we will secure our ponies and crawl through the tall grass with great stealth to within a short distance of their camp.

"We will wait until just before dusk, for at that time the bellies of our enemies will be heavy with food and their minds stupefied by wine. You may not know this, but their chiefs usually measure them three portions of wine before each battle to increase their courage and dull their sensitivity to pain. Okay, do you accept this plan?"

Since their "yes" was fervent, Mosheh instructed them to return to their own clans, inform their people of the plan, and prepare a short speech to inspire their warriors. He said they should remind their men that they were fighting—above all—for their families. He also said they had no more than half an hour to perform this duty, because their army had ten miles to travel before they could get into position at the right time to accomplish the task before them. After receiving a few more instructions, the chiefs left quickly to do as their leader said.

Mosheh succeeded in setting his fighters into position an hour before sunset. The grass being tall and thick, they managed to draw within a hundred yards of the enemy. The chiefs organized their warriors around the southern portion of the renegade camp in a semicircle so their attack would seem to come from several different angles.

Mosheh had a small whistle he would use to give the signal for the attack. It was made from the leg bone of an eagle, and he carried it with him at all times. His men knew the sound of that whistle well, for they had heard it often in past campaigns. As Mosheh expected, the enemy warriors were lying around, satiated with food, half drunk, and half asleep.

As time passed, they moved closer—fifty feet from the enemy camp. Mosheh waited until everyone was in position and then gave the signal. His warriors rose from the grass, bellowed their frightening war cries, and fell upon the enemy. The battle lasted only fifteen minutes, and the slaughter was terrible. About a third of the enemy managed to escape death and reached the glacial corridor, staggering and stumbling as they strove to escape their ferocious attackers. When he saw the last of them enter the passageway, Mosheh gave the signal to break off the attack.

The warriors of Shee Lo had lost only fifteen to twenty men during the assault. Hundreds of them stood waiting a short distance from the entrance to the glacier, watching the enemy disappear into the opening, waiting for

Mosheh to command them to pursue and finish their work. But Mosheh refused to allow it. Reluctantly they obeyed, and it was a good thing they did.

As it gradually grew darker, they beheld the glacial walls begin to melt, faster and faster, until they suddenly collapsed inward, entombing their foes and closing the corridor. Seeing the threat removed, Mosheh ordered his troops to return to their encampment. As they entered the camp three hours after sunset, their once fearful families ran to meet them, embracing them with joy.

It was the first week of October, and Gerald Galloway was furious. Before him, at a large oval table, sat the fifteen members of the World War Office and several UGOT associates. Lucienne Delisle, the associate charged with controlling the destiny of North America, sat as far away from Galloway as she could. They were meeting in the conference room of their own building complex not far from the Arc de Triomphe in Paris.

"Can any of you explain to me what happened? We spent billions mobilizing 300,000 troops and the best equipment and weaponry in the world. And what for? To annihilate one small nation in the American Midwest. According to Lucienne, your planning was perfect and should have accomplished the goal easily. Things did go according to plan at first because we slaughtered at least 100,000 of the religious fanatics in the first engagement. Yet what happened in the second engagement when our army was poised to wreak ultimate havoc? Nothing. No attack. No destruction. And no army. Can any of you explain it?"

A war minister, Lorenzo Giordano, ventured to speak up. "We received several reports from our spies embedded in New Zion, and they all differ. One report said the enemy had superior firepower and wiped out our armies in two hours."

Galloway shook his head in disgust. "That's impossible. We had fifty times as much weaponry." He continued to glare at the ministers and associates.

Another minister, Hayley Walker, who hailed from Australia, barely raised one hand off the table. "One of the secret agents told me that he believed our troops overestimated the power of the enemy and deserted in terror, scattering eastward for hundreds of miles."

"How does that explain the disappearance of thousands of vehicles and weapons?" Galloway said with contempt. "Disappeared without a trace."

"I heard General Dejiang made a grave mistake," said Julian Kennedy, tapping his fingers rapidly on the table. Kennedy was UGOT's associate for South America,

Galloway sneered. "And what mistake would that be?"

"Apparently he ordered his army to plunge into the Mississippi, not realizing how deep it is. He was thinking it was shallow like some of the great rivers of China. As a result, the army drowned, and the equipment sank to the bottom."

"That's the most ridiculous answer I've heard yet. Dejiang was an arrogant little idiot, but he wasn't that stupid. So basically you're all telling me you have no idea what happened, right?"

Their silence and anemic faces told him he was right. They had no clue.

"Maybe it was a miracle," Lucienne Delisle said simply.

For some reason those words struck a dagger into Galloway's heart, and he dropped his head, unable to speak for a minute. He refused to think of the implications. He finally looked up and said, "There's only one solution I can think of."

Lucienne threw him a sardonic smile. "And what would that be, Gerald?"

"Nuke them. Both the New Zion and the Old."

Lucienne's mouth opened in a broad smile. "When?"

"As soon as possible."

"How many nukes?"

"At least five on both Zions. You decide. We'll clean up the mess later."

Chapter 20

❧

Steven and Mary arrived at Spring Hill, Daviess County, on Saturday after two hours of driving. It was two days before the great council was scheduled to begin. They brought their two children still living at home: Gabrielle, who was fifteen years old, and Daniel, who was thirteen. Their oldest son, William, was still stationed in Illinois looking for survivors of the great battle. Their oldest daughter, Jennifer, couldn't come on the trip because she had to remain in Independence to care for her baby and two toddlers. Neil Roberts, her husband, was unable to get leave from his job.

Spring Hill was near the place that had been designated as the site where the council of Adam-ondi-Ahman would take place. That sacred site was a small flat square surrounded by a huge open-air amphitheater built into the landscape. The grass amphitheater extended outward a quarter mile from the square and rose in a vast circle to a height of two hundred feet. Beyond the top of the rise, the Church had erected nine hotels to accommodate the witnesses and participants in the solemn assembly.

An immense crowd packed the entire region, and the number of children was unbelievable. They were everywhere, running to and fro, jumping boulders and ropes, screaming, laughing, and playing all kinds of games. Steven and his family entered one of the hotels, hoping to get a private room, but soon realized their mistake. Every room was jammed with people, usually several related families. There were beds and cots in every hall and dining room and kitchen on all five floors. An old bishop told Steven and Mary that the crowds had begun to arrive a week earlier and quickly filled the hotels. He also said many of the visitors had brought tents and were camped around the periphery of the amphitheater as far out as a mile. He estimated that thirty thousand people were there with more arriving daily.

As his family left the hotel, Steven said to Mary, "Well, sweetheart, you were right. When the husbands go, the wives will know. And where the wives go, the children will show."

"Oh, you're such a romantic poet. So you actually admit I was right?"

"Yep. You got me there. I don't know what President Benson was thinking when he asked us to restrict this conference to ten or fifteen thousand priesthood leaders. I realize now he was hoping for the impossible."

"I think he knew some women would come, and maybe some children, but he was hoping to limit the number to help maintain order. You can't blame him for underestimating a little."

"A little! How about to the tune of over fifteen thousand people?"

Mary giggled and said, "Yes, yes, but President Josiah Smith, our late prophet, knew what he was doing."

"What do you mean?"

"Steven, you're the guy who's supposed to know everything. Now, however, you'll see how much you need your wife to keep you on the straight and narrow."

Steven dodged one small child and another collided into him. "Ouch! He got me. Please get to the point, dear."

"All this was planned by Josiah Smith. I mean the huge natural gallery rising high and extending far, all around the central altars. And the big grass campground expanding outward hundreds of yards. He knew how many people would come to this gathering, including women and children, and he knew most of them would need places to pitch their tents. He wanted all these people to come and be able to witness the proceedings in the best way possible."

Steven thought a long moment. "You know, you're right. He saw it all. I'm also thinking the scriptures must have been speaking figuratively."

"Figuratively? What do you mean?" Three eight-year-old girls thundered by, yelling at the top of their lungs. Mary held her ears until they were gone.

"Well, the scriptures say that ten thousand times ten thousand will come to Adam-ondi-Ahman, but that's a hundred million people. Look at the incredible throng we have now with only thirty thousand. Can you imagine what it would be like to try stuffing one hundred million people into the state of Missouri, or little Daviess County, or especially into the small area around Adam-ondi-Ahman? Obviously, it would be physically impossible. So I conclude that the number must be figurative."

"What does the scripture mean then?"

"I'm not sure. The old prophets didn't leave a key to their metaphors. Maybe it simply means a really big crowd and no more." Steven could see that Gabrielle and Daniel were getting antsy.

"Dad, what are we going to do?" Gabrielle said with impatience. "We have no place to stay."

Mary gave a smart-aleck laugh. "That's why I insisted on bringing the big tent, all that food, and the delightful camping gear."

"Wow! You mean we get to camp out?" Daniel cried, his eyes wide with excitement.

Steven hated camping and knew Mary felt the same way. "Yep. I guess we'll do some camping—for the entire six days. Right smack-dab in the middle of thirty thousand people. No trees or lakes, but a stream and lots of fresh air and good neighbors to keep us company!"

"And to keep us awake at night," Mary growled.

At that moment a boy about fourteen came running up, breathing hard. "Hey, are yuh . . . like . . . Brother Christopher?"

"Yes. Can I help you?"

"I been like looking all over for yuh. They gave me like a description and said about where yuh was. But I've stopped like ten different old guys, and none of 'em was you."

"No. I guess they weren't. What's up?"

"The prophet like wants to see yuh."

Steven tensed up as he always did when summoned by a prophet. "Where is he? Lead the way." He figured the young man was a recent arrival from Utah.

"You bet, man. Like follow me." The boy started off heading between two of the nearby hotels. He kept looking around to make sure the old people were keeping up.

Mary snickered. "Was that painful for you, Steven?"

"Painful?"

"Yes. All that like expressive English. I know like how sensitive you are to how everyone like uses English around you."

"Don't get me started, Mary."

Daniel said, "Dad, I don't like talk like that, do I?" Gabrielle giggled as Steven glared at him and tried hard to keep up with the rushing teenager.

He led them to a smaller, three-story building located several hundred yards north of the main complex of hotels. When they entered the building, they were surprised to see very few people inside. The boy continued halfway down a wide hall and stopped outside a door marked "President Wilford S. Benson."

"There yuh are, sir," the boy drawled. "The prophet said yuh should . . . like . . . walk right in."

"Thank you, young man. Can I offer you—"

"Nope. I don't take pay. I'm just here . . . like . . . to serve the prophet and the Lord." Before Steven could answer, the boy rushed away, apparently on another errand.

Steven felt a little ashamed. As he opened the door, he said, "You never can tell."

President Benson looked up from his desk. "Steven, I'm glad you and your family came a little early. Welcome to the Great Council." He stood up, walked around his desk, and shook hands with each of them. "I understand you lost a son in the recent war."

"Yes," Mary said. "Andrew. He was only twenty-five."

Tears welled in the prophet's eyes. "We've lost many valiant sons." He had trouble controlling his emotions. "I lost three sons myself. They all died in a great cause, and I know God will reserve a special reward for them in the hereafter."

"I'm sure he will," Steven said.

"Well, I suppose you're surprised at how many people showed up."

It was Mary who answered. "Yes. They say there are more than thirty thousand people here, including women and children."

"I guess I miscalculated the desires and ingenuity of the sisters. When I first saw families arriving, I was tempted to inform them that the council meeting was for men only. But when I saw their eyes gleaming with excitement and enthusiasm, I didn't have the heart to turn them away. Now I know they'll contribute greatly to the grandeur of the occasion."

"Aren't you concerned about the noise and ruckus the children will make?" Mary asked.

"Not now. I know this is what the Lord wants. When the children see all these marvelous events transpire, they'll feel nothing but awe and won't be inclined to make noise. These events will impress them and transform them for the rest of their lives. Besides, I believe the meetings will last only an hour or two on each of the six days, and they'll have plenty of time afterwards for questions, recreation, and rest. Of course, I'm not the one who will decide the program."

"Who will?" Steven asked, suspecting what the answer would be.

"The Spirit told me that Father Adam himself will create the agenda and preside over all the meetings."

Daniel looked shocked. "But he lived thousands of years ago. How can—"

"I'll explain it all to you later," Steven said, as if he hadn't already done so several times in recent months.

"We're using this building to house all the dignitaries," the prophet said, "such as general authorities and high-ranking government officials. Their families also, of course." Steven winced at the term "dignitaries." At important conferences held at the Marriott Center in Provo, he had always chafed a bit when he saw entrances marked For Dignitaries or For VIPs. He had always felt that every church member was a VIP, not just the leaders. Why not simply mark the entrances with For Church Leaders Only?

The prophet consulted a roster. "Let's see. We've assigned your family room C18. That's on the third floor. You can move in right now, if it's convenient." Steven and Mary nodded. "Good. I hope you'll find everything to your satisfaction. We're grateful to have you with us at this momentous event."

The rest of the day was spent getting to know the people in the same hotel and touring the holy site. Steven noticed that the officials had installed hundreds of long yellow poles five feet apart to mark four separate pathways from the top of the rise down to the square. The poles were joined by lines of yellow ribbons, and the pathways were about four feet wide and from a distance looked like four equally spaced spokes on a wagon wheel. Running along the ground near each pathway were wires attached to loud speakers every hundred feet. Near the bottom of the amphitheater there was a circle of yellow poles thirty feet from the square, and each pole was connected by a continuous yellow ribbon.

"What are all the yellow things for, Dad?" asked Gabrielle.

"I can only guess." He was still trying to figure it out.

"Well, Dad?"

"Um, I think the pathways are marked off so visitors won't sit on them.

That way people can walk up and down the hill without stomping on the other participants."

Mary elaborated, "You mean it's intended to allow people to walk from the top of the hill downward on the pathways until they can find vacant spots off to the sides to spread blankets and set up chairs?"

"That's what I assume. It seems to be a good idea."

"You forgot the yellow circle near the bottom," Gabrielle said.

"Huh? Oh, I don't know."

"I do," Mary said. "It's where they expect all the VIPs to hang out."

"Oh, yeah! VIPs like us," Daniel said with enthusiasm.

There's that term again, Steven thought.

They spent the remainder of the day playing games behind the hotel with a group of residents. After dinner they passed the evening with some neighbors discussing conjectures as to what would happen the following week. On Sunday they attended makeshift religious services, and later engaged in exciting speculations with numerous people concerning what divine beings would descend from above. People recounted many prophecies, predictions, and stories about every possible event that might occur at the council meetings. At ten in the evening President Benson visited Steven and Mary in room C18. He reminded them that the conference would start the next day at ten in the morning, and that they should walk down the hill to the special area marked off with ribbons near the central square.

The first pair of B-2 Spirit Stealth bombers left JFK in New York City on Monday at eight fifteen in the morning, heading for Utah. However, they would fly over New Zion without attacking, simply to strike terror in the hearts of the people of the new nation. The second two Stealths took off from the same airport an hour later, destined to drop their bombs on New Zion. All were loaded with three B83 nuclear bombs rated at 1.2 megatons each. Each bomb was capable of producing seventy-five times as much yield as the bomb dropped on Hiroshima, and all twelve bombs together had enough power to completely destroy both branches of the Mormon Kingdom. The bombers flew at cruising speed—560 miles per hour. The first wave would arrive in the Mountain West within three and a half hours, while the second wave would reach New Zion in less than two hours.

At the UGOT meeting with its World War Office on October 5, an angry President Galloway had commanded Lucienne Delisle to arrange for the nuking of their seemingly indestructible Mormon enemies. After the meeting she had used her considerable influence to set up the ultimate assault. The selected attack squadrons consulted with a number of tactical experts and high-ranking air force veterans to decide on the six precise locations to be bombed in the two targeted regions.

It was planned that the first target in New Zion would be Spring Hill in Daviess County, Missouri. They brought their recommendations to Lucienne and the War Office, and their plans were approved and authorized. At first, Lucienne thought it might give her a special joy to fly in one of the bombers to see the destruction in person, but then she decided against it, fearing something might go wrong and result in her own death.

By nine thirty Monday morning the outdoor amphitheater was packed with thousands of saints. Among them sat two thousand American Indians who had converted to the gospel. Most of the people were sitting on blankets or on folding chairs they had brought for the occasion. Nearly all wore light sweaters or jackets, sunglasses, and hats for shading. However, the sky was full of white clouds that offered some protection from the sun.

A vast murmur arose from the crowd, a sound that was soft and quiet but loaded with suspense and anticipation. After all, they expected to see things that none of them, nor anyone else on the planet, had ever beheld before. Steven and Mary sat in the "VIP" section close to the sacred square, and on the square itself chairs awaited the First Presidency and the Twelve Apostles.

At ten o'clock Elder Jason Widtsoe got up and walked to the microphone. At first he faced toward the west but slowly turned in a semicircle to the left and then to the right in an effort to see all sections of the huge crowd. He said nothing for at least three minutes.

"Dear brothers and sisters," he said at last, "how grateful I am for this great day, when the powers of heaven shall be revealed. I am also grateful that so many of you have gathered here for this marvelous occasion. We will begin by asking a deacon, Drew Lanning, to offer the opening prayer." A small, thin boy came to the microphone and gave a short but sincere prayer.

"Thank you, Drew. Now Brother Madison Hall will lead us in singing 'Come, Come Ye Saints.' After that hymn, President Benson will address us." The assembly sang their beloved song loudly and with heartfelt sincerity.

After the hymn, President Benson walked slowly to the mic. "Brothers and sisters. That was wonderful. Your beautiful singing brought tears to my eyes." He hesitated as if uncertain how to proceed. "I must tell you that I don't have a particular agenda for this meeting or those to follow because the program won't be decided by mortals but by those who will soon visit us, especially Father Adam. He will preside over all these ceremonies. While we are waiting, Brother Hall will announce one hymn after another, and we will sing each of them until our visitors begin to arrive."

In the middle of the fifth song, which was "Abide with Me," a great light suddenly appeared high in the heavens. It was so bright that the audience gasped at the sight. They could only look at it for a brief moment before they were forced to avert their eyes. Most expressed surprise, and many fear. When the light first appeared, the people seated on the holy spot moved quickly to the VIP section not far away, taking their chairs along with them. The light descended slowly in a dazzling shaft until it rested on the square.

The audience tried hard to see into the conduit, but still couldn't endure the brightness for very long. Soon the brilliance began to soften, and the people could see the forms of men standing inside the conduit. But then the shaft of light vanished and they clearly saw a group of men with glistening bodies standing in a circle, facing outward toward the congregation.

From their chairs near the square with their children, Mary and Steve also had difficulty tolerating the brightness in the sky, and it seemed as though the blazing pillar of light was falling directly upon them. However, when the light receded, Steven saw Adam, the young "superman," facing him not thirty feet away, their eyes at the same level. Adam walked forward a few feet, smiling at the crowd, and Steven saw that he appeared to be exactly the same as when he appeared to them before the destruction of the enemy army. White tunic, golden belt and sandals. The only difference was that his hair seemed to pulsate and change color, sometimes white as new-fallen snow, then deep, warm yellow like strands of pure gold.

Steven couldn't stop himself from thinking how unrealistic were the traditional paintings of Adam and the ancient prophets, assembled at Adam-ondi-Ahman. In many depictions the ancients were old men with long white hair and beards, wearing flowing white robes. Apparently the artists forgot that these holy men would all be resurrected, celestial beings with perfect bodies in the prime of their youth. In this assembly of divine ancients he saw many different styles of dress. Only one person had long white hair and beard and a full-length robe. Steven concluded that dress and physical appearance held little significance in celestial realms, and that freedom of choice was the norm.

Adam went to the microphone and said, "We won't need this." After turning it off, he looked up and contemplated the audience. There was not a whisper in the vast assembly as they waited expectantly. "My beloved children, I am so grateful to the Father to finally be with you on this great occasion." He spoke in a slow, soft voice, but every person could hear him distinctly as if he were talking directly in their ears. All were astounded that such was possible without the use of a loudspeaker.

"I have anxiously waited thousands of years for this time to come. Today I will question each person on this stage, and he will give me an accounting of his stewardship over his dispensation. Then each will lay his hands on my head and return to me the keys of authority that he received in his days upon the earth. If you listen carefully, you will be able to hear every word we speak."

Adam turned to the east and gazed at the sky as he spoke calmly. "First, however, we have a small matter of business to take care of. Within a very short time your enemies will be upon you from the heavens. Do not fear, for once again I shall fight your battles."

He said no more, and every eye went to the eastern sky. At first they saw nothing, but after several minutes two dark spots began to appear seven miles away and ten thousand feet up. They gradually took form, looking somewhat like the shadow symbol of the movie hero Batman. As they closed upon the amphitheater, Adam waved his right hand toward them as if greeting a friend. They flew by at over five hundred miles an hour, and the crowd cried out in fear, waiting for destruction to reign down upon them. Many dipped their heads into their laps.

But nothing happened.

Adam looked at them with disappointment. "Where is your faith, my children? I told you not to fear. Those flying vehicles bear tidings of fearful death in the form of what you call nuclear bombs, but they were not destined for you. They flew overhead only to intimidate you, for their real destination is Utah. The flying machines bound for this place will arrive in about one hour. Yet none of their bombs will possess the power to harm you. So, as I said, do not fear the might of your enemies." Those words were met with a sigh of relief from most in the assembly, but many faces were still white with fear. "Now we must return to the sacred work before us."

The Ancient of Days summoned one divine visitor at a time. After questioning them concerning their stewardships, he sat in a chair as the patriarchs laid their hands on his head and returned their keys to him. He interviewed Abel, Enoch, Raphael, Elias—known as Noah or Gabriel—another Elias, Abraham, Isaac, Jacob, Joseph who was sold into Egypt, Moses, Elijah, Nephi the son of Helaman, John the Baptist, Peter, James, John the Beloved, and Moroni. The audience listened with rapturous attention, hearing every communication. There was only one break in the ceremony.

After Adam had finished with Joseph, he addressed the audience again. "My children, we are about to be visited by two more flying machines. These metal birds intend to destroy New Zion with their nuclear bombs, but you must not be afraid. As I said before, they have no power to injure you."

A minute later, two Batman shadows appeared once more in the eastern sky, heading directly for them. The crowd gasped in tense anticipation, and in spite of Adam's reassurances, they couldn't completely control their dread. The first Stealth bomber roared by, flying low, followed closely by the second. As the second flew overhead, it dropped a 2,400 pound missile, which floated slowly earthward, its speed retarded by a parachute.

Women screamed and children cried. Once again Adam reassured them, but his words had little effect. The missile continued to descend and finally disappeared behind a hill a half mile away. Thousands of people covered their ears and buried their heads in their laps, waiting anxiously and expecting the worst. Yet all they heard was a muffled thump and a slight ground tremor as the bomb hit the prairie sod.

Still they remained tense, waiting for a terrible blast and a mushroom cloud. When nothing happened, they gradually gained confidence, and those whose heads were down looked up, laughing with relief, and soon laughter arose everywhere in the vast congregation. Many shouted praises to God, as others wept.

Adam raised his hand, signaling for quiet. His every movement and gesture revealed consummate health, strength, and power. Although the people saw his raised arm, they had trouble controlling their excitement but eventually mastered themselves.

"My people, thank you for your attention. I wanted to tell you that I simply deactivated the triggering mechanisms of the bomb you saw and the other eleven bombs meant for our people. I also assure you that none of the flying contraptions will return safely to base, for all will crash in deserted regions. Regretfully, the eight foolish pilots will perish for their role in the attempted attacks." After pausing, he added, "Now we need to continue the reports and ordinances."

The program for Monday was concluded by one thirty, and Adam turned the meeting over to President Benson. The conduit of light reappeared, and the heavenly visitors ascended instantly into heaven. Meanwhile, the clouds had dissipated, and the sun sent its fiery rays down upon the participants, who were beginning to sweat profusely and were trying to cool themselves with improvised fans. After a very short talk, the prophet dismissed the meeting until ten o'clock the next day. No one had said a word about what the agenda would be.

Steven and Mary were impressed by the kind consideration the celestial visitors and the prophet had shown toward the spectators, who were beginning to suffer discomfort after three and a half hours in the amphitheater.

The people returned to their tents, campers, and hotel rooms to eat lunch. Later they formed hundreds of small groups to discuss the events of the day. Most of them gathered outside under any type of shade they could find, and canopies and umbrellas were set up by those who had them. The teenagers assembled by themselves, discussing the godlike visitors, the nuclear bombers, and many other subjects.

After listening patiently for a time to what the adults were saying, the younger children left to form teams for playing games. During the evening dozens of campfires were started in areas beyond the amphitheater. Thousands of people participated, singing their favorite songs and telling their favorite tales, as most gazed thoughtfully into the flames. There were many silent and voiced prayers of gratitude to God for saving them from a horrible death, and much speculation as to where the enemy bombers would drop to the earth. Some of these impromptu gatherings continued far into the night.

Chapter 21

After their enemies had been defeated, the pilgrims from Shee Lo spent the remainder of the night in the glen by the ridges, doctoring their wounded braves, giving thanks to God, and sleeping until daybreak. When they had finished breakfast, they buried their dead in a solemn ceremony. Then, continuing their journey southward, they trekked on day after day, sometimes finding the trail easy, but also facing many difficulties, including rivers, mountain passes, deserts, and forests.

They were attacked regularly by wild bands of marauders. Usually the predators stole up to them at night, striking small groups of pilgrims as they gathered wood or camped a bit too far from the main convoy. Over a period of several weeks these evil men had killed twenty-five innocent people and had stolen their property and supplies. They succeeded in doing this in spite of the fact that Mosheh had commanded everyone to stay together, especially at night. At times, however, a few forgot his warnings and suffered because of it.

Mosheh increased the number of night sentries, but still the marauders assailed them, now from longer distances, shooting arrows at the pilgrims from a hundred yards away or farther. Mosheh supposed that the bandits expected the travelers to run away in terror or give them supplies, but maybe the renegades simply enjoyed killing for sport. Often he sent warriors on horseback after the assailants, but they always disappeared mysteriously into the wilderness like ghosts in the night.

Eventually Mosheh began sending out small troops of his best horsemen to patrol the margins of the moving caravan and the nighttime encampments. He figured that if he could completely eliminate the marauders once and for all, it would ensure the safety not only of this caravan but also those that would follow. He knew his countrymen would come, ten thousand at a time, to join their brethren in the land called Zion.

One day they were traveling across an undulating plain with many strange bushes dotting the landscape. The plain gradually sloped downward to a forest that extended as far as the eye could see. At first Mosheh didn't see anything unusual, but then someone yelled, "Look at that—above the tree line." He looked up and saw a small cloudless patch of light blue on the horizon above the timberline. He pointed it out to others, and they all were perplexed, not knowing what it was, for the rest of the sky was full of billowy clouds. They continued on for hours, and the patch of blue gradually became larger and wider. Mosheh was intrigued, marveling over what that curious object might be.

They soon entered the forest and saw tight growths of shrubs and densely packed trees, and the forest quickly turned from semidark to almost pitch-black. Here and there bright beams of light shot through the canopy overhead. They struggled through the dense forest underbrush, cutting their way past thick tangles of shrubbery—laboriously—with hundreds of long, two-edged swords. Since there were no trails here, except those made by forest creatures, they used small compasses to guide them, as they had many times on this journey. Someone lit a torch and immediately they could see, at least the people in the vicinity of the fire. Then all along the caravan others got the same idea and began to light torches.

After hours of struggle they stopped, their fatigue telling them it was time to rest and eat. Having gained experience in building fires during the journey, they knew they had to be careful that the fires were enclosed to prevent them from spreading to nearby shrubbery. As soon as they had cooked dinner, they spread out bedding on the wagons and the ground. Even though Mosheh was excited at what the next day might bring, it didn't take him long to become drowsy because of the pleasant sounds of the forest animals and the crunching of their horses consuming the lush vegetation around them. He especially felt warm and happy lying close to Chava.

The following morning they awoke early, ate a quick meal, and struck out at once. At noon they were still in the forest, but Mosheh felt that a great change would soon be upon them. He sensed a presence, colossal and inscrutable, not far away. The entity filled the air and struck his heart and mind with foreboding, like some great wild beast waiting patiently for them to approach. He asked others if they felt the same thing, and a few said they did.

Then suddenly they emerged from the forest and beheld before them what looked like a great blue lake. Not any lake Mosheh was used to, but infinitely more vast. He heard crashing sounds and soon noticed a series of tall waves rolling shoreward and breaking upon the sandy shore. In Shee Lo there were many lakes and hundreds of ponds, but none of them even began to compare with the grandeur and breadth of the body of water Mosheh saw before him. In its vastness it moved and sighed like a huge living being. Accompanied by Chava and several pilgrims, Mosheh walked across a wide stretch of beach, approached the water cautiously, and entered a short distance. As it lapped at his feet, he leaned over and touched it with his hand.

"I was right," he said. "It's just water. Still, there's so much of it."

Chava scowled at him. "What else would it be, silly?" Sometimes she questioned the sharpness of her young husband in everyday matters. She began to walk away from him in the water.

"Well, you never know." He licked water from his hand. "Wait, Chava, it's salty."

She turned quickly and looked at him. "Lake water salty? You must be wrong." She tasted the water on her wet hand. "Heavens! You're right. It *is* salty. Do you think it's poisonous?"

"I don't know. Maybe . . . no, probably not. It just means we can't drink it."

Other pilgrims overheard them and began to try the water. Their reaction was astonishment and delight, for none of them had ever experienced salt water before. Within minutes hundreds of people had entered the water, jumping, laughing, and splashing each other. Then someone suddenly cried out, "How will we ever cross this great lake?" Those words promptly dampened the enthusiasm of the others.

Chava reminded Mosheh that this great lake was nothing but another barrier between them and the promised land. He gazed southward, striving to see land across it, but he couldn't. In Shee Lo, he had always been able to spot land on the other side of any lake, yet these great waters seemed to go on forever. As he and Chava walked back to the beach, he began mulling over ways to solve the problem.

The company set up camp on a long stretch of sand near the lake and went about its usual end-of-day routine. Several groups of hunters went back into the forest to hunt for game, but Mosheh cautioned them to go no farther than an hour's walk and to use their compasses to return to the convoy. The three prophets stood on the shore for hours looking across the lake, as if by staring intently for a long time they might compel the lake to grow smaller. Mosheh learned later they had been hoping God would give them a miracle.

The people were silent as they worked, and Mosheh knew they were worried that their great journey, undertaken in obedience to God's command, might end at this lake, and they might never see the blessed Zion they yearned for so much. Just before dusk the hunters returned with a dozen game animals—only enough to feed a small number of people.

During the following week many pilgrims made suggestions to the prophets and Mosheh regarding how they might get beyond the lake. Some said they should travel either east or west and go around the barrier. They claimed that the distance around could not be more than a few days' walk, perhaps a week at most. After all, how big can a lake be? Others declared they should make sailboats or rowboats like they used to do in Shee Lo and cross the lake in them.

It seemed to Mosheh that the company was almost equally divided, half for one alternative and the rest for the other. Still the problem appeared to be insurmountable. In the first choice, they might travel for months and not find a way around the lake. In the second, they might drown in its depths during a storm or starve after weeks of sailing.

One woman reminded Mosheh and Chava that this was no normal lake because the waters were salty. Neither of them had any idea how that fact could be significant.

During one of the discussions among the leaders, Yaakov said, "If we venture forth upon the waters we may succeed or we may not, but our lives would always be in grave danger, because on such a great lake our boats might leak or we might perish in violent storms. Yet if we decide to take the land route, we would not have to go through the weeks or months of labor required to build ships. Also, it might take us a short time to circumvent the barrier, or a long time, or perhaps never, but at least we would not die on the trail."

"We might as well be dead if we can't reach Zion," declared one of the chiefs. The others seemed to feel the same. Still, Yaakov's words made a deep impression, and most of those who had chosen the lake route before changed in favor of going by land.

Mosheh raised his hand high to get their attention. "I suggest we act on both plans at the same time in order to not waste time. However, in testing the lake route, we should only build three boats, stock them with provisions for twenty days, and send out our most experienced sailors. Their goal, of course, will be to search for land on the other side of the lake.

"We all know from experience that the earth is round and that from where we stand on the shore, we can't see farther than four to seven miles beyond the horizon. So the land we seek might actually be only a few miles away. If after eight days our sailors see no land, they should return, and then we would know that a lake journey would not be wise. Of course, if they do see land sooner, they should return immediately."

Everyone approved that suggestion with enthusiasm.

Avram, another tribal chief, said, "We can save time also when we test the land route. Let us send two bands of warriors, one to the east and the other to the west, to see if there is a way around the lake. If they begin to turn southward as they follow the shoreline, they will know there is probably a way around. They should continue the same march another day to verify they are still traveling south, and if they are, they should halt and return to the main body to report the good news. However, I believe they must not travel along the shore for more than eight days before they turn back."

Mosheh was impressed with Avram's suggestion. "Yes, you are right, my friend. Do the rest of you approve our proposals?" Without exception the leaders accepted both plans.

After an hour of preparation the two groups of land explorers set out on their journey. At the same time dozens of men began work on the sailboats, and the job was completed in a week. The day after the boats were completed and stocked, the brave crews sailed away from land, and the pilgrims watched their brethren leave with prayers in their hearts for their safety.

The pilgrims waited impatiently for the return of all three expeditions. After sixteen days the explorers who had traveled east returned in the early afternoon with disappointing news. Their journey had taken them directly east and they had never begun to turn southward. Six hours later the west-bound group returned with the same sad report. This told Mosheh that the lake must be much larger than he had imagined. In spite of the discouraging news, he was happy his men had returned safely.

After eighteen days the seaborne explorers had not returned and were two days late. The pilgrims had seen storms far away on the lake and feared for the sailors, many wondering if they had drowned in the deep. They fasted and prayed for their return, but a few murmured against the Lord and silenced their murmurings only after receiving the rebuke of the prophets. On the twentieth day, the explorers still had not returned, and the entire company fell into a stupor of depression, believing that not only had they lost their brethren but also all hope of crossing the lake.

Just before dusk on the twentieth day, a boy with sharp eyes, who had remained half a day in a tree near the shore, shouted at the top of his lungs. At first the people didn't understand what he was saying but soon caught his words. "There they are," the boy called. "Three sails. I see three sails." Hundreds of people flew to the edge of the lake, babbling excitedly.

The sailors did return, and dozens of happy pilgrims pulled their crafts up onto the beach. After receiving a warm welcome full of hugs and kisses, they revealed that they had been hit by two storms, but they had not been violent enough to overturn the boats or separate them one from another.

Mosheh grinned with pleasure at several sailors making their report. "Why are you so late?" he asked when they paused to catch their breath.

A tall bronzed sailor, who had acted as a captain, explained, "The winds were favorable when we sailed south, yet on the return voyage we had little wind and needed to use oars to make headway. Only during the last day did the winds pick up again to push us along at a good speed."

Chava's eyes were wide with anxiety. "Did you see land?"

The bronzed sailor's face fell. "No. Just water as far as we could see." Hearing that, his listeners groaned and turned away with tears in their eyes.

Despite their terrible disappointment, the people spent the rest of the evening celebrating the safe return of their explorers. Near midnight they retired but had great difficulty sleeping. Mosheh knew it was because their minds were still filled with the same foreboding and frustration. The leaders circulated through the camp, trying to console them and promising that on the morrow they would solve the great dilemma.

The next day the tribal leaders held a meeting to discuss what they should do, but no one could present a reasonable plan of action. Karmiel was there too and he promised that the three prophets would find a secluded spot and consult with the Lord.

After being in the forest two hours, they returned to camp and declared that the Lord had answered their prayers. God had instructed the people to fast and pray for two days, and on the morning of the third day they would see his kindness and great power with their own eyes. Again the people were confounded, not knowing the mind of God, yet most decided to put their trust in the word of the Lord. They began to fast and encouraged their families and friends to do the same. They held three community prayers that day and the next, and also offered personal petitions.

Many found it difficult to asleep the night of the second day, for they wondered what the saying meant that on the third day they would see the infinite power of God made manifest. Some tried hard to stay awake all night, but by four in the morning a powerful sleep overcame them.

The next morning a strange noise shocked Chava awake, and she rolled over and looked into the sky. The sun was up, having risen several hours earlier. She gazed down the beach, looking for the source of the noise. Though her eyes were still bleary from sleep, she saw dimly—fifty yards down the beach—a man heavy with years who was partly in the water, making strange sounds and pointing at the lake.

Seeing no one else on the beach, she decided the poor old man had probably experienced a nightmare, was walking around in his sleep, or was mentally ill. Then she followed his pointing finger and saw a bizarre sight. It looked like a road in the middle of the lake, rising gradually from the beach and reaching a height of about thirty feet in the air. Chava guessed it was forty feet wide, and from the beach it extended outward across the lake until it disappeared in the distance.

Chava screamed, causing Mosheh to spring from the blankets. She also woke many neighbors, who sat up, gazing around in confusion. Soon hundreds of people were running to the beach, some treading water, others climbing to the top of the new construction, their feet sinking partly into the soft soil. The news spread quickly for miles along the beach, and thousands of people came running to see the miracle with their own eyes.

Before long, there were so many people crammed together in one place that no one could move the width of an arm without bumping into those around them. Mosheh stood up in his wagon and tried to get the people to listen, but his voice was drowned out by the racket of the multitude. A few minutes later he climbed down and pushed his way through the crowd until he reached Chava, who had worked her way to the edge of the lake. He hugged her tenderly, knowing that the Lord had provided the way for them to reach Zion.

After a few hours the people began to return to their tents and wagons. Since the area in front of the new highway was clear, the chiefs and prophets walked to the top of the curious construction to see what they could see. They noticed the top of the road was covered with small pebbles and a soil combining sand and clay. The surface was slushy, so they decided to wait a few days before allowing the company to travel on it. They believed the surface would soon dry, become smooth and hard, and support the weight of the caravan. There was much conjecture among the leaders as to how that enormous highway could have appeared there.

"It's possible," Yaakov said, "that the road materialized from the elements of the atmosphere by the miraculous power of God."

"Possibly, but not likely," Avram said. "I believe God marshaled forth the hosts of heaven, and they descended to earth and constructed the road in one night in some marvelous way."

"Still, that would require millions of angels," Liron said, "and where would they get the materials to make the road? It's more probable that God acted upon nature directly. For example, he may have caused a portion of the bottom of the lake to swell and rise until it reached the surface where it is now."

"Well, if Liron is right," another chief said, "that leaves the question as to whether the highway is floating on the surface like a huge barge or whether it descends without a break to the bottom."

Karmiel laughed. "Brethren, we can guess all we want, but the fact remains we have no idea how the highway got there. Like the scriptures say, God works in mysterious ways. The main thing is, the road is there now for our use." The other leaders laughed also and admitted that Karmiel was right.

The people were disappointed and impatient when they learned they had to wait. Mosheh tamed their impatience by warning them that the new highway might collapse under the great weight of ten thousand people with their horses, equipment, and supplies. It was important that the surface and top portion of the structure dry and harden. That afternoon the clouds disappeared, the hot sun beat down fiercely upon them, and an exceptionally warm breeze picked up from the west. Mosheh believed it was God's way of hastening the drying of the highway.

Chapter 22

❦

On Tuesday morning in Daviess County, the participants were in their places by nine thirty. They expressed the same joy and exuberance as the day before, excited over what new miracles they would soon witness. After the preliminaries, Madison Hall led the assembly in hymns of their own choice. It was during the third song, "The Spirit of God," that the shining pillar formed in the sky and descended again to earth. Brother Hall and the General Authorities rushed off the stage before being struck by the light.

When the conduit reached the empty square, the crowd could make out the figure of Father Adam smiling back at them. Steven and Mary still found it hard to believe that this young God was the same person who lived nine hundred and thirty years in mortality at the beginning of the human race.

Adam welcomed them and said they had many important things to do today. "This meeting shall be dedicated to missionary work. Will the First Presidency come forward." President Wilford Benson, Elder Bennion Hicks, and Elder Samuel Law came forward. After they took seats, Adam began asking each of them for an accounting of their stewardship regarding missionary work. As they spoke, the people were surprised once more that they could hear every word clearly without the use of electronic devices, in spite of the fact that most of those on the square were mortals.

Next, Adam excused the First Presidency and asked the Council of Twelve to make their reports, questioning them concerning their successes and failures. When they admitted mistakes, he gave them advice on how to approach their responsibilities more effectively, especially those dealing with missionary work. All these reports took a total of two hours.

"Now I have a special surprise for you," Father Adam said at noon. "Do you hunger and thirst?" The crowd said "yes" in unison. "I thought so. Our protective cloud covering has disappeared. Would you like to see it return?" Again thirty thousand yeses echoed through the amphitheater. "Are there any no votes?" The people laughed as they shook their heads. Adam grinned and said, "I thought not."

He looked up intently at the sky, and the assembly did the same. He looked down and smiled at the people, and they smiled back. He raised his eyes again and waited patiently. They followed his gaze, trying to be patient. Finally he said, "Sometimes the Father makes us wait." That brought a burst of laughter from the crowd. Three minutes later the clouds came, a colossal mass of them, covering the entire sky. Steven was worried they were going to get more protection than they wanted, especially when some clouds turned dark.

"Don't be afraid," Adam said. "It isn't rain, snow, or sleet you're about to get." Steven laughed inside because he noticed that Adam was getting the hang of English idioms and contractions. *I love a leader with a sense of humor*, he told himself.

Finally something began to fall out of the heavens, white and fluffy. At first the audience thought they were flakes of snow, and as the flakes fell, they covered their clothes and the ground around them. Children scooped up handfuls and put it into their mouths, exclaiming how sweet and delicious it tasted. Hearing the children, the adults did the same and expressed their delight to one another. The word "manna" was heard throughout the congregation.

"Yes," Adam said, "it's manna, a blessing from God. You can eat it now and gather enough for your dinner tonight if you have containers. Don't try to save it until tomorrow, because worms will breed in it during the night. Most of all, remember that this holy bread is a symbol of the great sacrifice of the Son of Man. Also, it's a reminder that you must live by every word that proceeds from the mouth of God, and not by the precepts and opinions of men. Eat it today as you contemplate the approaching visitation of the Savior to this congregation near the end of our conference."

Adam waited twenty minutes as the people ate all the manna they could hold and filled every pocket and container for later use. Soon the falling manna began to diminish until it came no more.

"As you know," Adam continued, "I have given your leaders instructions concerning future missionary efforts. Now I enjoin all of you, my children, to do everything you can to preach the gospel to every person you meet who doesn't already have it. You have received special witnesses as to the existence of celestial beings and the infinite power of God. Soon you will see the Lord himself. This special knowledge obligates you to do everything you can to further the work. I especially ask you to seek out the American Indians who live in your midst and have not yet accepted Jesus Christ.

"Moreover, in the near future thousands of the inhabitants of Zion will be called to go out into the world in one last great missionary campaign. Their job is to warn the world to repent and come unto Christ, for he shall spare none who remain in Babylon. This missionary effort will not take place until Zion greatly enlarges it borders, and the Lost Ten Tribes return from the land of the north to join you here in New Zion."

He paused for a moment to let his words sink in. "Tomorrow we shall take up matters of the greatest importance. Now I bid you farewell until we meet again." As he said this, a bright shaft of light formed around him, and he was drawn quickly upward into the heavens.

Most of the attendees spent the remainder of the day on Tuesday doing the same things as they had done on Monday. However, there was more speculation about when Christ would come and what he would do. The very idea that they would soon behold Jesus and hear his voice thrilled them beyond description. But it was also a little frightening.

Steven and Mary spent the evening in their room discussing various subjects, while their children socialized with newfound friends in a nearby meadow. They lay next to each other on the bed, which they often did when they wanted to talk about serious matters and their children were gone.

"Steven," Mary said, "you told me the scripture that says a hundred million people will come to Adam-ondi-Ahman is symbolic."

"Yes, obviously it is."

"I'm wondering if the same thing is true of John the Revelator's hundred and forty-four thousand. You know, all those exalted high priests who are supposed to follow Christ around in the last days. If that number is symbolic also, it might simply mean that the Lord will be accompanied by a large retinue of holy beings when he appears."

Steven had debated that in his mind for some time. "You're probably right, and there are other things to consider when discussing numbers. In some scriptures there may be problems with the accuracy of the King James translation. In others, the scribes who transcribed the prophets' predictions may have exaggerated the numbers to create a powerful effect on future readers."

"That's very interesting. So do you believe that the prophecy in chapter nine of Revelation might be symbolic when it declares that Gog will marshal forth two hundred million soldiers at Armageddon?"

"I believe it probably is. Gog will have a huge army, but he won't need two hundred million. Notice also that this Armageddon number is a multiple of the great council number. That suggests both are symbolic."

They continued to discuss other things and eventually got around to what was really on their minds—the visitation of the Lord. They asked each other how they might feel at the moment of seeing him, but neither could answer that question. Mary asked Steven if he thought the Lord might appear tomorrow. He admitted that he didn't know but he hoped it would happen.

On Wednesday the audience sang six hymns waiting for Adam to appear. Just after beginning the seventh song, "I Need Thee Every Hour," a light descended with Adam inside.

He smiled at the people in a loving way and said quietly, "Today will be the most important day of our conference here at Adam-ondi-Ahman." There was a sudden intake of collective breath. Steven heard many kinds of comments and exclamations across the audience. "He's coming today?" "Right now?" "Oh no!" "I'm not ready." "I'm afraid." He knew that many of those responses were spontaneous outbursts, unwittingly exposing secret hopes and fears.

"Soon we will receive the visit of the Lord," Adam said. "He will come today and the next three days. You will see for yourselves what will take place at that time. Now I would like Brother Hall to continue leading you in the hymn you were just singing."

After singing "I Need Thee Every Hour," they continued with other songs. As they sang they scrutinized the sky, their eyes glowing with expectation and suspense. Between songs, one small child said, "When's he coming, Mom?" No one paid any attention but proceeded with the next song, chosen by Brother Hall.

It was during "Redeemer of Israel" that the sky directly above them began to burn with fire. It grew until it filled a quarter of the sky with intense light. The spectators shielded their eyes from the brightness, able to glance at it for only a second, though they felt no heat from the blaze. It descended slowly, concentrating into a glowing ball about the size of a large cloud. When it was several hundred feet above them, the brightness began to diminish until the crowd could look at it without pain or discomfort. In the cloud they could make out hundreds of celestial personages, but didn't know who they were.

What happened next surprised everyone. Most of the beings began to return from where they had come until they disappeared from view. Only nine individuals remained, and Steven asked himself who they were. The soft voice spoke to his mind, saying, *"Those who remain are the Savior, Peter, James, John the Beloved, Moroni, Joseph the earthly father of Jesus, Mary his earthly mother, Mary called Magdalene, and the Prophet Joseph Smith. The first five are resurrected beings, the other four are not yet resurrected."* Steven looked around and realized that everyone in the audience had heard the same voice.

The shining cloud continued to move downward until it touched the square and then vanished, leaving the nine gleaming personages behind, standing next to Adam. In the middle of the group Steven saw a distinctive man who was slightly taller than Adam. No one had to tell him that the man was the Savior. He seemed to be about thirty years old, and was approximately six feet two with dark brown hair and beard. His hair fell to his shoulders, and his beard was of moderate length. He wore a glistening blue robe that reached almost to his blue sandals, and its sleeves extended just past his elbows. The robe was obviously very light in weight and was gathered at the waist with a white sash.

His very presence and every movement suggested elegance and grace and great physical strength, and his eyes were like glowing embers as he gazed upon the audience. Steven's heart burned as he saw the infinite love and compassion in the Lord's eyes and on his entire countenance. Jesus held his earthly mother's hand tenderly in his own. Steven turned to see tears streaming down his wife's face, and he realized that the people sitting nearby were also weeping.

The Lord stepped forward and spoke in a quiet, gentle voice. Soft and tranquil it was, yet it penetrated to the innermost soul, and no one missed a single word. "My love and my peace I give to you. Blessed are you for your faithfulness. My Father has sent me to tell you how pleased he is with what you have done in Zion. He accepts your temples, your sacrifices, and your great society. He rejoices at your courage in the face of danger and adversity. He is happy with your physical and spiritual growth. Through me he sends his everlasting love, for he is the eternal God of love. You have done great things, and you will do even greater things in the future, under his guidance, and in his name." At this Jesus stepped back and again took his mother's hand.

Adam came forward and said, "Now I will ordain the Lord, thereby returning to him all the keys that the patriarchs have given to me." He retrieved two nearby chairs and set them before the visitors. Jesus advanced and sat in one of the chairs. Adam went behind him and laid his hands on his head. The ordination was very short, but in it he bestowed all the keys and powers of every past dispensation upon the Lord.

Next Adam sat on the second chair, facing the Lord. He spent the following half hour giving his Master a report on his stewardship as the head of the human race. During this report the Lord asked Adam a dozen short questions, and seemed satisfied with his answers. The audience listened to every word carefully, and when the report was completed, both men stood and embraced each other in brotherly love.

Then Adam and Christ stood together facing outward. Steven could see their faces and eyes clearly as if they were no more than ten feet away.

"To all those in this assembly," declared Adam with solemnity, "and to the inhabitants of the earth, I declare, as the father of all mortals, that the Lord Jesus Christ is hereby officially declared the presiding High Priest of the holy Church on earth, and also the Great King and Ruler of the governments of this planet. By this all other governments are subject to him. In the near future he will assume effective command of his two kingdoms, at which time all other kingdoms shall be cast down and destroyed. This appointment and this authority have already been confirmed by the Father. Now I ask you all to ratify those rights by raising your hand high."

Every person in the assembly quickly raised his or her hand enthusiastically. No one objected. Steven knew this meant that the current governments of men, and also their churches, would remain in place temporarily, but that during the Millennium, Christ would return to earth to institute in person his worldwide theocracy. Today's ceremony was the official beginning of that holy government.

Adam was pleased at their enthusiastic response. "Now eight of your visitors will return to their home in heaven, while the Lord and I will remain to visit with you personally. We invite each of you to descend to this square, and we will talk with you individually face to face."

The audience could not believe its ears. To look into Jesus's eyes, to hear his voice, to communicate their hearts to him, would be an experience no one had been blessed to have for thousands of years, except a few of his chosen servants. Yet there he was, and the time was now. The conduit of light appeared suddenly, and the eight visitors mentioned were taken up into heaven. As Joseph Smith was drawn upward, Steven strained to get a good look at him.

Adam looked at the people sitting near Steven and Mary. "We first invite those who are sitting near us on this side of the yellow circle. When we have communed with them, the rest of you are invited to come forward in an orderly manner. Don't worry if you do not reach us today, for we will be here tomorrow and the following two days."

Mary and Steven and their children got into a line of "dignitaries" waiting to see the Lord. They progressed slowly until there were only a few people in front of them. As Steven drew closer, his heart raced faster and his face grew redder. He noticed the same reaction on Mary's face. Then finally they were there. He watched as Daniel talked briefly to Jesus, followed by Gabrielle. They took only about thirty seconds each. Jesus hugged each of them. Mary stayed about seven feet away until her turn, and as she talked to the Lord, tears streamed down her face. Surprisingly, Steven couldn't hear a word they were saying except when she first stepped up and Jesus said, "Mary." After a minute, Jesus embraced her and it was Steven's turn.

"Hello, Steven. It is so good to see you up close again." Steven looked deep into the Lord's eyes and felt his profound, unconditional love. His heart burned with a cleansing fire, which spread to every cell in his body. He felt enlightened and purified by that simple look into the eyes of the

Master, who had suffered exquisite agony, pain, and humiliation because of his love for all mankind.

"You were steadfast on the plains. You resisted the Evil One. You sacrificed everything to build my kingdom. And you were faithful in all things. I forgive your faults and trespasses. You are acceptable to me and to our Father . . . Do you have any questions?"

Steven struggled to control his powerful feelings. "Yes. Why me?"

"Why not you? You were the man for the job." He stepped toward Steven and embraced him warmly and very gently, as if he were worried about crushing him. "Go now, and my peace be with you. I have greater work for you in the future."

"What work?"

"You will see when the time comes."

Steven turned away and walked toward Adam, stunned and thrilled at the same time. Adam saw him coming and said, "Exciting isn't it? Meeting the Master face to face. I saw your reaction. I get the same feelings every time I meet him again after a period of absence. Steven, don't worry about the future. As he said, you're the man for the job." He hugged Steven warmly. "I can see it's going to take quite a while to meet this entire congregation."

"I don't know how you do it. I'd be in the hospital after two or three hours."

"That's because your body is not yet resurrected. If it were, all this would be what you people call a little piece of cake, especially when you already know every single person individually. It's somewhat like meeting family members at a great family reunion."

"You know the names of every person here?"

"Of course. There are only thirty thousand two hundred and twenty-three of them."

Steven grinned at Adam's precision. "Michael, may I look closely at your arm?"

"No problem." He extended his arm toward Steven, who took hold and examined it as though he were studying a new species under a microscope. He saw perfect, glowing skin, lit by some internal power, and he wondered what it would be like.

Adam chuckled. "Don't worry. You'll get yours someday. Well, I guess you'd better move along now or we'll be here forever. By the way, how do you like my English? It's such a terribly difficult language to learn. The Adamic language is sooo much easier!"

Steven laughed. "Very fluent. Very idiomatic. Great contractions."

"Thank you. A little praise doesn't hurt."

"Michael, speaking of the Adamic language, I don't suppose you could—"

"Can't do it. Takes too long. Besides, it's against the rules."

"Okay. At least I tried."

"Get going now, young man. The people behind you are going to have a heart attack." He smiled after Steven as he watched him move away.

Jesus and Adam descended also on Thursday, Friday, and Saturday, and remained from ten in the morning until two in the afternoon, communing with the saints individually. The divine visitors came and went in the same manner as before. The conference ended on Saturday afternoon, when the visitors returned to the presence of God. The saints set out on the journey to their homes, their hearts full of joy from the privileges and blessings they had received.

But the Lord didn't leave permanently. He returned to visit each of his temples and many of the private homes of the saints, both in New Zion and Old Zion. One night he visited the Steven Christopher family and spent the entire evening with them, eating dinner and sharing personal experiences. He ate Mary's carrot cake with zest and complimented her on her culinary skills.

The entire family was deeply impressed by his incredible wisdom and knowledge, and especially by his loving kindness and the fact that he accepted them without a hint of judgment. As he opened the door to depart, he explained that he would soon return to his celestial home and remain there until he saw them again at the time and place chosen by the Father.

Cuddling with Mary in bed that night, Steven reflected on the Lord's visit, thinking of a dozen questions he had forgotten to ask him. He mentioned this oversight to her and got a surprising answer.

"Sweetheart, why on earth didn't you ask him—when you had a perfect chance—where the Lost Ten Tribes are, and when we can expect them?"

Steven smacked his forehead with the palm of his hand. "Oh my gosh! You're right. I didn't think of that. I might have learned something no one else has a clue about. But maybe he wouldn't have answered my question."

"Well, dear, you never know for sure unless you ask," Mary replied in a wry voice.

Chapter 23

The unmasked sun beat down and the hot wind blew upon the miraculous highway for three days. On the morning of the fourth day billowy clouds appeared and the winds became mild and pleasant. Mosheh tested the road surface and found it hard and smooth. Two hours after dawn he commanded the company to move onto the highway, and they continued their journey southward.

One woman jumped off her wagon as it rolled by and asked Mosheh what they would do if the road began to fall to pieces as they traveled along it in the middle of the lake. Teasing her somewhat, he said, "Well, little sister, I suppose we might find ourselves drowning in the water, all of us." Seeing the shock on her sweet, innocent countenance, he quickly added, "But the Lord would not have given us this wonderful gift only to allow it to disintegrate beneath us." Instantly her face put on a happy look.

They traveled on the highway steadily for a month, stopping only at noon and dusk. Though it rained for an hour or so several times during this time, the highway showed no signs of breaking up. When the caravan made a halt, many climbed down the side of the road to fish on a ledge jutting near the water. The fish were abundant and the pilgrims replenished their food supply with a variety of strange creatures no one had ever seen before. When large white-winged birds swooped down to the highway to investigate the people and to steal what they could of the catches, the warriors managed to spear hundreds of them. Everyone enjoyed the taste of their meat.

Near the end of their second month on the highway, a great storm arose at midday. The winds howled like monstrous hounds, and great black clouds swirled overhead. A growling, twisting funnel fell to the lake a mile west of the road, sucking streams of water hundreds of feet into the sky. Gigantic waves rose high and crashed down on the road and the caravan, causing many to weep and cower in their wagons.

At times Mosheh felt that the wind would blow all of them off the highway and into the turbulent waters below. And indeed, it happened. After a dozen light wagons with their occupants and a number of small animals were hurled into the water, disappearing instantly from view, he sent a command down the line for the people to tie themselves to the heavier wagons and cover themselves with any protection they could find. He was also worried that the highway might begin to disintegrate at any minute under the onslaught, but it held firm. Then, after two hours of terror and misery, the storm abated.

They lost fifteen wagons, twenty animals, and forty-five people in the storm. Yet because of the violence of the tempest, Mosheh was surprised that more people had not perished. He asked himself why the Lord would let his obedient children suffer and die, but he knew it was not his place to question God. In spite of their losses, they gave thanks that the highway remained intact and its surface was hardly damaged at all. They started off again and traveled another week with no end in sight. Mosheh was beginning to believe this journey would never end, and he calculated that they had traveled almost a thousand miles on the highway.

He heard many complaints from his people, who were becoming more and more frustrated, wondering how wide this detestable lake was! They had plenty of food, but the water supply was getting dangerously low. During the ten rainstorms that had fallen, they had collected as much fresh water as possible, yet they could get no drinkable water from the lake because of its salt content.

A few days after the big storm, Liron the prophet hurried up to the wagon of Mosheh and Chava, who had stopped to prepare their noon meal.

"Good afternoon," Mosheh said. "Sit down and partake with us."

"Thank you so much," Liron said. "I am hungry and also sick of eating my bad cooking." Chava smiled as she handed him a plate.

After discussing recent events for a few minutes, Liron said, "I wanted to tell you something interesting."

"Oh? What? Mosheh asked.

"Last night I was reading in our ancient records and I came across a curious passage. I discovered that after our ancestors had first left the land of their captivity, over two thousand years ago, they traveled north for many miles and then along the eastern shore of a great body of water that was salty. The records called those waters a 'sea' because of the salt."

"A sea?" Chava said, intrigued.

"Yes, a sea."

"That is interesting," Mosheh said. "Was that great body of water as big as this one?"

"I don't think it was nearly as large as this one, but it was much larger than anything we had in Shee Lo. Like this so-called lake, it had salty water and high waves."

"Well," Mosheh said, "I suppose we'll have to start calling this endless monster a sea from now on."

Liron stuffed a huge bite of Chava's delicious food into his mouth and rolled his eyes in delight. After chewing as fast as he could for a minute, he grinned and replied, "Yes, indeed. That would be more accurate."

When they had traveled two months and three days on the raised highway, Karmiel, the prophet, received the strong impression that he should go to the front of the caravan. He did so and from time to time gazed intently at the highway ahead. In the early afternoon of that same day he saw something strange—a long dim line ahead that was a little darker than the horizon. Still, he was not sure. He hurried up the road, anxious to be the first to report that their journey would soon be over. After half an hour of rushing along, he was sure the line was growing darker and thicker. He chided himself for going on foot, for he knew it would take another hour of trotting before he could be certain.

So he walked slowly back to the caravan. Several warriors asked him why he had gone ahead, but he made some flimsy excuse, not wanting to embarrass himself. But later he confided his suspicions to Liron, who agreed to say nothing. Yet both of them felt a sense of relief without being sure why.

By late afternoon the whole company knew land was a short distance ahead and their long trek on the highway was almost over. A short time later the excited people traveled down the end of the road and onto a beautiful wide beach. It took an hour for the entire convoy to spread out along the beach. Many voyagers fell to their knees or dropped flat on their bellies and kissed the wet sand in gratitude. Since twilight was fast approaching, they hastened to pitch tents and build fires. While preparing their meal, Mosheh and Chava heard songs of joy throughout the company.

The following day they resumed their march southward. From the beach they moved into another forest, but one not so dense as that north of the mighty sea. Numerous narrow trails penetrated the forest, heading in all directions. They saw ponds of fresh water and animals of all kinds. Every species was new.

They traversed the forest for three days, and then moved suddenly onto a vast desert devoid of any type of plant. The desert soon took the shape of the sea in a violent storm, with curved hills of sand extending as far as the eye could see. Although they had replenished their water supply in the forest, filling drums and pouches, they hoped the supply would be enough to get them through this barren land.

The going was extremely difficult, for the wagon wheels sunk into the soft sand, and even the great shaggy beasts had to stop frequently under their burden. Soon every traveler had to drop down from the wagons and carry as much weight as they could on foot. The sun beat upon them with blistering intensity as if roasting them for its personal meal, and rising waves of heat blurred their view of the monotonous landscape. Their only protection from the sun was to cover their heads and faces with any make-shift shade they could fashion. They struggled up and down sand dunes for an entire day, making little headway.

On the morning of the second day in the desert, Mosheh directed his people to rest in the heat of the day, sheltering themselves from the sun and wind as best they could in the lee of high-arching dunes or under their carriages. Henceforth they would travel only at night, by the light of a bright moon. Mosheh was worried because he knew their water supply was almost depleted.

Two hours after sunup on the fourth day, just before Mosheh was about to call a halt, he saw what seemed to be a patch of green several miles away. Or was it a mirage? He mounted his horse and rode toward it with difficulty, looking up constantly to see if it was still there, or had evaporated in the desert wind. As he looked, the fertile cluster of trees seemed to waver and vibrate in the hot desert air.

Yet as he drew near the green patch, it remained intact, and he knew it wasn't a mirage, but an oasis. He laughed out loud, and the grinning travelers coming from behind rushed passed him to investigate this miracle. Within an hour the entire caravan had wrapped itself around the verdant haven, which was as large as a small lake. The people drank all they could and filled their containers. Many youngsters wanted to plunge into the six cool, inviting pools, but the leaders stopped them, explaining that they would muddy and pollute the waters. Later—deep in the night—Mosheh heard children giggling and splashing around in the water. He thought, *Ah! To be a child again, always willing to ignore rules.* He didn't have the heart to prevent them.

They spent the entire day at the oasis, replenishing their water supply and resting or sleeping in cool shade. An hour before twilight, Mosheh climbed a high dune a few hundred yards from the oasis and looked south over the desert to see what he could see. He saw a long green line, about fifteen miles away. He wasn't certain but something or someone spoke to his mind, impressing him that he was seeing a forest.

He hurried into the encampment and found Liron sprawled out near a pool, consuming a second helping of Chava's celebration meal of roasted venison and potatoes. "I need to tell you what I saw from a tall dune south of here," Mosheh said.

Liron groaned and stood up to greet the chief. "What did you see, my brother?"

"A forest some distance south of here."

"A forest! Several hours ago I climbed a dune and studied the land south and found nothing unusual."

"I know. It's hard to see, just a slim green line on the horizon. At first I was doubtful, but a voice spoke to me and confirmed that this desert would soon end at a forest."

"I believe you, and I'm grateful to hear it."

"In an hour we will march again and soon find the forest."

"Shall I spread the word?" Liron asked. "It might give our people hope."

"Yes, you are right. It might be what I need to encourage them to leave this oasis."

Many in the company complained because they had hoped to spend many pleasant days at the oasis, and they felt that to leave it was to put themselves in peril once again. It was only word of a nearby forest that convinced them to continue the journey.

As they left the oasis just after dusk, the company found travel easier, for the landscape began to level out, the sand turning into areas of hard gravel, with clumps of desert shrubbery appearing from time to time. A few hours before daybreak they approached the forest Mosheh had seen, and he stopped the caravan to allow his people to rest.

The next morning the sun was high in the sky when the company entered the forest. Mosheh was amazed at how abrupt the transition had been from forest to desert and later from desert to forest again, for it defied everything he knew about the natural world. The convoy wended its way through the forest for two days, enjoying its coolness and replenishing once more their water supplies.

On the third day they left the forest, and again the terrain changed abruptly. Now they found themselves on a rolling plain of soft ground that seemed to extend forever in all directions toward the south. They had voyaged on the plain for two days when several scouts came charging up on their steeds from the west, waving their arms and shouting excitedly.

They reined their horses in when they reached Mosheh, and one of the scouts declared in a loud voice. "We saw something very strange west of here."

"What?" Mosheh asked.

"Another miraculous highway. A five minute ride away."

"Show me," Mosheh said, finding it difficult to contain his excitement.

Halting the caravan and telling Chava to remain there, he jumped from the wagon and mounted his favorite horse. With a wave of his hand he summoned several other chiefs and waited until they arrived. The chiefs and scouts rode west to view this curious new sight. What they saw was a hard-surface construction about fifty feet in width, running north and south as far as the eye could see. It seemed perfectly level in its entire length, but was slightly convex from edge to edge. It was made of some black, semi-sticky substance that supported them perfectly well.

After they examined it and tramped their horses on it a minute or so, Mosheh decided that traveling on this pathway was much better and quicker than trying to roll wagons over soft terrain, which had uneven planes and was covered with bushes and boulders of all sizes and shapes.

Mosheh told the others to stay there while he hurried to the convoy in order to turn it west to the new road, and twenty minutes later the first wagons rolled onto it. Soon the company moved much faster as it continued its trek. Mosheh and the prophets believed that this road had been built, not by God himself, but by the people of Zion to lead them to the holy temple.

They followed the black highway all day long, stopping in the middle of the road at dusk to lead their animals to nearby forage and to make preparations for the night. It was almost night when they caught sight of a group of about twenty figures on foot, coming toward them from the east like phantoms in the dark. The pilgrims who caught sight of them were excited at first at the prospect of meeting the good people of Zion, and they walked into the night, hoping to make new friends. However, their anticipation changed to terror when they heard booming sounds and the thud of projectiles smashing into wagons and human bodies.

Instinctively, hundreds of pilgrims fell to the ground or sought cover behind wagons. Mosheh sounded the alarm with his whistle, and dozens of warriors grabbed weapons and joined their leader on the backs of fast horses. As the bullets whizzed by them on all sides, they charged the shadowy figures in a rush so violent and determined that the enemy turned and sought to escape, but the warriors ran them down and in minutes killed every man they found without suffering casualties. After the battle, Mosheh led warriors to the other side of the road to make sure that area was clear of enemies.

Mosheh and his men returned to the caravan with dread in their hearts, fearing to find family members who had perished. And indeed, six pilgrims had been killed in the attack and many more wounded. That night, Mosheh increased the number of sentinels. At a late-night council, the leaders concluded that their attackers were nothing but wandering outlaws, and not the people of Zion.

The next morning, after burying their dead by the side of the road, the pilgrims said prayers over them and marked their graves with hand-carved wooden memorials. Afterwards, they continued their journey, searching for enemies while looking for friends.

In the following days, other gangs attacked the rear of the caravan—this time in broad daylight. But Mosheh had added to the guards escorting the company by choosing an elite band of warriors and giving them special instructions. They occupied the last nine wagons, dressed in women's clothing, and when the outlaws attacked again, they leaped onto nearby horses and rushed the gang with spears poised. After a short time of fierce battle, the warriors slew every single outlaw. That same scene was repeated three days later with the same outcome.

The pilgrims met no further attacks and continued their journey, feeling an increase in peace and happiness at the prospect of soon meeting their brothers and sisters in the promised land of Zion.

Chapter 24

❦

On a beautiful day in early May they came from Canada and entered Minnesota on Highway 59. Ten thousand people in a caravan ten miles long. About a third of them rode shaggy horses, while others rode in wagons pulled by heavy horses. The wagons had wooden wheels, and from the wagon beds six poles rose upward about five feet. Attached to these poles was a canvas-like covering to protect the occupants from the sun. A few walked beside the wagons.

Their dress was similar in some respects to that of the early Seneca Indians when they lived in the state of New York before the American Revolution. Nearly every person wore a loosely woven, cloth skullcap with dozens of feathers of all colors projecting across the top and all around the edge to form a kind of brim. The cap acted as protection from the weather and as a tribal decoration.

Men, women, and children wore attractive multicolored gowns made of animal skins, always girded at the waist by wide strips of leather. The tops of the gowns on many men had several long slits that partially revealed strong brown chests. The men wore close-cropped beards and very long hair tied behind them in one long ponytail, but a few men had cut their hair so short that only a hint of it projected beyond their caps. The women wore two long bands of braided hair that were placed in front of the body, descending downward from their armpits. The children were smaller copies of their parents. Nearly all of them had black or dark brown hair. A few had hair that was light brown or almost blond.

They rode and trudged along slowly with utter weariness as if they had journeyed thousands of miles and endured incalculable hardships.

The men were unusually tall, averaging about six feet two inches. All of them carried bows and arrows attached to their backs, and broadswords and knives in handmade sheaths. Many bore long sharp spears. They looked as though they were fully capable of using their weapons to their advantage.

They were traveling through an area that had been devastated during the great Collapse, as had most regions of the old United States and Canada. It was only now beginning to recover. The number of settlers living in this northwestern corner of Minnesota, one of the seventeen states of New Zion, were so few that no one even caught sight of the newcomers until they were sixty-five miles south of the Canadian border and five miles north of the city of Thief River Falls.

A farmer was working in one of his fields with his three sons a quarter mile east of Highway 59, when his youngest son, an eleven year old, ran up to his father shouting excitedly. He pointed toward the road, and they all turned to look. Shielding their eyes, they strained to make out what that dark line was moving southward. The father walked thirty feet away to a blanket where he had placed their lunch basket, three rifles, and a pair of binoculars. As he studied the convoy carefully through the glasses, his sons joined him. At last he said something to his youngest and the boy scooted off toward their farmhouse six hundred yards away. The others followed him more slowly.

By noon four hundred citizens of Thief River Falls straddled Highway 59, a quarter mile north of town. Most of them had walked, but a few had brought solar cars, and one man had come in his small solar bus. They were armed with rifles and pistols, determined to defend their families no matter how numerous the enemy, and they knew how to do it. They had been attacked many times by roving bands of desperate, violent vagabonds, who would do anything to survive. Looking for any sign of hostility, they watched carefully as the strangers approached. Seeing none, they avoided brandishing their weapons. The newcomers continued to advance toward them with confidence, displaying no open fear. When the forepart of the caravan was fifty feet away, it stopped abruptly. Both groups remained in place for some time, waiting for the other to make the first move.

Finally, one of the rugged horsemen dismounted and advanced twenty feet before he stopped. At six feet six inches tall with a strong muscular body, he was a striking figure. His handsome face bore an attitude of courage and self-confidence, with no trace of East Asian features. Even from thirty feet away the townspeople could see the brightness and determination in his dark eyes. Many surmised he was the caravan leader. He raised his right hand toward them in what seemed to be a gesture of greeting and friendship. Next he removed all his weapons and placed them on the road in front of him. The men who were with him in the vanguard dismounted and laid down their weapons also.

Reassured, the settlers also laid down their arms and moved in to get a closer look. At their head was the town mayor, Ethan Reed. As Reed and George Barnes, the town constable, approached the tribal leader, the tall "Indian" reached out and locked his hand around Ethan's right wrist and shook it up and down three times, with shining eyes and a bright grin on his face. Ethan laughed heartily, figuring this was the stranger's way of shaking hands.

The young giant hit his chest with one fist and said, "A-luph." He actually said several words, but the only thing Ethan could pick out was *a-luph*.

"What's he saying, George?"

"Greek to me, boss."

Several other citizens came close as Ethan tried for five minutes to communicate with the big chief in English, asking what tribe they were, where they had come from, why they were traveling on the highway, and a dozen other questions. With great patience the stranger scrutinized his mouth and gestures during the entire interrogation, but clearly didn't understand a thing. All he could do is stare at Ethan with a blank look, a kind but indulgent smile on his face. His lack of comprehension was confirmed when he shrugged his shoulders, rolled his eyes, and raised one side of his mouth in a quizzical gesture.

Out of the corner of his eye Ethan saw that many voyagers had stepped down to the road and were heading toward them. He also noticed—to his surprise—that a group of children, a mixture of residents and travelers, were already playing a game that looked like hopscotch. Trust little children to make friends and break the ice quickly.

When Ethan had finished his questioning, the stranger launched into a long interrogation of his own in some weird language. Ethan listened carefully for about six minutes but couldn't grasp any more than the chief had. He returned his own blank stare and hunched his shoulders at the same time, both of his palms forward and up. The young giant hesitated a few moments, apparently thinking hard. Suddenly, his face lit up, and he raised his finger in the air, made an about-face, and spoke to a beautiful woman who had almost reached them, calling her Chava.

He said a few words to her in the mysterious language, and she returned straightaway to her wagon. While they waited, the tall Indian once again raised his finger into the air. Ethan was pretty sure he understood the finger gesture, assuming that the stranger wanted him to wait while this woman, no doubt the chief's wife, retrieved something from the wagon.

At that point, three elderly Cheyenne "braves" joined the growing crowd of townspeople. When the newcomer saw them, he walked up boldly with his usual grin and gave each of them the same three-stroke handshake. The Indians shook his hand but gazed at him enigmatically without a sign of emotion on their faces, as was their custom. The stranger said several things to them in his puzzling language, but they didn't appear to comprehend and said nothing in return.

"Don't you Indians understand him?" Ethan said. "He's obviously an American Indian, or maybe a Canadian Indian. Do you know what nation he belongs to?"

The nearest Cheyenne, a wisecracking old boy named Billy Circling Hawk, said in mock Indian English, "Him not Indian. Him not speak Indian tongue."

Ethan's eyes widened with shock. "He's not? How do you know?"

"Speaks no Indian words we know," Billy replied.

The ancient Cheyenne next to Billy shook his head feathers and added, "No, he doesn't speak Indian. Besides, he's got a beard. Can't be American or Canadian Indian."

"Indians never wear beards?"

"Nope," Billy answered. "A full-blooded Indian almost never grows a beard. They ain't got no body hair, or very little. In some tribes guys grow a few hairs but pluck them out as quickly as they can. They think face hair is very ugly. Need to attract available young women."

"So where does this man come from, Billy?"

"Hey, pale face, your guess is as good as mine."

"He used the word *Shee Lo* several times. Do you know what that means?"

"No clue." Billy scowled at Ethan for asking such a dumb question.

After searching her wagon for a minute, the woman called Chava returned and handed her husband a flat leather pouch, from which he extracted a piece of parchment. It was about a foot long and a half foot wide. The chief proudly shook his head up and down five or six times as he handed the parchment to Ethan.

Ethan studied the drawing for a while but wasn't sure what it was. He showed it to the people standing around him.

"It's obvious," Billy said with finality. "It's a picture of the big temple down in Missouri. At Independence."

"You're kidding, aren't you?" He rotated the parchment. "Oops, I guess I was holding it upside down." He studied the image carefully, then exclaimed, "By golly, you're right, Billy." He returned the parchment to its owner. "But how in the world could this uncivilized stranger get a drawing of the temple?"

The chief seemed to intuit Ethan's meaning. He picked up a stick from the road, waved the parchment so all could see, then pretended to write or draw on it. No one understood what he intended, at least at first.

Finally, Billy coughed loudly and said, "It's pretty simple to us Native Americans. Your foreign Injun wants a piece of paper and a pencil to write with."

"Yes, of course! Billy, you're a genius."

"Well," Billy said with mock seriousness, "I've been inhabiting these parts for over seventy years now, and I've had to get pretty creative when trying to get things across to you pale faces. Many times I've had to use pencil and paper, especially in the early days."

Ethan asked the crowd for pencil and paper, and after a bit of searching one man handed him a pencil, and a woman gave him a spiral-bound notebook. He passed them to the tall chief and the man began to do some drawing.

Ethan interrupted, touching his hand. "What's your name, young man?"

The stranger stopped sketching and gazed at him with puzzlement.

"Name. You know. Name." Still no comprehension. The mayor pointed to himself and said, "Me Ethan. Ethan." Then he pointed to Billy and said, "Billy." He followed the same procedure several times, pointing at different people and giving their first name."

"Aah!" said the stranger. Jamming his finger into his chest, he declared proudly, "Me Mosheh. Mosheh."

"Mosheh. That's a nice name. I wonder what it means."

The stranger finished his sketch and handed it to Ethan. The mayor squinted at the drawing with Billy and the constable looking over his shoulder.

"Okay," Ethan ventured. "We have here what looks like five horses. But what's that on their backs?"

With a touch of sarcasm, Billy said, "Ethan, I always wondered how you ever got elected mayor. It's perfectly clear. Five stick figures riding horseback. The little chubby stick at the end of the pack, the one with the beard, is no other than you. As for the two guys in front of you, I have no idea. But the stick in front of them is clearly a woman. Probably the chief's wife since she's smiling and has two long braids in front. The guy in the front, the tall stick with his legs nearly touching the ground, has got to be Mosheh himself."

"Yeah. All that's obvious," Ethan claimed. "But what's this at the edge of the picture?"

"Well, it's as plain as the nose on your face," Billy said, his voice laced with irony. "That's the stranger's tepee. See the arrow pointing to it. I think he wants you to accompany them to their tepee, wherever on earth that might be."

Fear passed over Ethan's face. "Go with him! Alone?"

"Yep, all alone," Billy said, clearly enjoying himself. "Just you and the foreign savages."

"No, you're plumb wrong, Billy," said Constable Barnes. "That's *obviously* the temple at Independence."

"No it ain't. That's a tepee. I oughta know. I lived in one for forty years."

"Let's not argue, boys," Ethan said. "I'll ask Mosheh." He held the drawing up to the big chief, pointed to the tepee-temple, and made several clever gestures indicating he didn't know what it was. Mosheh saw the problem, produced the parchment, and pointed to the image of the temple.

"See," the constable gloated. "It's the temple."

Billy was a poor loser. "I can't help it if the boy can't draw worth a dang."

"You mean Mosheh wants me to travel to the temple at Independence on horseback with him and others?"

"That's exactly what he wants," Billy said, smirking. "Hey, pale face, what's the problem? It's only about seven hundred miles give or take fifty. Us Native Americans do that kind of stuff all the time."

"Of course you do, Billy," Ethan replied. "You know, boys, I think there's something very important here. From the look of the caravan up

Highway 59, there must be thousands of these strange travelers. Coming from Canada. Not being American Indians or Eskimos. Having Caucasian-like features. Not speaking any language we're aware of. I'm telling you, we need to find out who these people are. Maybe some language scholars in the capital might be able to talk to them."

"Yeah, Mayor," said one of the nearby citizens. "We'd better get to the bottom of this. It has to be major important."

Ethan turned to Mosheh. Referring again to Mosheh's sketch, he gave him the thumbs-up and nodded his head several times. The gestures confused Mosheh briefly, but then understanding dawned. He started to return to the caravan, apparently to make arrangements for the long journey. Ethan stopped him. Pointing to the stick horses on the sketch, he shook his head and gave the thumbs-down gesture. Since the chief looked perplexed, Ethan pointed to the solar bus about thirty yards away and gestured for him to come along. Followed by Chava, they walked to the bus. Ethan opened the door, climbed the steps, and turned to invite them in. They hesitated, their eyes big, and Ethan figured they were afraid this metallic monster was just waiting there to swallow them up. But finally, seeing the smile and beckoning hand of Ethan, they ventured up the steps and turned to the left, gazing in wonder at the inside of the bus with its driver's place and ten padded seats separated by an aisle. At the end of the bus was an eleventh seat installed all the way across the inside.

Ethan gestured for them to sit down and grabbed the stick figure drawing. Using his pencil, across the top he sketched as many pairs of little suns and moons as he could, ending up with eight pairs. He made radiating lines from each sun and drew half moons to make a distinction between the heavenly bodies. As he showed this to the travelers, he used two fingers and trudged them laboriously across the sketch, his face grimacing and showing as much pain as possible. Several times, he wiped imaginary sweat from his brow.

Mosheh stared but didn't seem to comprehend. Chava popped him on the shoulder and said something in their native tongue. He understood but acted as if he was not the slightest bit concerned. Pushing his arms outward, he flexed his powerful muscles as hard as he could. Next he raised his right arm and proudly showed Ethan his flexed biceps, with Chava nodding her approval.

A bit frustrated, Ethan turned to a blank page in the notebook. This time he drew a bus with fourteen stick figures in it. After drawing speed lines behind the bus, he drew one big sun and one half moon above. Pointing to the sun and moon, he held up one finger and smiled, behaving as if the action depicted was quick and easy.

He watched for their reaction, doubting that his acting was doing much good. Then he turned to the page with the travelers on horses and counted eight pairs of suns and moons, holding up eight fingers, and indicating that the action described was difficult and painful. Going from drawing to drawing, he emphasized several times that horses meant five people and eight days while the bus meant fourteen people and one day. Again Mosheh was baffled, but his face brightened with understanding when Chava scowled and whipped out a ten-second explanation.

The mayor was delighted and hoped the problem was close to a solution. He was surprised when both of them made a gesture like whisking crumbs off their laps but not touching their bodies. Seeing his confusion, they shrugged their shoulders with a touch of disgust, looked at each other in a what's-his-problem attitude, and continued to make the crumb-wiping movement.

After watching them for a minute or so and seeing them make a half dozen other expressive movements, it occurred to Ethan what they were saying. He decided their gestures meant *well, show us what you can do.* He gave them Mosheh's wait-a-minute gesture, then exited the bus. They didn't follow at first but eventually waited at the bus door.

Ethan hurried back to the crowd. A large group of pilgrims had mingled with the townspeople, and they were sizing one another up. There was giggling, laughter, jabbering with only partial comprehension, touching of clothing, careful examination of facial features, and a vast array of expressive gestures, and even a sharing of gifts. Surprisingly, the two disparate groups were getting along fantastically well, especially the young children and the teenagers.

As time passed, more people arrived from the caravan and the town. It looked like the gathering would soon resemble a multinational fair at a large flea market. Ethan searched hard and finally saw the bus owner. He talked to him for a moment, and the conversation ended with the bus driver nodding his head.

They both went to the bus and invited Mosheh and Chava to get in with them. Everyone took a seat, Mosheh and Chava sitting on different benches. As the driver put the vehicle into motion, it lurched forward, and the two strangers screamed and sprang to their feet. The driver was only going five miles an hour. Both driver and Ethan burst out laughing. Seeing their amusement, Mosheh and Chava calmed down and began to laugh nervously. They fell back into their seats and plastered their noses against the window while the bus gradually picked up speed.

The going was hard because pedestrians and vehicles partially blocked the road. Consumed by curiosity, the townspeople were ambling up the road to get a look at the newcomers. It wasn't until they had driven past the city that they were able to accelerate. The driver stepped on the "gas" to show off what his new conveyance could do. The faster they went the more his passengers jabbered and the louder their oohing and aahing became. At thirty miles an hour Mosheh grabbed his window and tried to force it open. Thinking that the chief was trying to escape, Ethan jumped into action. Seizing Mosheh's arm, Ethan waggled his finger back and forth in a don't-do-that gesture. He didn't want to lose the chief right from the start.

Fortunately, Mosheh had no idea how to open a bus window. Ethan pointed to the right side of the seat and Mosheh moved to the aisle. The mayor sat next to the window, raised it about halfway, stuck his legs forward, leaned against the backrest, and tried to create a mini-scene in which he was enjoying himself immensely.

As for Chava, she was clearly shocked, intrigued, and a little frightened, but she seemed perfectly willing to embrace this new experience with open arms. Maybe her daily life had been humdrum back in Shee Lo. She laughed and squealed as she saw trees, fences, and houses whiz by. Quickly catching her mood, Mosheh voiced an occasional hoot. But Ethan really knew he had won him over when the chief put his hand out the window to feel the air rushing by, his hand moving up and down like a boat on waves. When they had reached forty miles an hour, Ethan asked the driver to return to their starting point.

Now all he had to do was make arrangements for using the bus, gather travel supplies, and convince Mosheh and Chava to make the trip with him. If they left early the next morning, he figured the trip would probably take a day and a half. When the solar panels stopped charging the batteries around seven in the evening, all they had to do was use the bus's backup electrical charging system. They could easily recharge the batteries at night at any convenient charging station. Later in the evening, the entire party would spend the night at some motel.

When they reached the big party created on the highway by the exuberant joining of two entirely different peoples, Ethan and several city leaders took Mosheh and a group of chiefs aside to make plans. They met in the same convenient bus parked nearby. After several hours of using gestures and drawing dozens of sketches, they had everything arranged.

That evening Ethan made several calls to the office of the governor of Missouri, Steven Christopher. Finally, at about eight o'clock he made contact. He described to the governor the events of the day, and their plans to drive to Independence the following day with a group of pilgrims. Steven was intrigued and asked Ethan to bring the travelers to his office at the capitol building. He asked if the newcomers had come with any written documents, and Ethan told him he believed they had. Steven asked him to try to convince them to bring some of those writings with them. He promised to contact several language experts he knew and have them available when their party arrived.

They departed at six in the morning the next day. Seven tribal members and seven citizens of Thief River Falls piled into the bus. From the mysterious tribe, Mosheh was accompanied by Chava, two other chiefs, the wife of one of those chiefs, and two singular men who seemed completely different from the chiefs or the warriors. One was tall, the other short, and both were dressed in full-length robes that reached to their moccasins. The robes were made of an off-white cloth with light brown trimming. Their buckskin moccasins were tan and laced with strings of leather. Their black hair and beards were long and uncut, and their demeanor suggested nobility, solemnity, and mysterious power.

Mosheh had indicated to Ethan that the unusual men were considered holy men who communed with God and wrote his words on parchment. They had brought pouches containing those holy writings. He had used the word *na-vee* when talking about them.

The townspeople included Ethan Reed, his wife Doloris, Constable Barnes, one councilman, Billy Circling Hawk, a prominent lady who insisted on coming, and the driver of the bus. The baggage of both groups had been deposited in compartments accessed from the outside of the bus. As they sped along at a blistering speed, varying from forty to fifty miles an hour, the pilgrims gazed in speechless wonder at the sights that rushed by them. The oncoming traffic that bore down on them and zipped by at nearly a hundred miles an hour threw them—at the beginning—into fits of panic. They covered their eyes or plunged their heads into their laps, apparently fearing that the approaching monsters would surely smash into them, causing their instant death.

After an hour of that, they gradually calmed down, but a few still held fear in their eyes. When they traversed small towns, the amazement of the pilgrims reached new heights as they strove to follow the movements of every pedestrian they saw. Around noon the bus went through a large city, and their eyes bulged with excitement. Using all kinds of gestures, Mosheh told Ethan, who was sitting across the aisle from him, that he had never seen so many people gathered together in one place.

⁂

The next day they arrived at the governor's offices in Independence shortly before noon. The mayor went into the building immediately, followed by the other travelers. The pilgrims were amazed at the marble floors and several knelt down to feel the strange new surface. One of the pages spotted them the minute they drove into the parking lot and hurried to inform Steven. Steven met them on the stairs as they worked their way up to his office on the third floor. After a few words of formality, he led them into the conference room that adjoined his office. They took seats around a long conference table that Steven used to counsel with state visitors. He was very impressed by the dignity of the pilgrim visitors.

"Thank you for coming," Steven said. "Which of you is Ethan Reed?" He had already guessed it was the gray-haired man in his mid-fifties with the ample belly.

Ethan raised his hand. "That would be me."

"Thank you for phoning me and for bringing these distinguished guests to Independence."

"Actually, I couldn't have held them back. They were bound and determined to visit the temple, especially their chief here, Mosheh." He nodded toward Mosheh.

"Do any of them speak English?"

"Not a word. We've communicated entirely by gestures, role playing, and drawing pictures."

Steven couldn't resist grinning. "I'll bet that was some experience. May I ask you another question, Mayor Reed?"

"Of course."

"You said on the phone that there were thousands of these people coming down Highway 59, and that they stopped and met you just north of Thief River Falls."

"That's correct."

"Where are they now—the main body of travelers."

"Well, we convinced Mosheh to ask them to wait a few days north of our city. They set up campsites the night before we left to come here."

"I assume they have sufficient provisions."

"They seem to have some supplies," the constable said, "but our towns-people and local farmers have started gathering foodstuffs to help them out. The city council will be making calls all over the county for contributions."

"What about leadership when their chief here is gone?"

"Mosheh told us there are quite a few other leaders in the caravan," Ethan said. "He's the principal chief but he has men below him. All the chiefs agreed that he and certain others be permitted to hurry on ahead in our solar bus. The one owned by Brother Carlson here." Carlson raised his hand briefly.

Steven was intrigued by the demeanor of the two natives with white beards and robes. "Who are the two men in white? They're dressed differently from Chief Mosheh."

"We have three chiefs with us, governor. Mosheh and the two men to his right, Avi and Even. They use the word *a-luph* to describe themselves. The men in white are considered prophets. The one on your right is Karmiel, and on your left is Liron. They are called *na-vee*."

"Interesting terms. I've never heard them before." Steven decided to get to the most important question. "Who are these people, mayor? Were you able to find that out?"

"We tried but didn't have any success. Mosheh said what they call themselves as a people, but I don't have any idea what the word means. It sounds like *am*. We asked him where they came from and he said something like *Shee Lo*. No idea what that means either."

"Did they bring any written documents?"

"Oh yes. I asked Mosheh to have them bring some documents. When I was walking up and down in the bus to check on how everyone was doing,

I saw the two holy men reading some pieces of parchment. So I guess I got my message across. We stopped to eat at a park yesterday, and I saw one of them writing on a piece of parchment with a wooden pencil and some kind of ink. I didn't recognize the words he was writing."

"Do they have any of these parchments with them now?"

Ethan talked to Mosheh using clumsy gestures, pointing at the holy men, and making a couple of sketches. He made sure Chava heard and saw everything because she was by far the most intuitive. Sure enough, after he did his best, Chava gave Mosheh another ten-second summary. Before the chief could react, one of the holy men picked up a leather satchel near his chair, withdrew a sheet of parchment, and handed it to Steven.

Steven examined it for several minutes while the others watched him expectantly. His face was grave when he looked up. "I need to call in our three Hebrew scholars. I don't speak or read Hebrew, but I studied it for a year a long time ago, and these symbols certainly do look like Hebrew consonants."

Chapter 25

Steven excused himself and went to his secretary's office. "Ester, will you please call the three scholars I've marked on this list." He handed her the list.

"Okay. These are the experts in ancient Hebrew, right?"

"Right. Two of them live here in town. The third doesn't live far away and should be able to get here within an hour. Also, call the catering service and tell them we are ready for them to deliver." Steven had arranged for a local catering service to deliver a special lunch at his office around noon. He had ordered several kinds of pizza, a vegetable salad, a fruit salad, a selection of nuts, finger foods, hot dogs with mustard and ketchup, red beans with rice, chili and beans, and strawberry shortcake. He returned to the conference room, and when he entered, the friendly talk ceased and all turned to listen.

"Okay, folks. All we have to do is wait a bit. My secretary is calling three scholars of ancient Hebrew. I hope I'm right that they're the people we need to communicate with our visitors from Canada. Also, I've made arrangements to have a nice lunch delivered to us by a catering service. They should be here within an hour."

"Governor," Ethan said, "may I try to explain all this to our visitors? After two days of practice, I think I've gained some expertise."

"Be my guest."

Ethan stood, and looking at Mosheh and Chava, made signs of eating and rubbing his stomach. The strangers understood his meaning instantly, and a few repeated his shoveling-the-food-in gesture. Then Ethan tore out the last page from the depleted binder and made a quick drawing of three faces. Next he retrieved the parchment the holy man had given to Steven, pointed to the writing on it, then to the three faces, and pretended he was reading the parchment text. Still nobody knew what he was saying.

No one except Chava. She gave her people a thirty-second summary, and the pilgrims nodded and seemed pleased that someone in Zion might understand their language.

Steven hoped at least that the look on their faces indicated accurate communication. Steven wanted the linguists to arrive first so they would be there when the caterers arrived with the food. He left for a while to procure a ream of paper and a box of writing instruments to facilitate the largely nonoral communication.

In the middle of all the sketching and gesturing, the caterers began to enter the room with trays of food. Each new dish was met with sounds of surprise and pleasure, especially from the pilgrims, who were not used to such lavish banquets. They all dug in immediately. The newcomers had trouble with the utensils, but friendly hosts showed them what to do.

A few minutes after the first round of dishes had been brought in, two experts in Hebrew arrived. They laughed when they saw the party and joined right in. Mosheh, who had few inhibitions, entertained everyone several times with his favorite native songs, singing in a strong tenor voice worthy of any performer in light opera. Chava did little to conceal her disapproval. From time to time other natives accompanied him, and the whites did their best to hum along.

But George Barnes, the constable, was not to be bested. After Mosheh had sung two songs, George let rip with the Toreador Song from the opera Carmen in a powerful baritone voice. Steven was surprised at the power of his voice and the accuracy of his French pronunciation, and the pilgrims were dumbfounded to hear him. Half an hour after the feast had begun, the third linguist showed up. Since there was plenty of food left, a place setting was made for him.

Steven kept an eye on the linguists, who from time to time tried to speak to the natives in Hebrew, and after some confusion, the pilgrims seemed to understand most of what they said. He concluded that there was a good chance these people were descendants of ancient Hebrew tribes. They finished eating around two in the afternoon, and the servers cleared away the plates quickly.

Steven was anxious to get to the main point of the gathering. "Okay, folks. Now we should probably get down to business. If any of you citizens of New Zion would like to leave to see the city or visit friends, please feel free to go." Not one person budged.

"Um, I see you're all as anxious as I am to know who these visitors are." He gave a sheet of paper to each of the linguists. "Yesterday, I spent some time wondering what we should ask these people, and I wrote down the most important questions that came to mind. Our experts can use them as a guide if they want. Of course, any of you can ask questions. Now, let me introduce our three experts.

"The man sitting on Ethan's right is Josuah Adams. He teaches classes in Biblical languages at the University of Missouri." Josuah was a slender man of forty-two with long brown air that reached his shoulders. He wore jeans, a blue dress shirt, and white sneakers. He was married to an Indonesian immigrant and had four children.

"The gentleman sitting on the constable's left is Malachi Kahn. He is an Israeli who used to teach at the University of Jerusalem. He taught ancient Hebrew and Aramaic and classes in paleography, which is the study of the historical evolution of manuscript families. Malachi immigrated to Zion six years ago and now has his own language institute in Kansas City." Malachi was fifty-five years old, six feet tall, and weighed a hundred ninety pounds. His short hair and beard were black. He was married to an American of German ancestry and was the father of five children.

"And finally, the man to my left is Nathan Daniels. He's an American of partial Jewish ancestry. He's an expert in ancient Hebrew and also speaks modern Hebrew. He has written several excellent textbooks on Hebrew and Greek." Nathan was sixty years old, short, chubby, and balding. He was married to a Spanish immigrant and had seven children. He was wearing a loose-fitting brown suit and a white shirt with an open collar.

"Okay. Let's begin. Who wants to ask the first question?"

"I suppose I can start," Nathan Daniels said. In Hebrew he told the pilgrims that Steven had just introduced the three people who wanted to ask them some questions. Most of the natives had trouble understanding his pronunciation and use of vocabulary, but Chava and the holy man named Karmiel exchanged a nod.

To increase their comprehension, Nathan asked Malachi Kahn to repeat the same things in a different way. Afterwards, Josuah Adams made the same points in his own words. By this time all the pilgrims were bobbing their heads. Steven could see the pleasure in their eyes at hearing their own language in the mouths of these strangers.

"It's understandable that there are significant differences from the Hebrew we have learned and the speech of these people," Josuah said in English. "After all, if they are who we suspect they are, their ancestors left Palestine over twenty-seven hundred years ago, and the language would have evolved quite a lot in their new homeland."

"That's right," Malachi said. "Their ancestors in Palestine wrote down parts of the oral scriptural tradition, and when the exiles left their original homeland, they probably took copies of those writings with them. If they hadn't done so, it's very unlikely we would be able to communicate with them at all. The evolution of their Hebrew was no doubt slowed by the existence of the written records."

"Oral tradition? What do you mean?" Ethan asked.

"Well," Malachi said, "the first five books of the Old Testament, or Pentateuch, had not yet been put into writing by the eighth century BC. Those scriptures, and often commentaries on them, were passed down orally from generation to generation. The boys and men spent long hours memorizing the scriptures, and many of them could quote the entire Penta-teuch from heart. However, as I said, there is evidence that parts of the oral tradition had been written down at the time the northern tribes of Israel were forced into exile."

"Thank you for that explanation," Nathan said. He consulted Steven's list of questions, and looking up at the pilgrims, asked in Hebrew, "Who are you? What people are you?" When several pilgrims looked unsure, the scholars used the same technique as before.

Finally, Karmiel answered, and Nathan translated it for the benefit of the speakers of English. "We call ourselves The People. We are the children of God."

"Thank you," Steven said, "but what race are you? What is the name of your nation?" Nathan translated Steven's questions.

Karmiel replied and Nathan translated. "The written record says that when our ancestors were forced into exile, they were called the People of Israel."

"I guess that about sums it up," Ethan exclaimed. "These people are part of the Lost Ten Tribes of Israel."

The citizens of Thief River Falls broke out clapping. Steven understood their sudden enthusiasm, for at last part of the great mystery concerning the Lost Tribes had finally been answered.

But Nathan wasn't satisfied. Now they knew *who* they were, but they didn't know *where* they had been living for twenty-seven centuries. He went on in ancient Hebrew. "But where have you just come from? Where have you been living?"

"We have come from the land of Shee Lo," Mosheh replied, his chest pushed out. "It is in the north country."

Nathan translated, then said, "I think Shee Lo is the word Shiloh in English. Originally, it was the first capital city of ancient Israel, but when Jerusalem was made the capital, it became the home of a sacred shrine, and remained a religious capital for 369 years. It was located in what later became the Northern Kingdom of Israel."

"By the way," Josuah Adams said, "Mosheh means Moses in English and Chava means Eve." There were smiles and laughter all around the table at that revelation.

"We understand, Mosheh," Malachi Kahn said, getting back to the main point. "But where is Shee Lo in relation to the country you are now in?"

"I do not know. It is north of here. God commanded our prophets, saying that now was the time for us to go south to join with our brethren and become one people. The Lord told us to prepare to leave in six months. So we obeyed—but not all. Two hundred thousand of our people stood and declared themselves obedient to God. The others—about three hundred thousand—were afraid and refused to leave their homeland. It is a land of milk and honey with beautiful mountains and valleys, and meadows and flowing streams. They did not want to lose what they had and expose themselves to the great trials that were prophesied.

"Because of sin and disobedience, our people have endured many wars, plagues, persecutions, suffering, and all kinds of hardships over the centuries. Yet each time we repented and obeyed, we received the blessings of peace and happiness, and the Lord multiplied our herds and our crops. So when the word came to leave Shee Lo, we desired most of all to obey the Holy One of Israel."

It took the linguists fifteen minutes to sort that out and to agree on the meaning of difficult parts. When Nathan translated it into English, the citizens of Zion were both shocked and intrigued.

Steven realized that Mosheh didn't know the answer to the question, but he was fascinated with all the information provided by the chief. "Who is the Holy One you speak of?" Malachi conveyed the question in Hebrew.

"He is the one who visited our fathers in Shee Lo after his death and resurrection in Jerusalem and gave us his gospel," Mosheh replied. Malachi translated.

"Why were the others so afraid to leave Shee Lo?" Nathan asked.

This time Liron, the second holy man, answered. "There were three main reasons. They were afraid of losing their land and their easy life, and they were terrified of the perils and tribulations the Lord said we would encounter during the journey. But the most important reason was the Lord told us that if we traveled south and continued for many weeks, we could never return to Shee Lo. Our homeland would be lost to us forever."

Billy Circling Hawk couldn't resist asking a question that had been bugging him. "Mosheh, in your caravan we saw no more than ten to fifteen thousand people. You said two hundred thousand had chosen to travel south. So my question is, when will the others come?"

Before Mosheh could answer, Chava said, "Soon the others will come. It would have been impossible for all of us to leave at the same time. Every three or four months a group the size of ours will head south to join us here. They will follow our footsteps and our pathways. They will suffer many of the same tribulations. They will obey God's word and will travel in all seasons, except the dead of winter. Why? Because he has promised to guide and protect them in their journey. We pray your great nation will accept us willingly. Together we have a great destiny to fulfill."

Josuah, who translated her words, looked into Steven's eyes, encouraging him to answer her entreaty.

Steven smiled at Chava and said, "I cannot speak for the whole nation, but I'm sure our people will welcome you as they have welcomed hundreds of thousands of other immigrants."

"I promise you that we will not come as beggars," Chava replied with sincerity. "The Lord has blessed us with much wealth and many treasures. We have gold and silver and precious jewels of all kinds. We have priceless furs and silks and many fine fabrics. Our men are skilled in building, commerce, and the hunt. They are strong and powerful, and most are skilled warriors who will fight to the death to protect your people. Our young women are beautiful, desirable, holy, and fruitful in bearing children. Even our older women have great beauty. All the women and girls of Shee Lo have many skills, and they know how to cook and sew and maintain happy homes. They are faithful and obedient to their beloved husbands—of course, not too obedient, I can assure you." She made the last statement with a twinkle in her eyes as she looked at Mosheh.

"Well, people," George Barnes said, "they have my vote, if it comes to that."

"Chava," Steven said, "I'm sure our people will be happy to see you and will welcome you with open arms."

Josuah translated the words of both George and Steven, and the faces of the pilgrims expressed relief and joy.

Steven wiped his eyes with a handkerchief. "Mosheh told us that the other three hundred thousand feared to travel south because they would lose their land and the life they had there. But most of all, the Lord told them they could never return to their homeland. Will one of you scholars ask him why they couldn't return? Did the Lord give them a reason?" Malachi transmitted the question.

"The Lord told us," Karmiel replied, "that as we traveled south to Zion, at some point we would migrate from our world to another world. He said such a migration would permanently change our bodies and our minds, and that it was not meet for him to reverse the process. The changes would be permanent."

"Ask him if they were mortal beings in their world, or something else," Steven said.

"Of course we were mortal, as you are," Karmiel replied. "We die the same as you do, but our mortal bodies in Shee Lo were adapted to the nature of that place just as yours are adapted to this realm."

"How did you know we were mortal and not translated beings?" Steven asked. Malachi had some trouble conveying the word "translated" and needed the help of Nathan and Josuah.

"We knew you were mortal because the Lord revealed it to us."

No one said anything for a minute or so, and they stared at the table as if pondering that answer. Steven was not surprised at Karmiel's statement that the Lord adapted or transformed their mortal bodies for particular purposes. After all, translated beings possess mortal bodies whose nature has been changed to permit them to live semipermanently and to perform special mighty works.

Also, the Lord transformed the bodies of the ancient patriarchs so they could live hundreds of years. Adam lived nine hundred thirty years, Noah nine hundred fifty years, and Methuselah nine hundred sixty-nine years. Then he transformed human bodies again over the ages to limit the life span of men and women to about one hundred years.

At that point, Steven suggested they take a break and go see the temple, for he knew the pilgrims were anxious to do so. Afterwards, they could return to the same room and hear the rest of the miraculous story. He asked Malachi to explain to the pilgrims that they could only see the outside of the temple today, but that at some time in the future they would be able to see the inside after special preparations had been made. He invited the three linguists to make the trip with him in his personal vehicle and they agreed.

As his guests left the conference room, heading for the bus, Steven phoned Mary and invited her to accompany them, and she said she'd like to go. Steven drove ahead, leading the bus to his home, which was on the way. He picked up Mary and continued on to the temple. When the bus reached the temple grounds, the pilgrims stuck their heads out of the windows and stared at the beautiful temple, their eyes full of awe because of the size and grandeur of the building with its towering spires. After the bus stopped, Mosheh got out, hurried to the nearest temple wall, and kissed it. It reminded Steven of the Jews who wept and kissed the Western Wall near the Temple Mount in Jerusalem.

They spent an hour walking around the temple grounds and finally climbed back into the bus to return to the conference room. Steven was anxious to get back because he wanted to learn more of the history of the Lost Tribes and how the pilgrims felt as they entered the land of New Zion.

Chapter 26

❦

When they returned to the conference room, the secretaries served the guests root beer, cookies, and donuts. While they ate, Steven asked the pilgrims how they felt when they finally realized their journey was almost over.

Josuah Adams translated and Karmiel responded. "As we traveled south on your wide black road, we began to see portions of land that actually looked like cultivated fields. The fields gradually increased in number, and we rejoiced because we felt we had entered the land of God-fearing, decent people. We even saw people working in the fields far away. We waved at them enthusiastically, but they could not see us very well. The main thing is, they did not attack us with their noise-making sticks. Then, we saw a city ahead, and hundreds of people walking toward us, and strange metal vehicles that rolled along the highway with no horses pulling them. That is when we met the seven citizens sitting here with us at this shiny wood table. They brought us to see the ruler of this people, who now sits at the front of the table."

After Josuah had finished translating, Steven laughed and said, "Tell them I'm not the ruler of the people, just the head of one part of this nation. They'll meet the principal leader later. Ask Karmiel also if he knows where the land of Shee Lo is in relation to the land he is now in. We've asked this before, but I'm trying again."

Josuah translated and Karmiel spent some eight minutes answering. The linguist briefly interrupted him several times to ask for clarifications.

After Karmiel's speech, Josuah said, "He gave another description of his country, but basically he said Shee Lo is in a region north of here. I asked him over and over where that land is in relation to Zion, but he really didn't seem to know. Despite all his descriptions, I don't recognize Shee Lo as any land on earth that I'm familiar with."

"Nor do I," replied Steven. "Do any of the rest of you have any idea where their homeland might be located on this planet, especially in the northern regions?" The citizens of Zion shook their heads. "Okay then. We'll do the next best thing. Malachi, ask Karmiel to tell us about his earliest ancestors. I mean the ones who lived in Assyrian captivity in the eighth century BC. I especially want to know where they traveled after they escaped captivity and what happened to them on the journey."

After the translation, Karmiel said, "We have only a few written records of that early period. I am not sure how accurate they are. What we have tells us that our ancestors in their pride disobeyed the Lord and turned to all manner of evil in their native land. This was over seven hundred years before the Savior was born in Jerusalem. Because of their sins, the Lord brought the Assyrians against them. After various sieges over a period of many years, the Assyrians managed to conquer all the Northern Kingdom and transport the majority of the inhabitants to Assyrian domains in the northeast. Only a remnant remained in Israel. In Assyria they remained in captivity for about a hundred years, and learned obedience and humility by the trials they suffered.

"After the hundred years had passed, the Lord began to remember his people and have mercy upon them. He stopped the waters of a great river called Euphrates to allow his people to cross over and then journey northward. At that time there were approximately three hundred and fifty thousand of them. After traveling north for several days, they entered a mountain pass that led them to the shores of a great sea, which they called the North Sea. They journeyed along the eastern shore of that sea another four days and saw an even higher range of mountains to the east. But they were still able to continue the same course by the sea, and eventually they ran into a branch of that sea that forced them to turn straight north."

During his translation Malachi interjected a personal note. "The North Sea he's referring to is probably what we call the Black Sea today."

Karmiel stopped to rest a moment. He ate a cookie and drank some root beer. The others waited breathlessly.

"Well, what's next?" asked Constable Barnes, anxious to hear the end of the story.

"They traveled northward for months and noticed that the weather became colder the farther they went. Of course, that was to be expected. They ran across hostile peoples in many regions and had to fight for their lives. Those foreign tribes did not want our ancestors to take their lands and their women. On the other hand, some tribes were friendly and seemed to find profit in inviting them to linger. Nevertheless, most nations were suspicious and inhospitable.

"Our ancestors suffered greatly from fatigue, disease, and deprivation. Many could not endure such tribulations and rebelled. They refused to remain with the main group, and began to corrupt themselves and worship foreign gods. Eventually, they broke off completely from their brothers and sisters and united with native populations. Some stayed in the same region, others traveled to the east, but most migrated to western lands.

"So our ancestors broke into two main groups, those who continued north as a group, and the rebellious who mixed with alien peoples."

"How many remained and how many broke off?" asked Doloris Reed.

"I do not know the numbers for sure," Karmiel replied. "Some records say that seven people in ten remained together and continued north, but other records seem to show that only half remained faithful."

"If half remained faithful," Steven said, "that means a hundred and seventy-five thousand continued on to the lands of the north."

"Yes, that is correct," Karmiel returned.

"What happened next? Where did the faithful end up?" asked Ethan Reed.

"Eventually the Lord led them to a beautiful land in the north. The descriptions in the records resemble our beloved Shee Lo."

"So you don't know where that ancient land was in relation to the other nations existing at that time?" Malachi said.

"No, sorry. We do not know the answer to that question."

"That would have been my guess," murmured Georges Barnes with a hint of sarcasm.

"Please go on, Karmiel," Steven said. "Tell us what the records say about the rest of the history of your people."

"Gladly, of course. It seems they lived mostly in peace and happiness in their new land. At least for about two hundred years. Then strife and dissension began to appear. Wealthy men became prominent, and they used their power and influence to gain control of the government. They fought against the laws of God and led the people into sin, for the people were not strong enough to resist them. Gradually the entire nation became wicked, and the land was full of murders, secret combinations, immorality, the love of money and possessions, and the pursuit of pleasure and idleness. Yes, the people abandoned God and idolized the rich, the famous, and the powerful, but despised the poor and humble. They persecuted the small remnant who remained faithful to God and his teachings.

"That terrible state of affairs continued for over four hundred years. Then one day the whole nation saw the sign of the Son of Man in the heavens. They all saw it at the same time. This happened about seven hundred and fifty years after they had been taken into captivity by the Assyrians. Great destruction fell upon the land. There were earthquakes, floods, fire from heaven, and plagues and pestilence of all kinds.

"Most of those disasters struck the houses of the wicked, but even the humble suffered. The people wept and mourned, yet only a small number repented. Many blamed God for their tribulations, and multitudes cursed the Lord as they perished. After the calamities reached their peak and began to subside, the Savior appeared in the heavens and descended in a cloud. Great fear struck the wicked and many repented of their transgressions.

"But the righteous rejoiced and embraced him with tears. He told them about his great sacrifice for the world on the cross and taught them his gospel. He established his Church among them and ordained twelve chosen disciples to rule it. He appointed righteous judges and governors to rule the people in their national affairs. Finally, he blessed them, committed them unto the keeping of the Father, and ascended back into heaven."

"Sounds a lot like what happened to the Book of Mormon people," Ethan Reed said.

"The people remain relatively righteous for many years," Karmiel continued. "But after four or five hundred years, factions among the people began to quarrel. Soon their dissensions led to hatred and outright war, each faction striving to destroy the others. Once again conspiracies and murders abounded. This sad state of affairs continued for over six hundred years, until the wicked factions left the capital of the land and became wild savages wandering from village to village in search of plunder and slaves. There were millions of them, but over the centuries they greatly decimated their populations with constant warfare among them.

"Then about a hundred years ago the Spirit of God spoke to many good men, directing them to preach God's word again in Shomron, the capital of the land. The people called those inspired men prophets. The prophets converted hundreds of honest people, who in turn preached the sacred word to hundreds of thousands and brought them into God's fold. Recently, the Spirit spoke to me and Liron, and several other prophets, commanding the faithful to prepare for the great journey southward to unite with the people of Zion.

"So, as we said, two hundred thousand people began to make preparations for that perilous voyage. They will come progressively in groups of about ten thousand. We hope to live in Zion permanently, except for some who plan to return to the original lands their ancestors possessed before the Assyrian captivity."

"Is there any more you can tell us, Karmiel?" Steven asked.

"No. That is all I want to say."

"Did you bring your scriptures with you, especially the ones written at the time Christ visited you?"

"Yes. We have some of them with us now, and other migrations will soon bring the others. We also have the writings that were recorded from the oral tradition."

"Okay, everyone," Steven said. "Are there any further questions?" The linguists and the citizens of Thief River Falls shook their heads.

Steven glanced at his watch. "Well, it's getting late. I guess that about wraps it up for today. I have made arrangements for all of you to stay at our guest house a block away. It has rooms to accommodate twenty-five people, several bathrooms, a recreation room, dining room, and kitchen. It is taken care of by a custodian, and a chef will prepare meals for you. I know for a fact that she is a great cook and has a supply room stocked with delicious food. Later in the evening, we'll take all seventeen of you on a tour of Independence in our tour bus."

"What about our people waiting on the highway north of Thief River Falls?" Mosheh asked and Malachi translated.

"I suppose you want them to continue their journey south."

"Yes, of course."

"All right. Ethan, can you contact someone there on the phone and get them to bring one of the pilgrims to the phone so Mosheh can give them instructions."

"I think so. Where's the phone."

"In my office. Follow me."

After Malachi had finished translating, Steven, Ethan, and Mosheh went into Steven's office, and they made the communication.

"Now all I have to do is alert the president and the other governors," Steven said afterward. "I know they will be excited to hear the news and will spread the word quickly. Everyone in New Zion will be thrilled that their long-awaited brothers and sisters from the land of the north have finally arrived. All along their pathway south happy people will welcome them and give them gifts and supplies."

Chapter 27

At the beginning of November, six months after the arrival of the first party of immigrants from the Lost Tribes, Steven and Mary held a little celebration in their home with close friends and relatives. Present were John and Tania Christopher, Paul and Maryann Christopher, Doug and Liz Cartwright, Ruther Johnston, Jarrad Babcock and his wife, Angel, and Andrea Warren and her husband.

Steven had told the guests beforehand that he hoped they could spend some time talking about the Lost Ten Tribes and the various theories concerning where they have been for so many centuries. John told him he had been studying those theories and had written down notes and scriptural references to bring with him.

After Mary served refreshments, they all sat down to talk.

"Well, Mr. President and Mr. Governor," Jarrad said, "how are the pilgrims from the north settling in?" Jarrad was now the lieutenant governor of Kansas and a member of the stake high council in his area.

Both Douglas and Steven laughed. "Jarrad, you don't have to be so formal," Douglas said. "We're all close friends here."

"Of course. I'm sorry. But how are they doing?"

"As you know," Steven said, "only a small portion of them have come as yet. About twenty thousand now. From what I've seen and heard they've been welcomed almost like royalty. Maybe they should sell book rights. Our citizens have invited them into their homes, and some communities have built houses for them. Not tents or tepees or whatever kind of shelters they had at home, but new Zion-style houses. Can you add to what I've said, Doug?"

"Yes, I can. We've tried to procure the services of every Hebrew-speaking person in the nation to teach them English. We also have about seventy people who don't speak a word of Hebrew but are skilled in teaching English as a second language. The tribal leaders have pretty much insisted that all their people attend our schools. For the most part, we are teaching them in church classrooms."

"When do you expect the next group to appear?" Andrea asked.

"We don't know for sure," Steven said. "Perhaps in two months. No doubt it will take several years for all of them to come. It's a good thing too, because it would be extremely difficult, if not impossible, for us to accommodate all two hundred thousand at once. We still have thousands of immigrants and refugees arriving each year from everywhere on earth."

John slouched in his armchair and yawned. The previous night he had spent too many hours reading and searching scriptures. "Steve, did you ever find out where these pilgrims came from? I mean, where their homeland is located."

"We tried hard, but all they could say is they came from the land of the north."

"So, basically, we don't know any more than we did before," snapped Paul, his voice tinged with irritation. "We still have no idea whatsoever where the Lost Ten Tribes have been for all these centuries."

"No, not really. Of course, we now know quite a bit about what their homeland is like, and we know a lot about them. Especially that they *are* the Lost Tribes and speak an evolved form of ancient Hebrew."

Jarrad scratched his head, looking unhappy. "That means we don't know which of all the location theories is correct. The ones people have been arguing over for hundreds of years."

"I guess not," Steven said. "I'm beginning to think we were wasting time speculating about their location. Maybe the real question should have been—when are they going to return?"

"What theories?" Ruther queried. "Yuh Mormons have so many theories about so many durn things that all that thar speculatin' makes my poor ole head spin." Ruther was now in his eighties and not caught up on all the religious debates concerning where the ten tribes were supposed to be. Apparently, the Baptists didn't get worked up about it, probably because they didn't expect the Lost Tribes to move in on them someday.

"You know, Ruther, I'm not an expert on all those theories. Maybe John and Paul can help us here. John, would you like to comment?"

John shook his head, trying to wake up his mind. He took a swig of root beer and cleared his throat for about ten seconds. "Well, let's see now. There seem to be five main theories that Mormons have entertained over the years. I've read a few books on them and I'm sure Paul has read some. Right, Paul?"

Paul looked at the ceiling musingly, as if counting. "Yeah, I'd say I've read three books on those theories, but it's been years."

"Which book is the best, in your opinion?" asked Andrea Warren.

"I'd give the blue ribbon to Clayton Brough's book," Paul said. "What do you think, John?"

"I agree. Clayton goes through each of the five theories, presenting all the evidence that supposedly supports each one. He objectively gives the pros and cons and doesn't try to make conclusions for the reader. In other words, he reviews the theories and doesn't push one pet theory like most other books do."

"What are the theories, John?" Douglas asked.

"Well, there's the Unknown Planet Theory, the Narrow-Neck Planet Theory, the Hollow Earth Theory, sometimes called the Concave Domain Theory, the North Pole Hypothesis, and the Dispersion Argument."

"Would you go through each of them for us?" asked Elizabeth.

After John spent half an hour summarizing the first four theories, his listeners agreed that those theories were based on conjecture and hearsay and should be rejected. Jarrad also noted they required God to expend an unusual amount of energy and resources.

"Thank you for going through all that," Mary said. "What about the last one—the Dispersion Theory?"

John removed notes from his scriptures. "Let's see now. Okay, here it is. The Dispersion Theory says that the Ten Tribes dispersed into native populations. Some went east into Asia, but most spread throughout Western Europe. In other words, they were scattered among all the nations of the earth and have been gathered into the Church for nearly two hundred years by our missionary efforts. This means they were lost as to their identity, but not regarding their location. Historically, most church members who expressed an opinion on this subject tended to believe this proposal. We know they were wrong because the Lost Tribes are now returning to us as a unified nation."

Ruther raised his brow and pulled his beard. "Why did so many of yuh believe the way yuh done?"

"For several reasons," John replied. "It was the only theory that seemed plausible and appeared to agree with the facts of science and history. The dispersion was considered to be a normal process and the gathering also. Many scholars found what they considered to be definite traces of Hebrew heritage in many of the countries of Europe, especially in England and Scandinavia. They studied shields, emblems, family crests, and coats of arms and believed they resembled similar objects among the ancient Hebrews. Also, they studied individual words that they felt were similar to Hebrew words.

"At first they claimed that all those similarities strongly suggested the Ten Tribes may have infiltrated Europe. But eventually they made a leap of logic typical of human nature and declared that all the similarities proved almost without a doubt that the tribes did move into Europe. Many would-be experts also supported their dispersion opinions by attacking the weaknesses of the other theories. Their logic worked something like this: since the other four theories are obviously ridiculous, that proves our theory is correct."

Douglas chuckled. "Okay, what were the arguments against dispersion?"

"Actually, there were more valid objections against the Dispersion Theory than against any of the other proposals. In spite of that, many members still adhered to the theory. In the first place, most General Authorities consistently taught that the Lost Tribes, or a significant number of them, would return to the world as a unified body. Only a few church leaders taught otherwise. In addition, the scriptures teach that the Ten Tribes would come to join with the people of New Zion. They could not do that until New Zion was first established and redeemed.

"Furthermore, Joseph Smith taught in the Tenth Article of Faith that 'We believe in the literal gathering of Israel and in the restoration of the Ten Tribes.' So it seems clear that Joseph distinguished between those two great events. They were not the same thing. Our missionary work would be a literal gathering, which suggests that new members would be brought into the fold piecemeal over a long period of time from many different nations. On the other hand, the word restoration indicates a bringing back to a former position or condition, and more closely implies an event happening to one object or group." John looked at his notes. "The same type of distinction is made in . . . D&C 110:11."

Still checking his notes, he continued. "D&C 133:26–34 describes unusual and singular events that could only refer to the Lost Tribes. For example, they will have their own prophets, who will perform miracles. It does not say those prophets are the same men who lead our Church today. Next it says there will be a great highway cast up in the middle of the deep to permit them to continue their voyage to Zion. It indicates that many other miracles will take place, and the tribes will bring their riches to Zion. This could not possibly refer to converts to the Church, especially during the first hundred years of missionary work, for most of those people were poor and therefore had great difficulty traveling to America.

"Also, in the Book of Mormon the Lord mentions three specific groups who will receive his word and write it, and each group will have the words of the other groups." John quickly turned the pages of his triple combination. "Okay. It's in 2 Nephi 29:12–14. The three peoples were the Jews, the Nephites, and the Lost Ten Tribes. The Lord made this statement around 545 BC. That means the Lost Tribes will have prophets to receive Christ's word at the time he visits them." John made another search. "In 3 Nephi 17:4, Jesus says he will go to show himself to the Lost Tribes. That was in 34 AD. So the tribes will bring their scriptures when they return. The people converted to the Church from Europe and elsewhere didn't have their own scriptures."

"Still," Tania said, "isn't there some truth to all those similarities between European culture and ancient Hebrew culture? How do you explain that?"

"I believe it's easily explained," John said. "Not all the people of the northern tribes were taken into captivity by the Assyrians. Thousands of them remained in Palestine and could well have had an influence on European culture. But most of all, when the captive tribes obtained their freedom and fled past the Black Sea into the boundary between Europe and Asia, a large portion of them rebelled and refused to continue on to the land of the north. They dispersed mostly to the west into Europe. That is no doubt why their language and culture had an influence on European civilizations."

Andrea Warren's face brightened. "So, they were the people who could have provided the chosen blood that leavened the nations of Europe and made so many Europeans willing to accept the gospel."

Paul didn't look happy. "I don't mean to hurt your feelings, but I've heard that blood theory many times. Frankly, it bothers me a lot. How on earth could such a rebellious people leaven anything? In the first place, the northern tribes had turned away from God in Palestine and lived in great wickedness for two hundred and nine years. So the Lord brought the Assyrians against them to chastise them into repentance. After about a hundred years of punishment, and their eventual repentance, he led them out of captivity by power and miracles.

"But instead of remaining faithful as they traveled north, about half of them rebelled again and rejected God's commandments, breaking off from the main group. They seemed to possess the same natural tendencies toward disobedience as the people of many other nations. So how could Israelite blood or genes have had the effect of quickening or purifying the genes of other peoples? I don't think it has anything to do with race. I believe many Europeans accepted the gospel because of their own personal character."

"I admit," Steven said, "it's hard to fathom. Still, God made a promise to Abraham and he's not the kind of being to go back on promises."

"I realize that," Paul replied, "but that favored race thing bugs me. When some maniacs get the idea that they come from the favored race, they begin to think they are better than other people, and before long they start persecuting the so-called inferior races. Sometimes this leads to genocide and ethnic cleansing. It has happened all over the globe. Think of Hitler and his master race. As I said before, people accept the truth, once they hear it, because of their personal character, not because they are English, Spanish, Indian, or Chinese."

"I agree that one race is not inherently better or smarter than another," Steven replied. "To think otherwise is to invite serious problems. I'm not sure how the chosen blood thing fits into the picture of who will be willing to accept the truth and who will be less willing. I'll leave that to the Lord, who has promised that he'll explain all things at the beginning of the Millennium. Meanwhile, I don't intend to worry about it." Paul buttoned up, apparently accepting Steven's position, at least in part.

"Well, folks," John declared, "I guess that about finishes our discussion on the location of the homeland of the Ten Tribes. We've covered all the theories."

"Not quite," Steven said quietly. Everyone shot him a surprised look.

"What do you mean, not quite?" Paul said.

"I have another theory."

"You're kidding, right?" John said in disbelief. "What theory?"

"Um, well, do you really want to hear another ridiculous hypothesis?" Even Mary stared at him with her mouth open.

"Okay, let's have it," John said. "Whatever it is, it can't be any more far-fetched than some of the others."

"Yes, Steve, tell us," several chimed in.

"As you wish, dear friends," Steven said with a pleasant smile. "I call it the Other World Theory, or I could just as well replace the term world with realm or sphere or plane. Any of them will do." He took a long pause to stretch his legs and take another gulp of Mary's herbal tea.

"We're waiting, Steve," Douglas said impatiently.

"Yes sirree, boy," Ruther said, "I'm a hankerin' fer another big laugh after hearin' all them wild Mormon speculatins I jest heard."

"I think it's possible that Shee Lo is located in another plane of existence," Steven said. "It's a plane that is right here around us on this planet. Kind of like the Spirit World the scriptures talk so much about."

"And what proof do you have for that?" John asked.

"The proofs of simple common sense and the economy of God."

Paul grabbed his scriptures as if to demand chapter and verse. "I understand what common sense means, but what do you mean by the economy of God?"

"It has to do with what Jarrad said about God's efficient use of time, energy, and resources." He went to a bookcase and brought back his triple combination. There were several slips of paper sticking out of the book, apparently marking specific passages. After plopping into his armchair, he said, "All right then." He flipped the book open at one of the markers. "The prophet Nephi in 1 Nephi 16:29 says, 'And thus we see that by small means the Lord can bring about great things.' "

He turned the pages to another marker. "And Alma the Younger in Alma 37:6–7 declares, 'Now ye may suppose that this is foolishness in me; but behold I say unto you, that by small and simple things are great things brought to pass; and small means in many instances doth confound the wise. And the Lord God doth work by means to bring about his great and eternal purposes; and by very small means the Lord doth confound the wise and bringeth about the salvation of many souls.'"

Andrea looked skeptical. "I don't see how you can say that God is using small means when he creates an entire separate plane of existence to house a few million people."

"I didn't say he created a completely separate plane of existence. He already has several realms he can use. Besides, we're not sure that producing a brand new sphere requires all that much energy and resources."

"What do you mean when you say he already has several planes of existence?" Mary asked. "I'm not sure I understand that."

"In the first place, we know we live on this planet in a mortal plane of existence. We also know there is a second world that the scriptures describe as the Spirit World. Do you all know where this realm exists and who lives there?"

"That's simple," Paul said. "The Spirit World exists right here on earth. It's a world we can't see that is all around us. It's divided into hell and paradise. Hell is where the wicked end up after they die, and paradise is where good people go after death. In paradise people in the know visit those in hell to preach the gospel to them."

"Good summary. How many people live in the Spirit World?"

"I don't think we really know," John said.

"Correct, but we can make general calculations. Demographers have made estimates as to how many people have lived on the earth and died. The estimates range from ninety billion to a hundred ten billion. We can reasonably assume that the figure is around a hundred billion, give or take a few billion. How many people live on earth now?"

"It's probably a little over seven billion," Jarrad offered.

"Right. So you can see the Spirit World must be pretty crowded with over fourteen times as many people there as are living today in our mortal plane of existence. And that doesn't even include the hundreds of millions or billions yet to be born and die."

"Oh yeah," Tania said, "but they're just spirits and maybe they don't need as much room as we do." Everyone laughed at what they took as Tania's sense of humor. "Well, they don't, do they?"

Steven smiled at his sister-in-law. "You're right. They probably don't, but still, even spirit beings need their space."

John swatted a fly and leaned back in his seat. "Okay, so the Spirit World is a bit overcrowded. Maybe there are different layers in it."

"You mean it might have different dimensions or planes?"

"I get your point, but who knows for sure whether or not it has different planes?"

"We don't know for sure because God hasn't revealed it. All we're doing here is speculating. Let's move on. What happened to the evil spirits who rebelled against the Father in the preexistence?"

"They were punished by being cast onto the earth . . . to tempt us," Andrea said.

"How many evil spirits were thrown out?"

"A third of the hosts of heaven, along with Lucifer," Jarrad replied.

"I mean how many individual spirits would that make?"

Paul did a quick calculation. "That would be fifty billion, based on a disembodied population of a hundred billion."

"Good, Paul. Now where did you say all these wicked unembodied spirits exist?"

"Right here on earth, as far as we know. Yet normally they're invisible to us."

"Yes, but do you think it's common sense to suppose they live in the very same realm as the hundred billion spirits from whom they were separated in the preexistence?"

"No, not at all," Andrea said. "They'd have to be in a separate realm. The Lord wouldn't want them to benefit in any way by being near the people who kept their first estate."

"That's a good assumption. So you see it's already possible that there are three separate spheres of existence: the mortal, the Spirit World, and the realm of Lucifer and his followers. Now tell me about translated beings. The scriptures tell us that in ancient times, during a period of twenty-two hundred years, it was common practice for the Lord to translate the righteous. It's possible hundreds of thousands were translated. And then we have the inhabitants of the City of Enoch, who probably numbered in the millions. So my question is, where are all those translated beings?"

Paul's face lit up. "I believe the scriptures say they were taken back into heaven."

"Yes, but the Prophet Joseph Smith clarified that." Steven took some folded sheets from the back of his triple and looked for the quote. "Okay, the prophet said, 'Many have supposed that the doctrine of translation was a doctrine whereby men were taken immediately into the presence of God, and into an eternal fullness, but this is a mistaken idea. Their place of habitation is that of the terrestrial order, and a place prepared for such characters He held in reserve to be ministering angels unto many planets . . .'

"We also know that some translated beings, such as the three Nephites, were assigned to teach among mortals. Yet no one has ever been able to point one of them out, as far as I know. So apparently, as Joseph said, translated beings live in a special order or habitation or place that seems to be separate from the other planes we just discussed."

"It's especially significant," John added, "that Joseph said God prepared a special place for translated beings. It suggests they don't live in the same plane as spirits or even mortals, in spite of the fact that translated people are still mortal too."

"Yes. They are mortal beings whose life span has been extended semi-permanently for special reasons. So now we have four possible realms of existence, all of them overlapping."

"What do you mean by overlapping?" Douglas asked.

"By that I mean these alternate realities or planes exist in the same general space. Maybe on the same planet. Yet there is no direct communication between them. That is, in everyday life people living in one realm do not usually communicate with people in the other realms."

"That's an interesting theory, Steve," Douglas said.

Steven smiled, feeling he might have won some believers in his speculations. "I think it has merits. But there are still other realms."

Mary groaned. "Don't we have enough yet?"

Steven chuckled. "It's not over until it's over. We also have the three degrees of glory: the celestial, terrestrial, and telestial. Apparently, each of these have different layers or degrees. I get the impression from gospel teachings that the people in the celestial world exist in the same basic plane, although there are, of course, three degrees of glory in this kingdom. Perhaps the same is true of the terrestrial kingdom.

"However, it may be different in the telestial kingdom. Doctrine and Covenants 76:98 indicates that in the telestial kingdom the inhabitants will receive a vast number of different rewards or glories according to their degree of unrighteousness in mortality, and they will receive bodies commensurate with their level. We don't know if this means they'll all exist in the same realm or in overlapping planes. Of course, we know there is a definite separation between the three primary kingdoms."

"Does that finish the different-worlds scenario?" Mary asked.

"Almost. There's another completely separate world that God has prepared for the sons of perdition. It's usually called outer darkness. In that terrible realm there will be a mixture of unembodied spirits and resurrected beings with immortal bodies."

"Of course," said Paul. "But what does that have to do with overlapping planes?"

"Maybe nothing at all, yet it does show that God has no problem preparing special planets or worlds for various kinds of people. And the populations in each of those worlds is vast, far more than a few million."

"Then why couldn't God prepare a special cave or hollow cavern at the North Pole, or a deep, warm valley in the same region?" Tania asked.

"Oh, he could if he wanted to. All things are possible with God. Still, I feel my theory requires a much smaller expenditure of energy and resources on the part of God."

"So you believe the Lost Ten Tribes were living in another plane of existence and moved into our plane without even realizing it?" John said.

"No, I don't believe it. I simply present it as another possibility. I believe there is more support for it than for the first four theories that are based on hearsay. As for the dispersion proposal, that contradicts the clear readings of the scriptures and the teachings of most General Authorities. In other words, I think my proposal is more plausible than the other theories, which I consider pretty ridiculous."

"So to create a habitation for the Ten Tribes, God simply used one of the life dimensions already in existence or prepared a new one like he did for translated beings," Douglas said.

Steven closed his triple and put it on a stand near his chair. "It's possible. Or perhaps all these dimensions have already existed from eternity."

"Do you have any other proofs for your theory, Steve?" Jarrad asked.

"Only a few hints that the pilgrim prophets gave us. Karmiel said they left the barren desert, walked through a forest, and then suddenly—in the blink of an eye—they walked onto a great plain. There seemed to be no normal geographical area of transition. That may have been the precise point or portal where they moved from their sphere of existence into ours. Also, Liron indicated that the Lord had told him and Karmiel that as they traveled south to Zion, at some point they would migrate from their world to another world.

"I also got another important hint when the pilgrim prophets said they couldn't return to Shee Lo. Therefore, once they moved into a completely different world, they couldn't return to the former one. Their migration would permanently change their bodies, and it was not meet for God to reverse the process. In other words, the changes would be permanent."

"Would you ever teach this theory in church?" Mary asked.

"Heavens no! It's not in the lesson manual."

※

In the next five years New Zion continued to grow and prosper. The Lost Tribes returned from the land of the north and received a warm welcome from the original citizens. The new people settled in quickly, built homes, and were baptized into the Church. They learned how a modern, scientific society worked, and they joyfully embraced many of the new wonders, while at the same time adhering to treasured native traditions. In many ways, they were like the American Indians who became members of the Church and citizens of the state. Most of the Hebrew descendants learned English quickly and contributed greatly to the growth of the political and spiritual kingdoms of God. Yet the eyes of many constantly turned to the east and their hearts yearned for their original ancient homeland.

Zion added nine new states from Old America, and the people chose to keep their original names, which they loved and honored. The new states that joined the union were mostly those to the west and included Minnesota, South Dakota, Colorado, Utah, Idaho, Wyoming, Montana, New Mexico, and Arizona. The total number of states was now nineteen. New Zion merged with Old Zion and became one united nation. The Lord blessed the land with rain and sunshine in good weather and bountiful snow in the winter, and he blessed their crops and gave the citizens the strength to help build homes for the great numbers of immigrants from other lands.

The citizens of Zion fervently believed that their nation had been redeemed as promised by the Lord—redeemed by the power of God and the goodness of its people. Someday it would expand throughout the American continent and become a beacon of hope, peace, and righteousness to the world.

Why did they believe Zion was redeemed? Because the nation had grown from its infancy into a great and powerful nation that no earthly power could cast down. The holy city—the New Jerusalem—had been built in

Jackson County, Missouri. The great temple had been constructed in that city, and many more in other areas. Father Adam had returned to the earth and defended Zion against the armies of the Antichrist. The great council at Adam-ondi-Ahman had taken place, and Christ himself had come, had received all the keys of the priesthood, and been ordained and ratified as the Ruler of the Kingdom of God.

And that is not all. The government of the land combined theocratic teachings and republican principles. The people used several terms to describe the same government. Some called it a theodemocracy. Others said it was a democratic theocracy. Still others preferred the designation republican theocracy. Steven Christopher and many others chose to call it a theocratic republic.

Christ was the ultimate lawgiver and visited from time to time to ensure that his house was in order. Other than that, he allowed the inspired constitutional government to manage the affairs of the nation. The ultimate goal was freedom and equality for all before the law.

There was a separation of church and state, but it was not an impenetrable wall like the imaginary barrier created by evil and designing men in Old America. The nation honored the Founders' original intent in the First Amendment, which declared that neither the central government nor state governments had the power to establish a favored state church or denomination.

Instead, it was a natural separation, based on different duties and focuses. Since it was forbidden for government to be involved in creating or financing public schools and other institutions, no one could claim that religious practices and teachings could not abound in them. The dominant religion was Mormonism, but one of the primary teachings of the Church was acceptance and tolerance for all other beliefs.

The only religion that was outlawed in Zion wasn't really a religion at all. It was the belief promoted by the government of Old America. Since Old-American lawmakers and judges had claimed there was an impenetrable wall between religion and state, then by default the only acceptable viewpoint in government had been secular humanism, which in practice had become atheism. In Zion, atheism was not declared illegal as a belief for individuals, but it quickly and naturally fell into disrepute because its proponents had no power to get their views written into the nation's laws.

For all these reasons, the citizens of Zion considered their nation to be redeemed in the eyes of God. Now all they had to do was continue in faith and courage to promote the cause of Zion and ensure that it fulfilled its ultimate destiny. Everyone knew that in the near future, they would yet face their greatest challenges in the land of the Jews, but for now they would live in peace and happiness in their homeland.

THE END

We hope you enjoyed *Promised Land*. If you did, please consider leaving an online review. The fourth and final book in the series will be out in the fall of 2014.

Kenneth R. Tarr taught French language and literature at Brigham Young University for fourteen years, and French and Spanish for three years at Snow College. He received a master's degree in French and Spanish at Brigham Young in 1965, and a doctorate in French at Kansas University in 1973, with a minor in medieval history.

Kenneth was born and raised in southern California and has been a member of the LDS church all his life, serving in many capacities. He and his wife, Kathy, have been married fifty-one years and have eight children and twenty-seven grandchildren. Currently they live in Utah where they operate an herb store. Kenneth enjoys writing, reading, exercising, doing repairs, and listening to good music.

Promise Land is Kenneth's third novel in his The Last Days series. A fourth and final novel for the series is in the works. The author welcomes questions and comments. You can contact him at tarrk@yahoo.com.

CPSIA information can be obtained
at www.ICGtesting.com
Printed in the USA
LVOW01s2323060417

529954LV00006B/160/P